Sanctuary Forever

WITSEC Town Series
Book 5

Lisa Phillips

Cover art by Blue Azalea Designs
Photos from Shutterstock

Also By Lisa Phillips

Love Inspired Suspense

Double Agent
Star Witness
Manhunt
Easy Prey
Sudden Recall
Dead End
Security Detail (Spring 2017)

Denver FBI

Target (A prequel story)
Bait

WITSEC Town Series

Sanctuary Lost (Bk 1)
Sanctuary Buried (Bk 2)
Sanctuary Breached (Bk 3)
Sanctuary Deceived (Bk 4)
Sanctuary Forever (Bk 5)

Dear Reader-Friends,

Because if you've read all four Sanctuary books so far then let's face it—we're friends.

First I want to thank you all for the wonderful emails I've received. The series so far has been a rollercoaster of highs and lows, and all of your warm words of encouragement have brought us this far…

To the final book!!

I'm so excited for this story. It belongs to Dan and Gemma, but it's about Sanctuary as a whole. The fate of every resident was part of this story's journey and it was a wild ride to write. I sincerely hope and pray that you enjoy reading it.

I learned so much through this series, some of it about Amazon pre-order uploads and the truth of keeping a series bible so all your character names/hair color/ages are straight and don't keep changing inexplicably. So yeah, Terrence (from Sanctuary Lost) did become Andy in Sanctuary Breached, but you'll have to just go with the flow as I rectify that in this book. And some other things.

Next year is quickly approaching on the horizon. I'm so excited to see what God has for me. I have a three book mini-series coming out with Harlequin's Love Inspired Suspense about Secret Service agents. I'm looking at writing a serial futuristic suspense novel with end times elements and of course—Ben gets his own series!! So there will be plenty to read from me.

As always, God richly bless you as He has richly blessed me through being able to do this thing that I love so much. And HAPPY READING!!

In His strong name,
Lisa.

Chapter 1

The past loomed in Dan's life like a ghost. The shadow of a time that was gone now but never really went away. Every time he passed the farmhouse the crack of a gunshot split his eardrums.

The flash of light from the muzzle.

He blinked and squeezed his eyes shut. Fresh air. The breeze on his face and the faintest tang of overripe tomatoes. His boots in the soft grass. The faint nicker of his horse.

He was an adult now, and that was a long time ago. Why wouldn't it leave him alone? Today of all days was the hardest—the anniversary of the night it happened.

Dan Walden opened his eyes and continued past the house he hadn't stepped foot in since that day, fifteen years ago. Curtains still drawn, paint peeling from the siding, and shingles torn off by that spring hailstorm. The inside was probably all dust and rodents by now. He halted on the grass and looked at his watch. Hour and a half and he'd be twenty-six.

Happy Birthday to him.

The sky was blue, and the breeze took the edge off the heat of the last week—*Thank You, Lord.* Warmth collected in the fish bowl where he'd lived his entire life. Every single day in this town with no way in or out, surrounded entirely by mountains; the comfort of their standing sentry over his farm, and over this town, wasn't far from the comfort Dan felt from his Heavenly Father. The protective hand of God. They'd needed plenty of that protection the last couple of years.

Things were finally calming down. The sheriff and his wife were having a baby soon, and in a few days Dan was going to perform the wedding of the town's doctor and their nurse. The town of Sanctuary had finally been guided to a place of joy and thanksgiving.

Bay must have heard his boots, because a nicker came from inside the barn. Dan smiled. He could take her out for a ride. Maybe head to the lake and lie on the dock until the sun went down. Some quiet prayer time tonight would do him good. Who needed a birthday anyway? It was almost dark, and apparently she wasn't going to come over. He'd be okay on his own for the evening. *The peace of God that passes understanding…*

Dan frowned. A golf cart headed down the lane. The mayor, Samuel Collins, was being driven over by another man. Neither of them he'd consider a friend. The mayor kept to himself most days, and his health was sufficiently bad that when Dan had paid him a visit, the mayor had his housekeeper politely decline. He'd tried two more times, but apparently Collins didn't want the company of the town pastor. Until now.

**

Gemma planted her shoe on the grassy dirt and froze. Those dark, round orbs stared back at her from maybe ten feet. She'd never been good at judging distances. The breeze shifted, and a branch swished against her arm. The deer blinked. Stared at her. *Superstition.* It was nothing but superstition, and one she wasn't even sure actually held weight since the last person to see the deer was still alive. This didn't mean anything.

The deer didn't move.

Gemma inched forward, slowly at first to see if it would run off. Then she started up walking. It didn't mean—the deer raced away before she reached him. Her. Whichever.

The path she was on wound through the woods from the diner to the farm, though Gemma would have to cut left, or she'd end up passing Dan's land altogether. Her visit was just one friend helping out another friend on an anniversary difficult enough it left lines on his face for days afterward. They did the same thing every year. Not a birthday party, it would never be that. But she couldn't let the day pass by unrecognized.

There were years Dan never would've survived it alone.

His friends didn't even know about his past, or what today was. Dan hadn't told anyone that it was the anniversary of the worst night of his life. And there were few who'd lived in Sanctuary, their witness protection town, back then. Apparently Gemma was in this strange category of "someone who knew" and "someone who cared." If his friends knew, they'd be all over it, bringing him dinner and making sure he was okay. It was how she knew they had no idea.

And then there was her. *Just friends.* They'd been "just friends" since that third grade field trip to the ranch when he'd forgotten his sandwich, and she'd shared her mom's homemade hummus and pita bread with him. He'd explained to her the particulars of the genus of cucumber she'd brought—a cucumber grown on his farm.

The trees rustled. Gemma glanced aside and saw the deer again, it's face concealed in part by foliage. Twice?

Gemma picked up her pace. She might not believe in superstition, but she couldn't deny the fact that once in a while it seemed like the world was trying to tell her something—like if bad weather was coming, or things were looking up. She got outside as much as she could and had written entire novels on her laptop, sitting on the grass outside at the library where she worked.

She'd never told anyone that it was as if the earth seemed to speak to her. Not in any magical or mystical way. Just a feeling. She'd told no one except Dan, and he'd suggested it might be the Creator. Gemma didn't know if she believed in a benevolent being, but she couldn't deny the strength of his faith. The Bible had navigated him through some of the hardest times anyone should have to face. Ever. She'd read every blog and most books that existed on the subject of childhood trauma and PTSD. The man should be seeing a professional twice a week, attending a support group and taking medication. But they didn't have two of those things in Sanctuary, and the stubborn man said he didn't want drugs.

If the deer was God's way of telling her He wanted her to keep Dan's secret, that was fine with her. And if God was using creation to send her a message then she would listen. If He was God, He could do whatever He wanted.

Gemma broke into a run, just in case. Who knew what seeing the deer meant? She sprinted fast enough the tote bag bumped against her leg with every step. At the edge of the trees where his front lawn started, Gemma slowed. The mayor stood with Dan outside the barn. Dan was one of the few people who still showed the mayor any measure of respect. Checkered shirt, sleeves rolled up so that she could see the defined muscles of his forearms. Jeans and brown boots. His hair had needed cutting three weeks ago, but apparently he didn't have time. Which wasn't a problem, because it seriously worked.

Just friends.

It had become a mantra. To the point that at least fifty times a day she wondered if she should tell him they couldn't be friends anymore. Maybe they should just avoid each other as best they could in a town of two hundred protected witnesses. She'd keep to her end of town; he could keep to his. She'd avoid the church, and he'd grieve that until he realized it was for the best.

But not today, on the anniversary of his mom's… disappearance. There was no way she could give him the break-up speech she'd rehearsed in front of the bathroom mirror a thousand times.

Maybe tomorrow.

The mayor looked… aggravated, maybe? Though he was trying to hide it. His gray suit didn't fit well anymore, and his silver hair had thinned. He'd ditched the rings he'd always worn, as though tired of pretending. The mayor looked like he was trying to convince Dan of something, while Dan was giving the man his characteristic nothing. Holding all his cards, giving not one thing away. She'd seen him stand perfectly still for a full five minutes of conversation once, before saying one word. The "tell" was in the corner of his mouth, and in his eyes. But she was too far away to see clearly. She had to get closer.

Gemma left the bag behind a tree for later and crossed the grass like she had something to say. The mayor didn't need to know she was there to hang out with Dan—that would mean theirs wasn't a secret friendship.

The route made her pass by the farmhouse. Dan had kept it locked since his father's heart attack. Then after the explosion had destroyed the ranch months ago, it had been condemned. Even though the bomb had exploded on the other side of town, the aftershocks had torn apart the earth and brought down the back porch on Dan's house. Not that he cared, or had any intention of fixing it.

She'd have burned the place down by now.

When she got close enough to hear, it was the mayor who was speaking. "You've lived here your whole life, Daniel."

Gemma winced even as Dan's lips pressed together. He hated that name.

The mayor's voice boomed across the clearing. "It's as a courtesy to you that I'm here to extend this offer because of your standing in the town. It cannot continue in the same greatness we have established if someone who does not understand how things work falls into the position of mayor through some kind of asinine voting system that should have been scrapped years ago. I wish to appoint my successor. Someone who has lived here their entire life, who understands that this town needs a guiding hand. A shepherd, as it were."

Okay so Dan might be the pastor, but that was pushing it. And what was the mayor doing? Gemma had lived here her whole life also, but he hadn't offered her his job. Evidently she was just the librarian, and not a valuable member of the community. No one even knew about her other job writing books. They just thought she sat behind her counter all day and checked out other people's books. They were all in witness protection, so they weren't big on sharing, but this was a small town. She had plenty of secrets, and no one had even tried to figure them out.

If she didn't have Shelby, the nurse at the medical center, for a best friend, she'd have gone crazy by now. Or signed herself out of witness protection and left the town forever.

She glanced at Dan again.

Okay, so she wouldn't have left.

Dan's gaze locked with hers. Humor sparked in his eyes. She'd given up trying to convince him that everything about her wasn't hilarious, but he thought her attempts to do that were hilarious, too.

"Good afternoon, Mayor Collins."

The mayor whirled around with far more agility than a man with serious medical problems should be able to. Gemma adored sneaking up on people. It was delicious. She smiled as sweetly as she could, channeling her inner Scarlet O'Hara. Maybe the tattoos would cancel out the debutante thing, but she could pull it off for a second. If she'd lived in the outside world and not closeted away in a witness protection town, she'd have been a world class con artist. *A grifter.* And she'd have written bestselling novels about her adventures.

"Ms. Gemma."

See? Totally southern. She turned to Dan, let go of her smile, and put her hands on her hips to seal the deal. "There was a caterpillar in my corn husk."

Dan said, "It's all natural, no pesticides."

"I don't like furry crawly things in my vegetables."

"Then buy frozen ones from the town store."

"Ew." As if.

The mayor butted in. "I'll speak with you about this another time, Daniel."

Dan turned his head to address the mayor. "I'll pray about your offer."

The mayor didn't give away how he felt about prayer; he just wandered off. Dan glanced at her. "Ew?" His eyes gleamed.

She whispered, "You know I was raised on an organic diet. I'd probably have a stroke if I ate a frozen pea."

The golf cart engine whirred, and the mayor was driven away by his crony. Gemma waited until he was well out of earshot. "I don't know whether to be glad or ticked off that he hasn't been by the library to offer me his position."

Dan didn't move for a second. Then he said, "I'm...not sure you should be the mayor." Why did he sound like he was trying not to anger her?

"I'd make a good mayor!" She waved in His Honor's direction, toward the road that led from the farm into town. "It's not like he actually *does* anything."

Dan's lips curled up. "I'm praying about that, too."

"Good." Gemma shivered. "Collins freaks me out about as much as Andy does. A few weeks ago Collins showed up at the library to 'offer me condolences.' The next thing I knew I was leaving him alone to lock up my library and going to see my mom to find out why she never told me Hal was my dad." She paused a second. "Do you think he knows mind control?"

"I think you've been reading a bunch of books about people with bizarre abilities."

Gemma shrugged. It was research for a new pen name, since the US Marshals declared she could write *with conditions.* She had to become an entirely new author every three years and switch genres, never to publish under that name again. This would be the fourth name she'd written behind, and she was in the mood for something interesting. Like urban fantasy, or some kind of historical fiction where the characters could do magic. Probably they'd try to steer her toward sweet romances—like they could control her *art*—and she'd have to write from the perspective of a Sunday school teacher whose biggest problem was that her grandson said a potty word. Yeah, right.

He hadn't looked away. His gaze was still on her. "I haven't seen you in a while."

She didn't want to shrug again, but she had to do something to off-set the effect those words had. Only it made it more of a sucker punch when he aimed that gaze at her and basically said he'd missed her. "I'm deep in the throes of researching a new genre."

It was entirely likely he read more books than she did, given how much he had his nose in that Bible always tucked in his back pocket. The thing was falling apart.

Gemma shifted on her Converse. "I brought a bottle of Coke and some cherry syrup. You wanna take a walk?" Like they didn't do the same thing every time they hung out on this exact day—that being an overload on sugar. With the way his dad had been and her mom's all natural, taste-free lifestyle, it had been their rebellion against this life, this town. And the people who were supposed to have taken care of them.

"Sure," he said. The edge that talking to the mayor gave him had left, and she caught a measure of peace. "Just let me go change."

He turned to the barn, and she saw the bulge of his pocket-size Bible in the back of his jeans. Gemma glanced up at the blue sky, and the valance of clouds. *Thank You for giving him that.*

She yelled over her shoulder before he disappeared. "I'll get the bag."

**

Dan left the barn door open because he was raised in it, and touched Bay's wiry nose on the way past. Everyone had gone home for the day. It was Friday, and those who lived in town didn't have any reason to hang around when they could be elsewhere. He employed six people, but only two full time—a husband and wife, Megan and Chase, who were in their forties, no kids, and worked as his managers.

Dan's farm produced thirty-six different kinds of produce, four varieties of raw milk, and the best honey ever—in his opinion. His greenhouses kept the town in vegetables three-hundred sixty-five days out of the year. Nothing that was flown in could compare.

It was almost an empire. Of vegetables. If he wasn't constantly half a step from losing his mind he might even take a moment to think on all he'd accomplished.

The last time he'd had an "episode" his manager, Megan—not Chase, thankfully—had gotten him back to his room before he could wig out all over the place in front of everyone. He'd actually punched Chase on one occasion. *Thank You, Papa, it wasn't Megan.* They knew enough to be careful around him, to not bring up anything about his family, the history of the farm, or the past in general. He had to live in the present. He couldn't even read one of Gemma's books because it would take him out of his life and the mental struts he'd erected around his memories. If they slipped and it all crumbled, Dan would…

He didn't even want to think about it, but it would probably involve a prolonged hospital stay in a padded white room where he couldn't hurt himself.

From the town of Sanctuary, I will cry to You. When my heart is overwhelmed, lead me back to You.

Dan flipped the latch and stepped inside the storage room at the back of the barn. He'd slept for years in one of the horse stalls because his father insisted. And as he'd had no intention of stepping one foot in that house, he'd moved into the storage room at the back of the barn after the old man dropped dead on the lettuce when Dan was sixteen. The romaine had never grown right since.

Dan had a tiny closet for his clothes, a three-drawer dresser, a bed his feet hung off the end of, and a desk with a wooden chair. The bathroom was a tiny room beyond that. His books were scattered across every available surface. Commentaries, devotionals, old works of Oswald Chambers he'd had Gemma find used online and shipped in.

Because they were all in witness protection, the town didn't have any phone contact with the outside world. Their landline phones only dialed internally, except for the sheriff's satellite phone which was separate. They had two hours of scheduled internet access each week per person via the library computers, but he mostly didn't use it. Mail could be sent in and out, and was delivered each week on Fridays now, along with supplies.

He stripped off his shirt and the T-shirt he wore underneath, washed up real quick since Gemma was waiting, and pulled on a clean tee.

Gemma.

Dan had heard the sheriff, John Mason, say many times that he had no clue what his wife was thinking. Matthias, whose wife ran the bakery, said the same thing. Like women were a great mystery they were trying to solve.

Dan wasn't trying. Gemma showed up when he needed company. They talked, and he felt better after he saw her. When she didn't come by for a few weeks, he sought her out. They hung out, talked, and he got her to a place where he could elicit a laugh from her if she was having a rough time. Not that she'd tell him what was up with her.

There wasn't much to figure out about Gemma. They were friends, and they made each other's lives better. It had always been that way, even back at school as kids. Through the dark and the light, Gemma had been there with him when he'd needed someone tangible. As adults they saw each other infrequently, but when they did there was something about her that…settled him. If he could figure out an adequate way to say thank you, he'd do it. But he didn't possess anything that immense which he could give her.

Only the knowledge of the Gospel.

He'd shared his faith with her a thousand times over in the years since he'd come to understand the enormity of what God had done. She knew what Papa had done, what He did every day for Dan, yet she didn't believe. She'd made no profession of faith for herself.

Now Dan was a pastor, and Gemma was his unbelieving best friend. He knew the others would frown on their relationship if it ever became public knowledge. Not out of judgment, but out of concern for him. It was why Dan had never told them, and why he and Gemma had decided to keep their friendship a secret.

Fifteen years, and not a day went by he didn't think of it. When he didn't remember the sound of that gunfire. The flash, the jolt. His mom…disappeared. His father, same old dad. He didn't want to think about himself, or he would end up in a head-funk he couldn't get out of.

Dan buttoned his shirt as he walked, then reached back and fingered the Bible in his pocket. He shut the door to his room and strode out. No point in locking his door. Not in a small town when he had nothing of note worth stealing anyway. Besides, any thief would have to get past Bay first.

Dan blew the horse a kiss, and she nickered back to him. He latched the barn door shut and scanned the trees for Gemma. She emerged with a canvas bag swinging from her hand that he didn't have to guess held two plastic cups, a bottle of Coke, and cherry syrup. It was what they did.

She walked with that loose-legged stride. Her milk-white skin with those freckles and her fire-red hair that flashed in the sunset's orange glow made her seem almost like some creature from a fantasy novel. He'd seen one of the covers once, at the library.

She grinned as she walked, and he kept his gaze on her so that it didn't stray to the house. She called out, "How about the lake?"

The town had elected to turn the hole the bomb blast had left into a man-made lake and stock it with fish. Dan never caught anything, though. He liked to dangle his tired feet in the water and lay back and stare at the stars while he prayed. Would it bother her if he took his boots off?

"Sure. That sounds great. Hey, you wanna take the horses?" He'd have to go back in the barn and saddle them.

She lit up. "Yes!"

Dan turned back to the barn. Out the corner of his eye, still a good fifteen feet from him, Gemma's footsteps faltered. She hesitated for half a second and a weird look shadowed over her face, but she kept walking.

The ground tremored. A branch cracked, and Gemma yelled, “Dan.” Her voice laced with worry.

“Don’t—”

The ground between them caved in and Gemma fell into it.

Chapter 2

Gemma had never seen a semi-truck in real life, but she got the expression anyway, because it felt like she'd been hit by one. She'd lived her whole life inside this ring of mountains with no cell phones, no vehicles except a Jeep, two designated pickup trucks, some golf carts, and a couple of ATVs to clear snow. The sky swam above her, inside the hole she'd fallen through.

The juts of rocks and uneven dirt were a painful bed beneath where she lay. She blinked and tried to move. Fingers, toes, her head. Pain sliced through her, and a feral moan emerged from deep in her throat. She was down, far down. *Dan.*

Gemma fought the pain and managed to turn her head to the side. What she saw made no sense, but the light revealed only the truth in all its ugly glory.

A tunnel.

She shifted again and everything went black.

**

Lord... Dan's thoughts drifted like smoke. He couldn't even say it. *Papa. You know what I can't say. She can't be dead. I can't handle that.* God knew if she was still alive, even if Dan couldn't form the words out loud.

She'd been swallowed up by the ground.

"Gemma!" He took two steps. The ground started to cave in so he jumped back.

No response.

"Gemma! Can you hear me? Are you okay?"

The closest phone was back in the barn. He could barely stomach the idea of leaving her, but if he was going to get medical help, that was his only shot. Dan raced back to it.

Ring. "Deputy Ling."

"Gemma—" He pushed out a breath and gripped the handset so hard it was about to crack. "It's Dan, at the farm. Gemma fell in a sink hole."

The new deputy was quick with the questions, her voice steady enough it enabled him to get a handle on the derby race of thoughts in his head. Dan pulled in a breath and pushed it out slowly. "I can't help her."

"I'll be there in minutes, and I'll get the doctor."

Dan hung up. He ran over toward the hole, but couldn't do anything except stand there and watch, yell her name, and then listen for any sound that indicated she might be alive. Waiting. *I have to be patient, Papa. Don't let her die. You incline to me and hear my cry.* They'd get her out of that *horrible pit, out of the miry clay.* Set her feet upon the rock. Establish her steps. A new song in her mouth. Psalms of deliverance and His faithfulness ran through Dan's head. *I'm trusting You, Papa.*

Dan got rope from the barn just in case. He secured it with a carabiner to the barn door and threw it as far as he could. When the end landed in the hole, he called her name. Nothing. He pulled the end of the rope back and tied it around his waist.

The sheriff's Jeep sped down the road that stretched from town, west of his farm. It was maybe half a mile of pitted concrete, but it gave him a sense of privacy and an escape from getting overloaded with being around too many people. If more than a handful knew how fragile his mental state was they'd never have let him be pastor. This town needed someone steady, someone who knew what he was doing. Instead they got Dan, who was a hair from falling apart nearly every second. He could barely get out of bed in the morning without Papa coaxing him into the light.

Dan lowered to his belly on the grass and started to crawl forward.

The Jeep door slammed. "Dan!" She called his name like a warning. "What are you doing?"

He didn't look back. "We have to get her out somehow. You have a better idea, Mei?"

"Let me do it."

That was actually a good idea. The deputy sheriff was five-three and weighed maybe one-ten all compacted into a tiny body. Still, she had this air about her, like she could bench-press his truck if she wanted to. That was exaggerating, but she was just one of those people who was more than what you saw. And people misjudged her. She knew it, and she used it.

He backed up and untied the rope.

When her fingers wrapped around it, Dan looked down into her almond eyes and didn't let go. "Get her out, but don't get hurt. I don't know how I'll get both of you out." It wasn't like they had a crane.

"Dr. Noel will be here in a couple of minutes."

Dan nodded and let go to watch her tie the rope and then crawl the same path he had. No one knew where the Chinese woman had come to Sanctuary from. She was maybe twenty-one, but looked like she could be years younger. Acted like she was thirty, had seen everything, done most of it, and lived to tell the tale. No one dared ask her who she'd been before she was sent to their witness protection town. Two months, and no one even had the guts to find out if Mei Ling was her real name.

Their last deputy had left a path of destruction behind him, and they'd gone without for more than a year. But John's baby was due any day. His family was growing and the marshal's chest was puffed out all the time, everything right in the world. Dan wanted to know what that would look like for him. A wife, a family. They weren't going to live in the barn with him, so it wouldn't work. *Papa.* He needed to give up that dream.

John had told them all that Mei was qualified for the job of deputy sheriff, and that she came highly recommended. John should know. He was a deputy marshal, and his brother was the former director of the entire US Marshal Service.

The tiny woman crawled on while the ground shifted around her. "Whoa." The American phrase came from her lips effortlessly, though he'd hurt her mutter in Chinese—he guessed—plenty of times.

"Be careful," he called out.

As if she wasn't? But he had to say it anyway, just as he had to pray. He barely took one step without praying, and now Gemma could be hurt. Was hurt. So he prayed it wasn't too bad. He prayed Elliot could help. He prayed Shelby—Gemma's best friend and the doctor's fiancé, a nurse herself—would come soon. That they all would help get her out of the ground.

"Almost there." Now it was her turn to say the obvious.

"Do you see her?"

Mei crawled another few inches, her body flat on the ground. He gripped the rope, keeping it taut between them so she didn't fall.

"I see her!"

Dan pushed out the breath he'd been holding. A golf cart sped down the road. "Elliot and Shelby are almost here."

Mei nodded.

When they pulled up, Elliot slid a backboard out. Shelby raced over and stood by him. "She'll be okay."

Dan nodded. He didn't know what Gemma had told her about the two of them and their longstanding friendship. The way she stared at him, he figured he looked sick so she just knew he cared.

The ground rumbled. "She's too far down to reach," Mei yelled, glancing over her shoulder at him. "Six feet, maybe seven. You'll have to lower me." She turned back to the hole. "Gemma, wake up!"

Did he want to ask if she looked okay? Maybe Gemma should stay unconscious, maybe that was better. She could have snapped her neck. She could be bleeding, or…

Shelby touched his arm. "Take a deep breath through your nose." She spoke the same way he talked to the mama goat when she got riled. Soft and slow. "Now blow it out slowly from your mouth."

The clean air settled his stomach.

"Again."

Dan held the rope and breathed.

"Okay, lower me down!"

Elliot crawled from the opposite direction with the backboard at an angle, toward where Mei lay on the dirt. She disappeared into the hole.

Elliot reached the edge of the hole and lowered the board. "Get her secure with the rope. Dan can haul her up, and I'll pull her out."

The doctor glanced at his wife, who stood beside Dan on the balls of her feet waiting for news about her friend. The look on Elliot's face said it all.

It wasn't good.

**

Gemma's head pounded. She pushed up from the bed. *Dan.*

"Lay back down!" Shelby was hovering like a mama cat that would bite the kitten to get it to comply.

"I want to know if he saw."

Gemma had been in here once before, when she broke her wrist at the age of twelve. But that was the other medical center, the one that had blown up. This one was new, though they'd used the same basic design.

Mei stared at her from the far side of the room. It made Gemma uncomfortable enough to wonder if she should write a spy thriller instead of just reading them. Mei might be able to help her with the details of interrogation. Maybe that was why she was so right for the deputy sheriff's job. Things did have a tendency to get a little crazy in the town of Sanctuary.

"Just concentrate on you, Gem." Shelby's nose crinkled. "Dan was shaken up, but he's fine."

"Are you sure?" She was giving too much away, but apparently having a concussion meant she had no filter. The cut on her head had stopped bleeding, and she was going to have a nasty gash—if not a full on scar—under her hair. Had Dan seen the blood? If he had, there was no telling where he was or how he was doing. "You need to send Elliot to check." She glanced at Mei. "Or John. Someone needs to make sure he's okay."

"I'm sure he's fine."

Gemma clenched her fists. "You don't understand!"

Shelby frowned. "If you can't calm down, Elliot will have to give you something to make you sleep, Gem." She glared at her friend, but Shelby stood her ground. "I'll do it. And I won't feel guilty at all. You're going to hurt yourself. You *fell in a hole.*"

Mei pushed off the wall and strode to the other side of the bed but looked at Shelby. "Why don't you get the patient a soda or something?"

Shelby glanced between them, then her gaze settled on Gemma. "No caffeine."

She whined. "Why do you hate me?"

Shelby actually laughed before she reached the door. As soon as she was out of the room, Gemma said, "John needs to see to Dan."

Mei lifted her radio. "Sheriff, do you copy?"

His voice cut in, "I did say you can call me John."

Mei didn't even smile at his response. She just asked him if he'd find the pastor and make sure he was okay. "Sure thing. *Deputy.*"

That made Mei smile, though it was more of a slight twitch of her lips. Mei perched with her hip on the end of the bed and pulled out a pad of paper and a pencil. "Feel like answering some questions?"

Gemma settled back against the pillows and shrugged. "I dunno, my head hurts pretty bad." It was true. Her body ached, and she'd bruised a kidney landing on a rock. But that wasn't why she didn't want to talk.

"What brought you to the pastor's house?"

Not Dan. The *pastor*. Gemma should remember that. "We hang out sometimes."

"So you're sleeping with each other."

"What? No!"

"Wow. That might actually be true." Mei tipped her head to the side and stared at her like Gemma was a zoo animal. "Huh." She blinked those long gorgeous black eyelashes. "Okay, so you hang out. What does that entail?"

"Talking?" Gemma didn't know what the right answer was. Mei thought they were having a romantic entanglement? Not that she'd all the way object. It was Dan, and he was her best friend, but he'd never been like that. Gemma had seen too many problems arise from sharing *that* with someone when there wasn't one hundred percent trust. Plus, those thousand books she'd read in her rouge period, before the steampunk novels. So much drama. Sex and drama. It seemed like the whole world turned on sex and drama.

Her life was far simpler than that, and wouldn't you know she actually liked it that way.

Mei wrote something down. "Talking. Okay." Like she didn't all the way believe it, but she was willing to entertain the idea. "Do you…talk…often?"

"It's not a euphemism. We're friends."

Mei nodded slowly. "I think I'm getting it."

That's was good, because Gemma didn't have the brain power to explain. "The mayor left and Dan went to change his shirt. I was walking back across the grass and fell in the hole."

"Did you know the tunnel was down there?"

"No." Gemma shut her eyes and remembered it. The dark expanse.

"And the pastor, does he know there's a tunnel under his house?"

"I don't think so." He'd have told her. Plus, didn't that mean he'd have to have gone in the house? No way.

Mei asked her about the Mayor and what he'd been doing there. She was still asking when Shelby came in. She pulled up short, a straw in an open can of clear soda. "The mayor?"

"Apparently if you're a lifer, that means he offers you succession." Except he hadn't actually offered it to her. Just Dan. Was it because she was a girl, or because she was a librarian? Libraries were institutions of learning that were the heart of a community. Who—in Sanctuary and out in the rest of the world—hadn't gone to the library as a child to check out a book for a school project? Adults frequented her shelves, and people held meetings in her rooms. Even those who didn't read came in to surf the internet. It was their only access.

"Okay." Shelby handed her the can and said to Mei, "Question time is over. She needs to rest."

Shelby adjusted the blanket. The ceiling light was off, and only the white glow from the hall gave any light, but enough it vaguely bothered her head.

"Did my mom get here?"

"I called her, but she didn't answer. I left a message." Shelby didn't react. They both felt the same way about Janice and the fact she'd withdrawn since the explosion rocked the town. Shelby just didn't know it was because that was the day Hal Leonard had died.

Her father. She'd told Dan that interesting factoid but not Shelby. Yet.

Gemma pushed all that aside. "Hey, Shelb—"

Her friend waved away the words. "Sleep first. Okay? We'll have plenty of time to talk tomorrow."

Gemma had wanted to tell her for weeks. She had a huge secret, and yet every opportunity to tell Shelby that Hal had been her father—that she'd never known all this time she'd been living in the same town as him—had passed them by. He'd been having a secret relationship with her mom for years. Gemma had met him, talked to him, and thought they'd had a rapport. At least as much rapport as a twenty-four year-old could have with a sixty-something biker. They'd laughed over tuna in the tiny town grocery store, and he'd never said one word about being her father.

Neither had her mom.

It didn't surprise her that her mom hadn't shown tonight. Janice didn't want to talk with Gemma about the past. Said she only wanted to move on, like Gemma had since she moved out a few months ago. Like Gemma could *move on* from being lied to for her entire life? One day normal, the next day John shows up like, "Hey, Gemma, your dead father left you an inheritance." He'd actually stuttered when he realized she didn't even know Hal was her father.

Hal was dead, all Gemma had was an archaic radio station and a giant secret.

She wanted to tell her best friend, but Shelby was getting married next week. Gemma would tell her when she got back from her honeymoon—to Frannie and Matthias's house up the mountain. She'd heard the view was spectacular.

The woman was planning a wedding. She needed to focus, not worry about Gemma. So Shelby left Gemma to the quiet, and Gemma closed her eyes. Only she didn't want to be alone. She didn't want those thoughts, all the questions swirling in her head.

"Knock, knock." His voice was a whisper. Probably didn't want to wake her if she was sleeping.

Gemma smiled and turned her head. Pain spiked through her. "Ouch." She groaned the word.

Dan winced. "That bandage doesn't look good."

"Are you okay?"

His eyes softened, and he sat in the spot where Mei had been. "I'm okay. It wasn't fun, but I'm glad you're awake. What does the recovery look like?"

"Headaches for days. Blah blah, muscle aches, blah blah, plenty of rest. Something like that."

He smiled with his lips. "I brought your bag."

"My Coke?" She grasped for her tote. "My hero."

Dan blinked at her. He shook it off and said, "Mei fished it out after they got you. It's probably going to explode if you try to open it."

She waved her hand. "It's all about patience. Twist the lid a little bit, count to five. Twist, count to five. You get it open."

His smile reached his eyes. "Did they give you pain meds? I don't think I've ever heard you talk this much."

Gemma slapped a hand over her mouth. "Don't let me say anything awful." Of course it came out like, dunlet musay anyafool. But he actually laughed.

Gemma waited while the sound cascaded over her. She could count on one hand the times he'd done that. And never on this day. She held out her hand. Dan waited a second, then placed his in hers. She had to say it. "You're happy." On his birthday. She couldn't say that word, but she knew that he got it. Because he nodded before he let go, and she thought that she might have seen the sheen of wet in his eyes.

Dan cleared his throat. He probably didn't want to be alone tonight any more than she did. "I saw Mei leaving."

"She was asking questions."

"She asked me some as well, though it was pretty obvious what happened since she showed up and was the one who got you out. She actually seemed more interested in what the mayor wanted."

"Same here," she said.

"I know John has been interested. The mayor isn't doing goodwill work. He's been sick for a while, and now he's touring the town and holding private meetings with people? It doesn't make much sense."

Gemma shrugged. She wasn't about to go try and solve that mystery. She had enough of her own with the file cabinets her father had left her, stuff he'd hidden behind a false wall in his radio station. She had planned to head over there tomorrow and do some reading, since a volunteer opened the library on Saturdays for her. Try and make sense of what Hal's papers were, and why they had to be hidden from the town. Not to mention why Hal had never told anyone about them but left the guarding of them to her in his will.

Why he'd been in love with her mother.

Fathered a child with her.

Lived in town and never said one single thing to anyone about that. So many secrets. Her father, and he'd never told her that. Not once. Never tried to get to know her, even in secret. Never. Not once, her whole life.

Dan planted his fist in the bed beside her and leaned in. "Gemma, why are you crying?"

Chapter 3

Shelby's smile was so full it encompassed her whole face. Gemma tried to return it but couldn't muster much enthusiasm. She relaxed into the armchair and tried not to wince. This was her best friend's dress fitting, and Gemma wasn't going to mess it up. She'd been released from the medical center an hour ago, and all that was better left there. Especially after Dan had asked her so sweetly why she was crying, and she'd told him to leave.

Because she was a big coward.

He knew about Hal, but he couldn't know what Hal left her.

Olympia sashayed her round figure into the room. The matron held a tray of glasses and a pitcher of lemonade, which she deposited on the coffee table beside two platters of desserts.

If she could move her head without it pounding, Gemma would have probably taken three of each. *Good thing.*

Olympia clapped her hands. "Okay, ladies." The woman's eyes were shadowed, but no one said anything about the fact Antonia wasn't here and apparently had no intention of showing up.

Olympia held out her hand to Shelby, who took it. "It's time to try the dress on."

At least three people squealed. One of them was Nadia Marie Carleigh, the town's hairdresser. Gemma did her own hair color. Andra, the sheriff's wife, sat with Nadia, who was round as a…not a house, more like a large farm animal—not that Gemma would ever say that to a pregnant woman, Andra least of all. Gemma would probably drop dead, alone, hours from now, and no one would ever know what killed her.

Andra waddled over and slumped on the arm of Gemma's chair with an oof. She glanced down and smiled.

Gemma smiled back, trying not to make it obvious the woman scared the Charles Dickens out of her. "How are you?"

"I'm carrying this thing around twenty-four seven, how do you think I am?" Andra touched her belly. Her words had a tone, but the way she rubbed her stomach softly was louder.

"Ready to pop. Isn't that what people say?"

Andra snorted. "I wish it was that easy to get one of these things out."

"I wouldn't know." Never married. Never kissed…okay, maybe there was that one time, but it wasn't Dan, so it didn't count.

Andra looked like she wanted to say something, probably like, *It'll happen for you.* But she didn't, which was appreciated since Gemma despised when married people thought that a wedding and babies were the endgame of every single person. Gemma got enough drama writing fiction.

"How's your head?"

Gemma shrugged but kept her attention on the door, waiting to see Shelby come back to the living room in the dress she would wear to marry Elliot in a couple of days.

"I heard you were at Dan's farm when you fell." Gemma didn't move. Had pregnancy destroyed Andra's interrogation skills? "Did you know he's officiating the wedding?" The woman was blatantly rooting around for dirt. Andra and Nadia had likely decided Gemma would be more receptive to Andra than Nadia. Or Andra drew the short straw.

Gemma held her facial expression still. "Of course he's doing the wedding. He's the pastor."

"I wasn't sure *you* knew that."

"Worried I'll corrupt him?"

Andra hadn't moved, either. And her face never gave anything away, ever. "Could you?"

"Nope." She'd kinda tried, years ago in a desperate move. She had way too much respect for him to do that "tempting" stuff anymore. It hadn't worked anyway.

"Well then."

Gemma looked away, not the winner in the contest of wills between her and Andra. It could be construed as a draw. *Better luck next time.*

Andra chuckled. "So you're feeling better."

"As better as anyone who fell in a hole yesterday."

"That was crazy," Nadia jumped into the conversation, like she'd been waiting for the perfect opportunity to interject herself. "Seriously, you fell through the earth into a hole. Shelby and Elliot told us all about it when we came to see you at the hospital—"

"You did?"

Andra nodded. "Shelby said you weren't up to visitors."

No one had told her. Why would they come to see her? It wasn't like they were "friends." Nadia and Andra had both come to town as adults. Frannie, who ran the bakery, showed up as an older teen. Antonia, Maria and Sofia, Olympia's grown daughters, had come as kids with their brother Matthias—now Frannie's husband. Gemma hadn't really connected with any of them. Not even in a school of fifteen kids. They didn't understand her, and she didn't understand them.

Maria brought her twin boys to the library sometimes these days, but she didn't give Gemma anything more than basic cordiality. The only one who'd tried to engage her was Beth, the daughter of the former president. But Beth was gone now. Gemma had seen in the paper a while back that she and her husband had a baby boy.

"I'm feeling okay," Gemma said. "Just a little sore and a headache." She had too many things to do to be out for the count. A genre to research, a mom to draw from her shell of grief, a library to run. A secret to protect.

Nadia nudged her. "Can I ask you a question?"

"Sure, I guess." Whether she would answer depended on what the question was. These women were entirely too prying, and Gemma wasn't the kind of girl who shared just for the sake of sharing. Shelby got that from her, and Dan as well—to an extent. But no one really knew everything. Gemma wasn't sure she wanted them to. Not that she was being mean, but she liked her privacy. Hal had too, evidently, so maybe it ran in the family. She might have inherited something from her father besides the radio station.

"Well, my question is…" Nadia drew it out. "You've lived here your whole life—"

"I don't want to be mayor."

Andra burst out laughing.

Nadia grinned. “This isn’t about that, it’s about the radio station.”

“Oh.”

“I’m thinking about getting it back up and running. Maybe renovating the place… Did you know Hal still used eight-track tapes?” When Gemma nodded, Nadia continued, “Anyways, I think it would be nice, you know, like a way to honor him. Re-open the radio station in his name and start broadcasting again.” Nadia took a breath. “I’ve already petitioned the committee about the funds. I figured I’d do it all aboveboard instead of just writing a check myself, so I’m asking everyone what they think, to see if anyone has any objections.”

Gemma had more than a few. The radio station was hers, not Nadia and Andra’s. Hal left it to her in a will that had been drawn up years before, when she was only a baby. Since he’d been killed in the explosion that blew up half the ranch, Gemma had inherited an aging building she didn’t want—along with everything it contained.

Nadia was right, it did need renovating. But they couldn’t start knocking down walls in the radio station, not when Hal had built a secret room into the place where he’d stored file cabinets full of decade’s old paperwork. Gemma hadn’t figured out what it all was yet, but she needed time go through it. She just wasn’t all that motivated. It would likely not yield any answers as to why he hadn’t told her that he was her father. It looked more like government stuff.

How on earth was Gemma going to explain it all to these ladies still waiting for an answer? She opened her mouth to spout something or other, but the door opened and Shelby walked in. White dress, modest neckline. Embroidery. She looked breath-stealingly beautiful. They’d picked out a white gown for Gemma from the same magazine, just for fun, though hers had been a whole lot shorter. But she hadn't bought it, because it wasn't like she'd ever actually get married.

With her luck, Dan would see her in the sweet bridesmaid's dress and have a heart attack. *End of story.*

Shelby's mouth curled up into a smile. "Well?"

The girls erupted into screams. Gemma winced. She might not have come if she'd known they were going to be so loud. While they squealed and hugged Shelby, and Olympia tsk-ed at them for touching the dress, Shelby's gaze never left her.

Gemma mouthed, *It's good.*

Shelby grinned.

After Shelby had been hemmed and pinned so that Olympia could make the final adjustments, she changed back into her normal clothes, and they all sat to eat. Shelby put two of everything on a plate and set it on Gemma's lap before she could object.

"Hush."

Gemma shot her a look. "So, wedding girl." She needed to deflect all this attention back where it was supposed to be. "Everything is all set for the big day?"

Shelby's smile turned dreamy, and she nodded. "Everything is ready." She glanced around, including the group in their conversation. "Elliot and I have been meeting with Dan, like John and Andra did. And like Bolton and Nadia will be doing one of these—"

"Not there yet." Nadia held her hand up, palm out. The one with the engagement ring on her finger. "Taking it slow."

They all laughed.

"We totally are!"

Andra shoved her shoulder playfully. "I give it four more months, tops."

Nadia's cheeks turned pink. "So… Shelby." There she went, drawing out her words again. "Olympia is in charge of the dress, and Frannie the cake, so long as she's not throwing up from morning sickness since the woman went and got pregnant again *straight away*. Dan is officiating the wedding…"

Shelby glanced aside at Gemma at the mention of Dan's name. Just a look, but Andra shifted. Gemma gritted her teeth.

"What was that?" Nadia's question was totally innocent. Still, Gemma glared at Shelby for a second. Why did she have to give stuff away like that?

"I think you should say Dan's name again," Andra said to Nadia like they were a tag-team. "More might happen."

Gemma shook her head. "It will not."

Shelby lifted her hands in surrender.

"I have to go." Gemma stood. "My head is killing me, and I have to check on the library." Which Shelby totally knew was a lie. The thing that killed her was leaving those two tiny cakes she could've eaten with one bite—

She grabbed them and stuffed them in her mouth, then said, "Bye," without spitting cake everywhere.

"Gemma."

She waved Shelby off, so her friend would know she wasn't mad. She just didn't want to talk about Dan with a bunch of women who thought he was their "friend." Sure, he was their pastor, and he'd even "led Frannie to the Lord." Which she was pretty sure he'd tried to do with her a bunch of times. Her life wasn't fodder for girl talk. No way. That wasn't sincere, and it would just end up being gossip.

Gemma walked, since she'd gotten a ride there with Shelby in the medical center's golf cart. She could go home or to the library. Or her mom's house. Instead she made her way to the radio station. Her life was her business, and if her father had entrusted something serious to her, she needed to figure out what that was so she'd know what she was protecting.

Dan's life wasn't fodder for gossip, either. Sure, he was their leader-guy for their church, but he had a right to the privacy he'd so carefully preserved all these years. He even managed to act normal around them, though she knew he would hit his limit after a few hours and need to recharge. All those women in that house were either members of his church or they attended sometimes. She was the odd one out. And not about to confront the fact she knew more about his faith, and what it meant to him, than any of them.

It's breath.

How many times had she heard him say that? More than she remembered. She hadn't understood it until the first time she'd seen him lose it. PTSD. Such a bland explanation for something that had rocked her world. She'd been so scared, and she wasn't sure he even remembered what had happened.

Gemma glanced down at the tattoos that covered her right arm, the ones Olympia insisted she cover up for the wedding. She ran her finger down the middle, where the scar lay underneath.

A scar Dan had given her.

**

Dan muscled the wheelbarrow back into the barn. Sweat-equity he'd heard it called. This farm had been grown on his weeding, harvesting, tilling, and planting. A lot of that was his father's relentless abuse: it had taken years, but he was able to call it what it was now. Still, even with all the hitting and shouting, and then more hitting, Dan saw life in those green shoots which peeked through the ground every spring and throughout the year in his green house.

Creation. He saw God in everything around him. His father—even just his memory of the man—wasn't able to take that away. Dan loved this earth. He'd bled for it, cried for it, begged for it, and survived it.

"Caught you."

He spun to see Chase lean against the wall then cross one foot over the other. Dan's manager grinned. If he'd had a piece of hay in his mouth it wouldn't have looked out of place.

Dan had figured one of them would corner him at some point today. It was safer if it was Chase and not Miranda.

Dan exhaled. "You caught me?"

"You've been avoiding me all day."

Dan pushed the wheelbarrow down the aisle. Bay nickered, and he clicked his tongue in reply. He should call over to the medical center and find out how Gemma had been doing when they released her. Or he could call her place. He had her number noted down somewhere. He could dig it out and ask how she was... over the phone. That wouldn't be weird. At least not weirder than him asking after her around town.

When he'd asked *Papa* what he should do, Dan heard only silence. He didn't know what that meant but mostly figured it was his choice, and it wouldn't have disastrous ramifications.

But what if God wanted their relationship brought to light in some dramatic revelation? What if Papa didn't approve? Dan didn't know if he could swallow that.

They didn't see each other much, but when they did, it healed him. Gemma had been there through so much of what he had gone through. Placing her tiny hand in his. That soft squeeze of her fingers.

He could barely think about his life and she wasn't in it. Gemma was God's gift to his sanity. Without her, the past would be a yawning chasm of darkness. She was His light to Dan, even if she didn't believe.

Chase's voice turned sardonic. "Speaking of avoiding…"

"Avoiding is such a negative word." Dan pulled off one glove and scratched the itch on his forehead that had been there for an hour. "What's up?"

Chase pushed off the wall. "Need a hand?"

"Nope." He liked it better when he worked by himself. All his staff knew that, and they only occasionally forced the issue to make him connect with someone.

"So we're not going to address this giant gaping hole of an issue in the yard? Is that it?"

"I'm thinking about it." John had set Mei on the investigation into a possible security risk that depended on where the tunnels went, but he hadn't seen her yet.

"Think harder," Chase said. "We need to know how far out we should walk to avoid stepping in a hole ourselves. We need someone who knows about this stuff to come and look at the property and figure out how to make it safe. The school is coming for a field trip in two weeks. They can't bring kids here if there's a risk one of them is going to fall in a hole like—"

Papa.

Chase's hand settled on his shoulder. "Whoa. Set the fork down."

Dan lowered the tool.

"Take a breath and push it out."

He wanted to push off Chase's hand and take two steps back, but that was both unloving and defensive. Chase didn't fully understand his aversion to having a bigger man touch him, especially when adrenaline flowed. He breathed. His friend only meant well.

"I'm okay." Dan waited another breath, while he debated how much to share. "I just keep seeing Gemma fall."

"How well did you sleep last night?"

Dan shot him a look.

"Okay." Chase's look darkened. "You know you're supposed to use those supplements I gave you when you need to rest."

Drugs probably would have been better, if Dan were willing to go to Dr. Noel. Get something to make him pass out that also left him unable to dream. He was not adverse to medication, not when he trusted Elliot far more than any of the other doctors Sanctuary had suffered through over the years. Elliot was astute enough he'd noticed something was wrong and had offered to help him. It was Dan who was hesitating.

He didn't have a chemical imbalance in his brain that needed to be regulated. What he had was a crazy past, and Dan didn't want to have to go through the process of discovering the right dose if it meant that past was going to rear its ugly head in the meantime.

In an ideal world he'd have a professional counselor and a support system of professionals who knew exactly how to help him. But this wasn't anything close to an ideal world—this was Sanctuary.

He'd rather pray and read his Bible. Which was exactly what he'd done. "I got half my sermon outlined."

"That's no good if you fall asleep during church tomorrow."

Dan motioned to his manager. "It's only you guys who fall asleep at church, not me."

"Nice deflection. As if I'd do that." Chase gave him a look. "Those supplements won't do you any good if you don't take them."

Dan acquiesced with a nod.

"If it's okay with you, I'd like to go in the house and take a look around. See what the damage is to the inside." When Dan started to object, Chase said, "I know after the bomb went off you condemned it, but I think you did that without even going inside."

"The foundation is cracked." That was obvious enough from the east side wall. He didn't need to go inside. "The basement probably caved in. It could fall to a heap of wood scraps any minute."

"I'll be careful. But if I can, I'd like to see if that tunnel Gemma fell into leads to the basement, or whether it's connected to the house at all." He glanced around the barn, like he suddenly wanted to be pacing out the distance between the walls and checking for false doors.

"It doesn't lead here. I've checked the whole barn."

"Did you know anything about it?" Chase's eyes lit up. "An honest-to-goodness tunnel?"

"I had no idea." He hadn't stepped foot in the house in fifteen years, so it wasn't like he went exploring around the place. Before that? The basement had been off limits.

"I'm going to look around in there. I'm also going to talk to the sheriff and see if he knows anyone who is a structural engineer, or whether we'll have to request outside help."

They could have someone flown in. A person with the required security clearance. Before the town had voted to break away from the federal government, and gotten the president's signature of approval on it, they would have simply put in a request and the military would have brought someone in. They had less help now, which was likely the government's way of punishing them for wanting their independence.

Dan let him go. If Chase wanted to go inside the house, Dan wasn't going to stop him. He didn't want anything to do with the place, but it was embarrassing to think of someone else seeing the disaster that was probably in there. His dad hadn't been the cleanest person in the world, which Dan knew first-hand since he'd had to clean up most of the messes.

The last time he'd been in the house, his mom had been in there. But he didn't want anything to do with that memory. Not even the good parts.

**

Night had fallen by the time Mei made it out to the farm. Chase met her at the rear of the house, skulking. The man wasn't good at hiding. She could see his agitation from here.

"Ready?"

Chase nodded. "He thinks we're going inside to see if it's structurally sound."

Mei didn't care what the reason was, or that they had a valid excuse. This town was a fishbowl, and the way the farm manager treaded around Dan Walden like he was made of glass was bizarre. She didn't know how they coped living so close to each other. She liked open spaces.

Chase used a key to get in the house, and Mei stood at the threshold of the door. "You realize you actually *should* have an engineer come in here, right?"

He nodded and disappeared into the house. "I'm just worried about Dan. He needs help, but there's next to nothing I can do if I don't know the extent of what I'm dealing with. I'm hoping the house will shed some light on it."

Mei wasn't worried about Dan. She rubbed her stomach and the left-over bruises from being lowered into that hole. She'd seen survivors before, many in way worse shape mentally than he was. He would be fine. Sometimes being left alone was the best medicine.

Inside the house was a cloud of dust thick enough Chase coughed. Old furniture, frayed from back when it was in use, was now ready to fall apart. Pictures on the walls were yellowed with age. Chase wandered into the kitchen, and Mei followed her instincts. Living room. She looked at the space. Couches laid out like that, only a man would place the rug in that spot. A man who didn't know a thing about interior design.

She knelt and slowly lifted the corner of the rug, tilting her head to see the floor below. Her flashlight illuminated the wooden boards.

With one glance to check Chase wasn't looking, she switched her flashlight to emit a black light.

Blood.

She let the carpet drop back down and got out her satellite phone. The town had spared no expense in keeping their people safe, though she'd had to wrangle a connected phone of her own. The sheriff wanted to give her a two-way radio. Like that would do.

Mei sent a message to her contact.

Get me everything you can find on Dan Walden's parents.

Chapter 4

"How is Mei settling in?"

Sanctuary's sheriff, Deputy Marshal John Mason, sat on the couch in his apartment, upstairs from the Main Street store front that was the sheriff's office. He shrugged to the TV screen, where he'd connected the video call, and answered his brother's question. "Seems to be doing fine."

His brother Grant was the former director of the US Marshals, so technically at one time his boss… but no longer. Now the town was unincorporated, and while he was still a marshal, John was more "on-loan" to this unique town. Full of federal witnesses, John was the law in a town of people with prices on their heads. And while he'd heard the story of the tiny witness protection town in Hawaii, from both Grant and Bolton, he was still sure that Sanctuary was the first—and the only—fully functioning witness protection town in the country.

Two hundred people who were his to protect.

"That's good, I'm glad Mei is doing well," Grant said, his voice tinny on the TV.

The screen display was split between Grant, a congressman from Utah, a representative to the Secretary of Defense, John's other brother Nate, and Dr. Elliot—Noel's father. John had a third brother, Ben, but the man never participated in their Monday morning update meetings.

John said, "Sure. Real good."

Nate actually snorted at this response. Grant knew just as well as Nate did how John felt about the timing of Mei's arrival and the fact their brother Ben had done a lot of work in Asia. Nothing that involved Ben was ever coincidental, and he figured this wasn't either. He just couldn't figure the woman out. She wasn't ex-military or CIA that he could tell. Black ops, maybe, given the way she moved. He'd read the file he was given. Whether it was true or not was a guess at best. John just couldn't shake the feeling Ben had been involved in the woman's coincidental arrival.

Grant said, "Nate, is everything set with you and Cyan?"

Nate had met and fallen in love with a woman who had lived in Sanctuary as a child and been signed out by her mother at eighteen. Still in danger, Nate had helped her through a hard time, and they'd fallen in love.

Nate grinned. "We should be in Sanctuary in less than a month, after Cyan testifies for the last time. After that it's all paperwork and packing."

John returned his smile. He'd be a father again by then. His son Pat was growing like a weed. The kid was best friends with the autistic young man who lived with them, Aaron. A new baby was just what they all needed, and this little one was going to change all of their lives. Not to mention his brothers would be uncles again, and his mom a grandma. It would be nice to have more extended family around full time.

Ben would say that John had gone soft, but he was happy to be soft considering the alternative was being alone.

"Now for business," Grant said. "You all have the file I sent about the witness from Hawaii who identified himself as 'Colt.' This man has requested to be transferred to the protected witness town of Sanctuary."

John opened the file on his iPad and scanned the text. He gaped at what he read.

Grant said, "Colt's real name is Malachi Molotov—"

"Absolutely not," Elliot's father said. His bushy beard moved as he mashed his lips together, his attention on the papers in his hands. "This man will not be going to Sanctuary, not now and not ever."

"I'm inclined to agree." The assistant to the Secretary of Defense closed the file, not even turning past the first page.

The words *Russian hitman* had stuck in John's brain, eclipsing everything beyond that point. He sighed. Colt might have made a good addition to the town, but now they would never know. Not when the committee viewed the safety of residents and the integrity of its security as paramount. John didn't disagree with that, not considering his wife was about to have a baby. But God's love had filled him, and when it did the job it was supposed to do, it meant that John was filled with grace, hope, and forgiveness. He could let his fear get in the way or his pride, but the purity and all-encompassing nature of God's love meant John viewed Colt with only possibility. An opportunity to love someone God had put in his path.

He couldn't do that if they didn't even let the man into the town.

The call wrapped up with everyone saying goodbye and clicking off until it was only Grant and John left talking. "Anything you need?" Grant asked.

"A structural engineer."

Grant's eyes bugged out. "I thought you were going to say 'baby stuff.'"

John told him about Dan's house and the ground falling in.

"Is Gemma okay?"

"She seems fine now, just bruises. She lost consciousness, but they released her the next day."

"Yeah, because you guys don't have an MRI machine."

John wasn't going to disagree. "Elliot knows what he's doing. He's a good doctor."

Grant didn't look convinced, but that only made John more convinced the man was worried about all of them, family or not, in the town. Sure, they'd had some crazy times lately, the last of which was a bomb going off in the mountain above the ranch. Then Nadia Marie and Bolton got lost outside town, and she came home with a teenage boy who was Bolton's son. Weeks later Bolton had shown up in a wheelchair.

John blew out a breath. "Some quiet would be good."

Grant burst out laughing.

"What?"

"Brother, you're about to have a baby. Kiss quiet goodbye."

"Oh yeah," John frowned. "Forgot about that."

Grant just laughed harder, so John disconnected the call. He didn't need that kind of negativity in his life. What he needed was to go check on Gemma but not because she'd fallen down a hole.

Gemma hadn't done anything with the radio station since John had explained both that Hal was her father—surprise—and that he'd given her everything he had. They didn't know anything about Hal. John had checked his file and discovered the man was one of the first to enter the witness protection town of Sanctuary—maybe even the very first.

According to his file, Hal had arrived with another man known only as Bill Jones. Neither of them had any file recorded anywhere. They either pre-dated John's paper files, or they simply hadn't existed before they entered witness protection. Not unheard of, but still rare. Whatever the reason, John was under the impression it was why Sanctuary had been founded in the first place. The secret that had built this town.

And one which had the potential to destroy it.

**

Gemma set the book down and sighed. Gothic horror was all well and good until she actually had to fall asleep. It probably wasn't a sustainable genre. The library was quiet, and the sun had fallen behind the mountains. Twenty more minutes and she could close up the library, head over to the radio station and do some more reading, figure out what all those Army division-something papers were all about.

She'd almost been tempted to go to church on Sunday morning. Just as it had been tempting to pound on her mom's door and ask why she wasn't calling back, like the woman could hide in a town like this.

The low-grade headache she had from her fall was manageable, though caffeine didn't help. Not in the quantities Gemma drank. Hers was what they called an "addiction" but she wasn't going to admit to anyone she needed help. She'd just swivel her chair so she could see the empty carafe on the cold and empty pot and stare at it. Shelby had set a limit on her intake. She sighed.

She needed a new book to write.

Urban fantasy. Something with magic and shapeshifters. A quest. No, a boy coming home because the dream of what he'd thought his life would be was now dead. He has a special power. No, everyone else does but he doesn't...

Gemma pulled her notepad over and started scribbling. It had potential. She'd have to flesh it out. She'd never done a magic-related genre before. Steampunk, yeah, and all those gadgets along with the Victorian outfits had been cool. Fun to get swept away in, even when she was the author.

"Knock, knock." His voice was like an old quesadilla where all that great melted cheese had gone cold and slimy. "Who's there?" Andy Evangeline sauntered into the library and headed straight for her. He didn't need a book. If she hadn't gone to school with him and seen it with her own eyes she'd wonder if he could even read.

"Hi, Andy."

He crossed his arms on the counter and smiled. "It's Terrence. I've decided to go back to my first name again instead of my middle name."

Seriously?

He looked like he expected her to say something, but she didn't. Why would she care if he was having an identity crisis? She didn't even like the man and never had.

Gemma had to use a lot of expressions in her writing that she'd picked up from other books and then hoped she'd used correctly. After all, there were no used car lots in Sanctuary, just a couple of cars and a few golf carts, and most people walked or biked where they wanted to go, but she got the idea.

Plus, she'd watched movies where the guy who sold wreckers had slicked-back hair, gold jewelry, and a silk shirt. Apparently Andy—*Terrence*—had as well, because he looked like a used car salesman from every movie she'd ever seen.

"Can I help you find a book?" *Please don't ask for one about dating.*

"Sure," he chuckled. "Got anything about asking the pretty girl for a date?"

Yeah, that was *so* funny. Ha ha. "Nope. After John didn't need the book, then Matthias, then Elliot *and* Bolton, I retired that whole section. The books were deteriorating from lack of use."

Because that totally made sense. Books totally degraded when you set them on the shelf and didn't touch them. She nearly rolled her eyes, but anyone that actually did that at themselves instead of someone else should be kicked out of the "independent woman" club.

Terrence coughed. "Yes, well." He strolled around the counter.

"No one's allowed back here."

"Except the volunteers." He kept coming toward her.

"Sure."

"And the school teacher."

She got up. "True, but—"

Terrence walked right into her space. Gemma's chair-back hit the edge of the desktop and she froze. His body almost touched hers. When she stepped to the right to escape, he stepped also. His gaze tracked down her body and back up, and he leaned forward to grasp the handles of her chair.

Gemma shoved at him to get away, but before she could bolt he grabbed her arms. "I just want to talk, Gemma."

This was on the top five list of freakiest things that had happened to her. Falling in a hole was only number two.

His face was all innocence, but she'd seen him hit Bolton over the back with a metal folding chair when the man hadn't been looking. He was practically the reason the former rancher was back in a wheelchair.

Some help, please. She didn't know who she was asking but was willing to accept whatever came and however it came about.

"And Terrence. Whatever you're calling yourself. You need to back up, then you can leave or I'm going to call the sheriff."

His innocent look hardened. "It's just a chat, that's all."

Gemma wasn't messing around. She wanted his butt out of her library. "Seriously, Terrence. We have nothing to talk about."

Movement over his shoulder brought her attention around, just for a second her gaze found Dan. Then she stared Terrence down. "I'm serious."

"I'm serious," he mock-echoed her. "Lighten up, baby." His fingers stroked her arm.

Gemma slammed both her palms into his chest and shoved him. Terrence stumbled back two steps.

Dan's voice drifted across the counter. "She's serious, Andy."

He whirled around. "It's Terrence!" Then he glanced between Dan and Gemma. Then Dan. Then Gemma again. "You guys? For real?" He shook his head, not confused, but like he didn't know where to slam his fist first. His gaze came to her.

"Baby, he is way too soft for you. You're wild, and you need someone who can handle that." He glanced at Dan. "You think you're up for the task?"

Dan said, "I have no idea what you're talking about, *Terrence*. I came to pick up a book I have on hold." Peace surrounded him, as though he put it on in the morning like a sweater and didn't take it off until bedtime. "You need to leave, or Gemma will call the sheriff."

"Over a conversation?"

Gemma said, "I have the right to ask anyone I want to leave my library."

Dan shot Terrence a look that almost made her smile. He wasn't staking a claim, they both knew he'd never do that. *Just friends.* But he was the guy who wouldn't let another man hassle her. Terrence gave her the creeps, and he needed to skedaddle.

The English language was so fun.

Terrence strode out, his head high. Gemma put her finger across her upper lip, like the lamest impression of a mustache ever, and found her most ridiculous voice. "You haven't seen the last of me…" She dissolved into evil-like cackles and then snorted. *Super attractive.*

When she looked up, Dan was smiling.

"Are you really here for your 'hold'?"

Dan's lips curled up into a smile. "You think I'd lie?"

"No, I don't. But I also don't recall you requesting a book."

"I put it in with Elma."

"I really don't need to interrogate you, sorry." She half-smiled and crouched to pull out the tub. His last name on a receipt poked up from the pages of a book. She lifted it out and handed it over. "Grace, huh?"

He shrugged. “I’m starting a series. You’ll have to come and hear it if you want to know what grace is.”

“Nice try.” She chuckled. “That was super subtle.” Gemma turned away. At the last second she caught the look on his face. Grief. Breath hitched in her throat, but she didn’t show him that or it would be worse. Gemma checked out his book.

“Are you busy right now?” She looked up in time to catch his shrug.

“I don’t have plans.”

Gemma bit her lip. “Can I show you something?”

Ten minutes later she’d locked up the library, and they walked outside. His truck was parked on the street. “You drove over?”

He shrugged. “You have to turn it on every week or so, or things inside start clogging up.”

“Oh.” She’d never actually ridden in a car. “Can we walk?”

“Still don’t want to?”

She shrugged.

“Okay.” When they got to the radio station he said, “I don’t get it. Did Nadia talk to you about renovating the place?”

Inside, they walked down the hall to the radio room. She had to check and make sure no one was there. “I know I can trust you. We’ve shared more than is normal—even between old friends—as far as I can tell. Maybe it’s normal for Sanctuary, but it could just be that it is what it is.”

“Why don’t you just tell me?”

“You know that Hal Leonard was my father, but there’s more. He left me something.”

His eyes widened. That was Dan, holding his reaction to himself and allowing her to deal with her own feelings and not his as well. Gemma shut her eyes and took a breath. “When he died, John came to tell me that Hal left this place to me. In his will."

"Wow. He left you the radio station? It was his thing." Dan shook his head, disbelief plain on his face. "I've been thinking about it since you told me. Hal… I don't know, but your mom? That's what I don't get. Why would she never say anything?"

"They kept their relationship a secret. They kept secret the fact he was my father. Everyone thinks my mom was pregnant when she came here, but that would mean she knew Hal before she came to Sanctuary, and he's been here way longer. For some reason, even here when there's no danger to them anymore, they still felt like they had to keep it a secret. From everyone. I can't make sense of any of it. The timing, the reasoning. Nothing." Gemma swallowed. "There's more."

He stepped closer to her. "What is it?"

**

Dan studied the room with its antiquated radio technology. He could hardly believe Hal was her father. The aging biker had been… maybe not a friend, but since Dan's father and the lettuce incident that sent him on his way to his eternal judgment, Hal had visited the farm almost weekly. It hit him now, though, that Dan had never even been in the radio station before. Why was that?

Over the years Hal had filled a void that should have been left by Dan's parents. They'd talked about everything. Not that Dan had to talk about God with everyone he spoke with, but faith was so natural to him it always seemed to come up. Hal had listened, and they'd even debated over creation and the existence of God.

Gemma stood taller and blew out a breath. “Okay, I was sworn to secrecy but that’s not what you and I do, so here goes nothing.” She walked to the wall and pressed. A latch opened.

Dan had no time to process the “no secrets” thing. He gaped. “What is…” His words faded as the door opened. File cabinets in a row beside boxes piled on boxes. Some had been opened, the contents disturbed. Everything was covered in a layer of dust, and the light fixture was pure seventies.

Gemma waited until he came to stand beside her, then she led him inside. The room was maybe eight-by-eight, but probably held thousands of papers. She showed him one. “They all seem to be military, like orders. Reports. Briefing summaries. Stuff like that. Lots of, ‘we moved from this place over to this place.’ I looked some of them up in the books I have on Vietnam, because of the dates. They seem legit. I found details of this one patrol, and it really happened.”

She squared her shoulders. “Hal left something in this room that I’m supposed to guard, to make sure it doesn’t get out into the world. Or just Sanctuary. But I have no idea what it could be.”

He waved his hand to encompass the room. “This could be the whole war, start to finish. Why would someone keep so many papers unless all of them were relevant?”

“Or unless you’re burying the needle in a stack of needles.”

“So it could be something, or it could be everything?” He walked to the first file cabinet and opened the drawer. “How do we tell?”

“We?”

He shrugged. “I figure you told me so I could help you look.” Obviously there might be other reasons. She knew practically everything there was to know about him, so why tell him about the room and not have him help? “We’ve been best friends for years." He hauled two chairs in from the radio room and set them down. "This is what friends do."

Her smile was hesitant, yet it didn't take much coaxing for her to brew them some coffee. He'd been up since dawn, but helping her solve the mystery of Hal Leonard being her father was more important than sleep he'd have trouble finding anyway.

Leather jacket, biker boots, and jeans. That long dirty blond hair tied back with a leather strap. As an image, it had worked for Hal. Maybe that had been the point, to deflect people's attention with the projection—a mask that allowed them to make assumptions about who he was and where he'd come from.

If it truly was a mask, Hal had worn it for years and even extended the guise to include his speech, his music tastes, and his eating habits.

Dan blinked. "What if Hal was one of these soldiers?"

"Or a spy."

He looked over at her, reading papers. She said, "A lot of people in this town have crazy, *crazy* stories about where they've been and who they were. Andra was an assassin. John was undercover, and Bolton was a criminal. How do we know Hal wasn't some kind of soldier, like you said, or a government agent?"

"I guess we don't. Until we find a paper that confirms who he was."

"It probably wouldn't even be his real name. How will we know it's about Hal?"

Would she be able to accept it if her father had been a killer? Dan knew what it was like to live with a monster. The old man could have been anyone and done anything before he came to Sanctuary. Dan didn't know the first thing about him, other than that he'd met Dan's mother—who was fifteen years younger—after he got here.

"Do I even want to know?" Her voice was soft, so he figured the question was rhetorical. "Maybe I'm better off being in the dark. I never knew he was my father before a few weeks ago, and I was happy. Sure, there was something missing from my life, but I was content knowing I would probably never get it."

Dan sifted through papers, while she aired her thoughts out loud.

"He asked me to protect this secret. Whatever is contained here in this room was important to him. Maybe I should just shut the door and never come back here." She shrugged. "Maybe I should burn it down. Why keep it all if it could be dangerous?"

Dan's breath caught. Dark eyes stared back at him from a photo, center of the stack of papers in his hand. "Don't burn it down just yet. I think I want to look through a few more of these."

"For what?" Gemma glanced up, and the frown disappeared as she saw what he held.

A picture of his father.

Chapter 5

Gemma jumped up and snatched the picture from his hands. Those eyes, jeepers they gave her the creeps. Like that gothic novel she'd been reading. Dan's father, even just a picture, set her skin crawling. No man on earth should be able to do that. Least of all a dead man.

She didn't want Dan here if this was going to be about his father.

"You should leave." She waved toward the door and hoped he didn't argue too much.

He hadn't moved, so Gemma pulled on his arm and tried to haul him out of his chair. His face contorted, and he reached for the photo.

She shoved at his hand, and the photo fell to the floor. "No!" He wasn't allowed to see that man. Gemma stomped on the paper, but it didn't help. That man had ruined everything, including Dan's whole life. Her life. His father had twisted and bent, broken and shattered everything Dan held as precious as though it were some kind of sick game. Like he got off on Dan's pain. On the power he held over all of them.

"Get out!" She tried to shove him, but he wouldn't move.

Dan didn't even touch her. His eyes filled with moisture, but all she saw was that frozen rage on his face.

"You have to get out."

He gritted his teeth. "I want to know what it says."

"It's nothing, it's just a photo." Her voice was frantic, her breaths coming short and sharp. "Just leave it. It's just a photo."

"What does that say?"

Gemma looked down. Under the dirt print of her shoe were two words. She leaned down close enough to read it. "Bill Jones."

"My father's name was Arnold Walden. Who is Bill Jones?"

"Someone who entered witness protection?" She shoved at him again. "Does it matter?"

"It matters to me, Gem." He stood ramrod straight.

"Why? He isn't here anymore. What difference will it make?" Gemma gripped the hair on the sides of her face so hard it hurt. Why did he want to know? What could he possibly gain from reading about horrible things his father had probably done when he already knew the depths of depravity of that human being's soul? Dan couldn't think it would make him feel better. There was no way.

"Dan, just go. Please." She would beg him if she had to. She'd made a mistake bringing him here, in sharing this with him. She refused to let him see any more of it. It was her thing, and she should have known it wouldn't be good telling him. Dan's God should have warned her. He couldn't possibly want

Dan to find out more awful things about a man who was supposed to have taken care of him. God had to be mistaken if He thought that would help.

The look on his face made her want to cry. "I need to understand. What if the answer is in here?"

"You can't understand a man who does what he did to a child, to his wife. There isn't anything to understand."

Dan started to shake his head. Tears finally fell, twin tracks that wet his face. Gemma swiped at the tickle on her face and realized she was crying, too.

"I want to know why he came here. I want to know who he was."

"It won't help."

"It might." His face contorted. "How could it make things worse? They can't *get* worse."

"You'll start remembering more. It'll bring things back to the surface that you've worked so hard to keep a lid on all these years."

"It's failing, Gemma. I'm failing. That stuff is so close to the surface that half the time I can barely breathe." His chest rose and fell rapidly. "I have to get it out."

"So talk to someone. John. The sheriff could help you." She would never suggest the shrink. That woman was nothing more than a file clerk, or some kind of washed up small town reporter. All she did was ask the newcomers a few basic questions.

Dan had talked to her once, years ago. She'd gone to his father afterwards and Dan had missed two weeks of school. When he finally came back he was still holding his arm funny.

She'd researched online and found infrastructure in society that was supposed to spot, and stop, abuse. Teachers, counselors, doctors, police, and other emergency services. In

Sanctuary they had none of these things. Dan hadn't even been able to get good medication to help him. He had to deal with it all by himself, and he said he was fine with that. She knew his faith was strong, and he counted on God to help him, but Gemma couldn't help thinking that a shrink and the right medication would have made his life far more peaceful.

Over and over again, every single time, it broke her heart to have to watch him go without those things.

"The sheriff can't help me." His breath hitched. "The only one who gets what I went through is you. Even Miranda looks at me funny."

Chase's wife needed to keep her looks to herself. Dan didn't need the added pressure of other people's emotions when he could barely contain his own. Gemma was going to go and have a talk with her.

"I want to know who he was." He swept his arm out to encompass the whole room. "What if the answer is in here? What if I can find out why?"

"And if there's nothing, if all you find out is that he was awful before he came here and then he was awful here, what then?" She couldn't bear it if that was all he got for this much heartache. "How will you move on?"

"I'll get up. Just like I get up every day, Gemma. I need this, even if just thinking about it is one of the hardest things I've had to do. Don't take the answer away now, when I've been handed a sealed envelope. The solution to a riddle that escaped me my whole life is in this room."

A single tear rolled down her face. What if it wasn't what he hoped for? "That man is nothing to do with you, and he never was." She pointed to the facedown photo on the linoleum floor.

Gemma said, "Hal wanted nothing to do with me. Your father terrorized you. Why do I want to know who my father was? Why do you want to know yours? Why can't we both just be happy with who we are. Who cares about the past?"

He reached for her, but she backed up a step. "No. I'd rather burn it down. Hal didn't care about me, and your father certainly never cared about you. Neither of our mothers were strong enough to handle the life they had, let alone really take care of us or protect us from getting hurt."

His gaze softened. "She still won't speak to you?"

"Don't change the subject. This isn't about my mom." Gemma folded her arms, the dampness of tears still on her face. "I'll read it all. If it's something that will help, I'll tell you what you need to know about your father. But you don't need to do this. Not if there's no guarantee of a result."

"Maybe I should read it instead of you." He stood toe-to-toe with her. "If there's something in here that will help you, I'll tell you what you need to know about *your* father."

"He wasn't my father, Dan. Not really. You know that."

"Maybe the secret he kept all these years, the secret that meant he couldn't know you…maybe it doesn't have anything to do with either Hal or my father." He shrugged. "Maybe it's something else."

"There's still information in here about both of them. Maybe we should tell someone else, because I don't want you reading about him." Even the memory of those black eyes staring at her made her flesh break out in tiny bumps. "Whatever is in here doesn't matter. We are what we make of our own lives."

"Unless God took the nothing that was my life and gave me *everything* in exchange for it."

"This isn't another gift, Dan. It's nothing but a curse."

"In my flesh dwells no good thing."

She sighed. "You've said that before, but I have no idea what it means. I was charged with keeping this secret for Sanctuary. That's it."

He looked like he wanted to say something, but then he sighed. "I know it won't be good. I know that. I don't need it to give me something; I already have everything I need. That's what I'm saying." He paused. "But I can't walk away from this. Not if it might help even just a little bit."

"I won't let you take the risk." She was pushing the boundaries of their friendship, denying him this. Dan would walk away if she made him. He wouldn't like it, but he'd walk away.

"If this secret cost you your father, it's big. No more being a lone wolf. It's not going to help you."

Gemma shook her head. "There's no 'we'. Not now. There can't be."

"Gem—"

"No. I won't let you do this."

"At least think about it."

"I won't. I can't do what you're asking." She couldn't watch the truth take the little his father had left behind and destroy that as well. "You need to leave. I can't talk to you, not now. Maybe not for a while. I can't do this friendship thing anymore."

Oh, God. I'm really doing it. She had to. *I'm breaking up with him.* "Don't come back. No more hanging out. No more chats. No more secrets. I can't do it. Not a single one of your friends even knows that we know each other more than acquaintances. And why is that?" He started to answer, but she cut him off. "I can't do this anymore, Dan."

Gemma sucked in a breath. It was for his good. She was saving him from this awful idea. "If we see each other it'll just eat at you, and you have to let it go. No one knows. This secret dies with Hal." She choked on her father's name.

"Gemma…" his voice was thin. She couldn't look at his face; she'd change her mind.

"You need to leave, Dan. I'm serious."

**

The same words she'd said to Terrence slapped him in the face. Dan took a step back, hardly able to form a complete thought. She was…

"You're breaking up with me."

"Our friendship, yes." And she wasn't going to change her mind. Dan had seen that look on her face before.

He sucked back all the emotion she didn't need to see, and said, "Fine."

Her gaze softened. "Dan—"

"No." He stepped back. "Don't do that. Not now." She'd made the decision, and she needed to stick to it.

Okay, Papa. Help me accept this. He cried to God in his head while they stared at each other. If he took one step away from her, who knew when he'd be able to come back? Dan shut his eyes, unable to spend any more time drinking in the sight of her. He turned away, walked away from his best friend in the world. Outside to the street. The library. His truck. He fired up the old beast, thanking God when the thing started.

He gripped the wheel but didn't go anywhere. She'd seriously thrown him out? Given him a gift, the possibility of understanding his father at least to an extent, and the chance to answer some of the questions of his past. Hot tears tracked down his face. It was years since he'd cried, but apparently today was his day. *Papa.* Why offer a gift and then take it away? It made no sense, although not much about Dan's life did.

He hit the gas and peeled away from the library. Didn't God want him to understand so that he could forgive?

Otherwise it made no sense. And he hated when things made no sense. Dan needed peace, and this was the opposite. His heart felt like it was on fire, flames of pain licking his chest. Life had happened to him. He'd never had the chance to make his own choices. Not even with the farm, not really. Only being the town's pastor gave him some semblance of control back.

Gemma.

Now Dan didn't even have her. God had given him enough, but Dan didn't have anything which he could give up. There was no margin, there was only God's hand on his life. Giving. Taking.

Dan clung to Him regardless of the fact he was falling apart. He was never *not* falling apart, it was just that it happened in differing degrees.

He pulled up outside the barn, across from where Gemma had fallen into the ground. Someone had taped off the area. They should have taped off the house, too. Dan let go of the steering wheel and squeezed the bridge of his nose. The sound of a gunshot, that *crack* which had filled his ears. He could never escape it.

He glanced at the house. Maybe she had the right idea to get rid of the issue by burning those papers. But if he burned the house down would that really make things better? He'd probably start a wildfire with as dry as things had been lately. The town's air quality would tank as the smoke had nowhere to go. Inversions were a killer here. The mountains didn't let anything out unless the incoming front was strong enough to scoop the air from the basin where Sanctuary sat.

If not for all that, he'd have burned the place down years ago. But it wouldn't get rid of the memories. All that blood. The searing pain. His father's laughter.

No one had even asked him what happened, and he'd never gone into that house again. His mother was gone forever. Dan had been left with little but a pain and rage he could do nothing about. The backlash from his father would put him in the ground as well.

It wasn't until he'd found God that he'd been able to let go of some of that furious helplessness.

Dan shifted in the seat and pulled his Bible out. He leaned his head back on the headrest and absorbed David's words, finding his feelings echoed there in the Psalms as the not-yet-king cried out for justice. For peace. Not an absence of fighting, but a state of mind that allowed God to be sovereign in spite of what was going on.

Everything had shifted, like that ground which should have held up Gemma. Was the answer in those files she'd banished him from? Dan hadn't only lost his shot at finding out who his father was, and maybe why the old man had been the way he had been, he'd also lost her. Sure, they didn't see each other frequently, but she'd been there. Through so much of his life she'd been *present* for him, a solid person he could hang onto. Maybe she didn't get the depth of feeling he had for her, the way he'd needed her deep down to his core. He would have said she knew what their friendship meant to him.

But maybe she hadn't.

Either way he wasn't going to be a burden. If she wanted him gone, fine. He'd honor her wishes and stay away. Try to forget what she'd been given and find his answers some other way. Now he had a name to research, a name Hal had known all along. *Bill Jones.* He should check the house for information, maybe look through anything his parents might have kept in the attic. If he could bring himself to go inside.

A curtain shifted. Dan frowned. Was someone inside the house?

He climbed out of the truck and walked around the bed. The sheriff's Jeep approached on the road. Dan looked back at the house one more time before he went to meet John as he got out of his vehicle.

"What's up, Sheriff?"

John shut his car door, then pinned Dan with a look.

Dan said, "Something is." Was it bad?

"How about you driving forty-five through town? That enough for you?"

"Uh…" He had? Dan had been so upset, he'd just driven.

"I'd ask for your license and registration if you'd been given any, or ever been required to take any kind of test." John sighed. "Want to tell me why you were going so fast I got calls from three different people? You blazed a trail through town. They said you looked upset."

Dan glanced at the window and the curtain he'd seen move. "I'm okay now."

Was it just his imagination, or had someone actually been in there? It was hard to tell anymore, what was real and what wasn't. So much of this land was pure memory, shadows of the past he couldn't escape or ignore. The house was a specter at best. Not a physical thing, but the sum of his memories. A past that beat at him, constantly.

"Dan?"

He turned.

"Is something going on?"

Papa. Dan waited for an answer on what to tell the sheriff, but it didn't come. He didn't want to lie, but neither did he want to explain the sad reality of his life to a man he respected. A man he considered a friend.

"You can talk to me, you know."

And tell the sheriff that he never went in his own house, and that he lived in the barn? John didn't want to know that. It was enough that Chase, Miranda, and Gemma knew what they did about him.

Dan scratched the side of his head. "I have a lot on my mind. I *had* a lot on my mind when I drove through town. It won't happen again."

"That's not what I'm worried about, Dan. You seem kinda…I don't know, out of it?" John shook his head. "I can't put my finger on it except that things seem to have changed since Gemma was hurt here."

"Okay." What was he supposed to say about that? "Sunday was fine, wasn't it?"

"I'm not concerned about your sermon. That's not the part of you that worries me."

"There's nothing anyone can change."

"Then tell me why you look at your own house like it's going to jump up off the ground and bite you."

Dan bit his lip. Weight hit his shoulder. Dan flinched from under it before he realized John had simply set his hand on Dan's shoulder. "Shoot." Dan ran his hands down his face.

"This is more than you being out of sorts."

Dan didn't want to say it all out loud. "Can't you just read my file?"

"You were born here. You don't have a WITSEC file."

"What about my father?"

John shook his head. “Him either, for some reason. He isn’t even listed. I read your mother’s and the police report. It was a blessing you weren’t there to see them argue badly enough she’d run off, though the file indicates you spent the night in the woods.”

Right. An argument, and his mom had run off. What had the previous sheriff thought, putting all that down? Had he seriously believed it? Thc sheriff before John…Dan didn’t even know how to describe Chandler. But he hadn’t helped anyone. He’d looked the other way far too many times.

Only Gemma had really seen Dan and seen the truth. Her mom had looked aside at him a few times, and Olympia had tried to get him to open up about himself, but by then it was too late. His father’s reign of terror lasted until the minute his heart failed, and he hit the ground.

“It’s over now.” At least, he wanted to be done with it. Though it seemed the past didn’t want to be done with him. *Is that You, Papa?*

“I’m here, if you want to talk.”

Dan shrugged but nodded as well. He didn’t know what to say, but it was clear that John cared about him. Dan couldn’t tell the story out loud. Gemma had known, and so there was never any need to speak about it.

John pulled a paper from his pocket and held it out. “Until then, here’s your speeding ticket.”

Chapter 6

The following Saturday afternoon Gemma saw the moment her mom arrived at the wedding. Ten minutes to start and Gemma dashed out of the dressing room. Shelby was ready; she was early for everything and apparently her own wedding was no exception.

"Gem—"

She was out the door before Shelby could finish, but then she glanced over her shoulder. "I'll be back in one second."

White chairs had been arranged in rows at the park for the wedding. The place was transformed in a way Gemma knew it would never be for her. Shelby hadn't missed a thing, which made the contrast all the more stark between Shelby's wedding and the wedding Gemma figured she'd probably never have.

Dan was there. She'd have to stand close to him and pretend everything was fine. Talk about awkward. She hadn't seen him since she'd kicked him out of the radio station, and it still hurt. Like something inside her had ripped open and would never be repaired.

It was all over town about the speeding ticket. Six hours of community service, whatever he chose to do. It wasn't exactly punishment, unless he chose something like trash duty, but John had made his point.

Law in Sanctuary didn't happen the way it did on those TV shows. Forty years and they'd only had one murder—at least that was recorded. She'd always figured the previous sheriff reported whatever he wanted just to prove the town was a success. Debatable. He'd probably been more of a fan of his assignment in a small town, than of actually policing people who pretty much just wanted to be left alone.

Gemma slowed as she caught up to where her mom stood. People gave her weird looks, but she ignored them. They'd never thought she was normal. Why get them to change their thinking now? Her mom's hair was down and unwashed. She hadn't bothered to style it, but it still gleamed strawberry blonde in the sunlight. Her mom had been so beautiful when Gemma was younger. She wasn't even fifty-five now, so why did she seem so old?

"Mom." Gemma tried to stop gracefully, but heels were not her friend. Shelby hadn't let her wear Converse, probably because she hated her and wanted Gemma to break her neck. Okay, maybe not. "Hey, Mom, wait up."

Janice turned. Her outfit was a dress that draped over her slender figure, swirls of color. Beads. A hippie headband to keep wayward strands off her face. She barely reacted. "Gem. You're here."

Of course she was here. She was a bridesmaid.

Gemma gathered her mom to her, whether she wanted a hug or not. "Hi."

Gemma readjusted the wrap that covered her shoulders. It was okay that she'd moved out. It was okay that she'd taken that step toward independence a few months ago, and it wasn't the reason her mom looked so haggard.

Gemma sighed. "How are you?"

Like there was nothing special to talk about, just checking in. Like Hal wasn't her father, and he hadn't left her the town's secrets behind a hidden door in his radio station for her to guard. Like her mom hadn't been with Hal for years and never told anyone.

This was just the way it was.

"Fine." Janice faked a smile, but Gemma didn't buy it. "I'm so happy for Shelby. I ordered her that pan set from her registry. I'm so glad it got here on time."

She should give her mom more of a break. Janice was grieving. "Can we get together later? I have some things that I need to talk to you about." She paused, but didn't want to give her mom too much time to formulate an excuse. "Would that be okay?"

"Sure, Gem. Why don't you come over for dinner tomorrow?"

"Oh. Yeah, okay. That would be great." Just like that. She'd been avoiding Gemma for weeks, and now she wanted them to have dinner? "Thanks, Mom." She kissed Janice on the cheek.

"There's Sam." Janice waved at Sam Tura, who ran the gym and the diner. "I have to go now and sit in the single-old-fogey's section."

Her mom jingled away while Gemma stared after her. What was going on? Except for that sadness in her eyes, she was acting like nothing had changed—as though Hal hadn't died, and Gemma hadn't found out her mom had kept her father a secret from her for her entire life.

Am I crazy?

Maybe it was her. Maybe Gemma was the one who was nuts, and everyone else didn't get it because they were still normal. Maybe a switch had tripped, and she'd gone crazy since John came to the library to talk to her about the details of Hal's will. Now Gemma had a million questions and no answers. She'd looked through some of the papers after Dan left and found a box all dated *after* Hal and Dan's dad were in Sanctuary. Reports from when Gemma had been a child, about Bill Jones and what he was doing. Concerns he might be up to something more than he claimed. Hal had been reporting to someone about Dan's dad, watching the man.

She hadn't found anything in there about his temper or any of the things he'd been doing to Dan's mom or the then six-year-old Dan. Not one reference, when Gemma knew for a fact there had been incidents back then. The school teacher, the nurse, the doctor, the sheriff. None of them had done anything to help Dan.

The one she was most disappointed in was her father. He'd been an observer to Dan's life, but not man enough to help a little boy who'd been hurt over and over again? Why was Gemma the only one who'd known?

"Excuse me." Someone strode past her, not even giving her eye contact.

Gemma wondered if she was invisible, and not for the first time. She projected whatever she projected, but no one really saw her, and now she had ruined the best thing she'd had going. First she'd sent her best friend away. Now Shelby was getting married. Things would change, as they should when her friend joined her life with Elliot's, but that didn't mean it would feel good to be alone again.

She'd always had Dan as a fallback. Now she wouldn't even have him to talk to.

Gemma turned in a circle. A crowd of people in their Sunday best, waiting for a wedding. Her town, happy and content. They thought they knew her—that she was just the librarian. They all got to go about their lives and be *fine*, while Gemma's artist soul wouldn't let her be satisfied. Something in her cried out for…more than this.

Her gaze met his, where Dan stood with Elliot beyond the front row. She wanted to smile back but couldn't. He didn't need to know more about his dad, but maybe they could still salvage their friendship. Because as much as she'd wanted to let go of him and live her life, Gemma had to face the fact that she needed him. Maybe as much as he'd seemed to need her. Dan tipped his head and motioned for her to get out of there. Gemma shot him a smile, glad they were still okay, and spun to see Olympia headed her way. She met up with the woman and took the tongue lashing she deserved.

Shelby stood with Elliot's father in an alcove where no one could see them, taking the last of their pre-wedding photos together. The bride frowned. "There you are."

"Sorry." Gemma rushed to her place.

"Don't know what you were doing," Olympia huffed, coming up behind her. "Standing in the middle of everything like a ninny."

"I'm here now, aren't I? Let's get this show on the road."

Shelby frowned, but Gemma motioned to her that everything was fine. Shelby knew she cared, that Gemma was happy for her, and that was enough. Gemma really liked Elliot, and he was good to her friend. So what was Gemma's problem?

Was she really so selfish she couldn't let her friend have her day without Gemma bringing her own drama into it?

Gemma thought about it as she walked down the aisle without tripping. *If that was You, God, then thanks.* She wasn't above thanking God for something as simple as her not falling on her face.

Dan's eyebrows crinkled into a frown. A smile played on his lips, and the notes were sweet, endearing. Before long he pronounced the married couple as Dr. and Mrs. Elliot Noel, and everyone stared while they kissed. Gemma couldn't look at Dan. She didn't want to know if he was looking at her. And if he did, it was likely he'd see everything she felt right there on her face. Just like every romance novel she'd ever written, the girl would give everything away, and the guy would know he just had to sweep her off her feet and she'd go with him.

But that wasn't going to happen to her. Maybe there was some kind of always-the-bridesmaid thing that meant single authors of romance novels never found love like they wrote about.

The crowd cheered. Gemma jerked out of her daydream and clapped. She looked across the rows of chairs filled with Sanctuary residents.

The mayor stood at the back, by himself.

Staring right at her.

**

"Smile," John said. "Otherwise people will think you're mad at me for giving you a speeding ticket."

Dan kept a straight face. "Who says I'm not mad?"

John's smile dropped. "Seriously?"

Dan couldn't help but laugh. "Don't worry about it, *Sheriff.*" He clapped the guy on the shoulder. "No harm, no foul. I'm thinking about helping with some landscaping at the library and the school. You know, for the children."

And had nothing to do with the fact he'd get to see Gemma. The idea had come to him when he'd woken that morning. She'd played the lead in his dreams, where he mowed the grass for her, and she brought him a lemonade. The kiss part would have to wait.

"Good for you." John grinned. "Nice wedding. That extra line, 'until Jesus comes for us' instead of the 'death do us part' stuff was good. I should've thought of that."

Dan took a sip of his soda. He did like weddings, even though part of him held himself distant from it because he knew he would never experience any of this except from his side of the proceedings. All it would ever be was a gift to his friends.

But not today. "Did you see the mayor earlier?"

John sipped his own drink. His eyes drifted across the crowd of people. "Left right after the service. With Janice, if I'm not mistaken."

Dan had seen Collins staring at Gemma. The man didn't need to bother her or get anywhere near her. The feeling rose up in him, inexplicably. Collins needed to keep a distance from Gemma. "Antonia is missing, also."

John's eyebrows rose. "She is?"

Like John didn't know. He held so much close to his shirt that it made the sheriff hard to read sometimes. "Last I heard, Shelby thought she might be involved with the mayor." Romantically, if Shelby was right. Not a couple that made any sense. Antonia was wild, but she was young. Why spend time with an old man whose health was failing?

"Is that gossip I hear from you, pastor?"

Dan pressed his lips together. "Just another wayward sheep to add to my prayer list."

"Okay, fine." John indicated toward the food tables. "Less people over there now that it's been picked over. Let's go."

Dan picked up a new plate even though he was full. There was one deviled egg and a couple of pieces of watermelon left.

John stood close to him, got a plate, and added a couple of carrots then twice as much dressing as anyone would need to dip them in. "Yes, Antonia is missing. Or at least just not here today, but she hasn't been around for a day or so. I'm not at the point I'm seriously worried something has happened, but I am close to it. I've got Mei out looking for her, since Mei doesn't like weddings."

Dan shot him a look.

"And since she's also not really a people person."

Dan smiled. "I might've noticed that, but I decided to let it go since she pulled Gemma out of the hole in my yard. So that's it, Antonia's missing?"

"Yes and no." John paused. "Back when the mayor first started acting weird, I noticed he paid…uh…extra attention to Antonia. I talked to her, and she was amenable to getting close to him and passing me information on the basis that if she gets even an inkling that she's not safe she tells me, and I get her out."

"She's undercover?"

John shrugged. "She wants out… of Sanctuary… and she needs money to do that. I'm helping her get set up in the outside world as soon as she's done, and in exchange she's doing this for me. Two more months and she's leaving."

"Does her family know?"

"She refuses to confirm whether she's told them or not, which probably means she hasn't, and she just didn't want to tell me that." John shrugged one shoulder. "I don't want to believe her plan is to leave without telling anyone. It's not a good idea."

"Not just because it leaves you in the awkward position of explaining to everyone your involvement."

"She promised me she'd be telling her mother."

Dan shot the sheriff a look. "Do you think the mayor knows she's not a genuine admirer?"

"I can't get a read on him," John said, scanning the area with his gaze even though the mayor had left. "I don't think she's blown, but then where is she? She was supposed to be here so we could talk. The only variable other than the mayor is the possibility that she might've made a move and exposed herself."

"He has guys, too, doesn't he? Men who agree with him."

"Yes. I know who most of them are because Antonia fed me their names, but there are holes in my information. The mayor barely speaks to me since he announced he wants my brother in cuffs for assault."

"Mmm." Dan nodded slowly while he chewed warm deviled egg. "I can see how that might hinder your fellowship."

John snorted. "Right."

"I'll keep an eye out for Antonia."

"Thank you." John studied him openly. "Sure you're okay?"

Dan didn't want to rehash their last conversation, so he said, "Tell me about your brother, Ben. The man clearly has more secrets than anyone should lay claim to. How does that affect your relationship, knowing there's so much he will never tell you?"

John thought for a second. "I take what I can get. I've never understood Ben. Even as a kid he was distant, shared what he wanted to share and no more. It can get under your skin, but then I see him with Pat and 'Uncle Ben' comes alive in the eyes of that little boy. Then secrets don't seem so important." John sighed. "I think he likely did assault the mayor, but I can also tell you he didn't do it without good reason. My brother has never done anything in his life without good reason. And he'd lay it down for any of us."

Dan nodded. He didn't even know what it felt like to be the recipient of that kind of love from another person. What would it feel like to be able to give that to someone? The richness of it escaped him in a way that made him want to grasp at smoke, trying to capture it in his palm. *Gemma.* She filled everything that he was. Papa had brought her into his life. Dan wanted to believe that was for a reason.

After all they'd shared, there *had* to be a reason. And not just because he'd been attracted to her for years. What was between them was so much more than that. She could be everything in his life—his whole reason—and that was what scared him so much. Papa should be his everything. If Gemma was such a part of his life that he thought about her even this much, did that mean he was losing his grip on God? Dan wanted to ask John about it, but the words just wouldn't come.

"Everything okay?"

He said, "You keep asking me that."

"You usually don't have this look on your face like there are a million things going on in your head."

Dan groaned. "I think I need to walk to the lake and pray for a while." He needed to find the balance between his relationship with God and a relationship with Gemma. Because she could break up with him as friends, but he wasn't going to let her take away everything else they could be.

Whether she ever told him anything about his father, or not, didn't matter. That wasn't what Dan wanted from her.

"Okay you're looking a little scary now."

"John?"

"Yeah?"

"How do you get a woman to change her mind after she broke up with you?"

**

Gemma strode over. Dan opened his mouth, but whatever he'd been about to say next, she cut off. "I need to talk to John." She crossed in front of him and faced the sheriff. "Can I talk to you?"

John blinked. "Uh…sure." He shot Dan a look and then said, "Let's go over here."

Good. She didn't want Dan to hear. If he'd told John anything about the room she'd found in the radio station, then she wanted to know. She needed to know. It was *her* secret. But she couldn't just ask that outright. She squared her shoulders and faced the sheriff. "How are you?"

"How…am I?"

"Yeah." She couldn't ask? "Andra? The boys?"

"Uh, good. Thank you." John seemed to think that was hilarious.

"And Dan?"

"You can't ask Dan how he is yourself?"

"I could, but you were just talking to him." She should have been a reporter. "So how is he?"

"Seems to be okay. Should I be worried about him?"

"Not unless he gives you a reason." If Dan wasn't going to tell anyone else, she wouldn't do it for him.

"What about you? Took a spill last week."

She shrugged. "A little achy, that's all. Can I ask you something?"

"Sure." The sheriff looked like he found this entire conversation completely hilarious.

"How much did you know about Hal and how he came to town?" It was tricky, given John had only lived in town a couple of years. And unlikely that he knew more about the man than she did, though he had access to all those files in his office. He would know who Hal had been before he'd come here, wouldn't he? Who Dan's dad had been, even. Official things she'd never have heard because once people got here, no one talked about that.

John frowned. "He arrived with another man, a Bill Jones. But there isn't any information on who that is, or why they came together."

Gemma absorbed the fact there was a solid connection between her father and Dan's—and that it wasn't good. "What about after they arrived?"

"You know who Bill Jones is."

Not a question. Gemma didn't know if she'd have answered even if it was.

"Gemma."

She didn't glance at him. "It's Dan's father."

"Hal helped out a lot, monitoring communications in and out of town before he was killed."

"He did?"

John nodded. "Hal maintained the phone connection internally, and when the town got internet he added oversight of people's allowance."

Which meant he listened in on everyone's phone calls. But the internet thing made no sense. "They book their time with me, at the library."

"Hal monitored what they spent that hour doing, and the Marshal's Service got a record of it. Couple of times people tried to look up old acquaintances or family members—check their Facebook page to see what they're doing, that kind of thing. Harmless, you could argue, but it is a breach of their witness protection memorandum."

"He kept tabs on everyone?"

"For security."

"But what—" She could hardly believe he would do that. It burned through her like *betrayal.* Maybe even more than his not having told her he was her father. He snooped on them as if they were just like Dan's father.

"These people have a right to privacy! You can't look at their internet time and police them like big brother."

"Actually we can. Each one of them signed away their rights to privacy and the freedom to go wherever they want and do whatever they want. It's the price of their safety."

"And me?" She waved her arms around. "I was born here. I didn't sign up for this life."

"You have the freedom to leave at any time." John paused. "Would you like to leave, Gemma?"

"Not today. Don't you know my best friend just got married? What's wrong with you?"

John grinned. "You need to ask me anything else?"

She ignored John's humor and glanced at Dan to make sure he wasn't listening. He was talking to Olympia. "Dan didn't say anything to you about… well, about his father?"

John's head jerked. "No, and I've gotten the impression that's an out of boundaries topic." There was a knowing look in his eye, as though now he knew about Bill Jones, and he intended to cross that boundary.

"It is off limits."

"Why?"

"I was just curious whether he'd mentioned his dad to you."

"No, I mean why is it out of bounds?"

"If he hasn't said anything…" She stepped back. "He didn't tell you anything about his dad?"

"No. Nothing."

Of course he hadn't. Though that didn't preclude John's looking the man up for himself—especially now he had a new name to search for. Still, she said, "Good. That's good." She nodded, more to herself than him. "It's best left alone, John." Gemma backed up and nearly bumped into a table.

"Whoa, there." John held her elbow in a soft grip. "You realize it would take me about two seconds to interrogate you to the point you'd confess everything, right?"

"And that's why I'm going to walk away, and you're not going to ask me anything else about this."

"Did you pick a new genre yet?"

"I'm thinking about it." Gemma took a breath, grateful for the change in subject.

"What did Dan's dad do to you?"

Gemma opened her mouth. She stopped herself before she spoke, then shook her head. "It's not about what he did to me."

"But he did do something."

She backed up another step. "I'm not talking about him. I have enough problems with my own father, to go and worry about Dan's, too. He's dead, and so is Hal. It should be done." It should. Why wasn't it? That's what she wanted to know.

How could two men cause so many problems from beyond the grave? Dan's dad was probably busy burning in hell, so she didn't have to worry much about him. Still.

"Gemma."

She shook her head. "I should go mingle."

**

Across town, Mei walked through the farmhouse to the living room. The place where Dan Walden's mother had been shot and killed, or so she figured. Mei surveyed each of the other rooms—master bedroom, a sad and lifeless place. No kid bedroom, which was interesting. Hadn't Dan had a room? Back down on the main floor she found the basement stairs off the hall and headed down there. Also no kid bedroom.

Mei shone her flashlight around the basement. Bare frame walls and insulation, wires but not even drywall. She circled the long tables in the middle of the room, the hanging lights. Processing what that meant in the context of US drug enforcement activities, in the late seventies and into the eighties, and setting it aside.

One wall had a square grate instead of insulation. Two feet by two feet. She wiggled the grate off and shone her light inside.

A tunnel. The floor looked like old tracks dug into the earth, like someone had carted something in and out of the house, many times. Mei climbed in and started walking. A tall man would have to hunch over. The walls were damp and the air musty, though it got cleaner as she walked. The moment she smelled fresh air, Mei glanced up. Stars.

This had to be the spot where Gemma fell in. Dirt and broken two-by-fours partially blocked the tunnel but she climbed over it, grunting when she sat on a splinter.

"Is someone there?" The voice was distant, outside Dan's house. In the yard.

Mei held still for a couple of minutes and then started moving again. Dan Walden was seriously hiding something. His mom's mysterious disappearance, death, whatever it was. Her contact hadn't been able to find much of anything on his parents. Then years after the mom is suddenly gone, his dad has heart failure? Dan Walden was a walking enigma. But good for her, she liked puzzles. And a tunnel from Dan's house that led to… where?

Mei was going to find out.

Chapter 7

Dan leaned against the wall outside Gemma's house. Night had fallen, the guests had gone home, and the happy couple were off on their honeymoon up the mountain.

The town only had four streets, then a collection of houses that were separate, like his farm. Main Street was in the center, the bakery, the bank, the diner, and the sheriff's office. The laundromat where he washed his clothes. Gemma lived on D Street. Dan didn't know how she managed to coexist with so many people in such close proximity, even if she'd moved out of her mom's house to live on her own.

He didn't think he'd be able to handle being in town full time. But then, none of these houses had barns for him to live in.

It wasn't long before she came walking down the street, shoes hanging from her fingers and her feet bare. Distant happy thoughts brightened her face as she stared up at the darkening sky. She'd had a good day, and it was a good look on her.

"Good wedding, huh."

She smiled, and for a while he felt like there was only the two of them. No past, no expectations. She said, "You do a good job as pastor. What you said about that cord was nice, too. Three strands."

He wanted things to go back to the way they had been before he'd found that photo of his father. Could they have that? Dan didn't know if it was possible. He also didn't know if he wanted to settle for that when he was pretty sure they could have more than a simple friendship. The possibility was always in the back of his mind—romance, however he was supposed to go about that. Yet she didn't know God the way he did, which put them at odds. It might work but there was every possibility it could crash and burn instead because they would never see eye-to-eye. Could he take the risk?

Dan braced and got it over with. "Wanna take a walk? We could hit the diner and get some pie."

Gemma grimaced. "I've eaten enough for two days. And a month's worth of cake."

"Then let's just walk. I could use some air."

She stared at him. "Why are you here, Dan?"

"I'm here because you're my friend, Gemma. Nothing is going to change that. It'll test it, maybe, but I'm pretty sure we've proven over and over that nothing will break this apart." He motioned between them with a finger.

Something flashed across her face, an emotion he didn't recognize. It made him wonder what he didn't know, and why she'd never told him whatever it was. Truth had always been their way. Now she was hiding something.

"Whatever it is, you can tell me." He paused. "It's me."

Gemma blinked, and the look disappeared. “Let me get my other shoes.” She held up the heels. “Can’t walk in these.”

She went inside, and he waited. The street was dark, quiet except for someone’s TV. Their front windows were open, so he could hear singing on the show. Sanctuary always seemed so calm after dark, but they’d gone through so much as a town, and the scars would be visible come morning.

The town had been under siege by a rogue Navy SEAL. The previous pastor, Father Wilson, had murdered people and tried to poison the water supply. The former school teacher, too, and the deputy sheriff at the time John showed up.

It was nice that the town had finally drifted to a peaceful time. They didn’t need any more bombs exploding in the caves that littered the mountains that was for sure. With the exception of the mayor, things were good. Who cared who took over for the man? There wasn’t much they could do to mess up everyone’s lives, given the committee that oversaw the town now had final say. It was little more than a title now. Dan didn’t even know why the mayor was so big on passing down the mantle of the job he’d monopolized for a decade.

When she came back still in her bridesmaid’s dress and wearing sneakers, he said, “What do you think the mayor wanted with your mom?”

“Probably asking her if she wants to be mayor.” Her voice was sardonic, but he heard the note of pain.

Dan nudged the outside of her arm with his hand. “I’m sure he’ll ask you.”

“Yeah, right. Doesn’t matter, though, because I’m way too busy to be mayor. I’ve got a library to run and books to write.”

“No wonder I hardly see you.”

She giggled. “Like you don’t have weeds to pull. Honey to harvest.”

"I know how you like your honey."

"I don't think I could put anything else in my coffee. I was raised on that stuff."

Dan wanted to grab her hand. Twine their fingers together, no big deal. He liked his space, and so did she, but sometimes connection was good.

"You realize you're being super weird, right? You're wearing dress shoes and we're walking through the woods."

Dan chuckled. "It's harder to hide sometimes, but I really like it. Us." The night was cloudy so he flipped on his flashlight as they entered the woods. He'd spent plenty of nights outside after his father locked the barn door. He liked this, too. Especially when she was here. "So where are we going? The lake?"

"Sure. We were going when I fell into the hole, and we still haven't been out there." Gemma stumbled.

He reached for her, found her forearm. Dan slid his hand down and found her fingers. "Don't want you to get lost."

"So we're friends again?"

They started walking again. "Why wouldn't we be?"

"Uh, maybe because I kicked you out of my business and my life."

"Maybe we can just ignore that room full of papers and be what we've always been." As if that would be enough. *Papa, I have plenty. Why do I want this when everything else should be enough?* Why did he want so much more than friendship? He'd been denying it for so long, and now it was hitting him all in a rush.

"Forgive and move on, is that it?" When he didn't say anything else, she said, "You're such a Christian."

A smile curled his lips. "You say that like it's a bad thing."

"You're just so darn reasonable it's infuriating." She stepped over a log. "Forgiving. Happy. I'd rather have a bad attitude. I *like* my bad attitude."

"Really."

She dragged his hand with hers as she motioned with her arm. "Yes! It makes me feel better. It's cathartic. Sometimes I want to punch something, so I go to Sam's gym and I do. Bingo. Feelings processed."

Dan chuckled. "Of course. Why didn't I think of that?"

"I've told you to try it. Not my fault you thought I was joking."

He cleared his throat. "So you don't need anything; you've got this."

"Maybe I do. Why is that bad?" She squeezed his hand but didn't let go. "I know you need God. It's great. I've seen what He does for you, and I know it wouldn't have to be that…drastic with me. No one else seems to see God like you do. I think people take as much of Him as they want, or need. Is that right?"

"I suppose. We let Him in to be Lord of our lives, but sometimes we don't want to give up everything for His sake. Like football or a hobby or what we think our lives should be. I do think some people miss what could have been had they given all, picked up their cross, and truly followed after Him."

"You mean like missionaries?"

"It can be anything. Even a stay-at-home mom or a Sunday school teacher, a prison guard or a sous chef. It only matters what it is God wants to do in *you.*"

"What if what He wants to do with me only has everything to do with you?"

Dan stopped. He tugged on her hand until she was facing him. "Why do you say that?"

She shrugged one shoulder. "He obviously cares about you if He'll help me make things better."

Dan hardly knew what to say. She saw all that, and she didn't see how God could do that for her? He'd be seriously honored if God allowed him to be the man who made her life better. Nothing could be better than her hand in his than marriage. Intimacy. A family of their own.

The question was whether she could handle it. Whether he could. That was if she even wanted that with him. Dan couldn't be sure of that simple thing. Maybe she was content with their friendship. She was still determined to protect him, and he loved her for that. He knew what it might do if he found awful things among that paperwork. Would she share what she learned with him? He was trying to be okay with it if she never told him anything, but it would always be between them. It might even turn things bad.

If he took this step, would it ruin everything they had that was good? Dan stepped closer to test the waters. Had he ever been this near to her as an adult? Thoughts raced through his head, and his temperature shot up. He was like a teenager trying to get up the gumption to kiss his first crush.

"Gemma." Her name came out like a whisper. *Papa, she's a gift. This would be a gift, too. If it's from You.* "Can I kiss you?"

"Are you sure?" she whispered back.

Dan nodded. "I'm sure." He lowered his head, one hand still holding hers. With his other hand he touched the outside of her arm. "I'm really sure."

It didn't matter what anyone thought. Okay, so it did a bit because he was their pastor. He could explain it, if he had to, tell them all exactly what had grown between him and Gemma over the last fifteen years. She was everything good in his life, and she'd been by his side through so much he'd never have survived if it hadn't been for her hand in his, walking with him through the woods wearing his coat because it had been snowing. Sharing her sandwich with him. Coming over with Coke and cherry syrup.

His lips touched hers, the smallest caress.

A twig snapped. "I think someone else is out here." The man's voice drifted to them through the trees.

Dan reached in his pocket and fingered the flashlight. He held Gemma close and prayed whoever it was didn't see them.

"Let's get out of here," she whispered.

Dan tugged on her hand, and they crept between the trees, away from the voice.

**

Gemma could hardly breathe. He'd kissed her! Years of wondering what that would be like, and some guy interrupted them in the middle of it? There was no privacy anywhere in this town. That, or maybe God didn't like her after all.

Gemma stumbled on a tree root. Dan grabbed her waist to help her along, and she giggled. She couldn't help it. This was bizarre. He was acting like he was her boyfriend, and Dan had never done that with her. Was it the wedding that had this effect on him?

They crept through the woods. As they walked, Gemma heard him laugh, deep in his chest.

She glanced back. "I think you've lost it." But she loved his laugh. "Let's go to the lake."

His smile. She couldn't get enough of it. "We got caught making out."

"I'll put out a press release. Pastor embroiled in hot scandal." Only there was nothing funny about this.

Dan trailed behind her. "Yeah, that might not be good. Maybe we keep a lid on what just happened, leave it between us."

"Fine by me." Like she wanted everyone talking about her business anyway. Everyone already thought they had a right to his. "If this gets out everyone will think I'm corrupting you."

"I'd like to think I can stand up to you."

She wasn't going to answer that, because he could. A lady was supposed to be tempting. Irresistible. He thought he could resist her? Fine. He didn't need to know he'd swept her away with that kiss.

"Why are you mad?"

She didn't turn back. "Who says I'm mad?" It wouldn't work if he saw her face. He'd know she was totally lying. But whatever, when a guy just out-right went and said he could resist her, how else was she going to react? "I'm not mad."

"Your voice gets higher in pitch when you lie."

Gemma kept walking. Dress-shoes back there was a little slower in pace, considering he wasn't hoofing it through the woods like she was. He needed to speed up if he was going to keep up with her.

"Somewhere you need to be?"

"I just want to get out of the trees," she said. "I like open space better."

"Since when?"

Gemma gritted her teeth. "Since right now, when I was kissing someone I care about a lot and someone saw us."

Dan tagged her hand and held on. "Gemma—"

"Do we have to deconstruct it? Can't it just be what it was, a very nice interlude?"

"It was *very* nice."

Gemma shook her head. If he wanted to be coy, fine. The lake wasn't too far ahead. She needed to jump in and cool off. Dan could watch, since he apparently wasn't in the least bit hot and bothered. Apparently she didn't affect him *at all.*

"And…you're mad again."

Gemma held her tongue, then decided to change the subject altogether. "I'm circling back to destroying that whole room. It's causing too many problems. And why does that secret need to be hidden, anyway? If it's so valuable, why not remove the possibility that it's going to get out?"

"Avoiding." She heard his muttered word. Then louder, he said, "I'm not going to tell anyone Hal had a secret hidden in there. Are you?"

Gemma shook her head. "I shouldn't even have told you." Her father should have left her some instructions along with his "gift." Gemma said, "Hal gave that radio station to me on the condition that I keep it safe and make sure no one ever finds it."

Dan sighed. "I can help you figure this out, you know. It'll go a lot faster."

"I still don't want you in there. I'm not going to budge on that."

"Stalemate."

They drew close enough she could see the lake. She didn't want to talk about the papers anymore, or even think about them. Bolton's ranch house had been destroyed, and beneath that house was where her father had died. Gemma had been holed up with most of the town in a bunker beneath the Meeting House. There was no ranch house now, just a pretty lake that hid the death beneath the waters and a grave she hadn't visited.

Gemma stopped. "This is the first time I've been here since John told me what happened."

Dan stood quiet beside her for a minute. "You have to believe that if he'd been able to, he would have told you he was your father. You have to believe that."

"So what was he protecting? The town itself, or me?"

"Or all of us. But my guess would be that he was protecting you."

"From what? That's what I don't get. I could leave if I wanted to, so why do I need protecting?" Gemma took a breath. "My mom came here by herself, pregnant with me. Or did she just tell me that so I wouldn't think any of the men in town might be my father? It was a trick. Like a horrible joke played on me, and now nothing about my life makes any sense."

"That doesn't change who you are."

"Only what I've always believed about myself." She stepped back from him. "That's why I wanted some space."

"Yesterday."

Gemma could've laughed. "New day, huh? So you want to go for coffee?"

"Why does that not sound like a good thing?"

"Let all your church-people see us together."

"I'm not ashamed of you. I could never be that, Gemma." Dan shook his head. "I have to handle it right, but it's not a lost cause." He took both of her hands. "*You're* not a lost cause."

"I know you say that. But they're Bible people, they aren't going to want me with you." Gemma sighed. "A few are already starting to suspect. That's why this shouldn't go any further. Aside from the fact we aren't ever going to agree on the papers thing, no one will think this is okay."

"Suddenly you need people's approval?"

"No. I want them to know I'll make your life better. That I'm the only one who can do that for you."

The only one who could love him the way he should be loved. Known to the core of his being the way she knew him and treasured the survivor that he was.

Gemma said, "They're never going to think that, and it isn't my job to prove it to them. I can't do that."

It would destroy her to have to try and convince everyone she was good enough for Dan. There would always be someone who wasn't satisfied, and Gemma would tie herself in knots trying.

She broke from his grasp and ran to the lake.

Maybe she should leave, as John had suggested. She would never really be happy here, separated from the one person she wanted most in the world. God had captured Dan, taken hold of his whole life. Gemma didn't even know how to do that for herself. And how would she compete with God, anyway? Dan was the thing she could never have but would always need the most.

Steps from the dock that stretched out over the lake, Gemma tripped. She sprawled on the ground in her dress and rolled. Dan slowed his sprint, his eyes on the ground between them.

He clicked on his flashlight.

Antonia lay on the dirt. Her lifeless eyes stared out, unseeing. Her skin was pale, her hair so dark it threw her complexion into Adams Family territory. Blood coated the front of her shirt, a macabre stain that soaked down into the dirt.

Gemma scrambled away, got tangled in her dress and fell back onto the grass. She climbed to her feet and opened her mouth. No words came out.

Garbled sound emerged from Dan's mouth.

Gemma stared at Antonia's chest, watching intently for movement. When she thought she saw the slightest rise, she moved across the grass on her hands and knees and pressed her fingers against the woman's neck. She was wrong. "No pulse."

She looked up. "Antonia's dead." Beyond Dan, Deputy Sheriff Mei Ling stood holding her gun.

"Both of you back away from the dead woman."

Gemma was happy to oblige. She got up and rounded the body, but Dan hadn't moved. His eyes were still locked with Antonia's prone form. "Dan." She grabbed his hand. "Come with me."

Mei was going to notice his reaction in a minute. The deputy sheriff crept around them in a wide berth, her gun still out.

"Put that thing away," Gemma told her. "You don't need it. Antonia's dead and it's just us."

His voice was a whisper. "I killed her."

Gemma whipped her head around. "Dan, come with me. We're going to walk away from Antonia right now." She grabbed his waist and tried to muscle him. He wasn't big. Why was he so heavy? "Dan, that's Antonia."

"I think Dan should come with me."

"No." Gemma wasn't going to let that happen. "Dan, come with me. We're going to walk away from here. Together. Everything is going to be fine, but you need to walk with me."

He reached up and grasped her arms, his fingers gripping her biceps hard enough he was going to leave bruises. How could she snap him out of this? "Dan."

"I killed her." His voice was the broken whisper of a child.

"It's Antonia," she whispered back. "It's just Antonia."

Mei said, "You need to step back. Dan Walden is coming with me."

"No." She couldn't step back, and neither did she want to. Dan wouldn't let go of her, and she didn't want to let go of him, either. "You're not taking him anywhere."

"Step back, Gemma."

She tried to turn, to stand in front of Dan like a sentry so Mei couldn't get to him. His grip on her wouldn't let her move much, but she twisted. "Back off. Dan's going back to his room, not to the station with you. He doesn't need that."

"It's not up to you, Gemma. I have a gun and a badge and you don't. Now back off."

"No."

Mei moved forward. Dan shifted her, and suddenly Gemma was behind him. The force of his moving her sent her to the ground again.

Mei lifted her gun. "Stand down."

"Don't talk to her like that."

Gemma got up. This time, she grabbed his arm. "She said stand down."

Mei looked between them. "I will shoot…one of you! Now both of you back off. My trigger finger is itchy." Mei pointed her gun at Dan, then at Gemma.

"Don't point that at her!" Dan's throat turned red. Color spread to the top of his head. He launched at Mei, his hands reaching for the gun. Mei let go with one hand and punched him in the face.

"Don't touch my weapon." Her left hand, still holding the gun, shifted to point it at Gemma. "Get off me, or I will shoot her."

Dan's whole body solidified.

Gemma grabbed his shoulder and tugged him back. "Dan, come here."

He spun her into his arms, probably to put her behind him again. To defend her. Gemma's elbow flung out and connected with Mei's temple.

The deputy sheriff cried out, but it sounded more mad than like she was in pain. Gemma hauled Dan away from her while Mei rallied.

She blinked, dazed, and her eyes narrowed on them. "On your knees, hands behind your head—"

She couldn't be serious. "But—"

"Both of you are under arrest!"

Chapter 8

John took the stairs two at a time and flew out the door from his apartment into the sheriff's office in socks, pajama pants, and a T-shirt.

Mei's eyes widened, and she motioned to his pants. "SpongeBob?"

"They were a gift from Pat. And that's not what we're talking about." It was for real. Mei had locked Dan and Gemma in the jail cell. Gemma was still cuffed.

Mei motioned to her to turn her back and lift her hands, then un-cuffed the librarian.

"Seriously?"

"Antonia is dead, and these two assaulted me." Mei turned her face so he could see the color, high on her cheek.

"That was an accident," Gemma called across the room.

"I don't doubt that." John scratched his head and turned to Mei. "Where is Antonia's body?"

"On the ground at the lake."

He didn't want to call Elliot back the night of his wedding, but John might not have a choice. "We need Dr. Noel to act as medical examiner and bring her to the medical center. He can do the autopsy there."

"She was shot."

"And there will be evidence on her body that needs collecting." John blew out a breath. "I know you haven't been a cop long, but you're not supposed to leave a body. Evidence could be tampered with. Anything that points to who her killer was is basically worth nothing at this point, given it could have been planted there or something could have been removed."

Mei pulled something from her pocket. Her fingertips were bloody. "Bullet."

John opened his hand as a reflex. She dropped the round into his palm. Had she dug it from Antonia's body? "It's a really good thing we don't actually have a court system in this town—"

"I might actually get to kill someone." Mei wiped off her hands and then poured herself a cup of coffee while John just stared.

"—because you've single-handedly destroyed any case we might have." There was nothing else he could do. "You're probably going to be fired after this."

"Probably?" Gemma's eyes were wide. "I've never been a cop, but I have read a lot of detective novels. I think she might be some kind of…" She blanched. "Andra doesn't, like, recognize her or anything, does she?"

"She isn't an assassin. I wouldn't hire an assassin to be my deputy."

Mei lowered her cup from her mouth. "But you did choose one to be your wife."

"Andra doesn't kill people anymore." Why did he keep having to tell everyone that?

Mei shook her head. "That's just something civilized people say to try and convince themselves they wouldn't make an exception if they seriously hated someone."

John stared at her for a moment. "Mei, let them both out. I have to go to the scene and see to Antonia. I don't want Gemma and Dan in my cell when I get back." He wandered to the door that led to his upstairs apartment. "I cannot believe you arrested Dan Walden."

After a second of quiet, Gemma said, "But you can believe she arrested me?"

Like he was going to get in the middle of *that*. "You either, Gemma."

Mei folded her arms. "This man confessed to the murder of Antonia Hernandez."

"He didn't kill her," Gemma yelled. "He officiated a wedding, and then he was with me!"

Mei huffed out a breath and wandered over to him. Her gaze on his was serious. "You're too close to them, that's your problem."

"My problem is there's a dead woman at the lake who was left alone instead of being taken care of with the respect she deserves as somebody's daughter, somebody's sister. We might not have a lot in this town, but I thought we had *that*."

Not to mention it was likely John's fault for drawing Antonia into this "mayor" thing. If Collins had killed her, John was going to have a hard time conducting a fair investigation. Collins would bring up what Ben had done to him, and no one would ever be satisfied the right thing had been done.

Olympia deserved justice for her daughter.

John ran a hand down his face. He was going to have to tell Olympia that her daughter was dead and Matthias, Maria and Sofia, that their sister had been killed. They deserved to know the truth, but things were so sticky he might not be able to do that for them. Mei likely wasn't going to be all that much help, either. Especially if he needed someone impartial. Any other day, he'd have chosen Dan to be with him for this task.

Mei said, "I have evidence. My investigation is almost complete, and the pastor is smack in the middle of all of it."

"Investigation?" John shook his head. "What investigation, Mei? You're supposed to be getting to know these people. Making sure the tunnels aren't an active security breach." He motioned to the cell. "As for the pastor, his name is Dan."

Mei waved away his words. "I don't like to use their names."

"You used Antonia's."

"She's dead. What does it matter what I call her?" Gemma gasped, but Mei continued, "Once you start, you start to build something that'll turn into a *relationship*." She said it like it was a dirty word. "And then you end up actually caring about them. It's a slippery slope."

John couldn't speak. Finally, he got out the word, "What?"

"What?"

"You're supposed to be a deputy sheriff. I explained this, Mei. There are procedures."

"You think that's why I'm here?" She cocked her head to the side. "Procedures?"

John shut his eyes. "I'm going to get dressed, and then I'm going to Antonia. Then I'll be informing her family that she was killed." *Lord, this is going to hurt them. Help me do this right.* "When I get back, Dan and Gemma need to be out of that cell, and you and I are going to have a talk. About *procedure.*"

**

The sheriff went back upstairs, and Gemma turned to Mei. She caught the deputy's gaze between the bars of the jail cell and said, "I told you that you weren't supposed to leave Antonia's body."

Sure, it hadn't made Mei super happy to hear that she shouldn't just shove them both to the sheriff's Jeep and drive them into town, but that wasn't Gemma's problem. Mei should have read the deputy sheriff's manual better.

"I don't need any help from you." Mei actually looked a little chagrined. Gemma wouldn't have thought that was possible. "Not when you're so obviously going to cover for him no matter what." She motioned toward Dan.

"Because he would never murder someone!"

Dan flinched. Gemma strode to where he sat on the cot, his gaze on the far wall like he wasn't seeing anything. She crouched in front of him. "Dan?"

He hadn't spoken to her in the car. He'd only sat there. It was she who had grabbed his hand.

John came back in, shrugging on his jacket. "I'm taking the car."

"If you're getting ahold of Elliot to see to Antonia," Gemma called out, "maybe you could have him come and see Dan as well."

John stopped, one hand on the front door handle, about to go outside. "Why does Dan need a doctor?"

Gemma wanted to get mad, but none of them knew. Dan had never told them even the first thing about his issues. Even people who'd lived in town their whole lives, or most of Dan and Gemma's lives, knew only some. Not all of it.

Gemma touched his cheeks as softly as she could. "Dan." She kept her voice soft. It was the only thing that worked. "Dan, can you hear me?"

He didn't move.

"Dan, its Gemma. Everything is fine now."

"I killed her."

She flinched, even though he spoke in a whisper. "No, you didn't. It wasn't your fault, Dan. It never was."

"He's confessing to the crime." Mei's voice was low but excited. "He's the one who killed Antonia."

Gemma glanced at her and hissed, "That's not even what he's talking about."

John shook his head. "We're going to have to do this later. I have to get to Antonia."

Mei stepped closer to the cell. "Oh, so he's talking about his mom, then?"

Gemma froze. Dan actually blinked. "Dan, you have to come out of this. Come back to me."

"Barn."

"I'll get you home."

Mei said, "He must be talking about where he hid the body." She gripped the bars. "Did you bury your mom in the barn, Dan? Is that what happened? All that blood on the living room floor. Was it a gunshot? Did you kill Antonia just the same way you killed your mom?"

Dan shifted both hands out, his arms flailing with them. Gemma was shoved with the force of his momentum. She fell back on her skirt *again*. "Dan!"

His face almost pressed through the bars. He yelled right in Mei's face. "You don't know what you're talking about!"

"But you did kill someone. Right? You said it. You killed her."

Gemma scrambled to her feet. "Mei, you need to back off." She set her hand on Dan's arm. "Dan?" He shrugged her off, and her arm whipped out at an awkward angle. Gemma hissed and held it with the other hand. "Seriously, Mei. Back off."

The deputy folded her arms. "I don't think so—"

John set his hand on her shoulder. "Mei, I think you should back off. Something is happening to Dan, and you're not helping."

"It's called a confession. That's part of police work, isn't it?" Mei said. "I'm not letting him go if he's telling us he murdered a woman."

"How about I go to the murder scene and get us some evidence? Then we'll actually know who killed Antonia."

Dan stepped back from the bars. He glanced around, saw Gemma holding her arm, and frowned. "Are you okay?"

She nodded.

"You shoved her," Mei said. "A couple of times by my count."

Gemma said, "Yeah, but when I elbowed *you* in the face it was way more fun."

"Gem."

She looked at Dan. "It's fine. We're both okay. Antonia's the one who isn't."

"I'll be back," John said. "If you're not going to let them go, then don't talk to them, either. Make them coffee, but don't ask them any questions and don't engage."

"Fine." Mei moved away from him and sat at one of the desks.

"You okay, Dan?"

"Yeah, Sheriff."

"Gemma?"

She didn't glance away from Dan. "Yes."

"I'll be back." John shot the deputy a pointed look. He'd seen Dan have what he called an "episode." Did that mean he was going to do something about it?

Gemma had tried for years to figure out what would help. All she'd been able to work out was that she simply accept Dan, give him friendship, and let him be the man he wanted to be.

John shut the door behind him. Gemma looked once at Mei to make sure she wasn't listening—she totally was—and then spoke low. "I'm sorry I kicked you out the other day. I shouldn't have done that. Whether the info would help or not, I should have let you stay and let it be whatever it was going to be. So I'm sorry. That's all."

Dan touched the back of her neck with his hand, leaned in, and kissed her forehead. "Thank you, Gemma." He gave her a small smile before it disappeared. "Did I hurt you?"

She opened her mouth to deny it.

"Yes, you did."

"Mei." Gemma shot her a look. "This is none of your business. Stay out of it." She turned her body, so her back was to the deputy. "I'm fine."

"Don't lie. I hurt you." She could see on his face that he hated the fact he'd left a mark on her, even if it was just a little bruise. That wasn't the care he wanted to take with her—the kind she took with him. Both of them knew that, but she was going to convince him it was all good.

"It's not important."

"It's important to me."

"Well then call it even," she suggested. "I hurt your feelings, you..." She turned her arm so he could see the red mark.

Dan hissed out a breath between his teeth. "I don't like it. Not at all."

"It is what it is. Don't worry about that."

"Antonia is dead." He ran a hand down his face. "Olympia will be devastated. Maria is going to need help, and Sofia will have to find someone to assist her at the nursery. All of their lives will be irrevocably altered, and there's nothing we can do to soften the blow. I don't even think we're supposed to be able to."

"Aren't there people at the church who will rally around them when something like this happens?" That was what church people did. She'd seen the pies being delivered.

Dan nodded. "Yes, but Olympia is usually the one doing it for others."

"Then I'm sure there are plenty of people who will want to repay that favor."

A smile curled his lips. "Thank you, Gemma. You're right. Most likely they will want to help out."

She'd helped him. That felt good. Dan never liked when he disappeared into his own head, and she hated seeing it. Blank-faced Dan was scary, especially considering what he'd done the last time. It was mercy that he didn't remember.

Gemma folded her arms to trace the scar on her bicep with a finger and walked to the other end of the tiny cell. Something needed to change, otherwise Dan was going to disappear into himself at the wrong moment. Someone could get seriously hurt, and not just her.

Or he could do it during a sermon and wind up saying something that made him sound crazy. She didn't want him to lose his position. Being a pastor meant so much to him. He hadn't asked for it; he'd just filled a need when it was evident that there was one.

Gemma glanced back at him. Hands on the bars, he hung his head. What was he asking God for? Dan's "Papa" helped him. She'd seen the evidence enough to know that when he was done he'd be more peaceful. Happier, even. Gemma would still be jittery.

Did she want that peace?

**

Dan lifted his head. Mei didn't bother to hide the fact she was watching him. Gemma moved behind him, and the bed creaked. But he didn't turn.

"You have to admit, finding you both standing over a dead body was pretty suspicious."

Dan figured that might be the closest thing to an apology Mei Ling would ever give anyone. At least without killing them afterwards. Maybe he was on the wrong track, but occasionally there was that look in her eyes, and he wondered who was underneath.

Mei said, "Your mom disappeared, didn't she?"

Dan nodded. That was the public story, while the truth of what had gone on was far different.

She motioned to her computer screen with one finger. "The sheriff's report from back then says he asked around, but no one had seen her leave. She was never seen again. Clothes gone. A suitcase she'd brought with her."

Gemma said, "I never heard about the suitcase. I was nine at the time, and my mom used to work at the farm back then.

Dan's mom went missing one night, and everyone was really freaked out. I wasn't allowed to play over there after that day."

"No one looked for her, and after a couple of months the sheriff closed the case." Mei paused. "Which makes me wonder where her body is. No point in searching for a dead woman."

Dan flinched. "I actually don't know the answer to that."

"But you do know what happened."

Gemma slammed the bars beside him. "John told you not to ask him anything! Can't you see it's been *enough*? He was eleven years old. Do you know many eleven-year-olds that have buried bodies?"

"Gemma." Dan took her hand and led her away from the bars.

"I don't like that woman. I don't want her insinuating anything about you."

"I'm good, Gemma." So long as he didn't let go of her, he figured he could keep his head.

"Are you sure?"

He nodded. Part of him wanted to tell her he was strong, or that he didn't need her to defend him, but that would be a lie.

He wanted to be strong. He wanted to be a man who didn't need anyone to defend him. But God had given him so much to take on that it forced Dan to admit he needed help. And why would that ever be bad? God was the one who held him up, who held him together. Had he not endured life with his father, Dan would never have known what it was like to be nothing… and to be given everything. He'd never have known the extent of God's sufficiency in his life.

"I just want you to be good."

"I know." Dan touched her cheek. They were past the point where he needed to hide how he felt with her. Mei was watching, but Dan figured it would be out sooner or later that they'd been together tonight. Nothing was set between them, but they had time.

"So," Mei said. "You guys *are* sleeping together."

Gemma whirled around. "I told you we weren't. That hasn't changed, not that it's any business of yours."

When she turned back, Dan mouthed, *Sleeping together?* Gemma's eyes widened, and he laughed. "Not that it wouldn't be pleasant, I'm sure."

Gemma chuckled. "Yeah, I'm not that type of girl. But thanks for offering."

"I know you aren't that type of girl." He grinned. "Good thing I'm not that kind of pastor."

"Yeah," she grinned. "Good thing." Then mouthed, *Awkward.* Dan smiled, and she couldn't help but chuckle.

Mei said, "I'm confused. What are you two talking about?"

Dan said, "How about that coffee John mentioned?"

The door flung open. Olympia rushed in, and the bell above the door swung so hard it clanged and got stuck. "Is it true?" Her face was red, flushed. Sweat beaded down from her temples. She breathed hard, as though she'd run all the way from B Street. "Is it true my Antonia is dead?"

Gemma stepped away from him like he had a bad cold. All the amusement of the moment before evaporated like smoke. "Olympia." Dan didn't know what to say. A woman was dead. "I'm so sorry, but she's gone."

"The caller said it was you, but I didn't believe them. Not Pastor Dan. He would never have *killed my child.*"

Gemma said, "We found her; that's what happened." She paused. "I'm sorry, too, Olympia. She was a beautiful girl who had so much to give the world." She looked guilty almost, as though ashamed they'd shared that humor a moment ago.

The matron blinked. "Thank you, Gemma."

Mei rounded her desk and waved toward the waiting area. "Let's sit." She looked as though she didn't know what to say, either.

"Let me out." Dan wanted to sit with Olympia. To pray with her.

Mei shot him a suspicious look.

"Just do it, Mei. He's not going anywhere." Gemma did the stand-off thing again, and it worked. Mei strode over and unlocked the cell door.

She pointed at Gemma. "You stay with him so I can watch both of you. No funny business."

Gemma held up both hands. "Got it."

Dan passed both of them and sat beside Olympia. "What about the others, do they know?"

She nodded, a tissue balled up in her hand. "I called them. They're on their way."

"That's good."

The door opened, and more people poured in. Six. Seven. Eight. Asking for the sheriff, and demanding to know what had happened. The room filled fast. Mei got on a chair and yelled for quiet, but no one listened.

Maria pushed through the crowd. "Mama, Antonia is dead?"

Dan nodded so Olympia wouldn't have to answer.

"What happened?" She glanced between them as people crowded around to hear the answer. "How did she die?"

Dan swallowed. "It was by the lake. We" —he shook his head— "Gemma and I found her by the lake, but it was too late. She was already gone."

"Gone?" Olympia's eyes darkened.

"She'd been shot."

Maria gasped. "She was murdered?"

Matthias and Frannie pushed through the crowd. People moved so close they touched his knees. Dan had to stand. It was getting hard to breathe. He needed air so he could reassure them, answer questions, and try to point them to the peace of God. *That passes understanding, thank You, Papa. I need that right now.* He tried to breathe and managed to get some air in.

"Dan." Olympia tugged on his sleeve.

"I'm sorry." He looked around for Gemma. Where was she?

"People—" Mei's yelling was drowned out by the talking. Shouting. Questions. Those who thought they knew what had happened, or who had done it.

Dan stood on his chair. Better air, and a vantage point. But he didn't see her anywhere. "Gemma?"

Mei glanced around. "Where is she?"

He shook his head. "I don't see her."

Maria yelled across the crowd. "Maybe she's been murdered, too!"

Chapter 9

Terrence pushed her farther down the alley and shoved her against the wall. "Finally. I never thought I'd get the opportunity to get you away from all of them."

Brick bit into Gemma's shoulders above her dress. "Terrence—"

"No, shh. You don't have to thank me, Gemma. I'm glad I could get you away from that crazy pastor."

"Dan?" Gemma had been hauled out of the back door of the sheriff's office and dragged halfway through town in the middle of the night because Terrence thought he needed to rescue her from *Dan*?

She hadn't even seen him until he grabbed her. All those people in the sheriff's office, Antonia's mom and sisters crying, and Mei yelling at them all to calm down. It was chaos, and she'd only wanted to escape. But not like this. The escape she'd wanted was into Dan's arms for a hug. He'd hide her from the world when she needed to retreat. They'd given that favor to each other so many times over the years. But now he had someone else to help, as their pastor. Their friend.

There wasn't anything Gemma could add that would make Olympia or Maria feel better. Antonia was gone. All that blood made her want to gag and lose the wedding cake on the ground.

Terrence stood close but not touching her. "I heard he killed Antonia. You're probably going to be next." He sniffed. The man didn't stand still for more than half a second. He was constantly in motion, even now that they'd stopped. "I had to get you out of there."

"And you did." She kept her voice as soft as she could. He'd grab her if she tried to run, just like he'd done in the library. "Now I'm safe, thanks to you, Terrence."

"Right." His head jerked in a nod, but she could hardly see his face in the dark. Was it midnight yet, or had that hour come and long-gone already? "Thanks to me, getting you out of there."

She was going to have to talk if she wanted out of this. Appeal to the hero-persona he seemed to think he had. "Maybe you could walk me home?"

His body jerked like she'd slapped him. He turned his head to her, his chest still facing the end of the alley. "No. We should wait where it's safe for a while."

Terrence pulled a pack of cigarettes and a lighter from his pocket, shook one out, and lit it. He touched her bare shoulder with his free hand and blew smoke to the side. "I'm so glad I could help you get away from that psycho. He's just as bad as the last 'father' Sanctuary had, thinking he's so righteous and then murdering people while no one in town suspects. Antonia was probably just one in a string of people."

Gemma blinked. No one else was missing, so who else exactly did he think Dan had killed? She didn't even know for sure if Terrence wasn't the one who'd killed Antonia. He very well might have, as she'd seen her hanging around the mayor before, the way Terrence did sometimes. She'd thought the mayor brushed off his attempts to be with the "in" crowd. If he'd killed Antonia it could have been to win their favor.

"Then there's Bolton," Terrence went on. "Forget the wheelchair, that guy has it in for me. Every time I see him he gives me this look, like he'd like nothing more than to stick it to me."

Seriously? That was all Terrence's fault. He'd been hitting on Nadia Marie—back in his "Andy" phase—like a crazed stalker. "You hit him over the back with a chair, Terrence. Now he's almost paralyzed."

"Like I was supposed to know he had this pre-existing condition!"

Right. Because Bolton hadn't bought insurance from Terrence over the phone. The company didn't cold call people in the town, only people in other states. Not a very interesting job, or so she'd heard from a couple of her book club ladies.

Terrence waved his hand holding the cigarette around so frantically she flinched, then held still as he decided it was time to touch her. The lit end glowed yellow in the dark as he took another drag. Was he turning his "crazed stalker" toward her now? That was the last thing Gemma wanted from him. Top of the list being that he'd *leave her alone*.

"Maybe you could back up a little, Terrence. Give me some space." She waved a hand between them. "I can't really breathe."

"It's okay, Gemma." He moved closer. "There's no reason to be scared when I'm keeping you safe."

"I do need to get home, though. It's really late. You could walk me if you want."

"I'm not done talking with you." The tone of his voice deepened with frustration. "You're not leaving me, Gemma."

"What are we waiting here for?"

Cripes, how did she get into these situations? And where was Dan? He needed to walk up, all peaceful and pastorish, and tell Terrence to back off like he had in the library. *Okay, God. You could tell him where I am.* Maybe it didn't work like that, but she knew they talked to each other. *I could use some help before this gets more out of hand than it already is.*

"Gemma." His fingers ran down her face, her neck, her shoulder.

Ice flooded her veins, and she couldn't move. Dan retreated into his head when he couldn't cope with what was happening around him, and she knew why because she'd done the same thing. But only once. And she absolutely did not want to think about that. It wasn't going to help her right now.

He grabbed her hand, twisted it, and pinned it against the wall.

"Terr—" He touched the lit end of the cigarette to the inside of her arm. Gemma cried out.

Terrence shifted, and the soft flesh of his other arm pressed against her mouth. Her eyes met his, so she shut them. Shut him out.

She needed Dan. Why wasn't he here? For once she wished it was *her* that he was helping. She needed him right now. *Papa.* The first image her brain conjured was not the way she wanted to think about him.

Someone was crying.

Gemma lowered the book and reached out for the lantern switch. If someone knew where her secret camping spot was she'd need to find a new one. Tomorrow, anyway. She was just getting to the good part of this book.

There it was again, crying. The sound hitched, like the person was running.

Gemma snapped off the lantern, bathing the inside of her tent in darkness. She knew where everything was. Her sleeping bag, pillow, and bear. The secret stash of candy bars she'd hidden from her mom.

Terrence pressed the cigarette against her skin again. Gemma's body tightened, and a tear rolled down her face. "He said when this is over, I can have you."

A thump. The person cried out again, like they'd fallen. Who would be out in the woods in the middle of the night on Halloween besides her?

And besides her guardian angel. Gemma didn't know who put the supplies in her tent sometimes, or who had tied up the canopy that protected it from snow.

She crawled to the door and raised the zipper. Every snick of the teeth echoed through the woods like a tree falling.

In front of the door was a wide fern tree. Gemma peered under the lowest branches and then crawled on her belly to the edge, where she could see the path. The crying was almost right on top of her. The edge of a white sneaker flashed in the moonlight. She knew those shoes.

"Dan."

He cried out, tripped, and fell. Gemma ran out, still in a crouch and tumbled onto the dirt path beside him.

"Dan."

He didn't stop crying. His eyes were swollen, his face wet. Gemma touched his cheek. Had his dad hurt him again? She hated when his old man did that. She didn't even have a dad, just a mom, but she knew fathers weren't supposed to hurt their kids.

When she'd asked her mom about Dan's dad, Janice told her to hush about it and never ask questions about that man again. Gemma wasn't supposed to let Dan's dad even know she existed. She didn't understand that part, since Janice worked on the farm, but she'd told her mom "okay" anyway. Janice had seemed so desperate.

"Dan?"

His hands were a dark color, his shirt wet with something. What was that? It was sticky. "You're bleeding."

He shook his head, frantic. "Not me."

"Get back here, boy!" His father's voice boomed through the trees.

Dan cried.

"Shhh." She pressed her hand over his mouth. She could taste his skin, cutting off all the sound she made. No one could hear her. *The old man would find them if he made too much noise. Sometimes he scared her until she thought she might pee a little. Of course he was going to know who she was. What was her mom thinking?*

He yelled again. "Daniel!"

Still on the ground, Dan flinched. Gemma tugged on his arm. "Come with me and hide."

Terrence did it again. The sting was like being stuck with a knife. Gemma's cries were muffled against his doughy arm. She pushed against him, wrestled while the pain coursed from her arm to her fingers and up to her shoulder. She could hardly breathe.

"It's coming," he whispered in her ear. "No one can stop it."

Dan shook his head, the whites of his eyes huge in the moonlight.

"Come on," she said in as loud a whisper as she could. "Now!" She pulled, and he crawled. He'd just turned eleven, so he was too

heavy for her or she'd have dragged him in there. When they entered the tent, he gasped. Crawled toward where her pillow was.

"Shh." She put her finger to her lips even though he couldn't see her. "I'll turn on the lamp in a minute." Gemma rummaged and found the tissues she had left over from after she read Call of the Wild. She found his arm in the dark, then his hand and pressed it in there.

"Daniel, you get back here boy!"

Gemma reached out again. She found his hand and squeezed. Didn't let go. "We're safe in here."

They sat together in the still and the dark well past when his father's footsteps moved away and the yelling stopped.

Gemma found the switch and turned the lantern on. The stain on the front of his shirt was dark red, on his hands. His fingers. "What happened?"

Dan looked up at her, his face half-swollen. His eyes so puffy he could probably barely see. "I killed her."

Gemma kicked out. She opened her mouth wider, forced the bile back down, and bit Terrence's arm with every ounce of strength she could muster. He cried out and let go of her.

Gemma kicked him. She gripped her arm, but there was no relief for the burns which marked her skin. Four of them. Every time the inside of her bicep touched her shirt she had to bite back the cry. She could still taste him in her mouth.

"Hey!" Someone yelled from the end of the alley.

Terrence threw the cigarette at her along with a nasty word and ran off in the opposite direction.

"You're safe." Hands gripped her shoulders, and her head swam as the present blurred with the past. Boots slapped the concrete in a retreat, but there was someone in front of her. Cologne.

Gemma pushed off the wall, out of the person's arms. She shook off the feeling of unwanted touch and glanced around. "Where is he?"

"Who was that?" It was the mayor.

Her arm was on fire. She was aware of every second of what happened, exactly what Terrence had done, even while her mind had been elsewhere. She hated the fact she'd frozen like that.

"Who was that with you? You didn't look like you were okay, so I called out. He ran off, but I didn't see his face."

Gemma looked at the mayor. She couldn't really see him and couldn't hear anything but plain sincerity in his words. Had he simply stumbled upon her and Terrence? She hated that she was backing up again, but Gemma pushed the feeling aside and started walking toward Main Street. "I have to go."

**

"I hardly think she's been murdered," Mei said, shooting Maria a disapproving look. The room was in chaos. Dan couldn't move for the press of people.

He got up from the chair and turned back to take Olympia's hand. "I'll be back soon, but I just have to—"

She nodded. "Find her." Olympia sniffed and pressed the tissue to her nose. "Go find her. Don't let Gemma end up like my…" Her voice cracked, her face screwed up, and she began to cry again.

Dan didn't want to leave. They needed quiet to pray, which meant all the people crowding in the sheriff's office needed to vacate. Dan clapped his hands. The noise level dropped almost immediately. Mei shot him a look much like the one she'd gifted to Maria. Apparently the woman just enjoyed seeing other people as a disappointment.

"Okay, listen up. We don't want this tragedy to beget yet another tragedy on top. If you're able, I'd like you to pair up, or groups of three. Go out and walk the town, see if you can see Gemma. If you do, find the nearest phone and call the sheriff's number."

People began to dissipate.

"Since when do you get to decide what people do?"

Dan ignored Mei's stance. "Who took her?"

"She was beside those old-lady twins, then she was gone." Mei gritted her teeth. "I only lost sight of her for one second. I cannot believe someone hauled her out. Could she have just left and not told us? Maybe she just walked off."

"There's no way," Dan said. "She would've said something."

"You realize she can just do whatever she wants, right?"

"Sure, she could have left because she felt like it. But some people tell a person, 'bye.' Especially friends. My guess is you haven't met too many nice people in your life."

Mei didn't even respond. "Right. So people are looking. What are we doing?"

"Looking for her as well." He sighed. "There's something I need to tell you about Gemma."

Dan led the way out the back door. He quietly explained as they walked about Hal, his relationship to Gemma, and that room full of documents.

"You think she's being targeted?"

"I think it's possible at least," he said. "Someone might know Hal was hiding something, and she doesn't even know what it is yet. All we have right now are a whole lot of questions." Most of them about Hal's connection to Dan's father.

"Any of those questions have to do with Antonia?"

"I would've said no two hours ago. Now I have no idea."

He'd have to tell Gemma that Mei knew about the radio station room. He hadn't told Mei the location, just the fact it existed. Gemma was going to have to forgive him for telling the deputy sheriff, but if her life was in danger because of what her father had left her then he wasn't going to feel guilty for doing it.

Help me find her. Lord, keep her safe.

"Over there." Mei pointed with one hand and with the other dragged him over to the back of a building, where she hugged the wall. "Who is that she's talking to?"

"It's the mayor." Dan didn't like this, not one bit. If that man had hauled her from the sheriff's office there had to be a reason. And it wouldn't be good.

"Let's get closer."

**

The mayor held out his elbow. "It would be my pleasure to escort you to your residence."

Yeah, like she was going to buy his suddenly chivalrous act. Gemma took his arm like it was a snake in danger of biting her and said, "I appreciate it."

Tension tightened every inch of her body until she thought she would snap. Her arm hurt like she couldn't believe. She needed Shelby and her creams and sticky things like giant bandages, but her friend was on her honeymoon.

She needed to talk to John and tell him what had happened with Terrence, but the sheriff was at the lake taking care of Antonia's body. Olympia was grief stricken. Gemma couldn't burden them with this right now. It had to wait.

"Of course, you'll have to remind me where you live." His white teeth flashed in the dark. A shuffle behind them made her glance back. "Probably a cat."

Ah, yes. One of the new residents had brought a cat with them, an old and mean tabby that did not like the tuna she'd set out at the library to try and win it over. Hadn't worked, and she'd been scratched for her troubles.

They continued along the street.

He said, "How have you been recently?"

"Fine, thank you." Like she was going to answer that for real? She nearly snorted out loud.

"It's okay to be honest, Gemma. I'm aware you've had…difficult news. That Hal Leonard was your father, and that you never knew this fact. How is that possible?"

He sounded so genuine, so caring. Gemma steeled herself against getting sucked into it and ignoring the fact he'd just parroted all that off like it was common knowledge. "He never told me, and neither did my mother. So how did you know?"

He tsked with his mouth. He'd been speaking to her mother earlier. Had they talked about it? Collins was precisely the kind of man who kept relevant information to himself until it suited him, so he might not have found out tonight. Either way, he was probably here to gather more information. It certainly wasn't about being a gentleman. She didn't believe that for one second.

"And you?" she asked. "You seem to be feeling better."

"I've gained a new lease on life."

But not from that pseudo-relationship with Antonia. She hadn't believed for a second that it had been genuine. Gemma didn't want to be the one to tell him the woman was dead. Good thing she had no problem keeping secrets exactly the way the mayor did. It didn't bother her one bit to leave the job of informing him that Antonia was dead to someone else. It wasn't like he's actually cared for the woman.

So Gemma changed the subject. "I heard that you're actively seeking a replacement for the mayor position."

"I have been." He patted her arm with his free hand. "And I think I've found the perfect person to take over for me."

"Isn't it typically a position where people vote for the candidate they feel would represent their beliefs and oversee the town in a way they agree with?"

"That's precisely what's wrong with the electoral system in this country today. People don't know what they want, and if they do they don't do the required research to be well-enough informed to make an intelligent choice." He snorted a laugh that actually sounded gentlemanly but also incredibly snooty. "That's why my choosing a successor will yield much better results. Everyone will be considerably happier after I make the announcement and turn the office over to my choice of mayor."

"So who is it?"

"Ah, my dear. I do not reveal secrets until the time is right." His eyes gleamed, and he winked at her. "I'm sure you can understand the need to conceal certain things."

"Um…sure." He couldn't have known she'd just been thinking about that very thing. This was way too bizarre, and she was sweating. It was cold. Her arm hurt, but they weren't far from her house. Gemma needed to sit down.

"Secrets. They make the world go round," he said. "Much like what brought us all to this town—though not yourself, I suppose. Your father, your mother. They arrived separately, did they not? Years between."

"That's right." The mayor had only been here maybe a decade. She remembered seeing him for the first time. She'd had exactly the same impression of him back then as she did today.

Totally hiding something.

He said, “And do you know what brought Hal here?”

“Why would I? I had no idea he was even my father.”

He nodded slowly, his face thoughtful. “That’s a shame. Not truly being able to know someone who meant something to you.”

“Many people in Sanctuary wished to leave their pasts behind when they came here. It seems Hal was no exception.”

“And others have plenty of secrets, new ones made in this place.”

Gemma didn’t know who he was talking about unless he was referring to himself.

“Take you for example.” They stopped outside her house. “An incredible author, each of your pennames in their own right have made a mark on the world.”

Maybe in the sense that her art had been appreciated by someone, somewhere in the world. “Sure, I guess.”

She’d had books that sold well, and ones that didn’t sell at all. It was the nature of it, but it kept her from being bored. Had Collins actually read any? She doubted it. He’d probably searched for one of her names online and read some reviews on one of those sites where people happily trashed the author’s character, forgetting that they were a real person with real feelings.

“Well,” she said. “This is me. Thanks again for walking me home. I’ll be talking to the sheriff about what happened, and he’ll likely want to speak with you and get your take on it as well.”

“Don’t hold your breath on that.” The mayor held his body still. “The sheriff seems to devote entirely too much attention to the things he wants while ignoring every other valid case. I'm sure he won't care that Terrence hurt you."

A trash can fell over. There was a scuffle across the street and a thud. "Good night, Gemma." The mayor bowed and walked away.

Gemma turned to her front door, ready to bolt every lock she had and hide under her covers until daylight.

It was open.

Chapter 10

Dan rubbed his aching head. Mei had actually hit him, just to keep him from running over and walloping the mayor. Or going after Terrence. He hurt her? Rage burned through Dan's body. Rage upon rage at what might have been done, and the fact he hadn't been there fast enough. Hadn't known she was taken. Hadn't helped her.

He needed to get to her. Gemma!

Dan scrambled off the ground, unable to believe Mei had seriously punched him because he'd wanted to help Gemma. Because *she* wanted to be the one to go to Gemma and talk to her. What did Mei think was wrong with Gemma that she needed Mei right now, not him? And why couldn't he go have a man-to-man chat with Terrence about how one treated ladies?

"I don't think I can handle another conversation." Gemma's voice was distorted, but he could hear the edge of fear. "This has been the longest night ever."

Mei didn't stop until she was within arm's reach of Gemma. "You don't need to wait for John. You tell me what Terrence did."

Dan stretched out his tweaked muscles and felt the pull of the scar tissue on his back. His cheekbone smarted where Mei had planted her tiny fist in his face. The woman had upper body strength for sure.

"I—" Gemma's voice was tentative. "Maybe we could go inside, but…"

Dan walked over. She looked seriously shaken.

"The front door is open." Mei glanced at him. "Stay with her—" She drew her weapon. "—I'm going inside to check things out. I'll put the call out that we found her."

Mei walked inside, and he gathered Gemma into his arms. He felt more than heard her sigh. "Is someone in there?" Did Mei think it was a break-in?

Only one of her arms was around him, the other was tucked close to her side. "I really want to go in my home. I need sleep." There was something in her voice, something he couldn't decipher.

He shifted his hand up and rubbed the back of her head. Her hair smelled fruity and made him want to close his eyes and stay there for a while. "If you can't get in there or don't want to now, I'm sure your mom will let you stay on her couch."

Gemma nodded against his chest. "I didn't need this."

Antonia hadn't needed this night, either. None of them had. *Papa, a woman is dead. Help us figure this out.* "What happened in the sheriff's office? Who took you?" He wanted to ask why she hadn't called out, said something.

"I was listening to Mei, watching what was going on with everyone in the sheriff's office. Terrence touched my arm, said he wanted to talk to me but we wouldn't be able to hear each other. He didn't grab me until we were outside."

She shivered, and he collected her close to him again. They'd shared a kiss earlier that evening but affection could wait. Right now she needed support, and in a short while she would need space.

What Dan needed was answers. "No one standing close to you saw him?"

She shrugged one shoulder. "He pulled me through town to the alley between one of the offices and, I think, the laundromat? No one saw us, no one even looked. He—" Gemma's voice broke.

Dan didn't want her back on that whole 'I'm invisible' thing she used to talk about. No one missed Gemma. If they ignored her it was because they were intimidated. She was a knockout, and she didn't try to hide it. Her tattoos weren't about drawing more attention, and they weren't a statement against authority. He hadn't figured them out. But Dan was still blown away by her half the time, and they'd been best friends for years.

"I want you to talk to Mei about what happened, okay?"

She had to tell someone, and there might be too much pressure with him. She'd leave parts out because of the need to have be careful with his feelings. Mei was an impartial third party. She could take the statement, build a case. As much as Dan wanted to get his shotgun and… Terrence needed to be behind bars. Dan wasn't going to kill him. He hadn't pulled a trigger to kill anything bigger than a cougar in years.

"Tell her everything that happened. And call someone if you don't want to be alone later."

Gemma pressed her lips together, then said, "I'd rather go to the tent."

He stared at her. "You want to be in the woods by yourself?"

"I didn't say I wanted to go there alone."

Dan sighed. "Gemma—"

"I know." It was her turn to sigh. "That was a long time ago, and we were kids hiding from the world. We didn't know it was weird that we were alone for long periods of time."

He shifted again and touched her cheeks. "I would know now that it was fine, but others wouldn't." When her face changed, he added, "I have to care about other people's opinions. At least to an extent. There will always be someone that isn't satisfied, but I have to keep things as open and honest as I can. If there's nothing to hide, then I don't have to work at hiding anything."

"Dan. You hide *everything.*"

He dropped his hands and stepped back. She was right. No one knew how hard it was for him to function, or how difficult it was to maintain a balanced normal without the assistance of meds.

It was so bad it had led to him confessing to Antonia's murder when he'd had nothing to do with it. *Papa, help John figure this out. Help Mei see the truth.* Did he want to come clean and tell everyone about his past? No. But maybe he should tell his closest friends. Shame and fear had covered him like blankets for so long, would he finally be able to throw them off and stand free of their weight?

Dan needed to go and pray about telling John and Matthias.

Mei stood at the door, then came toward them. “It’s clear. No one is inside now, and nothing looks disturbed.” She glanced at Gemma. “Are you sure you didn’t just leave your door open by mistake? It happens.”

“I remember locking it.”

“Then if someone took the trouble to break in, it wasn’t to take anything. Unless they knew exactly what they wanted and took nothing else.”

Dan said, “Or they didn’t find it here.”

“Could this be about the room of papers at the radio station?”

Gemma gasped. She looked at Dan, at Mei, and then back at Dan. “You *told* her?”

“You’d been abducted! We didn’t know where you were or who took you. Mei is a police officer, and she needed all relevant information.”

“You told her.”

Why did she look like he’d betrayed her? That wasn’t what had happened. “Gemma—”

“No. Don’t give me excuses. I trusted you, and the first chance you got you told someone?”

“Gem—”

Mei cut in. “Enough. He told me, it’s done. Now answer the question, do you think this break-in could be about the papers?”

Gemma thought for a moment. “I don’t know how someone would even know about them.”

“The mayor did ask about Hal,” Mei suggested. “It’s conceivable Terrence and the mayor planned that whole episode just to draw you away so that someone could enter your house and search for anything related to Hal.”

"You think that might be what they did?" Dan asked. "I didn't even know people thought like that. It's… vindictive."

Mei stared at him like an alien just grew out of his head. "Are you for real?"

"I don't know what you mean."

"I didn't even know there were people like you still left in the world."

Dan shrugged. "Maybe Sanctuary could be a good thing for both of us."

Gemma took a step back and lifted her chin. She was holding her arm funny. "What if it wasn't good for any of us so we just checked out and left?"

She wanted to do that? Dan said, "That's what John said Antonia was planning to do. She was working for him, undercover with the mayor. The mayor and his friends must have figured out she wasn't for real and killed her because she knew something she wasn't supposed to." He turned to face Gemma. He could ask about her arm later. "Did she ever ask you about Hal?"

"No, I don't think—"

"Whoa there, Nancy Drew." Mei chuckled. She shook her head at Dan like he was a cute little kid. "The Sanctuary Sheriff's Department doesn't need your help solving the murder of Antonia Hernandez, but thanks for helping me brainstorm."

Gemma cocked her head to one side. "You've read Nancy Drew?"

"Movie trailer. I got the reference right, didn't I?" When Gemma nodded, Mei said, "Good. Not everything translates right."

"What language?"

Mei's eyebrows lifted. "You think I'm going to give you personal information so that you can figure out who I am and then use it against me? No way."

Dan watched the interplay between the two women, hardly knowing when to remind them it was the middle of the night, someone was dead, and they still had to figure out if Gemma was sleeping here alone or not.

Gemma said, "Wow, you're really paranoid."

"Actually it's just being 'smart,'" Mei told her. "The opposite of which, is 'dead.'"

"Huh."

"Okay, ladies." Dan clapped his hands. "Mei, if you could take Gemma's statement about what happened with Terrence, I'm going inside to check all the doors and windows and make sure it's secure for Gemma to go to bed. Right now we all need some sleep."

Mei shot him a dirty look. "Don't think I don't remember you confessed to a murder earlier. But since it's looking less likely that you did it, I'll just slide you over to the list of possible suspects along with Gemma here. Okay?"

"Uh, sure. That'd be great."

"But I'm still watching you." She turned to Gemma and her grimace morphed into a smile. "Let's go talk, yeah?"

Gemma chuckled. "Living room."

They went inside, and Dan discretely checked all the windows. He spent extra time outside, walking around the yard and the back. Gemma needed space to say what she wanted to say, and he took the time to stare up at the stars and pray for her that this wouldn't linger. That she wouldn't suffer nightmares the way he did.

When he caught himself falling asleep on his feet, Dan knocked on the front door.

**

John ran his hands through his hair and paced the barn. He'd closed up the sheriff's office for lunch because Dan asked him to, but he had a murder investigation to get back to soon. Especially since he also needed to oversee Mei's search for Terrence. She hadn't called in to say she'd located him yet, which better mean she was still out looking.

Now he knew why Dan called him and Matthias out to the farm. And it wasn't for a sandwich.

Matthias blew out a breath, his gaze on the pastor. "Brother…" His voice cracked and died. "I don't even know what to say."

Dan wiped his face, and his gaze met John's. He nodded to his pastor, his friend. "Thank you for telling us."

"It was time." Dan paused, head high in the middle of the barn where they'd first met. Dan had seemed almost intimidating that first Battle Night right after John arrived in Sanctuary. Now he only looked broken. "The time to talk about this was probably a while back. But I didn't know how you'd react, so I didn't say anything."

"What made you tell us now?"

"Just something Gemma said." Before he'd walked back in to the house and found Mei putting Band-Aid's on the inside of her upper arm. Injured because Terrence had burned her with cigarettes. Dan knew exactly what that felt like.

Matthias's eyebrows lifted. "Gemma, huh? Guess that explains a few things about why y'all were so tight in school." Matthias shook his head. "I'm kind of surprised you haven't married her by now."

Dan's face screwed up. "We can't get married."

John knew why, even though Matthias argued otherwise. It was the same reason Andra had waited, tested the waters, and told him about her faith. "They'd be unequally yoked."

Though John figured that Dan was in love with her, and if he had to guess he'd say Gemma felt the exact same way.

"Is that even a thing anymore? Unequally yoked." Matthias lifted his hands.

"If you want less reasons divorce is going to cross the table, yes," John said. "The idea is to have the best situation possible, so that you minimize the issues. And if you'll listen, the Bible will tell you what those issues are so you can avoid them. It's called wisdom."

"Huh," Matthias said, a smile only in his eyes. "Guess I missed that one."

John decided he was just playing dense to inject some humor into the situation, so John said, "I feel sorry for Frannie."

"You see my wife around town. Does she look like she's having a hard time to you?"

Every time John saw her, the woman was all smiles. But he wasn't going to give his friend that credit. "I guess she's coping just fine."

Dan stood. "There's one more thing."

John said, "Tell us."

"Actually it's more of a showing thing." Dan walked to a closed door at the end, not the storage room but a door to the right.

"What is this?"

John followed him inside. At first he thought it was Dan's office, then he saw the bed.

"This is where I live."

"Wait," Matthias said. "What about the house?"

Several things clicked into place for John. "He hasn't been in there in years."

Dan nodded. "First it was because he didn't want me there. Then after the old man died I didn't want to go in there. I still haven't."

"So it's just going to sit untouched?"

Dan shrugged at Matthias's question.

They didn't stay much longer. Dan looked worn out. John drove Matthias back into town and dropped him off at the bakery before he unlocked the back door of the sheriff's office.

Andra was at his desk, the computer on. "Bye." She spun in his chair and smiled. "Your mom says 'hi.'"

"Hi." He leaned down for a kiss and didn't pass up the chance to place his hand on her belly and feel their son kick. "How are the two of you?"

"We're fine, but I don't want to talk about us." She waved away his concern. "How is Dan?"

John gave her the highlights of Dan's childhood.

Andra looked like she was going to cry. "If he wasn't dead, I'd kill the man myself." When he gave her a look, she added, "If I did that kind of thing anymore."

"Uh-huh." He folded his arms. "Now get out of my chair."

Andra held out her hands. He helped her up and swatted her behind as she passed him. "Fine, fine. I'm going to take a nap. Pat and Aaron went to the park to play catch."

John looked up Dan and his father in the town's files. It was all paper, and he'd barely started entering the backlog into his computer system. Arnold Walden's death had been labeled natural causes. No autopsy had been done. And there was no mention of Bill Jones anywhere. The previous sheriff's report was spotty, but basically the man had collapsed in the sun onto his lettuce, and no one had been able to revive him.

Had anyone actually tried? John wasn't sure he'd have expended much effort, though he'd have done his duty.

That duty would have included pulling the child, Dan Walden, from the house years before that day. Years before his mother had disappeared and been assumed dead. He might even have relocated them out of Sanctuary. Or he'd have sent Arnold to solitary confinement in a secret prison somewhere. Ben had to know of one.

John blew out a breath. Hindsight was a beautiful thing, but he couldn't change Dan's tragic past. It was possible his father had been poisoned. There were substances—even natural ones—that could mimic a heart attack. The old man hadn't been tested for them. If someone did kill him, John figured they'd done the world a favor. Or at least one little boy.

He pulled up the file on Dan's mother, Emilia Walden, next. The sheriff had labeled it a disappearance. Like it was possible for someone to simply up and vanish in a town with no way in or out. Back then there was no communication with the outside world but by snail mail. If she'd been killed, her body had never been found. Who knew what story she would tell, even in death? Probably one similar to Dan's.

John couldn't let go of the pain he felt for his friend. He bowed his head and prayed for peace to fill Dan's heart. The man might be his pastor, but John needed to pray for him.

So many people looked to Dan to help them fix their problems, and they had no idea Dan had so many of his own. The man had been hurt over and over again, the mental and physical scars still with him to this day. John couldn't help but wonder over the fact Dan had it as together as he did.

"Sheriff, come in."

John grabbed his radio. "Yeah, Mei. What is it?"

"I'm at Terrence's house. You should get over here."

Two minutes later he pulled his Jeep up and parked outside the house. This section of the street, the houses had been divided into upstairs and downstairs apartments. Gemma's was a downstairs apartment, right across the street from Terrence's second floor place.

John took the stairs two at a time and knocked on the frame at the same time he pushed the door open. "Mei?"

"Bedroom!"

John crossed the living room, resisting the temptation to hold his nose. Evidently Andra had humanized him, because this place had a distinctly "bachelor" smell to it. Or that was just the dirty clothes on the floor and the dishes in the sink.

He stopped at the door. "What is it?"

Mei pulled back a pillow on the rumpled bed. On the grimy sheet was a 9mm revolver.

"For a town where there aren't actually supposed to be any weapons, there seem to be an awful lot of guns around." John sighed. It wouldn't be registered to Terrence, or anyone else in town. That would be a violation of WITSEC rules. Who knew where on earth this had come from? Unless they got a print or a confession, it would be a pain to find out who it belonged to.

"Want to bet this is the gun that killed Antonia Hernandez?"

"We can certainly get it tested and find out."

"Twenty dollars, or fifty?"

"I'm not betting on a murder weapon, Mei." He blew out a breath. "A woman is dead."

She almost reminded him of… no. There was no way.

Mei had come here like everyone else, yet her qualifications—if you could call a finesse for weapons and a bad attitude that—were clear.

She wasn't some kind of plant sent here to help him. He was mostly sure. Though if she was, would he be mad exactly? Maybe initially. Then after Andra had the baby, fine, he might be a little grateful for the help. He might actually be able to take a day off.

Still, there would be a point of contention if she had been sent there by his brother. Mei was exactly the kind of person Ben would hire for his business of private investigators, or security experts or whatever it was they did. And she was Chinese. Ben had spent a lot of time in China, but John was pretty sure that his brother's interest in that culture went way back to this tiny girl in high school. Dang, he hadn't thought about her in years. Never did know what happened to her, why she left. Ben was never the same after that.

Did Mei remind him of his old flame? Ben was old enough to be her father, but John knew for a fact he had a soft spot. He just managed to hide it really, really well.

She cocked her head to the side. "Why are you looking at me like you just figured something out?"

John pulled an evidence bag from his pocket he'd stashed there just in case she found something. "Drop that in here, but don't get your prints on it."

"As if." She took the bag from him, slid one side of the open edge under the gun and scooped it up. "Now what?"

"Any luck finding Terrence?"

Mei shook her head. "He's proving…elusive. I don't like it at all. No one should be this hard to find in such a tiny town. I stopped by the library this morning and gave Gemma some pepper spray."

"Good. Let's get this back to the office."

The doorbell rang downstairs. Mei wandered to the front window. "Great. Terrence's parents are here."

"Yoo-hoo, Sheriff!"

John groaned. *Your son is a crazy psycho who burned a woman with a cigarette last night, and how are you?*

Chapter 11

Gemma pulled a new stack of files from the first cabinet. She was barely halfway down the drawers. Plenty to do, and it was better than sitting at home pretending to watch TV while her arm hurt, her mind raced, and she wondered who was going to come at her next. She was beyond exhausted, up half the night, and dreaming monstrous images the rest of the time. There was no way she would try and sleep now.

The ice cold terror of what happened had thawed and left her with the knowledge that she'd frozen. Again. Not completely, but enough that it bothered her. Just like the other time she'd been confronted—years ago now—Terrence had hurt her, and she'd done not one thing to fight him off. Was she weak? Maybe retreating into her head and not giving everything she had to get away from the situation from the first second meant she didn't have enough strength. Perhaps she had nothing to draw on when someone came at her like that.

But if that was true, it meant Dan was weak for doing the same thing to survive his father. She'd read about coping mechanisms before and knew the mind could splinter under extreme stress. A child might not remember something which happened to them, when in any other situation they'd know exactly what went on. But she'd been far away, deep in her memories, while Terrence could have touched her all he wanted.

She needed to write another book and put in a character, who by all accounts should be strong, and make them face a situation where they were unable to defend themselves. Just so she could figure it out, wrestle with what had happened and the fact she'd *done nothing*. Gemma let out a growl of frustration.

The paper.

She set down the file pages and tried to smooth out the crumples she'd just made. She needed this. Needed to focus on something that didn't involve her at all.

This stack was nothing but more mission logs. It seemed like they were carried out by a single man team, instead of a group. Hal? Bill Jones, maybe. From the little she'd gathered, mostly from Hal's tattoos, he'd been in Vietnam. Had the man run solo missions back then? But why, and what on earth was he doing in the jungle alone? The text made it seem so benign, she didn't understand any of it.

These papers didn't even say which part of Vietnam he'd been in, just a bunch of numbers. She'd have to look on the library computers tomorrow, see if they were latitude and longitude references or what. But all this was forty-plus years ago now, and most of the people who took part in it were older. A lot of them would be dead now. It was all a history most people only wanted to forget, or they wanted to remember it with some kind of rose-colored sense of honor while current affairs were only history repeating itself, and everyone claimed it was some kind of "new problem" instead of people being selfish just like every bad thing that had ever happened all through history.

Gemma loved to read about history. She couldn't imagine being called to give so much—maybe even everything—as some politician's pawn in a global chess match that could never be won. She'd always been a pacifist, raised by her mother. An earth child.

But it was easy for the both of them to spout litany about peace from behind a wall of mountains that protected them from nearly every threat in the world.

If she was outside of Sanctuary, things would be different. It was why she couldn't be as vocal on her stance as others were online. Gemma didn't know what it was like to live in the real world, and the people she knew who had… well, the real world hadn't done them any favors, had it? If she'd grown up in Kabul or New York City, she'd probably have a different stance, but she'd grown up here.

Mostly Gemma figured nowhere on this earth was perfect. If there was she'd sure like to live there, but maybe they didn't let people like her in. There had to be some kind of standard, otherwise it wouldn't be perfect anymore. People would just mess it up, like they had over and over again, all through history.

Marched eight miles to location. No one left alive. Target still unaccounted for.

This was a little more serious. But she wasn't going to know what it referred to if she didn't know who the players were. Someone had died. Someone was being hunted. Gemma sighed. Was she going to read anything at all in this mess that made sense?

At least she could figure out whether the words that had filled out the boxes on the form were Hal's handwriting or not. Gemma wandered out to the radio room and rummaged around. *Bingo.* A sticky note with Hal's writing on it. A pang of something that made no sense hit her. She hadn't really known the man who wrote this, only as an acquaintance in passing.

Was that her destiny also, to die alone and unknown? Dan's face filled her mind. She'd never be unknown. But the alone part was entirely too familiar to be comfortable. She'd always been at ease by herself. It was simpler than explaining to people who didn't understand why she was the way she was.

Gemma went back to the paper, laid both side-by-side on the desk, and flipped on the lamp. She wasn't a handwriting expert, but she'd watched enough CSI that she knew to look for unique loops and swirls. The slant of the words.

They looked like a match to her. He wrote at an angle, and the scratches of the letters resembled one another, which meant Hal had sat in a tent somewhere in Vietnam and written this report. *No one left alive.* Who had he been chasing? She and Dan had found that picture of Bill Jones, Dan's father. Was that the man Hal had pursued through the Vietnamese countryside?

The front door of the building hit the bell she'd hung above it, with a loud clang. Hal hadn't needed a bell, and there were probably legitimate questions going around town about who'd installed it but Gemma didn't care. She had no key, so she couldn't lock the place, and that would only invite more questions anyway.

Gemma ducked back into the hidden room and pushed the door shut. From the other side it would simply look like there was a wall here. She pulled the pepper spray Mei had given her from her back pocket and held her breath. It was probably nothing. Just Nadia Marie, or someone else feeling nostalgic and missing Hal, so they'd decided to come for a visit. The person would leave after a while, and she'd be able to open up the door again.

Not the person—whoever it had been—that had tapped on the wall like they were trying to find a hidden door all those months ago. Right?

Footsteps. She could hear them, though muted. That meant if she made too much noise they'd know she was here as well. Gemma backed up from the door. How thin were the walls? Could someone just punch through them? Maybe they wouldn't even need a hammer.

"Okay, so you're not in here," the man's voice was a low rumble. "This was a stupid idea."

Dan?

"You're probably at home sleeping, not rooting through papers at almost midnight. That would be crazy. Just because I can't sleep a wink doesn't mean—"

Gemma cracked the door.

Dan turned back to her, eyes wide.

She said, "Uh…hey."

"Can I come in?"

Gemma opened the door wide enough he could enter, then said, "Open or shut?"

"No one knows we're here, but open is probably better."

Suit yourself. Like she cared about propriety. Maybe a torrid affair everyone talked about was just what she needed.

"How are you?"

Sigh. No torrid affairs today. Maybe next week. "I'm fine."

Dan's eyebrow rose.

"Okay, so I jumped out of my chair every time the door opened at the library. I nearly set off the pepper spray about six times and could have permanently damaged some old lady's eyes, but I have it handled."

"And now you've settled in for some… light reading?" He motioned to the papers.

She shrugged, which shifted her long sleeve shirt over the little bandages on her arm. "I'm going to try the tent tonight, see if I sleep better there. If I find anything good here, I'll take it with me."

He sat on the edge of the desk. "Is that tent even still standing?" Never mind that it hadn't been her secret hideout since childhood. He still didn't really get why she liked it so much.

"I don't know. I haven't been out there in years." She tried to remember the last time. "I don't think I've even thought about the place in forever. It could be rags, or some kind of animal habitat, by now."

"Probably the deer."

"Don't say it." She clapped her hands over her ears. "That deer doesn't like me. I think she might be stalking me."

Dan chuckled. She knew he didn't believe all the superstition around town about the deer. He'd seen it so many times himself, which meant both of them were the walking dead. Or as good as. It was nothing but a dumb legend told by people who'd left their interesting lives and come to the most boring town in the world.

"Find anything good yet?"

Gemma handed him a pile. "Find something good yourself. Why should I do all the work?"

Dan was still laughing when he sat and started to read the first page. She didn't even want to know what that was about. Yeah, so she was letting him in after telling him to leave. A woman could change her mind.

Fifteen pages later she came across something that might actually yield helpful information. "No way," she breathed. "Bill Jones was working for the CIA. Maybe even as an agent. They called him 'the asset.'" Gemma frowned. So who was "the target" she'd read about earlier?

"What does it say?"

Gemma scanned the paper. "The CIA was going to take heroin they'd seized and trade it back to a Vietnamese drug dealer, a rival to the one they'd confiscated it from. I'm not even going to try and pronounce his name. The asset's job was to make the deal, but it went wrong. This report" —She checked the sticky note— "I think was written by Hal and says he was supposed to have been on surveillance for the Op. He turned up at the meeting location, a farm, but it was too late. The drugs were gone, the dealer and his crew were dead, and sixteen women and children who'd worked the farm had also been slaughtered."

"So Bill Jones betrayed the oath he took with the CIA and became a killer?" He'd read that book on the history of American intelligence that she'd given him. This came straight from the pages of that book. They were reading real history, an operation. A killer.

His father.

"The bottom of the page has been written on by someone else. It says they determined the asset was a liability. They advise that the target should be killed on sight."

Gemma looked up. Dan's face was pale. She swallowed, "This was years ago."

"He killed people. A lot of people."

Gemma might've argued that what he'd done to Dan and his mother had been a whole lot more evil. Sometimes death was a mercy denied the living. But she didn't figure he'd consider it mercy, considering everything his father had done to him.

"See what else you can find."

Gemma looked at the next few pages. "One is a hospital report. Stab wound. Then I have a log where it looks like he was chasing Bill Jones. His handwriting is different, thicker pencil strokes like he's pressing down really hard."

"Frustrated." Dan paused. "Though it could have been from some kind of injury."

Her father had pursued his father through miles and miles of Vietnamese war zone? "This one indicates Bill Jones was captured. When Hal was sent to retrieve the asset, he wasn't there anymore. Hal found bodies. Prisoners and guards, Americans and Vietnamese." She blew out a breath. "Bill Jones—"

"My father."

Gemma sighed. "He had no discretion, no sense of discrimination. He just killed." Whether there was a reason, maybe they would never know. Hal had been tasked with bringing in Bill Jones, but "the target" had eluded him.

"And then they came here?" Dan shook his head. "This makes no sense. Why, years later, would he be a farmer living a normal life? He met my mom and got married." Dan paused. "Why did Hal let him do that?"

"If he hadn't, you wouldn't be here. And your mom must have seen something in him." Gemma didn't want to think what the alternative was.

"She was my best friend."

Gemma pressed her lips together. "I know."

"And he took her away."

Gemma wandered over and set her hand on his. "I know."

Dan closed his eyes, and his head dropped forward onto her shoulder. She waited for him to pray through whatever was in his head. It was the way he lived his life.

If his faith enabled him to withstand everything that had been thrown at him, there had to be something to it. Some people might call it a crutch he leaned on, but it was more than that. It was everything to him. It was *breath.* What his father had done would have broken someone who didn't have the connection with his Heavenly Father that Dan had.

Maybe she should go to church on Sunday, hear him talk more about it.

"I told John and Matthias everything."

That was huge. He'd told them everything, like… *everything?* Gemma opened her mouth to ask him how it went.

The bell clanged.

She swung around. Dan shifted beside her, and she reached for his hand. "Do you think it's Nadia?"

Dan shut the door. "Less questions about us and the room would be good at this point. We can just wait them out."

Gemma turned and went back to her papers. He wasn't worried about her marring his reputation?

She handed a page to Dan so he could read about Hal's fruitless search for what he was now referring to as "the target." Things weren't any better in this round of mission reports. The CIA agent had gone out of control, and Bill Jones was being hunted. Hal—and whoever he'd worked for—wanted him dead.

Footsteps crossed the radio room beyond the door. More than one—several people were out there. Someone tapped on the wall.

She swung her gaze back to Dan and mouthed, *They know we're in here.* Dan nodded, but it wasn't okay. There was no way out. No way to get past this but to confront whoever was there.

The door opened a crack. A fist-sized canister flew into the room, hit the floor like a firecracker and sent a flash of light and a great bang through the room.

Gemma fell backwards as booted feet rushed around them. The ceiling swam, the walls. Big black figures. Shouting. Her brain sputtered like strobe lighting, stunned and unable to do anything to stop them. *Papa.* They needed Him.

"No. Leave them alive."

Dan grunted, then cried out in pain. The rubber tread of someone's boot crushed her hand.

"Get everything."

**

Mei strode through town toward the radio station. Yeah, she probably should tell them she was going to break in and look at all those papers Dan told her Gemma had found, but she wasn't a people person. It wouldn't help her tactic to stay disconnected from the ones who lived here, especially the ones she might actually like to be friends with if she "connected" with them.

They all thought she was Chinese, probably because of the lilt of her accent. Truth was, she was as American as most of them. She just hadn't been in this country that much, until now.

Terrence had disappeared. Totally dropped off the grid—if this town had one. Now she needed to find the evidence that proved he killed Antonia, and this whole thing would be wrapped up. Would she be able to leave? The question of why she was even sent to this town passed through her thoughts again. There did seem to be more brewing here, and the mayor was quite likely in the middle of it.

The man played his part like a pro, but Mei had understood the rules of that game her entire life. She might be barely twenty-two but she'd travelled the world. Her mom hadn't agreed with her choices, not when she found out what Mei was doing. But after all that had happened there was no way she could deny Mei anything—a fact Mei counted on, probably more than she should. Besides, it was the family business. What was she gonna do, get a real job?

But this wasn't about her. Or her issues that tended to lead to people either dead or missing. This was a real assignment. He'd sent her on an honest-to-goodness real assignment! Sure, he sent work her way every now and then. After her mom found out she went ballistic. Mei should probably have told him to shove off and go fix Sanctuary himself.

Next time she would. For sure.

The deputy sheriff gig was kind of boring, but the job put her in the middle of everything relevant that was happening—that could not be denied. And neither could the fact it was slightly obvious that John didn't believe she was some normal girl who happened to have excelled at deductive reasoning. He'd never have bought a military background, not that she had one anyway. Still, it would've been more straightforward to apply to that separatist group who enjoyed pillaging Eastern Europe. Not that they'd let her in, after…

Anyway. Mei sniffed and glanced around. At least none of her enemies could find her here. That was a plus. Sunshine, and people she enjoyed observing. The bakery had cream cheese wontons, and her mom couldn't call her every day just to make sure she was alive.

A man dressed in black with a ski mask on his face—an oddity she had yet to see here—dumped a full box in the back of Dan's truck. But it wasn't Dan.

"Evening." Mei tried to look not scary. The way his eyes narrowed, she didn't think it worked.

"Walk away."

She didn't recognize his stance or voice. Left handed, scar on his forearm probably from a knife wound, but his boots were clean. Out of practice. "Make me."

Another man walked out of the radio station in similar clothing.

Mei snorted. "Stealthy. Wow. Robberies generally go better if you try to hide the fact you're stealing something. Just saying."

The second man blanched and dropped his box. Both of them pulled guns.

"Don't just stand there," first man said. "Get her inside with Gemma and Dan."

Mei pulled her gun. "Don't think so." Though she was going to go in and check on them. "Guns down, now."

The first man fired. The shot hit her in the left shoulder. Mei fired back but hers went way wide.

Man that hurt. Like, *hurt.* It was like fire that blinked across her vision. Where did the other one…

She fell to one knee, and her gun skidded across the ground. Crap, this wasn't going well.

The truck revved. Men ran past her, and gravel flew as they tore away from the radio station. Mei touched the wound on her shoulder. Ugh. She didn't like to bleed, but blood on the buttons of her satellite phone was the least of her worries.

"Sheriff." She let go of the button and moaned.

"I've asked you to call me John." He paused. "Did you find Terrence yet?"

"That's not why I'm calling." Half the town was probably listening on police scanners. Normally it was way less, but with Antonia's death, things were getting entertaining. "I need your help at the radio station. Now."

He had better understand. She wasn't going to spell it out.

"And get the doctor." Gemma and Dan might need medical attention.

Mei forced her legs not to give out and made it to the radio room. The open door in the wall was probably the worst hidden room she'd even seen. She'd have found it. Blood ran from Dan's mouth and he lay, out cold, on the floor. Gemma lay a few feet away, out as well, but with no visible injuries. A flash grenade lay discarded on the floor, probably what had incapacitated them.

Mei landed on her knees. A squeeze in the vicinity of her chest didn't help the situation. Feelings were not her friend, and they did not help her do her job. Mostly she just ignored them, except that one time, with that Swedish guy… *Don't think about that.*

She tapped Gemma's cheek with her fingers. "Hey."

Nothing.

"Gemma, its Mei."

She wasn't going to admit to anyone that she'd lied to the sheriff. Names were good. They told you who you were, and where you came from. A name was a gift, and she remembered every single one she'd ever heard.

Now she was in a town full of people whose names—new and old—indicated they'd been through the worst a person could endure. People like her, who had seen too much and had to live through it. Ugh, she was starting to care about them.

This might be the worst assignment ever.

Chapter 12

Gemma turned her head to watch Shelby walk in the medical center room. Sadness, grief. Not the face of a woman who had gotten married less than two days ago. Shelby stopped beside the bed. "It's all gone. John said they cleared out the whole room."

Gemma shut her eyes and turned away. Her headache was back, but other than that she'd been unharmed. Except for the blast of what John had called a "Flash-Bang." But that wasn't what filled her mind at the moment, or for the whole day, as she lay here doing nothing just because Elliot said it would be good for her.

She'd heard the commotion, the moment when Dan had woken up. His shouting, then John's shouting. The crash that came from his room down the hall.

"How is he?"

"Good now. Calm." Shelby settled on the edge of the bed. "I don't get why he would react like that."

Gemma pressed her lips together for a second. "Pain plus disorientation. A man's voice, or his touch. Doesn't matter if Elliot just set his hand on Dan's shoulder." She paused. "Even I would be wary about getting close to him right when he woke up. He tends to do it swinging. He gave me a black eye the last time."

"The last time, when? When did you have the opportunity to have Dan wake up beside you?"

"Okay, I know it sounds bizarre, but it was a long time ago. We were kids, and there was nothing weird about it." Gemma sighed. "We've been close a long time; that's just the way it is."

"Hon." When Gemma didn't turn to her, Shelby touched her arm and said, "You don't need to defend it to me. Yes, he's my pastor, but I know you better than that. If you tell me it's on the level, why would I question it?"

When it came to Dan, she went into defense mode. Ready to fight for him to the bitter end. The nearest she could figure was that since she couldn't have everything she wanted with him, she would have the friendship part—and all of her feelings had concentrated there. It was love, but what had grown between them was a hefty dose of friendship-love, the tendency to jump up to bat for each other and a whole lot of unrequited feelings.

But there was nothing she could do about it now.

"What about Mei, is she okay?"

She'd heard Mei's voice at the radio station before they were taken to the medical center, reassuring her that everything was going to be okay and not to worry about Dan. Gemma thought there might have been blood on her shoulder. "She was hurt, right?"

"Shot." Shelby nodded. "Dug the bullet out herself."

Gemma had to swallow, fast.

"Elliot did the stitches, but only because she couldn't focus on it, and she kept passing out. He waited until she couldn't argue and then did it fast." Shelby smiled. "When she woke up she didn't say anything about the fact it was done, and then asked for this cream we put on, asked for it by its actual name. Who knows stuff like that? When Elliot offered her a sling for her arm she said she didn't need one."

Gemma shook her head. "That woman makes no sense, unless she's some kind of spy."

"So long as she finds Terrence, I don't care who she is." Shelby shivered. "That man always gave me the creeps. Now he outright terrifies me."

Gemma nodded.

"Which is why John asked Bolton to keep watch outside your room. No one will be disturbing you while you're in here." Shelby grinned. Her eyebrow twitched. "Unless you want them to come in."

"He's your pastor."

"It's sweet," Shelby said.

"There's the woman who just got married." Gemma grinned back, then said, "Sorry your honeymoon got cut short."

"Don't worry about that. Elliot and I understand what it means to live in this town." She patted Gemma's arm. "If someone broke their leg or had a heart attack, it would be no different. We'll get our time away. I just still can't believe Antonia is dead. I saw her the other day, and now she's been *murdered?* Things keep getting worse."

"I need to find out why this town was created in the first place." It was a germ of a thought until she spoke it out loud.

"So that people in witness protection whose faces were recognizable could hide somewhere."

"That sounds like a party line." Gemma tapped the blanket over her leg as she ran ideas through her head. "I think there might be more to it than that. Because, tell me, how many seriously famous people are there here? Six, maybe? The rest of the residents just live here so that the town can function. We need a doctor, a sheriff, a farmer, a rancher, store owners, families, and a school teacher. But what if there's some other reason for the town?"

"I don't know, Gemma. It's a good theory, but you'd need some way to test it. A way to find out if you're right."

"Where were you when I needed a lab partner in Chemistry?"

Shelby grinned. "I never would have let you cheat off me."

"Figures. Dan didn't, either."

"Want me to ask John about Sanctuary?"

Gemma shook her head. "He's only been here a couple of years. I need to talk to someone who would know, if there even is anyone still here who was also here back then. Someone who knew Hal, who knew Bill Jones. I have no idea where I'm going to find that person."

She'd also have to get on the computer, do some research. Find out more about Hal in Vietnam, about Albert Walden and the CIA's connection with Bill Jones. Like she could just Google all that.

Shelby said, "What about your Mom? She has to know something about Hal."

"Sure, if she'll actually tell me the truth."

"She was here earlier. You could call her, ask her to come back and talk to her."

"She was?" Gemma didn't know who was behind the attack on them. "What about Dan's truck? Did they find it?"

"John said he found the truck abandoned on the side of the road that leads to the ranch. Or, what used to be the ranch. No papers in the back. It had been completely cleaned out. And he said Mei had given him a decent description of the men she came up against. Not physical features, but enough he knew who to talk to. He's going to do that today."

Gemma couldn't shake the feeling that the mayor might be behind all this. She didn't know what his intention might be, but there was no doubt he was capable of murder and subterfuge. And she also couldn't shake the feeling that things were going to get worse before they got better.

Gemma shivered in the bed. "Did Elliot say when I can get out of here?"

"Technically you haven't been admitted, he just wanted you under observation for a while to see if your head is right. I told him not to bother, that you were loopy anyway and it couldn't be fixed, but he insisted."

Gemma felt the corner of her mouth curl up, but didn't dignify her friend's comment with a response. She flipped the bed covers back and sat up. "That means I don't have to stay."

"It does if you're going home alone. If you drift into unconsciousness because you're bleeding in your brain and no one's there to find you, what do you think will happen?"

"It's not like Elliot is even equipped to do emergency brain surgery anyway." Gemma glared at her friend. "Maybe I don't want to be cut open."

Shelby gasped. "How can you say that?"

Gemma shrugged. "I'm going to talk to Dan, and when I can explain it better then I'll tell you."

"You weren't just trying to get a rise out of me?"

"If I was, it was only because you were trying to get a rise out of me." She had on her jeans and One Republic shirt. All she needed was her Converse. "Did you take my shoes?"

"Get back in bed, Gemma. If you want to leave you have to talk to Elliot. And when he says you can, then you'll get your Converse."

"Why hasn't Terrence been found? Why does no one know where he is? He's left to run around town, stealing my papers that Hal left *me,* and shooting Mei? Why can he do that?" Left with no air, Gemma sucked in a breath. "He *shot* Mei."

"She's fine. And she says it wasn't him."

"It wasn't." Mei stood at the door. "And don't worry about Terrence. He isn't going to come after you if I have anything to say about it."

Shelby's eyes were wide. She looked like Mei had just professed Gemma to be her brand new best-friend-for-life, leaving Shelby firmly in the "old friend" category.

Shelby looked away. "I'll go fetch Elliot. Maybe Mei can see you home."

Mei glanced at Shelby's back as she left, and then at Gemma. "Did something just happen?"

"Yeah, you."

Mei said, "Not the first time. And for the record, I'm good with camping out in front of your place and making sure no one bothers you. The sheriff will probably let me borrow his Jeep to sleep in."

Gemma stared. She'd been planning on visiting the tent, but Dan was probably right that it was rags by now. She sighed. "You could take the couch. If you want."

"Even better."

"I just have to go see my mom first."

**

Dan jotted the scripture reference down on his notepad.

"So this is what you do?" John stacked one boot on top of the other on the side of the medical center bed. Casual, like he hadn't seen Dan completely lose it. "Read your Bible. I'm guessing you're preparing your sermon?"

"What else would I do?"

"True. And I can see how it would help to think about something else. With the added bonus that it's calming. Hopeful. Now I see why so many of your sermons focus on good things that come out of hard times."

"Every pastor has one sermon," Dan said. "Isn't that what they say?"

"We preach what we know. If all you know of God is shallow, then that's the extent of what you have to give people. But if what you know of God is that He is *everything*—life, hope, goodness, and the answer to all the evil in this world—then that comes through, too. And with you, I don't think you could hold it back. You need it to be bigger than what you're capable of controlling. A lion that jumps into the fight for you, because that's who He is to you."

Did Dan need to tell him that he was exactly right? "Don't you have police work to do?"

"I have a deputy. I share the load now."

"Figures." Dan glanced over. "But couldn't you be out finding Terrence?"

John chuckled, then sipped from the paper cup. "Every time I ask Mei about that, she tells me not to worry about it. Actually, I think she might have already found him."

"So where is he?"

"That, my friend, is a very good question." John sipped again, thoughtfully.

"You're not worried about her running around town, and what? Disposing of people?"

"It's with the committee. And I have no evidence, only a suspicion anyway. But if this is what I think it is, heads will roll. We've had enough rogues in this town. That isn't something I can tolerate when law abiding citizens deserve that respect." John sighed. "Still, I've been without a deputy for a while. It's kind of nice."

Dan was used to being counsel to people who needed to talk. Or vent. He didn't always know what to say, or always understand what their problem was, but God did. That wasn't an easy answer to give someone, but it was the best answer, and it helped him to have faith.

Half the time when he reminded someone to trust God, or to go back to His word and see what the truth said, it helped him as much as it helped the person. Dan had to take every thought captive, or else he was going to react before he could do anything about it. His flesh, scarred and traumatized, was trying not to get angry again just because he'd been kicked out of malice by those guys in the radio station. Dan didn't want to feel that pain again. He didn't want to go back to that place where he was helpless. Finding Antonia's body had been bad enough.

The blood.

He'd heard that gunshot all over again. The flash of the barrel. The present had blurred with the past in his mind. Pain and blood, washed together into one nightmare he couldn't be rid of.

"Where did you just go?"

Dan swallowed. He shook his head and flipped pages in his Bible. "I'm okay."

"You realize lying is a sin, right?"

"Never said I was perfect. I just didn't want to answer the question."

"You wanna talk about Gemma?"

Dan sniffed. "What about her?"

"Is that a wise decision as a pastor, to spend your time with a woman who..." John's words trailed off, and he left it hanging.

"Runs a library? Writes novels? Follows the rules of witness protection? Seriously, I'd like to know what exactly your opinion is of her. Clearly you have one."

"Dan—"

"No. You know what? When you wanted to marry an assassin I counseled you to be cautious. I didn't tell you it was a bad idea."

John set his boots on the floor and sat forward. "If I do the same, will you listen?"

"I don't want you bad-mouthing her." He would kick John out if the guy was going to talk bad about Gemma. Truth be told, he'd be disappointed in his friend for jumping on the bandwagon the rest of the town seemed to ride. Gemma was just an introvert. She liked who she liked, and that was it.

"What did she get you into, in that room?"

He told John about the papers and about his father.

"I can look into it. Find out what happened."

"You could, but I don't know if you'd find anything," Dan said. "What we really need to know is who knew about the papers, who wanted them, and why they needed to know what was in there."

He'd told Mei, but she'd been shot trying to help. Dan said, "Hal kept this secret, but why is it so bad that no one can know what it was?"

"And now that it's out, what do they plan on doing with it?" John paused. "There's a big difference between information being released in this town and straight up posting it on the internet."

"A big difference." He thought for a second. "What if it wasn't about the totality of what those papers contained? It's possible someone only needed to know one thing they didn't. Maybe it was just getting an answer to their question, the way Gemma and I were doing. After that they might have no need to keep the rest of it."

But how would they know? Unless John found the culprit and the person explained it all.

"Did you see any of their faces?"

Dan shook his head.

John's radio chimed twice. "Well, I'm glad you're good." He got up. "I'm going to take off, let you get your studying done. I'll let you know when I figure this out."

Dan chuckled as the sheriff practically ran from the room. Even if he asked what those chimes from his radio signaled, John probably wouldn't tell him. He didn't mind that John only hung with him because he'd had a spare moment. The sheriff was a busy man with a baby almost here in a town where strange things were happening. Only one of those was a variable in Sanctuary. The rest was the day-to-day of living so closely with other people.

Dan tried to serve the town as best he could, but days like today only cemented the fact he had no qualifications. He'd done nothing to help Gemma, or to keep those papers. At best, he only functioned. But until God brought someone else to the town, to lead His people here, it was Dan's job to set himself aside and do what God wanted him to do.

Just as he needed to set aside whatever had been in the papers. It was John's job to find out now. And Gemma? Dan was going to have to set her aside as well. As much as he might want it, she couldn't be persuaded into being a Christian. She was going to have to make up her own mind in her own time. And Dan would be waiting.

Right now he needed to refocus on what he was supposed to be doing. Gemma was a beautiful distraction that was for sure. But he couldn't serve the people in this town as their pastor if he spent all his time with her and got preoccupied trying to find out who his father had been. He had to do what was best for the residents here. Not himself.

As much as he might want for things to be otherwise.

**

John slammed the door of his truck and made his way inside the sheriff's office. Matthias stood in the middle of the room, an anxious look on his face that John hadn't seen in a long time. Bolton was in his wheelchair by John's desk, way more practiced at hiding his anxiety than Matthias. They'd been in the basement of the library looking at computer records.

"What did you find?"

Matthias wrung his hands together. "No one's even looked at any of it since Hal" —Matthias swallowed— "since he died.

Everything was still there, so we spent some time listening to the back-recordings. Rewinding the files and listening."

"And you found something?"

Bolton nodded. "A call made to Sam Tura's gym ten minutes before Gemma and Dan were attacked. Two words. 'It's on.'"

"Who's phone?"

"Terrence Evangeline."

"So he went home, knowing we were looking, and took the time to make a call?" John aired his thoughts aloud. "Or, someone is framing him for it while he isn't around to defend himself. And either Sam is involved, or he's being pulled in on purpose to distract us."

Bolton nodded. "Teams are out checking every storage shed, out-building, cabin, and empty inch of grass in this town. If Terrence is out there, we'll find him."

"And if someone is hiding him, we'll never get our hands on either of them."

"He has to come outside sooner or later," Matthias said. "Someone will see him. Terrence can't hide forever, and he can't live in hiding forever, either."

John said, "He could try and wait us out. But in the meantime whoever incapacitated Gemma and Dan and took those papers is framing him for it. And they'll probably try and frame him for Antonia's murder as well. That is if he didn't actually do it." He sighed. "It isn't in his best interest to hide."

"So put out a call to all the phones. Announce it to the whole town," Bolton said. His mouth thinned. "But when you do, you'll want to add that there's a line of people more than happy to kill him for what he did to Gemma. Did you see that bandage on her arm?"

John didn't disagree, but still, "You want me to arrest you for murder?"

Bolton grinned. "You could try and find enough evidence."

"That's exactly what I'm worried about." He shot both men a look. "I'll go check out Terrence's house. The two of you talk to Sam. Find out who in the gym was on the phone at that time. Radio me when you find out."

"Yes, sir."

John shook his head. "If I was your 'sir,' I'd have a cup of coffee in my hand by now."

He took a moment to check in upstairs with his family. When he was satisfied they were all safe and resting, he walked to Terrence's house. It wasn't worth using his Jeep after dark if he didn't have to. People were used to quiet, and the noise would disturb them. So many of the people who lived here were on alert, watching for him to do something—shoot someone, arrest someone. This week had been more exciting than the last four months, what with Gemma falling into a hole and Antonia being murdered. A deputy being shot and a theft made it a record week. Now everyone knew Hal had been hiding a secret in the radio station.

John didn't knock, the door was unlocked anyway. Terrence's place had been trashed. Someone angry had gone through everything Terrence owned, most likely after his parents were there looking for him. Mr. and Mrs. Evangeline were the kind of people who saw reputation as more important than truth. They couldn't believe their son's good name was being tarnished by Gemma's lies.

John walked through the house, the crunch of broken glass and ceramics under his boots. The bedroom was a disaster, clothes everywhere. The bathroom, same. The back door was open and the yard overgrown. Not a man who saw appearance as everything. All this only cemented the opinion John had of Terrence Evangeline. Especially the magazines under his bed. This wasn't a man trying to grow or better himself in any way.

The only thing which confused John was the shovel and pickaxe in the closet. Both were smeared with fresh dirt. What had Terrence been digging?

And where in Sanctuary was he hiding?

Chapter 13

John jumped out of bed and stepped into the hallway before he answered the phone. "Ignore my calls much?"

A car horn in the background obliterated whatever Ben had been about to say. Why return a phone call if Ben was somewhere he wouldn't be able to hear?

John said, "What was that?"

He went into the living room and downstairs so he didn't disturb anyone. He'd rather be within earshot of Andra this close to her due date, but he also had to figure out this mystery.

"—little busy here, brother."

"Where is here?" The caller ID on his satellite phone had given him numbers, and he wasn't all the way studied up on his country codes.

"Doesn't matter, John. What do you need that my secretary couldn't answer?"

"Sanctuary."

"What about it?"

"Everything there is to know, you know it, Ben. So you tell me. What secret was Hal Leonard keeping?"

Back when Hal had died, Grant had discovered Hal's handler had been killed under mysterious circumstances. The police still hadn't figured out who did it or why. A plan was unfolding, and it had reached Sanctuary, once again putting their entire town in jeopardy.

A woman he'd been responsible for was dead. Gemma and Dan were involved in something they didn't understand that might get them more hurt than simply being incapacitated. He couldn't be certain, but John could feel it. Something was happening. Again.

"I can find out," Ben said. "Give me a little time, though."

"How will you find out?"

"Don't ask me how, John. I can find out. Leave it at that."

Probably he was going to call some CIA contact he had. John was pretty sure Ben had never been a spy, but then Ben would move, and it looked military. Either way, he had to have contacts. Ben also had Remy on his payroll, and the world-class hacker could probably dig up the answer to John's question.

So John probably could leave the "how" alone. As long as Ben came up with answers and no one else died. He had to accept that Antonia's death was his fault. She'd been gathering information for him. Unless he knew for sure otherwise, he had to assume that was what had gotten her killed.

John gripped the phone. "You know what I'm not going to leave alone? Mei."

"What about Mei?"

Did he really want to ask this? John took a breath. *God, don't let this push him farther away.* He'd been praying for his brother since John had first become a believer. If anyone needed hope, love, *life,* it was his brother, Ben. John hadn't figured out a good way to broach the subject yet. Maybe soon his brother could come to town when they actually had time to spend with each other. Ben's last visit had been in and out.

"Ask me now, John. Before I hang up."

John took a breath and then said, "Is Mei my niece?"

**

Mei walked two steps behind Gemma through town. She glanced back at the deputy who had spent the night on her couch and made sure no one bothered her.

"Do you need your gun out?" Surely she didn't intend on shooting anyone. Not really. Terrence, maybe. But no one else needed to be shot, unless Mei had figured out a way to tell who had taken the papers.

Gemma shook her head. "I don't get it."

Mei's eyes moved continually as she scanned the street. "Not much to get. No one messes with you, and I'll shoot them if they try. That's it."

"Um…"

"Don't ask. It's better if you leave it alone."

"Oookay." Gemma wasn't going to argue with a woman who was armed. "What if you get called out for sheriffly duties?"

"This town? It's usually only neighbors arguing over who took whose plastic flamingo from their yard. No one's going to mind if you're there with me. Might diffuse the tension."

"Mr. Carten and Mr. Norris."

"Once a week." Mei sniffed. "So I TiVo my shows and watch them later, when I can fast forward through commercials. It's not a bad life, and it's a lot less dangerous than some of the places I've lived."

Gemma said, "Bad things happen everywhere. Humans aren't different, no matter where they live." There was more to say, but they were at her mom's house. Painted yellow. Same white trim. The flowerbed was where it came alive, though. Janice was a regular at the nursery.

Maybe she would answer the door this time.

What was parked out front caught Gemma's attention. "That's the mayor's golf cart." One of the mayor's friends stood by the cart, arms folded. He scowled as they walked up. At her, or at Mei?

"Is that one of them?" Gemma whispered.

"I think I'd need a warrant to pull his sleeves up and find out," Mei said. "But the judge doesn't like me, because I told him his grandbaby wasn't cute."

Gemma pressed her lips together to keep from laughing. It wasn't a lie, but Gemma knew you weren't supposed to *say* that.

She pushed open the gate that led to the front door. Gemma didn't bother knocking; her mom never locked the door anyway. Her mom decorated in hippie chic, and Gemma didn't understand any of it. She might have grown up in this house, but she'd decorated her own in "books" and hand-painted her favorite Emily Dickenson poem on her living room wall. Gemma's tastes were simpler because there was no reason to want more in a town like this. She didn't even take a salary from the library, because what she made off her books was enough to live on.

Gemma motioned to Mei that they should be quiet, to which Mei gave her a look and then moved through the hall to the living room. What was the mayor doing here?

"You'll have so much sway over this town, Janice. You can make it a better place to live. Being the mayor has meant everything to me, and I'm proud of the job I've done. Now I'm ready to pass the mantle, as it were, to someone else—someone of your caliber. A woman who has faithfully worked in this town for years, raised a child to be a success, and continued the legacy that is Sanctuary."

He'd still never once asked her if she wanted the mayor's job. He must see her as a child and nothing more, even knowing about her books. She could hardly believe he was offering it to her mom. Weeks after Hal's death. One day after Antonia's. At Shelby's wedding the mayor had told her that he knew who he wanted to be his successor. Her mom was his choice?

The mayor didn't miss a beat. "Say you'll think about it, Janice. Promise me you'll give it all the consideration you can. The people of Sanctuary deserve the best in leadership, and I just don't think the committee is doing a good job keeping people safe. Antonia was murdered, for goodness sake! When will it stop? So what do you say Janice? Are you ready to usher this town into a new era?"

She could almost see her mom in the role, though Janice would be way lower key about it than Collins was. Plenty of people in town liked Gemma's mom, even looked up to her.

Gemma waited for the answer.

"I'm a retired gardener, Samuel. I hardly think that qualifies me to run a town. Besides, the committee oversees everything now. A mayor and a town council would be redundant at this point. I'm sorry to say, perhaps there isn't as much of a need for a mayor as you may have previously thought. I think Sanctuary has evolved beyond the need for that kind of government."

"The people need a voice." He sounded agitated almost.

Gemma stepped into the room, Mei behind her, still out of sight. "I think she gave you her answer, *Samuel.*" Collins blanched, and her mom's eyes widened. Gemma knew she didn't look good. She'd fallen in a hole, been stuck with a cigarette, stunned, and had her hand trodden on.

He motioned to Gemma but said to Janice, "That's why we need leadership, so that incidents like this don't occur. Ever since the sheriff showed up, things have grown steadily worse and worse. From my wife's death, all the way to the town being blown up." He spat the words. "When will it stop?"

Her mom stood up. The tray of tea on the table hadn't even been touched. Collins hadn't been here long. "I believe it's time for you to leave, Samuel."

Gemma held up one finger. "Actually, I have a question for you."

Collins motioned for her to ask it, though it was clear he didn't care what the question was.

"Are you planning on speaking at Antonia's service? I understand the two of you were close. I could speak to Olympia if you want me to."

"Close? Where did you get this idea?"

Probably from Shelby's story about seeing Antonia at his house, and the mayor looking disheveled right after. As though they'd been intimate. But maybe it wasn't about the mayor having real feelings for Antonia. Gemma shrugged. "I guess I was wrong."

He turned to her mom. "Thank you for your offer of herbal tea. I'm sorry I can't stay."

Collins moved so fast it ruffled her hair. When she turned to see Mei's reaction, the deputy wasn't there.

"Gem?"

She was staring at the open door. Where had Mei disappeared to? Gemma shut the door and went into the living room. "Yeah, Mom?"

"Did the doctor release you? How are you feeling?"

Her mom had dropped off a book with Shelby the day before. Gemma had finished it. "I checked myself out, I'm okay. It's just a couple of bruises."

"Added to the bruises you already had from falling through the ground." Her mom waved her hand, and her bracelets clacked together. When she sat, her long floral skirt flared out around her. "What is going on in this town? I feel like I'm going crazy."

The edge of grief was still present, but her mom was more like her old self than she'd been since the bomb blew up the ranch. Since Hal had died.

Gemma sat in a wicker chair across from her. "Can I ask you some stuff?"

Her mom's brow crinkled. "You write all those books, and you're so eloquent, and then you say 'stuff'? I don't get it."

"Neither do I. But this has to do with the bruises."

"And falling in the hole?"

"No, not that." Gemma squeezed the arms of the chair. "It's about what was in the radio station."

Janice shifted.

"I need to know about Hal." Before her mom thought this was going to be another conversation about how they never told her he was her father, Gemma said, "He had a secret room full of papers in the radio station. Maybe you've heard about that because someone broke in and stole everything."

Janice pressed her lips together. "I'm not talking about your father. That is private."

"Not from me. It's my life. Don't I have a right to know about the man I came from?"

"It's none of…"

"None of my business?"

Janice shook her head. "It was supposed to be private. That was the only way it could happen, the only way I could have him."

"By denying me a father?"

"It was dangerous," Janice hissed. "I was not going to put your life in jeopardy just for some juvenile dream I had of happy families. That is not the way the world works."

"And even after Dan's father died, things were really still the same?" Gemma couldn't understand what was so huge that, even when Hal and Arnold Walden were both dead, her mom still wasn't able to say it. What on earth could be that huge?

"I need you to tell me. If you know, I need you to tell me why someone took all the papers." Gemma decided to play on her mother's instincts. She pointed to her face. "Why someone would do this to me."

Janice paled. "That was never supposed to happen. You weren't supposed to be involved. I can't believe Hal left you that radio station in his will. He had to know you'd ask questions, that you'd go in there and read it all. He probably figured he was dead, what did he care? And you know what? I'm glad you didn't get to read it all. I'm sorry it's out there now, but some truths cannot be stopped. At least you're safe from it now."

**

Dan hauled the wheelbarrow in from the fields. He stopped outside the barn and looked up at the stars. The knot in his chest eased. Time to sleep.

The Jeep pulled up. The engine shut off, and Mei got out the driver's side. Dan turned to her as she rounded the hood of the vehicle, cutting through the beam of the headlights that lit up his parents' house, and stood in front of him. "Doing okay?"

Dan said, "You care now?" He'd heard her in the sheriff's office, telling John she didn't get involved.

Mei shrugged, but he didn't buy her nonchalance, as she glanced at the house. "Has to be hard for you, coming home to this place every day. Waking up here. Working here. I don't know how you do it."

"It's my home."

"But this is where all that history of pain lives. It's in the ground. The walls." She glanced around. "Don't you feel like it's screaming at you?"

He studied her face, the twitch of her fingers by her side. This wasn't why she was here. "Do you want to tell me about it?"

She shook off whatever she'd been thinking. "It doesn't matter. He's dead now, and I won't ever go back to that time in my life. My life is mine. I do what I want." She glanced up, caught his gaze, and narrowed her eyes. "What about you? Doesn't look like you've moved on."

He couldn't deny that part of him was still back there. And yes, maybe living here didn't help the memory to fade, but he had worked hard to build good memories to replace those bad ones. "Maybe moving on looks different for different people."

"I'd like to show you something, if you're up for it." She motioned toward the house.

Dan froze.

"I'm aware you haven't stepped one foot in that house in years."

"Since my mom—" Dan stopped himself.

"Did he kill her?"

"She disappeared. Didn't you read the police report?"

"Please. It was like the plot of a bad soap opera, and I didn't believe one word of it." Mei held out her hand for him to lead the way. "This is important."

Dan shut off his thoughts as he walked. He breathed the first few lines of his favorite psalm and touched the door handle.

"Don't think about it, just keep moving."

"Says the expert in revisiting the places that hurt the most."

Mei touched his sleeve. It surprised him enough his thoughts jerked out of the past. "Humor is a very good sign. Or so I'm told. I'm not that good at making jokes." She covered his hand with hers, and they opened the door together.

Dan stood on the threshold, while Mei squeezed past him into the darkness of the house. "I'll turn my flashlight on when we hit the basement stairs. That way you won't have to look at anything in here."

She didn't want to go to the living room? Dan didn't understand. Why were they here if she didn't want to see where it had happened? She didn't want to ask him about his mother, about those things he'd buried so deep he could barely process that they were real. He had to leave them tucked away, or they would destroy him.

Mei reached the door to the basement. It was already open. She clicked on the flashlight and shone it on those wood steps.

"Can't go down there."

"What?"

He couldn't move. "Not supposed to go down there. Ever."

Mei touched his arm again. What was with her and touching? It was gentle, benign even, but something about it kept him anchored to the moment. "We are going down there."

Dan said, "Why are you doing this? There's nothing good down there."

"What is down there?"

"You know the answer to that. Otherwise you'd just go down there. You wouldn't be asking me just so you can see my reaction." Dan didn't move. "I've never been down there."

"He's not here. He can't do anything to you, tell you where you can't go or what you can't do. This is *your* life, Dan."

How did she know that? Dan wanted to pour her a cup of coffee and sit somewhere she could talk to him about it. He'd tell her about the peace he had found in the Lord. She'd survived something using pure will, which increased his respect for her tenfold. She'd had to find the strength in herself, and that was a hard thing. Dan had his relationship with God to lean back on. Mei had no safety net.

"Would you like to go downstairs, Dan?"

He appreciated the choice. He didn't need to trade one authority figure for another. Even John had become… softer with him. Gentleness wasn't either of their strong suit, but he appreciated the effort they were putting into easing him.

Dan stopped at the bottom of the stairs. When Mei joined him she shone the flashlight around. "Where is… where is, ah-ha." She pulled a chord, and the light came on.

"What—" He could hardly process what he was seeing. "It looks like a jungle of weeds down here." Chest-height tables covered with plastic bins six inches deep. Soil. Green leafy plants that had withered and died. It smelled musty, earthy. Lights hung in rows above the tables.

"You don't know what this is, do you?"

Dan shook his head.

"Your dad was growing marijuana in your basement. That's probably the real reason why you were never allowed to come down here. You'd have seen it. You'd have told someone." She snorted. "Not that it's even illegal now in a bunch of places."

"I wouldn't have known what it was," Dan said. "We are in Idaho, though. It's illegal here."

Mei said, "He still didn't need you blabbing about the basement full of plants your dad was growing." She walked down a row. "Especially considering you'd eventually have seen this."

Dan stared at the hole in the wall. The track. The cart. "The tunnel. The one Gemma fell into led to my house?"

Mei nodded. "He transported the weed out by cart."

"Out of Sanctuary?" When she said nothing, Dan shook his head. "You can't get out of this town, that's not possible. Where does this even lead?"

"To the mine."

Dan blew out a breath. "This is unbelievable. First he's a CIA agent, then he's a rogue and a killer. Now he's a drug manufacturer, and probably a dealer?"

"Some guys have all the fun."

"Excuse me?"

Mei swallowed. "My bad. Crime never pays. Just say no to drugs." She took a breath. "Uh… you wanna take a walk?"

"Have you been in there? How do we know it's safe? Gemma fell down it. Maybe it's blocked off."

"Pretty convenient, having an escape tunnel under your house. Come and go anytime you please…"

"Sure, if there's an exit other than just ending up inside a mine." Dan shivered. "I'm not a big fan of underground. Or tight spaces. Or the dark."

"How about spiders?" Mei's voice was grave, but she stepped into the tunnel and started walking. "Those things creep me out. You think it's just an itch, but then there's this *thing* on you. Blech. Cockroaches are only half a step up. Or anything else with legs. And eyes."

Dan had no choice but to follow. He wasn't walking back through that house by himself. Bizarrely, the deputy sheriff made him feel better. Even though she was smaller than him, she did carry a gun. Though he felt like she could easily turn on him, and he'd hit the ground, dead, before he even realized she'd killed him.

Was that why she was walking him to a mine? Did Mei plan on killing him and dumping his body where no one would ever find him?

His steps faltered. Of course. "Mom."

"Dan?"

He couldn't answer. He always figured his father had buried her in the woods somewhere. Had he hauled her through the tunnel and hidden her in some crevice of rock?

Dan sucked in a breath and locked his knees.

"It isn't much farther."

Papa. Dan put one boot in front of the other. Again. Again. He couldn't think. Didn't want to. Just walk. The tunnel narrowed. He walked with one hand on the ceiling and his head bent.

Light shone on his face. "Keep going. Don't stop now."

The tunnel opened up. They followed the track as it bent left and then right. It had to be three miles from his house.

Mei slowed. She turned and lifted the light so he could see her face. "I need to show you something, Dan."

"Is it her?"

"No."

His heart sank.

"But it's what's left of her."

She held his arm and they walked around a corner. A rumple of fabric. Bones. Lay against one wall. Discarded.

He couldn't look at the face, where her eyes should have been.

Dan looked at the fabric below her neck. The gold chain, and that locket. The one he'd given her for Christmas.

"Is this your mother's body?"

Dan shut his eyes. "It's her."

Chapter 14

"The secret's out now, Mom." Gemma shifted to the edge of her chair. "Whoever has those papers can spread this wide, and everyone will know who Dan's dad was. Who Hal was. There won't be any hiding it."

"I suppose you think the mayor is behind it."

"Why not? He's a bad guy, and I don't trust him at all. I think he set me up, brought Terrence into it, and used the opportunity to have my house searched while he occupied me. Every time I turn around, the mayor is in the middle of things."

Gemma's strength was flagging. She pulled up her feet and curled into the chair, unable to lose the memory of when Terrence stood right in front of her from her mind.

"He just wants someone to take over for him. He's sick."

"If you mean ill, that's debatable. Sick is probably right," Gemma said. "I think he killed Antonia, or he ordered it done."

Janice rolled her eyes. "You always did have a wild imagination. At least you put it to good use instead of getting up to trouble like I did."

"Mom, will you tell me how you came to live in Sanctuary?"

"You know we don't talk about that."

"Maybe friends don't, or acquaintances. But I'd like to know your story." What if this was their one chance to find footing as adults? There had to be something that would bring them together, something with the power to sever this wedge that had always been between them.

Janice sipped her tea. "My story is Hal's story. That's why I never told you."

"Because I'd know what the two of you were hiding."

Her mom nodded. "Some things are best left alone. Secrets, when they are revealed, don't always heal. They can wound. Or kill."

"You didn't come here together, did you?"

Janice shook her head. "We were enrolled in witness protection around the same time, but I spent ten years in Hawaii before I was allowed to come to Sanctuary. I still have no idea what island I was on, I just woke up and I was there. But it was necessary. There had to be distance between Hal and I. No one could know we were together."

"You succeeded in that. I never knew." Gemma didn't care there was an edge to her voice. Her mom had to know how much it hurt that this had been kept from her for her entire life. Only after he was dead had she found out. "Would you ever have told me?"

"No. Even though he's dead, I still never would've told you." Her mom's eyes flashed with hatred. For Hal? "It's the agreement I signed with the Marshal's service."

"Tell me what happened, Mom. Please." Gemma was desperate, but she couldn't force her mom. She would only shut down the way she had after Hal's death.

"I was a reporter. You can find some of my articles online, still."

"There's no Janice Altern online. I'd have found you."

"My real name is Bridget Tunston."

Gemma felt her eyes widen at the name of a popular feature writer rumored to have disappeared. "But… your face."

"It's why I had to be hidden and all record of me removed from the internet. Every photo ever taken." Her mom gave her a wry smile. "The Marshal's service is so thorough, if I didn't have a mirror, I'd have forgotten what I looked like."

This was unbelievable. Her mom was a famous writer?

"That's where you get your writing from. I even toyed with the idea of a novel once. But it never worked out." Janice sipped her tea, set the cup down, and sat back. "I was daring. Wild. I thought I could go anywhere. Do anything. Thought I was untouchable. For years I wandered the world and never settled down. Australia. Indonesia. China. India. Thailand. I saw it all. I was free to go wherever I wanted and write whatever I wanted. Magazines. National Geographic articles.

"Then war broke out in Vietnam, and so many men were dying. I'd been a child of the world for so long it was strange to feel so *American*. I cried for them. And then I bought a plane ticket, a boat ride. I made my way there and began to report on the war. I met GI's and intelligence people. Interviewed locals and drug runners. Everyone on both sides. I didn't play favorites. I did it all. I said it all."

Janice's gaze drifted away. "Then I stumbled on a story. It would have been huge, and it was the first time in my life I was genuinely scared of a story and what it might mean. What might happen to me if I wrote about it."

She paused. "American intelligence in Vietnam was... well, they had barely any idea what they were doing, what they wanted. Or how to go about getting it. Trying to undermine the enemy was a nightmare I wrote about over and over again. It was hard to find a success story or even a human interest piece that showed us in a good light.

"From what I was hearing and finding, it looked like the CIA was in bed with drug runners. The Vietnamese mafia had something on the CIA, and they were getting weapons in return for whatever it was. I hiked in the dark to a village under the thumb of the Vietnamese mafia to meet a contact of mine. I'd seen CIA officers there before. When I got there this man was—"

Janice coughed. "I walked into the middle of a slaughter." She lifted her sleeve and showed Gemma her shoulder. "One of the bullets caught me. I landed in a pile of blood and bodies he'd left in his wake."

"Bill Jones."

Janice's eyes widened.

"I know he was Dan's dad."

"He killed them all without mercy. I think under orders from the CIA to get rid of everything. That's the only way it made sense, though they should have been clearer about how. I was just collateral. Afterwards he burned the village, and I just about managed to crawl out before he saw. That's when Hal found me."

Gemma could hardly breathe. Dan's father had colored her life, just as he had colored Dan's. Not in the same way, but the impact could not be denied.

"Hal was with the military police, but he worked alone. He was the one they sent to rein in Bill Jones. He was out of control, the CIA's puppet who cleaned up their messes and left no one alive to tell the story."

"Until you."

Janice nodded. "Hal stayed with me for days in this hut. The woman who lived there didn't speak English, but we knew enough of the language we got by. While I healed, he told me what was going on. That he was trying to get to Bill Jones to stop the man before the CIA could allow him to commit any more atrocities. He wanted me to go on record with what I'd seen and what I knew.

"Hal kept me from any of his reports. He didn't want any chance the CIA would find out that I'd witnessed what Bill Jones did. He couldn't trust anyone within the military, or the intelligence services, to keep the secret. Not if he was going to bring down Bill and the CIA. We travelled to Saigon, and he called a friend of his in the US."

"A Marshal."

Janice nodded. "I was sent back to the US in the custody of the Marshals so they could keep me safe. But it wasn't official. It was all off-book, and this was before witness protection even existed, so there was no play book for what we were doing. It's why I think it went so badly wrong."

"What happened?"

"Hal went after Bill Jones. He found him. The plan was to arrest him, threaten him with charges, and bring down every crooked intelligence agent in the East. But in return for testifying, Bill Jones wanted no prison time." Janice paused, and Gemma waited while she collected herself. "Bill rolled over on his handlers, but only after the Marshal's Service agreed to grant him immunity and hide him away for the rest of his life. It was unheard of, but since he came with all the paperwork he'd copied—reams and reams of covert orders, documents, memos, and TOP SECRET files all on microfiche—they had to agree."

"But he killed all those people."

"And if it had gotten out that American intelligence was actively undermining what our men in uniform, dying for their country, were doing, what do you think that would have done to the war rhetoric? Both sides would have exploded over it. All that death for nothing, they wanted to sweep it under the rug. They were ordered to contain the situation, and Hal was ordered to contain Bill Jones.

"The CIA officers who ran Saigon base all disappeared. Bodies showed up—military officers, Hal's commanding officer, another reporter who looked like me. Even the Marshal that Hal had called. All of them, dead. The CIA agents were going to kill everyone who knew what they'd done and then walk away.

"Hal and Bill were back in the US. Moving around all the time, they never stayed in one city long. But the death threats didn't stop coming. I was in Hawaii, no communication but the little I heard from my handler who boated in groceries for me. Hal and Bill were nearly killed in a highway collision one night. The Marshals Service decided they needed somewhere completely secure to place Bill Jones."

"Prison would have been good."

"They decided on Sanctuary. Nothing but grass and trees inside a ring of Idaho mountains. It was a permanent solution to an impossible problem. No one could get in, and Bill couldn't get out. So a senate committee was formed, and the witness protection program was born out of a need to hide witnesses from the active threat against them. Hal and Bill came in by parachute with a backpack each, and the town of Sanctuary came into effect."

"How did he get all those papers in the radio room?"

Janice's breath hitched. "I located them and sent them to him, page by page. Hal wasn't under the same mail strictures as the rest of the town now, and he wanted proof of everything that had happened, so I got it for him. He watched Bill Jones every day of his life. Reported back to the Marshals. Got regular deliveries. Wood to build houses. Furniture and appliances. Seeds. Animals. No one ever found them.

"Years later the Marshal's Service had a high profile witness whose face was too recognizable to simply relocate him to another city. They sent him to Sanctuary. We got a sheriff. More people. A doctor. When it was safe, me."

"And then me."

A smile curved the edge of Janice's lips. "It had been a long time. Attraction is a powerful thing."

Gemma didn't want to know that about her parents, but she knew what her mom meant. She felt that with Dan, and it was worse now that he'd kissed her.

"But we kept it a secret. Bill Jones would have used anything against your father. Especially a child."

"There's a whole lot there that I have something to say about, and we'll get to it, but that's not what bothers me most."

"What is it, Gem?"

"Sanctuary isn't a haven at all. It wasn't supposed to be safe place to hide, it was a prison cell for Bill Jones."

"Sometimes they are the same thing."

**

Dan took a step back. Mei crouched over the body and pulled out her phone. She keyed the radio. How on earth did that thing even work down here?

"Sheriff?" Her voice swam around him. "…body. Yes I'm sure, Dan confirmed it… backup. Because…"

Dan's back touched the wall, and he slid down, as his thoughts dissipated and air whooshed through his ears. Had she brought him here just to identify his mother's body? Mei could have shown him a picture. She could have confirmed it was his mother using DNA or something other than him being there.

His chest rose and fell as he struggled for each breath. Perhaps God had brought him here so that Dan could finally face what he had done. *Papa. Did You bring me here?* Dan shut his eyes and started to whisper. "Surely the darkness will fall on me. Darkness shall not hide from You. Darkness and light are the same to You."

He should just turn himself in now. Tell Mei exactly what happened.

John would get there just in time to see her slap the handcuffs on him, as she had the last time. This time he would stay in that cell. He'd be sent to prison. A nameless, faceless inmate just like all the others. But it would be justice. He would never be able to return here, never see his home again or his friends. Gemma.

"Dan?" John's face came into focus in front of him, crouched, a frown crinkling his eyebrows.

"Hey."

"I'm sorry. Your mom—" John stopped.

Dan shut his eyes.

"Let's get you out of here. You don't need to stay and see this." John pulled on his arm. Dan didn't have much choice but to go with it. He locked his knees to keep from falling. Sweat beaded on his hairline. "You're in shock."

Mei stepped up beside them. "What happened to her, Dan?"

"You don't see that bullet hole in her shirt and the stain, Mei? Back off."

A low, guttural noise came from his throat. He couldn't tell them what had happened. They would never let him be pastor if everyone found out what he'd done. Dan dipped his head and planted his hands on his knees. He still couldn't get air in. "Can't… breathe…"

"Dan." John's voice sounded pained. "Come with me, okay?" He put his arm around Dan's shoulder and tried to maneuver him away from the skeleton.

"What happened to her, Dan?"

"Mei." John barked her name.

"Did you kill her?"

Dan's body jerked. John swung around. "Seriously?"

"It's a legitimate question!"

"He'd have been what, eleven? You think an eleven year-old pulled the trigger and killed his mom?"

"It's happened."

Dan tried to interject. "Jo—"

The sheriff ignored him. "Mei, I'm not even kidding right now. You need to back off and let me deal with this. I don't need you wading in when you know basically nothing about investigating a murder."

"Seriously?" Mei set her hands on her hips. "I've read every manual you gave me. And I've seen every episode of Psych! I know how to solve a murder, thank you very much."

"Mei." He said one word, but neither Dan—nor Mei—missed the fact it meant, *Mei I can't believe you just said that. I don't even know what to say, so stop talking right now.*

Dan tried again. "John, I—"

Mei's phone rang. She lifted one finger to them and said, "Hold that thought." She turned slightly away and said, "Did you get it?" Pause. "Then why are you calling? Oh. Sure, that's fine, but I need a rush on that info." Pause. "Because I'm looking at a *skeleton*, Remy. That's why!"

Dan blinked.

"I knew it." John muttered, "I've been played."

Mei covered the phone with one hand. "Like you didn't suspect?"

John said, "That is so not the point right now."

Mei went back to her call. "Seriously, Remy, I need that information as soon as possible." Pause. "What do you mean?" Pause. "Huh. Okay. Well let me know when you get something."

Mei stowed the phone. "Apparently neither of your parents existed before they showed up here. We know your dad was, you know, a bad guy and all. Whoever your mom was, she changed her name. It was long enough it predates computer records, and the place where the records were kept was destroyed by a fire in eighty-three. Which means I'm back to nothing."

"Nothing but the crazy idea that Dan killed his mother."

Mei turned to him. "When you saw Antonia's body by the lake, you said 'I killed her.'"

"I did?" He barely remembered. Gemma had filled in most of the gaps, but she hadn't mentioned that.

John's eyebrows rose.

Dan said, "It's complicated."

"I'll bet it is," Mei muttered.

"Look," John said. "There's a lot here for us to cover. We can't do all that tonight, so let's call Elliot, and we'll go back to the sheriff's office. Then maybe Mei can tell us why she works for my brother."

"You knew?"

John shrugged. "It was too easy. And you're a pain in the backside, but that made it more obvious. If you'd been a cop already I'd never have bought it. The fact you're a complete maverick makes way too much sense, in a completely bizarre way."

"Okay, then," Mei said. "But I want to know who killed this woman and why she's been laying in the dirt for fifteen years."

"So do we all."

Dan nodded. "I can tell you what happened."

**

Gemma didn't want to believe her mom had been a party to bringing someone like Dan's dad into a place where he could mingle with innocent people. He should have been in prison, then he'd never have been able to hurt Dan, or kill his mother. But then Dan wouldn't have been born. Gemma would have had to live here without ever meeting him.

Did she wish to give all that up just so he wouldn't have had the life he had? She didn't want to say yes, because then she wouldn't know him, but what kind of friend was that selfish? He should have had a happy childhood, a good life. Instead he'd been basically tortured for years.

What kind of God allowed that to happen? She'd asked the question many times, and she knew Dan's answer: that God was the one who'd saved his life, not the one who condemned it.

Her mom spoke to the window. "If Bill… Arnold Walden… knew that Hal had a daughter, he'd have used that against him. Hal continued to report to the Marshal's Service, because they had to know he was, you know, *contained* as well as protected from the CIA agents who wanted to kill him. But he was allowed to live his life. Hal figured a wife might mellow him. A son."

"It didn't," Gemma bit out.

She turned, her eyes filled with tears. "I know." Janice swallowed. "That hurt Hal most of all. But there was nothing he could do. He thought Bill was up to something, and couldn't put his finger on what it was. Aside from keeping watch, Hal laid low until Eme—"

"Eme?"

"Dan's mother." Her face flushed. "Until she came to Hal, willing to let him in the house so he could search it."

Gemma shut her eyes. "That's why she was killed."

Janice nodded.

"There was nothing he could do to stop it?" Gemma breathed. "Did you warn her? Did he do anything to help Dan?" Her mom blanched but Gemma ignored it and said, "When the man who murdered an entire village of Vietnamese people got married, did you tell her what to expect, what she was getting into?"

"It wasn't my place." Janice shook her head, the tears flowing now. "She had to know something was… *off* about him. It was obvious. Even as young as she was, she had to see it."

"So was there something wrong with her, too. Is that it? Is that what you tell yourself to justify not saying anything?"

"Gemma—" Her mom's voice broke, and she covered her mouth with her fist.

"How about when Dan came to school with bruises on his face? When he walked around all the time scared out of his mind that his dad was going to show up? Or scared that he wouldn't, and he'd have to go home and face him." Gemma paused. "You worked at the farm. You had to have known."

"It was surveillance. My job was to report on day-to-day activities, not be a family counselor."

"Is that what you tell yourself so that you can sleep at night?"

"Who says I sleep?"

Gemma stared at her mom. "I don't even know you. I can barely look at you, and I can't believe I come from someone who would swing a woman and child out to dry for a *secret*."

"It was more complicated than—"

"Nothing is more complicated than someone being hurt. You see it, you stop it." Gemma's chest heaved. "What's wrong with you?"

"I know you love him," Janice said. "He had you, and he had Hal watching out for him."

"But he didn't stop it. Not any of it. I tried, and I was only a child. What does that say about Hal?"

"He loved you!" Her mom's voice filled the room like a screech. "How do you know your precious Dan wouldn't be dead right now if it wasn't for Hal?"

"His mom *is* dead. Dan's dad killed her."

"She disappeared."

Gemma stood, unable to stomach being there anymore, and said *again*, “Is that what you tell yourself so you can sleep at night?”

Chapter 15

"Sit back down, Dan."

They'd come all the way down to the sheriff's office. Because John really, really didn't want Mei to overhear? She was with the body, with Elliot. They were bringing Dan's mom back to town, where they could run tests. It was enough to make him want to throw up.

"Dan, sit down."

He settled into a chair in the waiting area and sighed. John should probably just put him in a cell. He should at least be cuffed after what he'd done.

"Talk to me."

Dan shut his eyes and said it out loud. "I was the one who pulled the trigger."

"You were eleven."

"I don't need you to explain it away, or convince me that I'm not responsible. I know what it is, and I know what happened." Dan opened his eyes. "You weren't here. You never met him, and you don't know what he was like."

"So tell me."

"From the moment he got up in the morning until he went to bed at night he never let up. Not for one second. Do this. Do that. Why did you do this? Why did it take so long? Why didn't you do it right? I don't remember one single moment of peace in my life until my ninth birthday. Not one single second where I was happy, or at rest."

"I thought he died when you were fifteen."

"The peace I found wasn't him dying."

"And your mom? What was she like?"

"Her hands shook, all the time. She never smiled, not even when I drew her pictures of us. Taking walks in the woods. Flying, leaving this town. At the beach—I saw it in a movie once. She'd look at them, tell me 'thank you' and then tell me to put them in my drawer so he didn't see."

"What happened on your ninth birthday?"

Dan felt the ghost of a smile curve his lips. "Gemma brought me a cupcake. I'd never had one before. For half an hour I was actually happy."

"And the barn thing?"

"You mean, sleeping in there?"

John nodded.

"I had to stay out of his way after he found out about the cupcake thing. So I hid in the barn for days. He beat me black and blue when he found me, then he locked the door and didn't open it for I don't know how long. It felt like a week. Gemma said I missed three days of school. After that he made me stay out there. Now its home."

"Can you tell me how your mother died?"

"He was mad that night, but it was different. She didn't have her usual look where she cowered. Her chin was up. I don't know what happened. Gemma asked me about it, but I didn't hear what they said. I was in the kitchen. He hauled me by my arm, dragged me into the living room. He had a gun."

Dan took a breath. "She started screaming, telling him she was sorry. But it was like she had something to apologize for, and she really wanted to take it back. She was crying, telling me it wasn't my fault. That she was so sorry. That she loved me, but she had to end it.

"She told him not to kill me. That I hadn't done anything wrong, and that I didn't deserve to be hurt. It was the first time I heard her say that, and I've never forgotten it. I didn't think she cared, honestly. We were a team, and he hurt both of us, but I didn't think she ever saw it like that. I think she just thought she was alone."

"She didn't try to protect you?"

Dan shrugged. "I don't know. A lot of those years I don't want to remember."

"What happened next?"

"He pulled the gun on her, and not me. I'm sure I screamed. I was crying. I tried to get away but he grabbed me. She was still screaming. I was screaming. It was so loud. His elbow hit my head, and I halfway dropped to the floor, but he pulled me back up and made me face her. Twisted my finger onto the trigger." His breath hitched in his throat. "The gun went off…"

"He made you do it.

"I killed her."

"Dan—"

"No." He stood. "Don't try and explain it, or tell me I'm wrong. I know what happened."

"You were a kid."

"I was a killer. And I killed her."

"He forced you to do it. He was the one who knowingly pulled that trigger." John meandered over, the way Dan would approach a skittish goat. "There is no way you are responsible for what happened to your mom. No way. You were nothing but a scared kid."

"John—"

"Did you want her to die?"

"No!"

"Did you pull that trigger because you wanted to?"

"Of course not! I—"

"You didn't kill her, Dan. He did."

"I had my hand on the gun. On the trigger."

"Did you take her to the mine?"

"No. I ran to her after she fell." His breath heaved in his chest. There was no air in this room. "He hauled me off her, threw me across the room. There was so much blood. It was all over her, all over me. He turned to me, pointed the gun. He was going to kill me, so I just ran. Outside into the woods. I don't even remember how I got as far as I did. Gemma found me."

"And he took her through the tunnel to the mine. Told everyone she ran off, got lost in the woods, or whatever ridiculous story I cannot believe they actually bought." John shook his head. "The sheriff filed a report on her disappearance. Though you can hardly even call it a report, it's so flimsy. He should have launched a full investigation, but apparently he didn't even set foot in the house until after your father had cleaned up the place. Moved the rug to cover the stain. He had to have been a great liar. A man who killed all those people, kills your mother, and no one points a finger at him."

"I always thought the sheriff might have worked for him, or something."

"What do you mean?"

"He didn't show him any respect, but then my father didn't show it to anyone. Still, the sheriff acted more like my dad was the one with the authority."

John shrugged. "Could have been for whatever reason your father came here. The sheriff before me was a marshal for the witness protection program. He'd have known something about your father, surely, and if he didn't, then your father could have told him whatever he wanted to."

"He was charismatic enough when he wanted to be. I figured that was how he fooled my mom into marrying him."

"And he left you alone after that night, didn't try to kill you?"

Dan blew out a breath. "I'd be dead if he'd tried. There was no stopping him. But as you can see, he didn't kill me. I wouldn't say he left me alone, either. Things changed, that's for sure. We'd shared a moment we couldn't avoid, and I think he might have been worried I would tell someone. He kept me close, but he couldn't stop me from going to school."

Why hadn't his father killed him, if Dan could have told someone? Had the old man assumed Dan would take the blame for it? Or that no one would believe him?

"And no one ever asked why you had bruises?"

"Unless you count Gemma, no. She was pretty vocal about the way he treated me. Until…"

"Until what?"

Dan shook his head. "I don't know. One day she just stopped talking about it. No one listened. Maybe she just gave up."

"Or he got to her."

Dan's stomach dropped to the floor. "He didn't." He shook his head. "There's no way…" But there was. It certainly explained why she would quit trying to tell people he was being hurt. "Oh, no."

"This town swung the two of you out to dry. I feel like I should apologize, even though I wasn't here. Children being hurt is not uncommon. This world is so full of evil I can't even imagine. But I don't like the idea of it happening in my town."

"You weren't here yet."

"I know."

"If you had been, would you have done something about it? Would you have helped me?"

"Of course I would."

"I know," Dan said. "That's why I appreciate your friendship. And value the job you do as sheriff of this town. Because you would never have let that lie."

"They let you down. Both of you." John's voice was soft. He glanced over. "I can see why you hang on to her, why you two are friends. You've been through a lot, and Gemma fought for you when no one else would."

"In a lot of ways she was the only good thing in my life." Dan found a small smile, down deep in his memories. "She was actually the first one to tell me I should read a Bible. I'd seen my mom reading one, and I told her about it. Gemma told me to see what I'd find. We figured it couldn't hurt."

"And she didn't take her own advice?"

"She's always been a free spirit. It's one of the things I love about her. In all these years, she's never lost that fight. It just got squashed and then redirected into her work, into keeping our friendship going when by all rights it should have fizzled out." He shrugged. "I'd have let her go, but she never not once let me do it. I don't think she knows any other way to love someone."

"So she's it for you?"

Dan frowned. "Who else am I going to meet that can be what she's been in my life? Gemma is the whole package. Shared history, shared pain, shared joy, shared hope and happiness. When you add in attraction and decades of friendship, it's hard to say no."

"I can see that. And I understand, but I don't know what it's like. I only have family that have stuck with me that long."

"She is my family."

"So why haven't you married her yet?"

**

Gemma glanced over her shoulder and then kept walking. She couldn't stand to be in her mom's house any longer, but walking around without Mei felt wrong. Now she knew for sure Dan's childhood had been ignored, for whatever reason they thought was important. He'd endured a nightmare, and no one even cared, or if they did they hadn't done anything about it. She'd been a child herself and helpless. Powerless to save her friend.

Gemma stopped in her house for ten minutes to get changed into her workout clothes and then wiggled her feet into her tennis shoes without untying them. Who had time for that? She fast-walked to the gym, with a little jogging involved. It calmed her and made her less inclined to glance around like a crazy person who thought she was being followed.

There hadn't been any word about Terrence or any sightings of him. But then she hadn't seen Mei lately, either. At least she knew Terrence hadn't "disappeared" the way everyone said Dan's mom had. Gemma couldn't even tell them the truth, because Dan would have been in trouble. They'd hidden in her tent for a whole day, and then she'd gotten him supplies, and he stayed longer. She'd made him tell her what happened. He'd choked out how his father held his hand on the gun and pulled the trigger.

The hindsight of an adult was a whole lot different than the perspective she'd had on it as a child. For so long they'd stayed silent about it for fear Dan would get in trouble. Then one day she couldn't stand the lies any longer and went to the sheriff to tell him exactly what had happened to Dan's mom.

Dan's father had come over that night while her mom was out.

The hindsight of an adult on *that* whole thing wasn't something she wanted to dwell on, either. Now she knew he was truly evil—not that she'd needed a piece of Hal's paper to tell her that. She'd known even before he confronted her.

No one had stopped him. Not even Hal. Her mom was probably at his house that night, and they'd left her to swing. Completely vulnerable, like this town was a safe place to live. They hadn't known Dan's father would pay her a visit, but a child shouldn't have to live with that fear.

Gemma didn't need a shrink to tell her that Hal, Dan's father, and the sheriff had all played a part in her inherent distrust for authority figures. It wasn't rocket science, though mostly no one in town had figured out why she was the resident "rebel." Such a ridiculous label, but one she'd been stuck with nevertheless just because she was different. And she'd been vocal enough in her life that people noticed.

She didn't need that kind of notice. She had Dan, and he said God knew everything she'd never told anyone. That had been a strange thing to think about. God was a little bit "Big brother in the sky" spying on her, but she'd gotten over that invasiveness when she realized it meant she was never alone. Not even that night.

Gemma stopped at the corner of Main Street and looked up at the sky. Not this night, either.

I'm sick to death of being helpless and unable to stick up for myself. Gemma wiped the tear from her cheek. *Is there something wrong with me? You could have done something. Maybe there's something wrong with You. Maybe that's it. Maybe You're not good like Dan says. Like the Bible says.*

Yeah, so she'd read that thing. And she didn't totally understand why a collection of historical stuff, poetry, and letters made Holy Scriptures, but she'd just take their word for it. She had been swept away in parts, disgusted in parts, and completely confused, but there was something about the Bible that made her want to come back to it. To sit a while, and think on it.

Gemma had way too much energy for that right now, though. She had to punch a heavy bag for a while and try to figure out why Terrence had made her freeze. It wasn't like she couldn't defend herself, like she hadn't gone to Sam at the gym and begged him to teach her. She'd used some of those moves on Terrence, but it hadn't saved her.

Gemma sighed and pushed open the door to the gym. The lights were on, but it was empty. "Sam?"

Sometimes he worked in his office when no one was there and the diner across the street—which he also owned—was closed. A chair lay on its side.

"Sam, are you here?"

A low moan answered.

Gemma circled the boxing ring in the center. That was when she saw him. Or his legs, at least. Sam was on the floor, half-in, half-out of his tiny office. She ran over and knelt by his side.

"Sam?" *Please tell me he's not dead.* She touched his back and felt his chest lift underneath her palm. He wasn't dead. *Thank You.*

"Sam?"

"Gemma." He moaned her name.

"What happened?"

"Couldn't stop…" Sam's eyes fluttered closed. "Couldn't help…"

"What, what happened?"

Sam didn't answer.

Gemma hopped up and stepped over him. She ran to the phone and dialed the town's emergency number. *Please don't let Mei be on duty.* She'd ditched Gemma at her mom's house and disappeared. Who knew where the woman was?

"Sheriff Mason."

"John, its Gemma. Something happened to Sam, and he's on the floor. He's unconscious now. I think he was hurt."

"I'll be there in a minute." His voice came breathy, like he was already on the move. He said more, but she wasn't focusing on his voice. Just Sam Tura on the floor.

"Gemma, does he need a doctor?"

Gemma leaned down to look at Sam's face.

John said, "Elliot is dealing with something, but I'll call Shelby."

Gemma nodded, then realized he couldn't see her so she said, "Good idea."

"I'm outside now. We're coming in."

We? Gemma stepped out of the office and saw John, followed by Dan, enter the gym. "Let me see to him, okay?"

She nodded and stepped aside. John crouched and touched Sam's neck, followed by his face. His chest. He dialed a number on his phone. "Shelby, its John."

Dan touched her elbow. "Hey."

Gemma didn't want to bother with awkward pleasantries. They'd kissed already, hadn't they? She slid her arms around him and touched her cheek to his chest. Dan's arms wrapped around her, and she smiled against his shirt. "Hey."

Neither of them let go until Shelby rushed in with a duffel bag. "What is—oh. Hey, Gem."

"Hi, Shelby." She didn't feel like talking much more than that.

Dan rubbed her back, which she took as his signal they should let go. She looked up at him. "Are you okay?"

"I was going to ask you that."

"Dan's good," John called over to her.

Dan raised his eyebrows. "I guess I'm good."

Gemma didn't look at the sheriff. Whatever had happened between them might be "good," but she wanted Dan's take on it before she accepted the sheriff's declaration. Finally, they had a sheriff she respected, but that didn't mean Gemma didn't remember very clearly what happened when authority was misused.

"I told John everything."

Gemma frowned. "Everything what?"

"My mom. Everything."

"Oh."

"Mei found her remains."

Gemma touched her mouth. "She did?"

"Among some other stuff. I'll tell you later. But I am okay. I feel better, better than I've felt in a long time."

She smiled at him. "That's—"

Shelby said, "My goodness."

"—good." Gemma turned back to Shelby. They'd turned Sam's body over, his shirt open. The aging black man, once a boxing champion, was covered with bruises.

"They're from a boot. You can see the imprint of the heel," John said. "His face, too. His throat. It's a wonder he can breathe."

"Elliot will have to look at him. He could have massive internal bleeding with this much bruising." Shelby's voice wobbled. "I'm scared to move him, but we have to."

"We can put him in my car," the sheriff said. "But it'll take the four of us to move him."

John was right. By the time he shut the door and drove off, Gemma was breathing hard. "I hope he'll be okay. I'd hate for him not to recover." Sam was a huge part of town, and not just because he owned two businesses. She'd learned so much from him and not just how to fight. Sam had believed she could be more than what everyone said she was. He was the one who'd encouraged her to write.

"He said he couldn't stop. Couldn't help. Then he passed out." Gemma hadn't been able to help him. "Who did this to him? Everyone likes Sam."

The man was practically harmless. So soft spoken.

Dan set his hands on her shoulders. "Let's walk to the medical center. They'll tell us if he's okay."

Gemma nodded. "I hope he isn't seriously hurt. Who could…what if it was the same person who killed Antonia? Or the same people in the radio station."

Dan's hand tagged hers and didn't let go. "It could be. But they can't have wanted him dead, or they'd have killed him. Just like they didn't kill us." He squeezed her hand. "I'm glad they were gone when you got here. But I don't like thinking how long Sam laid there before you found him."

"I know." Gemma wanted to pray Sam would be okay, but she didn't know where to start.

"We should talk."

She nodded. "I went to my mom's. The mayor was there, and she told me all about your father and Hal and why they came here. They started Sanctuary because of your dad."

"They did?" Dan stopped. He shook his head. "That isn't what I wanted to talk about."

"Your mom, then? You said you were okay, but you did see her."

"She was a skeleton and rags."

"That must have been hard to face."

"Yes, but that isn't what I want to talk about, either."

"Okay, then. What—"

Someone ran over, their shoes clacking on the sidewalk. "Gemma! Yoo-hoo! We'd like to talk to you! Gemma!" The woman's long floral skirt tangled around her legs. Her husband struggled to keep up.

The man's big belly and bald head hadn't changed. Neither of them had, not for years. If they had, then hearing them share their political and religious opinions over and over again might actually be interesting.

"Uh. Hi, Mr. and Mrs. Evangeline."

It was Terrence's parents.

Chapter 16

"It's late, Sam has been hurt, and we're on our way to see him."

Despite Gemma's statement, Dan didn't see either of Terrence's parents even blink. "Was there something you needed?"

Terrence's parents ran the town's art programs. They put on a dinner theater every year, and people treated it like they were forced to do what John called "jury duty." Dan had no frame of reference for a court as they didn't have one, but he got that it was apparently torturous. Kind of like being forced to watch a great work of Shakespeare twisted into a contemporary rendition performed by nice people—some of whom could not act in the slightest. At least the dessert had been good.

Terrence's mom nodded, and much of her features wobbled along with the motion. "We need to speak with you, Gemma."

Beside her, Terrence's dad huffed and said, "We'd like to know why you're spreading these lies about our son."

"Lies?" Gemma's eyes widened.

Of course they would insist Gemma lied about Terrence's actions.

"Yes, of course," Terrence's mom said. "What else would they be, but lies? You take the good name of our son and smear it with dirt, like some kind of...*smear* campaign. What is wrong with you?"

"Lies." Gemma said that one word carefully.

"Lies!" Terrence's dad's face flushed. "Now you go to the sheriff, missy. And you take back what you said about our son."

"He burned me with a cigarette. It's not a lie, and I'm sorry you don't believe me—"

"Hiding in that library. Probably gave you a wild imagination. People don't go around doing things to other people like that."

"You think I'd spread something like this if it wasn't true?" Gemma's reply was soft, hurt. Not like this couple Dan had respected, yelling in her face. She said, "Terrence is responsible for his own actions. Where is he? Not here, defending himself."

"We took him to church every Sunday. He's a good Christian boy!"

They thought that was what it took? That being a "good person" was the point? Dan interjected, "Uh—"

Terrence's mom cut him off. "He applied for the deputy sheriff position and got passed over for that Chinese girl. Who knows what the sheriff saw in *her*? My Terrence is a lifer, and we're proud to have raised him here in this town. He was perfect for that job. Honest as the day is long, he is. Instead we get a woman who's only been here a few months. She doesn't know a thing about how Sanctuary works, or the people who live here!"

Gemma said, "If he'd have made such a good deputy why did he hit Bolton over the back with a chair?"

Terrence's dad closed her mouth. Swallowed. His mom said, "Because he was being noble! He thought he was helping Nadia get out of a bad situation."

"More like a jealous situation," Gemma muttered. Then louder, she said, "Bolton was nearly paralyzed because of that."

"That injury is because of his sin. That's what caused him to be in that wheelchair. Father Wilson always said—"

"Father Wilson was a murderer," Dan said. Then he realized what that meant. He wanted to lay down and cry, ask Papa why he insisted on having such flawed men lead His people in this town. Maybe they just weren't supposed to have a pastor. Or a church. Maybe a couple of home Bible studies would do.

Dan cleared his throat. "Terrence's guilt or innocence is for an investigation to decide, and whether he'll be convicted of something, we'll find out with time. John is in charge of all that."

"Did you know," Terrence's dad said, "that out in the world, a sheriff is voted in?"

Gemma shrugged. "This is a witness protection town. John is a US marshal."

"He's not in charge of this whole town. He isn't the mayor, but he thinks he is. I think we should be able to vote for a sheriff. We're not run by the government. I'm going to petition the committee, have everyone sign it. We should be able to vote in our own sheriff."

Dan said, "Why choose someone else? John was the one who figured out who killed the mayor's wife and made sure the school teacher and the previous deputy didn't hurt anyone else. John was the one who saved Frannie from Father Wilson, and helped me make sure the whole town wasn't poisoned. John was the one who got stabbed fighting off that rogue Navy SEAL. John has protected this town for years, and he deserves our respect for it. He's a good man, a good husband and father. A good sheriff."

"I'd echo that, but apparently you guys think I'm a liar anyway." Gemma looked down her nose. Dan could see how people might misconstrue that as her thinking she was above them, but he knew it was only a mechanism to protect herself from being hurt. No victim deserved to have their trauma questioned because someone didn't believe they were telling the truth.

"Mr. and Mrs. Evangeline, if you'll let us go we need to see Sam Tura. Make sure he's okay, or if he's even woken up." He started to walk away, guiding Gemma to walk with him. "Come on."

Terrence's parents sputtered after them, murmured, and talked to each other. Dan needed to explain a few things to them about being a Christian vs. being a good person. Too bad he couldn't use the pulpit for his own agenda, not even what—in his own mind—he believed God "laid on his heart." Dan simply preached what the Bible said, and God spoke through His word, not Dan's. He needed to pray for Terrence's parents.

Gemma's steps were leaden. He didn't think she wanted to stay back there with Terrence's parents, but something weighed heavy on her.

"I know you were telling the truth. I was there right after. I saw Terrence leave, and I saw Mei helping you bandage your arm." Dan had seen that face before, and he'd forced her to tell him then as well. "You weren't lying."

Gemma didn't say anything.

He squeezed her hand. "You can't make everyone believe you."

"I know that. I don't try anymore, but it still hurts."

And yet she stood. She faced it, and she was working on moving on. Gemma had so much will it blew his mind every time he saw it. He'd never met a woman like her, so different than his mom's shaky hands and soft voice. Gemma had strength, even if she didn't know it.

Dan's mom had cowered. And he understood why. Mentally, he could comprehend the fact she'd lived with a tyrant who probably hurt her in countless ways. That life would weigh anyone down, it could take the strongest person and reduce them to a shadow of who they were. But Dan hadn't been in that position. He'd been reliant on his mom to protect him from his father, and she hadn't. Or she had somewhat, and that was why he hadn't been killed that day when she did stand up to him.

God's hand had been there, even in ways Dan didn't see because he'd lived it from a child's perspective. He'd only seen a woman he adored, a woman he wanted to be strong, drift away. Fail. Get scared. Lose her fight. Lose her hope. In the wrong situation it could happen to Gemma, but Dan only saw the friend she had been to him for years.

Dan stopped right outside the medical center and turned to her, took her free hand so that he held both of them. "Gemma."

"This looks bad. Is it bad? Because I don't think I can handle much more."

Dan pulled her in and hugged her. "It isn't bad."

"It is serious, though."

"I think you need a vacation."

"Where am I going to go? We can't leave this town, and it's not like we can camp out in the woods now."

Sure, they'd done that as kids. Stayed up late reading—actually *she'd* read, and he'd listened to her words. The inflections of her voice added life to every story. *The Lion, the Witch and the Wardrobe*. The *BFG*.

"I don't know. Maybe we can work it out." If they got married no one would object. They'd have no reason to object.

"What are you talking about, Dan?" Her whole face had come alive. Mission accomplished. The idea had taken root since John mentioned it. The sheriff had only made the suggestion because he was happy. Married people did that all the time, wanting everyone to experience the bliss they had. Dan had seen the opposite as well, in his congregation. It was never perfect, but it was good. He and Gemma would be able to figure it out. They'd been friends forever, and he was pretty sure she felt the same way he did. At least, she did if that kiss was anything to go by.

She said, "You're so concerned about your reputation, we've never even had dinner at the diner, and now you want to disappear together into the woods? You're crazy. How will everyone think that's not the worst idea they've ever heard? The only way they'd accept it is if we were…" She stepped back. "No."

"Is it a horrible idea?"

"Getting… I can't even say it. Can you?"

Dan swallowed. "Elliot and Shelby are married. John and Andra. Frannie and Matthias. Nadia and Bolton are getting there, but they have a teenage son to worry about so that's complicated." He clenched his stomach and shrugged. "Why not us?"

"Why not us." Gemma's voice had a low tone. That wasn't good. "Can you at least *try* to act a little more like a romantic? I'm not expecting hearts and flowers and chocolate, but something more than 'why not' wouldn't be an awful idea. Maybe you could think on that while we go inside and make sure Sam isn't dead, since it took us so long to get here."

She turned and grabbed the door handle.

Dan stalled her with a hand on her elbow. When she turned back, he said, "I love you. I always have, and I think you've known that for as long as me. Why don't you think on that?"

He moved around her and held the door. Gemma glanced aside at him, her face full like she had a million thoughts in her head.

If she didn't want to find some good together, he wasn't going to push her, but he knew what they could be. He knew the peace and love they could find together. Yeah, he wanted to marry her. It wasn't a complicated decision. She was his best friend, and the woman he loved. Yes, she was right that he wasn't the most romantic person, but Dan was convinced if they opened themselves up to see what love could be between them, that he would find a way to show her how he felt. He'd make sure that she found everything she ever wanted with him.

He was finding life now, instead of walking that valley of the shadow of death. It would probably take the rest of his life, but he was inching away from it slowly and gaining ground.

With Gemma beside him.

**

The man was crazy. He loved her? Okay, so she knew that, but marriage? Gemma didn't even know if she was a marriage kind of person. Nor could she think of one example of a good marriage that had lasted that she could mine for tips. She wasn't going to ask Terrence's parents what their secret was, and who else had been married that long? She didn't want her and Dan to turn into crazy people.

John stood by the front counter. He and Andra were happy, and he'd come through a bad marriage. She knew his first had ended in divorce. Maybe John knew how to do a good job at it.

She glanced back at Dan. If she agreed, would they be setting themselves up to destroy the good that they'd found together? What if they tore each other apart because they didn't know how to coexist? There was a chance it might be good. Great, even. But how did she know it would be for sure?

The sheriff lifted his chin as they approached. "Sam is in a coma."

In the end, Gemma spent the night in the medical center with Shelby, who insisted she used a spare bed to sleep. When there was no change in Sam's condition in the morning, she walked home. It was just after eight, and a Sunday. No one was out and about.

Gemma stopped abruptly and spun on the street.

No one was there. She was turning herself inside and out in knots. Terrence wasn't waiting in the shadows to accost her again.

Gemma showered as fast as she could and dressed in one of her more demure outfits. These jeans only had a rip in the knee, not up her thighs like some of them. Her boots had heels, and she added some jewelry.

What did people wear to church anyway?

Don't think about it. Don't think about what anyone is going to say, or what they'll think. This is about you and Dan, not anyone else.

Her people didn't go to church. But if anyone could break the cycle it was her, and Dan. They had to walk free of the past if it was going to lose its grip on them. She wasn't going to pretend to be something she wasn't, but she'd spent all night thinking about it. Church was a huge part of Dan's life, so why shouldn't she get to know him in that context?

Gemma ignored the surprised look and took the folded paper the person gave her. She stepped inside the Meeting House and saw a lot of the town was there. The volume of talking in the room dropped, but didn't go to dead silence. Because that would have been embarrassing. Still, Gemma felt her cheeks flame, ducked her head, and made for the back row. She stopped at the middle seat and slumped into it.

The sheriff's son said, "Excuse me." Gemma shifted her knees and let him pass. The sheriff followed him, and they sat on the end of her row. Andra came along a second later, her pregnant belly protruding in front of her. That looked uncomfortable. Could she even breathe?

Andra sat on the seat right beside Gemma.

She turned to say "hi" to the sheriff's wife but only got as far as opening her mouth before someone sat in the seat on the other side of her.

"Morning." It was Nadia Marie.

"Uh, morning." Gemma had been ambushed. Though they probably thought they were being supportive. Bolton, Nadia Marie's fiancé, came over in his wheelchair. A gangly teenage boy moved a chair from the end of the row and walked off with it. Bolton maneuvered into the space and took Nadia's hand. Frannie and Matthias, both of whom had been at the school for a time when Dan and Gemma were there, made their way down the row in front of her. Matthias had one of those baby carriers, which held their daughter.

Frannie sat and glanced back over her shoulder. "Hi, Gemma."

"Uh, hi." Yeah this was super awkward, but they'd boxed her in. There was no escape now, even if she wanted to run out in front of everyone. "How are you, Frannie?"

The baker made a puking motion and then pointed at her stomach.

Gemma didn't even know what to say, while beside her Nadia Marie chuckled.

They all stood. Gemma jumped out of her seat so she didn't look like she had no idea what was happening. Dan was at the mic, a guitar around his neck. He started to sing about a lion and a lamb; she didn't know what that meant but he seemed to think it was important. She didn't think it was about that lion in *The Chronicles of Narnia*, but that was the only lion she knew. She'd heard him sing before, but his voice had grown. It was deeper now.

Everyone sang along, which was also awkward. Gemma didn't know the words, so all she could do was stand there. His singing voice didn't help. Probably church wasn't the place to think this, but it was kind of...sexy. A low rumble. He didn't do it like it was a show, but clearly he meant every word he sang. He believed it, and she knew that was true because he lived it.

He stepped away from the mic, saw her, and his eyes widened as he walked to the front row and sat.

Another guy got up and prayed. She didn't know the man too well, but he was older. Then everyone was told to stand up and say "hi" to someone around them. It was torturous. The girls smirked but hugged her, even while they laughed at her discomfort.

"Jerks."

Nadia burst out laughing. "Worth it, though. He saw you."

Gemma rolled her eyes. Beside her she heard a low groan. When she looked, Andra had leaned forward, one hand on the back of the seat in front of her. "Wow."

Gemma moved closer. "You okay?"

"I thought it was just these uncomfortable plastic chairs."

John turned from talking to someone. "Andra?"

"I think I'm okay." She straightened, then let out another moan.

"Mom?" Pat, Andra's step-son, looked worried.

Andra turned to him. "Might be time to meet your brother."

His smile was something Gemma wouldn't have said she needed to see. He was so happy it was blinding. This wasn't really her business. But when she did, it was something she would never have wanted to miss for the world.

Dan walked up to the podium this time. Not a grand piece of furniture, it was actually a simple mic and a music stand. He smiled at the room. "If you'll sit, we're going to get in the Word."

John said, "Andra?"

"I'm okay." She waved him off. "Let's sit for a bit. You know these things take time."

John didn't look convinced, but he sat. Dan shot them all a questioning look. Gemma motioned at Andra. Dan nodded. He prayed, adding a prayer for Andra and the baby, and then started to preach.

She'd heard him call it that before, but she'd never heard him speak like this. He captivated her. Gemma watched his face light with it. He lost years of pain and hardship in that moment as his arms waved and he explained a passage about talents. She didn't know what that was, and he didn't dumb it down for her for which she was grateful. She got the gist of it—God wanted her. Not what she could do, but who she was. And not part of it, all of her. All that she was willing to give Him. Though Dan called it "surrender."

Beside her Andra hissed, one hand low on her belly.

Could Gemma do that? Could she give God her life just because He wanted it? She couldn't deny that the Being who had done so much for Dan would deserve that—and probably more—from her.

Andra stood up. Her hand flailed and landed on Matthias's shoulder. Her knuckles went white, and John shot up. "Andra!"

Matthias turned back. Andra cried out and a puddle of wet hit the floor right by Gemma's Converse.

Chapter 17

Dan stood beside her in the medical center's waiting area. How she got here was anyone's guess. Gemma had tried to gently extricate herself from the press of people rushing Andra to the sheriff's office and then around back where he parked his Jeep. She'd stepped away from the group several times, only to have someone grab her hand and pull her back. There had been nowhere to go, and she just got swept along with them because the alternative was elbowing people out of the way and making a scene.

"Pretty exciting church service, don't you think?" He grinned and squeezed her hand, which he hadn't let go of. "It's not like that all the time."

Gemma couldn't help but smile back. "I'll take your word for it."

"Come on, we can check on Sam while we wait for word about Andra."

And apparently she *was* going with everyone to the medical center. Gemma didn't know that she really needed to wait for "word" about Andra and the baby. She'd hear around town, wouldn't she? But being part of Dan's life meant she was part of that kind of thing. Part of these people and their lives.

"So what did you—"

"Do you know what—"

Dan grinned. "Go ahead. Mine can wait."

Gemma shrugged. "I guess I just don't really know what's going on. I mean, the papers were taken from the radio station days ago. Why haven't they shown up like your truck did?"

"It's hardly a truck now," he said. "More like the stripped-down shell of what's going to be a nice planter."

"Okay, but… I'd think whoever took them at least had an idea what they might be. So why haven't we heard about it? No one has made a move or said anything."

"They'd incriminate themselves if they did."

"But whoever it was had to have known it was there, or why else take it like that?" She didn't want to think about being stunned by that flash grenade, but it had happened. She wasn't going to sweep it under the rug. "They had to want those papers badly enough they couldn't wait until after we left."

"I don't know why it's like they've disappeared. And why did Antonia have to die?" It was just so senseless. "What if someone else is killed?" Okay, so she was talking about herself, but Dan probably didn't need to know that. She could barely go home without thinking someone might be waiting to kill her. Those papers had belonged to her. Terrence—even if only because he was a sicko—had targeted her, and the mayor had interjected himself into her life. Gemma couldn't help thinking she was a part of this.

What if Terrence came back and hurt her when she could do nothing to stop him? Sam was hurt, and the same might happen to Dan. What would she do if he was in a coma, lying in the medical center where there was nothing she could do to help him?

"Gemma." His voice was soft now.

Her breath hitched. "What?"

"You're crying."

She swiped the tears from her cheeks. Why did she not know when she was crying?

"Why are you so sad?"

"I'm not, I'm scared. I'm scared to death that something is going to happen, and I won't be able to do anything to stop it." She sucked in a breath. "Hal left me that room, and why? It wasn't a gift, it was a curse. Which is pretty much what your father left you. Nothing but evil. More hurt, more pain. And I didn't need more of any of that. I didn't. I don't."

Dan's hands slid across her cheeks, and he cupped her face in his palm. "I'm right here." He touched his lips to hers.

People passed them on the street. Someone gasped.

"People—"

"Don't worry about them." His lips were so close she felt the words as he spoke them. "Just focus on me right now."

"Okay." She sucked in a breath and tried to get enough air.

"I need you here with me."

She blinked. "You need me?"

"Gemma." Dan's eyes crinkled at the corners. "You didn't know that?"

"I think I might have." Still, she hadn't relied on it when she was overwhelmed and couldn't see a way out. God knew what was going to happen, and she had to trust Him to hold them together.

Dan touched his smile to hers. "I'll find a way to make sure you're safe. I can't stay at your house without… okay, we still need to talk about that whole thing. But maybe there's someone else you can stay with or someone who can sleep on your couch, to make sure you're safe when I can't be around. But I'm not going to leave you alone, okay?"

Because he would fall apart without her. Gemma bit her lip, then made the decision to just say it without worrying about the consequences. "That's why I never left."

His face softened. "Tell me."

"I wanted to." She shook her head. "I wanted to leave so many times. I even went to Sheriff Chandler about it and got the paperwork started. It never went anywhere. He said the senate committee didn't have time to discuss my case. Then I guess I just put it aside and went back to work. To life here."

Dan circled her loosely with his arms. "Gemma, did he offer you the option of moving away when you turned eighteen?"

"No, did he do that with you?"

Dan shook his head. "I've heard John talk about it, that anyone who lives here should have the option to go or stay when they turn eighteen. We should have been able to choose."

"He didn't tell me that. Chandler, I mean. He never said that was an option for me."

"Me either."

Gemma shook her head. Everything in Sanctuary was upside down. She thought she knew how it worked, and she didn't like the way she'd grown up with so many lies, but she'd been working on accepting it. Learning how to be happy in spite of everything.

"Someone wanted to keep us here?"

Dan nodded. "The question is whether they needed us to be here, or whether they just needed us to not be anywhere else."

"Loose in the world." Gemma had never even thought about it. "It was about controlling where we went and who we spoke to. The sheriff." She breathed. "I always knew there was something between him and your dad. He could have stopped your dad so many times, but he didn't. And when I went to him, he sent your father."

Dan didn't speak.

The sheriff and his father had tried to destroy her, but it hadn't worked. They'd tried to contain her, but she'd gotten her books out. Part of her roamed free in the world every time someone read one of the novels she'd written.

Dan's brow crinkled. "What are you thinking now?"

"I need to go write something. I'm having another book idea."

"Medical center first." He grabbed her hand and tugged her along. "I'll find you a pen and some paper. You can work on it while we wait."

"I can work on it at the library on my computer."

"You can find out how Sam is doing at the medical center."

Gemma sighed. "Fine. Hopefully Mei is there. I want to talk to her." Mei had to explain why she'd ditched Gemma at her mom's house when the mayor had been there.

"I actually had something I wanted to ask you."

Mei hadn't found Terrence yet. He was still out there. Terrorizing her, if only in her head. Antonia's killer was roaming free as well. Even if it was Terrence who'd done it, two people or one didn't make much difference. Sanctuary was under siege, because someone else was dead, and it was like everyone had something better to do than look for them.

Dan continued, "What did you think of my serm—"

What Mei *had* found was Dan's mother. She gasped. "Do you want to have a service for your mother and bury her properly?"

Dan's face softened. "That would be really nice, Gemma. Will you help me figure it out?"

"Of course. I have no idea how to do it, but I'll find out, and I'll get people to help. She deserves to be placed at rest, finally."

"Thank you for thinking of it, Gemma. I didn't know what I was going to do." Dan squeezed her hand. "But I want to talk about church. What did you think of my sermon this morning?"

"It was fine."

"Fine?" Dan's question was tentative. "That's it?"

Gemma shrugged. "There's so much going on now. I guess we could talk more about it later, if we need to." He didn't look happy. "What? What did you want me to say?"

"It was just… You know what, never mind. Don't worry about it."

Gemma blinked. "We can talk about it more. Later, okay?"

"Okay."

It wasn't. She could see that much. It mattered to Dan that she tell him what she thought of his sermon, and she needed to remember that for next time. And there would be a next time.

Dan pushed open the door to the medical center. The crush of people was enough to make her want to pull her hand out of his and run away, but she straightened her shoulders and walked in hand-in-hand with Dan Walden. The rebel and the town's pastor. People could think what they wanted.

She was here to stay.

**

Two hours and no word. The crowd in the medical center's waiting area had thinned. Dan sat with Matthias, Bolton, and their women. Pat and Aaron were there, playing a board game on the floor with Olympia's grandsons. Gemma had made a run to the library and grabbed a stack of books for people to read. Olympia and her daughter Maria, and the elderly twins, as well as the sheriff's dispatcher, had jumped on the stack. Now Gemma was sitting with them, talking about some book they were all reading.

The mayor had shown up as well, and he hung back not really mingling with the crowd. Dan didn't like the way he eyed Gemma over the top of his fishing magazine. Why was Collins here, anyway? He didn't care about John or Andra. He didn't care about the baby, or finding out that John's newest son was healthy.

Matthias elbowed him.

Dan glanced over.

Matthias had looked up from his book, a beat-up Peter Leavell novel Gemma had given him. Dan didn't like cliffhangers.

"You don't actually have lasers in your eyes, you know."

Dan stared at him.

"It isn't actually possible for you to set him on fire with your eyes, even though it looks like you're trying."

Dan rolled his eyes.

Bolton chimed in. "You got a beef with the mayor?"

"Nothing concrete I can put my finger on."

"Do you think he was behind the theft of those papers and Antonia's death?"

"Like I said, nothing concrete."

"So go smoke him out," Bolton said. "If he's guilty, then sooner or later he'll mess up. Then you'll know for sure."

"And if I ask the wrong question I'll end up dead just like Antonia."

"You know John feels bad about that," Matthias said. "He's been asking around, but he's getting nowhere. He thinks it's a group, and he has some names Antonia gave him but he can't just go ask them straight out. You all reported it was multiple men in the radio station. John is working on the problem."

"A group." Dan glanced between them. "Doing what?"

"John doesn't know, and he can't penetrate the group. They all know he's the sheriff. But it could be about anything, and no one's talking. They're all shut down tight, waiting for something. Whatever plan they have in place, Antonia was a casualty of it."

"If John is on it, though, I'm not going to get in the way. Isn't that what happened to Antonia?"

Bolton shrugged with his mouth. He'd lost weight over the last few months but looked happier and more open than he had in any of the years Dan had known him.

Nadia stood. "More coffee, guys?"

Dan grabbed the mugs from her. "I'll get it." He strode to the carafe Olympia had brought over from church. It was running low, but they should be able to get a few more cups out of it.

"Daniel."

Just the sound of his name made him nearly drop the mug. Dan gripped it so hard it could've cracked in his hand. "Collins."

The mayor poured his own coffee, but all Dan saw was Antonia's body. He did not want to end up another casualty of whatever was happening in town under the cover of secrets and lies. And murder. *Help us get past this death. Help John find the truth without anyone else getting killed.*

"Such an inspiring sermon this morning."

"I'd love to have coffee with you and talk about it some more. If you'd like to discuss it and pray about it." It was so much easier to do that with the men in this town. If it was a lady he usually hooked them up with Olympia, but the woman was grieving. He needed to ask her how Sofia was doing at the nursery after her sister's death.

"That's not necessary," the mayor said. "I don't want to take up more of your precious time. You're a busy man."

"Right."

He just wanted to compliment Dan on being eloquent, but the mayor had no intention of actually surrendering anything in his life to God. Mostly Dan figured there was a swatch of people in his church simply because they were bored and wanted to get out and socialize on a Sunday. They had no intention of seeing his words as more than happy sentiments that might get them a better life. Dan had prayed about it a lot but figured if someone wasn't willing to listen to the Lord, there wasn't much he could do except keep talking.

He filled the last cup.

"I would like to bug you about something right now, though."

"I'll just deliver these over there." Dan motioned to the group with one of the cups. As he walked, he caught Gemma's gaze. She sent him a questioning look, which he responded to with an, *I don't know* motion of his mouth. Dan wandered back to the table and got his own mug. The mayor motioned him to a far corner of the waiting room and they sat.

"I was wondering if you'd given any thought to the possibility of being the next mayor. I can understand things have been interesting for you these past couple of weeks, but you did promise to give it some consideration. To *pray* about it."

Like that was just something Dan said, not a real part of his life.

Dan nodded and sipped his cup. "It has been interesting, as you said. I still have the bruises and lingering aches from the radio station attack, and I know Gemma is feeling it. Antonia's death has hit the church hard. It's going to be a rough time over the next few weeks as the town re-orients itself when one of their number is missing."

His face had frozen for a second when Dan mentioned the bruises, but the mayor shook it off. "And who better to lead them at this time than their pastor?"

"I'm just not sure that job is for me. Though I thank you for thinking of me."

"That's a real shame, Daniel." The mayor sighed, like Dan had genuinely disappointed him. "This town is going to you-know-where in a handbasket. There are those who will fight it and those who will watch the show. It's sad to know you'll be on the side of ones who will do nothing to ensure the future of this town."

"And passing the title of mayor to another person is your endeavor to safeguard Sanctuary?"

"I do my part." The mayor shifted on his chair. "The mayor position is just one portion of my activities."

Now what did that mean?

Over the mayor's shoulder, Dan watched Gemma move from her spot and head to the back hall, where the rooms were. He didn't blame her wanting to go sit with Sam Tura—unless she just had to use the bathroom. "I suppose I'm not as altruistic as you," Dan said. "The people are what I care about. More than the town."

"And you'll watch this town sink for the sake of holding some hands?"

Dan shrugged. "Why would it sink?"

"This town is circling the drain. Things are in motion. And when it's done, likely there won't be a Sanctuary left."

"Antonia's death?"

"She was a casualty of war."

Gemma didn't come back. Good. Dan didn't want her anywhere near the mayor. "Did you kill her?"

The mayor barked a laugh. "Of course not. Terrence took it upon himself to end her life. It was not any of my business."

So Collins had waited until John was otherwise occupied to share that with Dan? Whether Terrence actually killed her, was ordered to, or it was simply being pinned on him, remained to be seen. Dan didn't trust the mayor farther than he could throw him.

"Why share that with me?"

"You're part of it," the mayor said. "Gemma is part of it. Hal left her that secret in the radio station for a reason."

"Was that Terrence as well?"

The mayor shrugged, all innocence. "Who knows?"

"How do you know about the radio station?"

"It's all over town. Papers missing. Everyone figures it had to be a big secret, and most have gone to see the hidden room for themselves."

No one had told Dan that. "Do you know who took the papers?"

The mayor said nothing.

"Some secrets should never be brought into the daylight. This town doesn't need to know that it was originally a prison to keep my father in." He wanted to see the mayor's face. He wanted to watch when he said the words, to see what Samuel Collins did. Dan studied him, waiting for a reaction.

There was none.

Which meant it wasn't a surprise. "My father grew marijuana in the basement of my house for years. As far as I can tell, he got it out of town somehow."

"Through the mine." The mayor still didn't react. "He grew it in the woods also. Cornered the market in the Northwest, across the border into Canada, and all the way down to Colorado. Why do you think these are some of the states that are the biggest proponents of smoking pot? He got in the business early and set up an empire, a culture. Your father did that."

If he had, then he had to have made a bunch of money. Yet it hadn't saved him, and he'd never spent it. Dan's dad's heart had given up. That shriveled up, black member in his chest had simply quit. He'd fallen in the romaine instead of enjoying his ill-gotten gains.

"If you agree to become the next mayor, I will personally ensure that no one in town ever finds out that you are descended from a murderer and a drug dealer."

Dan stared into the mayor's eyes and tried to pray. Tried to think what the sheriff would tell him to do. He trusted John. The mayor was drawing him into a plan, and Dan had no idea what it was about. Collins wanted to blackmail him into the mayor's job? Why?

Collins also seemed to know all about his father's activities—as Sheriff Chandler would have. Who else in town had been involved?

A loud scream erupted from down the hall.

Gemma.

Dan ran to the open door, Sam Tura's room. She stood in the doorway, her face pale and one hand on her chest. "I just went to the bathroom. I was going to sit with Sam for a while. He—"

Xander stood over the body, dressed in his uniform, Sam Tura on the bed. The big security guard backed up. "He ran past me, down the hall. Nearly knocked me over." Xander blinked. "Terrence tried to kill Sam, but I stopped him."

Dan turned back to the waiting area beyond the crowd of people who now filled the hall.

The mayor was gone.

Chapter 18

It didn't matter how long they banged on the door or how many times Dan called out to her through the window. How many times the phone rang. Gemma sat on the library floor in the dark with her back to the check-in desk and didn't move. Didn't speak. Didn't cry.

All she could see when she shut her eyes was Xander standing over the bed. Sam Tura's face so pale, she didn't know someone with dark skin could look that pale. She'd thought Sam was dead, and she'd thought it was Xander who'd done it, but someone else? Gemma hadn't seen anyone running away. Could it really have been Terrence?

She gripped the sides of her head and breathed. Sam was in critical condition now. Terrence hadn't been there for her.

Life wasn't supposed to be like this. She forayed into fictional worlds to get excitement. Reading and writing. Both had plenty of drama for her, especially since Dan's father had died and it seemed like life had finally calmed down and had a rhythm to it. But now everything was upside down again. Secrets. Lies. Pain. Death. People were being sucked in, left and right. When was it going to end?

And what was she supposed to do?

Papa. She didn't even know where to start. *I—*

Creak.

Gemma's head shot up. "Is someone here?"

A door handle clicked and then creaked open. Gemma got up, grabbed the closest thing—a stapler—and held it high above her head. She wasn't going down without a fight.

"Gemma?"

She dropped the stapler. "Sheriff?"

John clicked on a flashlight and crossed between the shelves. "There you are." His smile was soft.

"Shouldn't you be at the medical center?" Andra was having a baby, and he was here?

"It's a boy." His smiled widened. "I mean we knew that, but still. Six pounds nine ounces. They're both fine, sleeping. Olympia is with them."

"Oh."

"And Mei took Xander to the sheriff's office. She's talking to him."

"Okay."

His smile wasn't so excited now. It was the smile of a man inherently happy but forced to face things that weren't. *Back to reality.*

"Wait a minute." She held up one hand. "How did you get in?" She walked to the bookshelves where he'd emerged from. "Where did you come from?" John shone the flashlight over her shoulder. Gemma flipped the nearest light switch and said, "There's nothing there, just a wall."

John tapped the outside of her arm with the back of his hand. Gemma winced when the burns Terrence had given her smarted. She moved aside, and he touched the wall. Just like the radio station, the wall revealed a secret room. "Seriously?" She could hardly process it. "In my library? Please tell me this one is not full of classified documents, because if it is, then I don't even want to go in there."

"It does have to do with Hal," John said. "But not in the same way."

Gemma took a step back. "This was in my library the whole time?" When John didn't answer, she said, "How many more secrets are there in this town? Because I'm not sure I even want to know. I barely want to go in there. Hal couldn't have mentioned this in his will? He gave me the radio station, and I got attacked there. Why not tell me about the secret room in my own library? That's not important enough that I know about it?"

John sighed. "This isn't about Hal, Gemma. It's just another entrance, and it leads through the basement."

She could tell he wanted her to quit freaking out. Gemma took a big breath and let it out slowly. "What is down there?"

"Let me show you."

Gemma didn't move. "Would you ever have told me if you hadn't needed to get in this way tonight?"

"No, but I'm about as done with secrets in this town as you are. So you might as well know, that's all. And it's not bad, but it might be part of what's going on."

John led the way. Gemma stopped at the bottom of the stairs and sat on the bottom step. The room was full of computer screens. A bank of servers, like she'd seen in a movie. "Is this what connects us to the internet?"

"From the satellite, to here, then to your computers upstairs."

"But that's not it, is it?"

John shook his head. "Hal was in charge of oversight of town surveillance. He logged every phone call on the town's internal system, and flagged anything that might be suspicious. He was the point person for the military's surveillance of our mail."

"I already know they opened everything going out of and coming into the town. It's part of security."

"Now that's done by a private company that mainly employs former TSA agents."

"That makes me feel super secure."

John gave her a small smile. "After we got internet and satellite TV, Hal's part was done by computer, though he still oversaw everything. It was his job from the beginning."

"Because he had to report back to Congress about Bill Jones. Not that it did any good, since Bill was supplying pot to the Pacific Northwest out of his basement."

John's eyebrows shot up.

"Dan told me before I came over here. He's worried what the mayor is into, and I'm worried which one of us is going to be the next Antonia."

"That's a valid concern."

"Seriously?"

"It pays to be smart," John said. "There is nothing wrong with awareness that leads to caution. It could keep you alive."

Gemma blew out a breath. "And all this was below my library the whole time?"

John nodded.

"Because town security means we all have to sacrifice a little of our privacy," she said, her voice completely sardonic.

"Except it's not a little. It's a whole lot, because a dead man who was a bad man made it that way, and the culture of this town hasn't changed one bit in the forty years since the first person set foot here."

"It's kept a lot of people alive."

"And now you're just going to tell me? What about all your friends? Don't Nadia, Frannie, Bolton, and Matthias deserve to know they live in a fishbowl?"

"Some of them know, some don't."

"And they're fine with it?"

"This isn't a discussion about invasion of privacy, Gemma. You deserve to not be in the dark about this, as it's your library, and this whole thing has been hard for you. Hal put a lot on your shoulders, but what I'm trying to get across is that it's been for the best. He helped me save a lot of people when this town was under attack."

"It got him killed."

"No, his love for this town, and the people who live here, got him killed."

"He was in the ranch house, protecting Beth and everyone over there."

"Yes, he was. Because you were safe under the Meeting House with everyone else." John sat on the edge of the desk. "That's the man who was your father. A man who gave everything he had to give in order to make sure the people he cared about were safe."

His gaze was so intense that Gemma had to look away. She'd rather be mad at Hal, because being mad meant she didn't miss what she had never learned about him while he was alive, and it meant she didn't grieve not getting to know him now.

Gemma made her way back upstairs and sat in the first chair she came to. John pulled another chair over and sat so their knees were almost touching. She leaned her head in her hand. Her body still held the bruises from falling through the ground. The headache was only just starting to diminish. She felt like she weighed an extra hundred pounds, or like she'd aged thirty years.

"Tell me what you saw in the medical center."

Gemma didn't open her eyes, or look up. "Xander. No one else. He stepped back with his hands still stretched out. Both, like he'd had them around Sam's neck. I guess he could have been checking for his pulse, but at first glance I thought he—" Her voice broke.

John asked her what Xander had said, so she told him. Then Gemma added, "I don't know what to believe." It was like a million-piece puzzle, and she didn't know what the final picture was supposed to be. "I hope you guys can find out what really happened, because it just doesn't make any sense."

"Murder, even attempted murder, almost never does make sense. Even when you know the reason." John stepped closer. "It's often senseless and horrible, but you have to set that aside and think about what you have in front of you. Alive. The people who care about you. The good parts of your life."

"Is that what you do?"

John nodded. "I have to."

"How do you do this? How do you be the sheriff in a town like this, where it never shuts off? There's always something happening, and lately it's been so much worse. I can't wrap my head around it, but it almost feels like something is brewing."

"I compartmentalize as much as I can, but it never completely works. Hal was better at that than I am, though he did it with lies. Thankfully, Andra understands that the town needs their sheriff almost as much as she needs me at home as her husband. And I don't keep anything from her."

It would be that way with Dan. If he married—when he married—his wife would have to deal with the demands put on him as pastor. Gemma hoped she'd have enough grace to deal with it like Andra did, but she didn't know. She'd probably just get mad and then kill-off someone from town, in a book. But John was right. Truth was better than what Hal did, even when it hurt.

"This is too much." Her head was so full of thoughts she didn't even know where to begin. She couldn't take any more of this.

"Let Dan in the door. Talk to him about it and stay safe. Be careful, and I don't want you to be alone, okay?"

Gemma nodded. "I know you need to get back to the medical center."

"Thanks for being cool about that, Gemma."

The alternative was being a jerk, so she just nodded. "Why don't you go out the front and let him in?"

John patted her shoulder. "I can do that."

She'd had enough secret doors to last her a lifetime.

**

Mei folded her arms. She'd rather roll this desk chair off a cliff than listen to this guy cry for one more second. *Tears make you weak, and weakness will get you killed.* Just the memory of his voice made her shiver.

"Security guard."

He swallowed a sob and looked over. "My name is Xander."

"Whatever." She'd learned a couple of their names, and where had that gotten her? Mei rubbed her shoulder. *Still hurts.* Revealing pain was also a weakness. She could see his craggy face in her mind as he said it. The crinkles around his mouth, and the stubble that grew gray. Mei shook off the memories.

The security guard was like a ten year old in a man's body. She marveled that he'd kept anyone safe, let alone that he might've actually planned to kill someone. Though the gym owner had been in a coma so there probably wasn't much fight.

He blinked at her. Mei got that a lot, there weren't many people who understood her. She mostly just ignored it. "You tried to kill that man. The one in a coma."

"Sam." The security guard broke down again. "And I didn't."

"And I'm supposed to believe it was Terrence? Maybe instead of crying, you could explain to me why you tried to kill him."

"I didn't try to kill Sam! Why are you saying that?"

He hadn't had a gun issued as part of his security guard gig for the medical center. That was more of a night-watchman kind of a deal. Making sure no one broke in to steal prescription meds, stuff like that. Guns weren't technically allowed in this town, except the sheriff. Though the farm had one, and a couple of ranchers. The bullet that had hit Antonia had come from a revolver registered to an old lady in Kentucky. Mei was still waiting on word as to whether it was the same gun used to shoot her outside the radio station.

"So it was Terrence?"

The security guard sucked in a breath and pressed his meaty hand against his mouth. If he started crying again she was liable to strangle him the way he'd strangled that other guy.

"I didn't see his face. He had a big jacket, and his hood was up."

"Isn't that weird, since it's been so mild lately?" She hated the weather here, it was so *blah.*

He glanced at her. Confused. Then got up and grabbed the bars of the open cell. He reared back and then slammed his head against the metal.

"Whoa, whoa!" Mei rushed over and tugged on his arm. "What are you doing?"

"You don't believe me. You think I want to kill him!" Blood ran down his face. "You're going to send me to prison because you think I hurt Sam!"

She hauled on his arm until he let go of the cell bars, but only one hand. He seriously felt so strongly about being accused of trying to kill that man that he was willing to hurt himself because of it? "Xander."

It was like he didn't even hear her. "You don't believe me." He grabbed the bar, dragging her with him and leaned back to hit his head on there again.

Mei ducked between his arms and came up between the big security guard and the bars. When he moved forward, she grabbed his cheeks, and kissed him quick on the lips. He sputtered and stared at her.

"Don't get any ideas, it was just to distract you."

**

Dan didn't say anything, he just stood in the middle of her library and held up the bag. Everyone outside had left, as he'd politely asked them to give him and Gemma some space. His friends headed home. They'd seen the baby—and the aftermath of an attempted murder—and now it was late.

"I feel like you should say something about birth and death, or the circle of life."

He lowered the bag. "Do you want me to?"

"No. I'd rather drink Cherry Coke and not talk about anything at all."

"It has been a crazy day."

"Same old, same old?" She shook her head, like he could even think things were normal right now.

"I'm not ignoring what's happening, Gem. I'm just choosing not to let it get to me." He took the contents from the bag and made them both a drink. Then he pulled out the vanilla ice cream.

"A Cherry Coke float?"

"Desperate times call for desperate measures."

Gemma laughed. "I love you." Her eyes widened, and she slapped a hand over her mouth.

Dan closed the gap between them. "I actually already knew that." He smiled, his face close to hers. "And for the record, I also love you."

She smiled. So sweet. "I know."

"So what now?"

Gemma motioned to a table. The chairs had cushions but they'd been comfortable thirty years ago. "Here or the bean bags in the kid's section."

Dan grabbed both cups and the long handled spoons he'd brought and headed for the bean bags. He waited until she'd taken her first sip and swallowed before he said, "Do you want to get married?"

Gemma's head whipped around, her eyes wide. "Right now?"

"People are dying. And I've been trying to talk to you about this for a couple of days."

"What about the yoke thing?"

"Being unequally yoked?" When she nodded, he said, "It is important, but I think that even if it does cause issues, we have so much of the rest of us that's straight that we'd get through it."

"What if I never make a commitment?" She didn't mean to him, and Dan knew that. He knew she meant what if she never became a Christian.

"Do you think there's a chance you might not?"

Gemma frowned as she thought. Her thinking face was very cute. "I don't think so, but I don't know how long it's going to take. He's not pushing me into it. Which is good, but I don't feel like it's urgent, though."

God wouldn't pressure her into believing, but it *was* urgent. That was life, and it could end in a moment. "What if you died?"

"You don't want me to go to hell?"

Dan stared at her. "Do *you* want you to go to hell?"

Gemma cocked her head to the side. "Are we sure that we believe in hell?"

Dan nodded. "I've lived it. I don't want that. I want nothing but peace now. Forever."

"Okay. Bright side, things aren't going to get worse."

"There might be challenges for us, Gemma. But we can get through them together."

She was quiet for a moment and then she said, "I always knew that what happened with us would roll hand-in-hand with me and Him." She pointed one finger at the ceiling. "You're just so much a part of each other, that's how I see you. Both of you." She smiled a sweet smile. For him, and for God. "So yes. I accept—"

She glanced at the ceiling. "—I'm ready." Then looked back at Dan. "Because people are dying. Because things are crazy right now, more crazy than I know how to handle, and you've always been my haven in the midst of all of it. No matter what. You always have been, and even with everything that's happened that's never changed."

"It won't."

"I know. I trust you. And I trust Him. You've both always had my back."

Dan scooted to the edge of his bean bag, braced one foot on the floor, and leaned over to her. "Kiss."

Gemma obliged, along with another smile. "How long do you want to wait?"

"Well, there's no jewelers in town, so I gotta order you something online. Guess I jumped the gun on asking."

Gemma shrugged. "I don't care. It can be our secret. But I don't want to wait too long."

"We also have to find someone who can marry us. I'm the only pastor, and I'm not even officially a minister except from this random website. I don't even belong to a denomination, I kind of have to cover them all because people come from everywhere."

"Huh."

He frowned. "Guess I really didn't think it through all the way, either."

"Who marries the pastor when the pastor gets married?"

"Something like that." He shot her a grin.

"Let's put a pin in that."

"What?"

Gemma chuckled. "Just something I saw on TV. Hang onto that thought for later. We'll come back to it."

"And in the meantime?"

"I don't know, but it'll take some planning. Not that a wedding should be a big deal. Me, you. Someone to marry us. Witnesses. Cake—I guess that's Frannie's department. A dress and some flowers."

"I'm really glad you don't want a huge thing."

"Would you marry me if I did?"

"You wouldn't be you, but I'd still think you're cute." The best friend he knew didn't want fanfare, ever.

Gemma set her cup aside. "Can I ask you something?" Dan shot her a look, and she said, "Okay, fine. But sometimes I just have to say it so that you'll brace."

"I'm braced."

"Do you want to stay here?" Gemma's breath hitched. "I know you have your farm and your friends. The church and all the people here, but..." She picked at a thread on her jeans. "Maybe, would you think about whether or not, if we could leave?"

"Leave Sanctuary?"

She nodded.

"Is that what you want?" He had to tread carefully, or she'd shut down. Gemma didn't like having her feelings dismissed, or feeling like she was trapped. It was important to her to have freedom after being cooped up for so long.

Gemma bit her lip. "I think we should talk about it."

"You said it yourself. I have the farm, the church. My friends." She had Shelby, and now Elliot. Did Dan want to think about leaving? Sure, he'd been here his entire life as well and unable to leave, but then he'd never really wanted to the way Gemma had.

Dan stood to pace the kid's area. Could he navigate the outside world? It would likely be akin to moving to a foreign country. He wouldn't be doing it alone, though, would he?

Gemma stood as well. "Never mind. It's fine."

It was not fine. There was no way she meant that. "Gem—"

"Forget I said it. I'm tired, and I'm going to head home and try to sleep."

She didn't mean that, either. "Gem—" He tried to catch her as she swept around, cleaning up and grabbing her purse. "Lock the doors behind you."

"Gemma!"

Two seconds before the door shut after her, Dan heard the hitch of her breath. She was crying.

Chapter 19

"We don't have to go in the living room."

Dan ignored Mei's comment and glanced in there anyway. It was getting easier. "Remind me why we're even in here again. Do you think Antonia's killer has been in my house? Or has Terrence been hiding out in here?"

"We're in here looking."

Dan didn't need this after that disastrous conversation with Gemma. Now Mei was evidently done with Xander, and she'd come back. The woman clearly knew a bunch of things he did not, because from his perspective it made no sense.

He still hadn't been upstairs in his parent's house. What did he expect to find up there but more evidence of the sad existence of his childhood? Before he could think about it, Dan trotted up the stairs. The air in the hall was dense with memories. He could hardly take one step without hearing his dad's voice or remembering being shoved against the wall.

Doors were open. He walked to the first room. Dust had been disturbed but still sat thick in the air in his parent's bedroom.

Drawers had been pulled open. The contents of the closet lay on the floor. Disarray, but not as he remembered it. "Someone was in here. But recently?" It could have been years ago, and he wouldn't have known. Dan turned and saw Mei in the doorway behind him. He pointed to the mess and said, "This your doing?"

"You think I'd search for something and you'd be able to tell after?" She looked disgusted. "Please." She surveyed the room. "Sloppy. Searched all the normal hiding spots." Mei folded her arms. "And they have no imagination."

"Okay, so someone was definitely in here, and it was for nefarious reasons."

Mei lifted both hands.

Dan sighed. "Could be they were looking for something related to the papers from the radio station."

"Ah, the papers."

"What does that mean?"

Mei shrugged and blew out an exasperated breath. "It's just that… you know, you'd think if what's in there was so explosive, then whoever took it would have spread it around by now. Blown the whole thing wide open, and all that. Wouldn't they? I'd have spread that stuff wide."

"Gemma said the same thing. Am I supposed to know why they haven't?" Dan wasn't doing well knowing the answer to a woman's question.

Gemma had stormed out of the library because he'd taken too long processing the idea of living somewhere other than Sanctuary. He didn't even know if he would be safe if he left this town. He had to find out from the Marshal's service if the

CIA agents who'd wanted to kill his father for turning on them would come after him. Were they even still alive?

Dan had no idea.

It might be that the Marshal's service wouldn't have the first clue what he was talking about. A lot about Bill Jones went under the radar back in the seventies, and it seemed like only Hal knew what had really happened. And Janice. Hal's contact at the Marshals had known—a man John had told him was killed a few months back. The list of people who knew Bill Jones was shrinking. Soon no one would be left to corroborate.

There were so many questions. And yet, when he didn't answer fast enough to satisfy her, Gemma had walked out.

"Are we going to the basement, or what?"

"You're not going to, like, dust for prints in here?" Evidently Mei didn't want to do police stuff on his possible break-in. "You said they were sloppy. Maybe they left fingerprints behind."

"Do you have any idea how long it takes to run a print?" When he said nothing she said, "Besides, I'd have to go all the way back to the sheriff's office for the stuff, and it's nearly dinnertime."

"It's after ten."

She ignored him and pointed to the door, as though leading the charge. "To the basement."

Rather than figure out what on earth Mei was talking about, or what she wanted, Dan said, "One second." He wandered down the hall to his bedroom. His bed was still inside. No mattress—that had been tossed in the horse stall. No toys. Nothing hung on the walls now. A couple of shirts in a drawer, but not much else. Rags, like the towels still on the rails in the bathroom.

A scuffle caught his attention, probably rats in the walls. He wouldn't be surprised to find birds in the attic. Or bats. There had been bats when he'd been shut up there, in that dark empty space. *You can sit here until you've learned your lesson.*

"Someone's downstairs." Mei's voice was low, guarded.

"Rats, probably." Dan wasn't that worried.

She shook her head and pressed a finger to her lips. Dan signaled— he would go first—and then he pointed to the wood floor. He stepped to the top of the stairs, avoiding every creaky board. Same as they descended to the first floor. Muffled talking came from downstairs. *Thank You, Papa, the walls are thin.* They always had been, and it had driven him crazy when he lay awake at night listening to his father yelling and his mother crying.

Mei tapped his arm. Dan nodded. He had no intention of confronting anyone, though he wasn't about to let her go alone.

Mei crept to the stairs and started down. "Police! Freeze, both of you!"

There was a crash and then the sound of feet running. Dan headed down and caught up in time to see Mei disappear through the tunnel. He raced after her and the punishing pace she set. There was no let up, not until she reached the opening where they'd found Dan's mother. Mei stood with her hands on her knees, her head forward. "Lost them."

"They went different ways?"

She nodded. "Couldn't tell which was in charge, but they were both fast."

There were more than two tunnels here. His mom had been removed so that he could set about burying her. "Two guys?"

"Spindly. Young, probably. Still kinda teenage-lanky."

"I know them." Dan gave her their names, and the houses where they lived. One was the kid's mom's address. "If they've been dragged in, it isn't like Xander was. They probably volunteered, figured it would be more exciting than their lives. I can see that. Part of something big, so they might get noticed."

Mei said, "I'll go talk to the mom and confirm, add them to John's list of those involved. Then I'll find them."

"In there?" Dan motioned to the tunnels that branched off from where they stood. "It has to be a maze."

"There must be a way out, maybe to the woods. That might be how they got in, whatever they were doing in your basement. But one of these tunnels leads through the mountains out of Sanctuary. Your dad used it; it has to be there."

His breath still came fast, and now he was going to have to go all the way back to his house. "I can hardly even comprehend the idea that there's a way out of Sanctuary. All this time, the 'safe, secure town of Sanctuary' was wide open for someone to make their way here. My dad conducted illegal business out of the house. He breached the security of this town, how many times?" He sucked in a breath. "And for money? Where is it?"

Mei nodded. "I have someone looking for it. Do you remember Remy? She used to live here. And I am going to pass that information to you when I find out. It's technically yours, as his only living dependent. Though it's ill-gotten gains. I'll have to ask about the legalities, but I'm sure we can work something out."

Dan didn't know where to start. Why would he need money when he had no expenses? The business paid for itself. But what if he had a brother or sister out in the world? Maybe

Mei could find that out. They would be much older, but Dan would like to know. He could have family. Good or bad, they'd been related, but maybe they'd be good. Another gift from God.

He'd have to talk to Gemma about that idea. If she would listen to him, or even let him talk. When she didn't want to, she absolutely would not, and there was no changing her mind.

Help us, Papa. Don't let a stupid misunderstanding ruin what's between us. He still intended to get that ring. Dan had thought about giving her his mother's ring, but he didn't want anything that his dad had touched. This wasn't about the past, it was about who they were together and the future they could build.

"What now?"

Mei walked to each tunnel in turn, then went back to the second one. She stuck her head in and sniffed. "This one smells like fresh air."

"Let's try it." If it led to the woods they'd still have to make their way back to the farm, but Dan didn't want to walk that dark tunnel again. And he didn't want to stay in his mom's grave any longer.

**

The fifth time John shifted in bed Andra said, "What's wrong?"

"Sorry. I'll let you rest and sleep on the couch." The baby—their son—was in a bassinette John's mom had sent them, in the corner of the room, sound asleep. Pat had never slept so much the first week of his life. Was this normal?

"I can hear the thoughts spiraling around in that head of yours from here."

John rolled over and shoved his face in the pillow. "Sorry."

"You keep saying that, but you have yet to do anything you actually need to apologize for."

John shifted to his side and faced his wife. "Did you figure out what to call him yet?"

"Anton."

"No."

"Ridge."

"Closer, but no."

Completely straight face, she said, "Frankfurt."

"No way."

"Jalapeno?"

"Funny." John sighed.

"How about Nicholas?"

"Nick?" He let the name roll off his tongue. "Nick Mason." John smiled. "I really like that one."

"Me too."

John leaned closer and spoke where their lips almost touched. "You could have said that one first."

Andra grinned. "Go to sleep."

He couldn't. Too much was happening in Sanctuary. "I'm close." John could practically grasp it in his fingers, almost like the answer to this riddle was a tangible thing.

"If you rest and let your subconscious work on it you might wake up with the answer. Have you thought of that?"

John sighed. "It has to be about the mayor. There's no other explanation. But what? What is he planning, what is going on? It's like he's cultivating an army, but for what?"

He hated that Antonia had been killed because of this—because of him. John could hardly stomach the responsibility he had for it, and he hadn't been able to talk to Olympia since she first found out. Antonia had been a wild girl, determined to push the envelope. Her mom was right about that, and she said she didn't blame him, but it didn't matter. He blamed himself.

He'd told the girl to tread carefully, but she hadn't wanted to go slow. John had considered the fact she might have gone too far and gotten all the way caught up in it. He'd seen it happen undercover. He'd even thought about it himself, in darker moments. Taking the money, ditching the job. Leaving the light and falling into darkness.

He figured that was what had happened to his brother Ben. Too many times he'd fallen into black for, and now he couldn't find his way back. Now he insisted on this ridiculous distance. The go-betweens. Greeting cards instead of phone calls. Half-answers instead of real information. John sighed. Was he ever going to break through with his brother? It would take something huge. That was for sure.

Ben.

Antonia.

Mei.

The mayor.

John ran his hands down his face. Then he prayed.

He didn't know how long he slept, but he woke up to a ringing sound coming from his charging iPad.

John barely lifted his head off the pillow, flipped the cover back, and swiped to answer. "Yeah."

"I can't see you." Grant. Why did his brother call so early?

"What time is it?" His voice was muffled by the pillow, but he wasn't about to move.

"Just after four, mountain time. Breakfast awaits, dude. Wake up."

"Maybe on the east coast. We're supposed to sleep when the baby sleeps. Didn't you know that?"

Andra shoved at his back with her palms. "Speak for yourself. Which one of us got up twice during the night?"

John left the bed and took his iPad into the kitchen. He punched the button on the coffee he'd prepared the night before, and hung his head.

"Where's your ugly mug?"

John glanced up. Humor before coffee was never a good plan.

"You're going to want to sit down."

John sighed. "That good, huh? And here I thought this was a social call. A, 'hey, John, how's your wife and new baby? That growing family of yours.'"

"You're still not sitting."

"I know."

Grant shrugged. "You're the one who chose to live there. Don't know how you stomach some of those people. Or how you babysit them all."

"They're an acquired taste. And if I recall correctly, it was your idea. You said it would be *good* for me." John sat at the table. "So, I'm thinking you're on FaceTime because of… the mayor?"

Grant smiled, more of a grimace really. "However did you know that?"

"Wild guess."

"Last night Samuel Collins filed a motion with the committee that oversees the town of Sanctuary. For several reasons, which he explained in an incredible amount of detail, he's putting forth the request that you be removed from your duties as sheriff of the town of Sanctuary. For good."

"He wants me fired?"

"It's unprecedented. There isn't even any legal basis for this. There's no legal basis in Sanctuary for anything. It's more like a sovereign state at this point, since you're out from under the Marshals service and the federal government. He wants you gone, says the town is going to govern itself. That's the proposal he's making."

"On the basis of what?" The fact he was kind-of on leave with a new baby couldn't be coincidental. Nor could anything else that had been going on in town. This wasn't the time to remove the sheriff from his position. There would be anarchy at worst, and complete chaos at best.

Grant lifted a paper and read, "You hired a deputy he claims is unsuitable. And he actually has good reasons—stuff we didn't know that I have no idea how he got his hands on, but I'll be talking to Ben about. Evidently you give certain people preference over others. You haven't found Antonia's killer. You let Ben go after he assaulted Collins, and you never followed up on the case."

"He never went to the doctor, and he didn't tell me until he was fine, and the man wants me to investigate an assault, base on nothing but his word against Ben's?"

Grant shook his head. "He also says crime has gone way up since you came. Something about how the previous sheriff kept the stats low, so you must be responsible for the outbreak in lawlessness."

John got up and poured his coffee. This was insane. The previous sheriff's record hadn't been stellar, more like nonexistent. Chandler had left town when he'd been diagnosed with terminal cancer. John hadn't heard much since he arrived, but the word he got was that the man wasn't well liked. Now that Gemma had told him how Chandler had overlooked Dan's being abused, he knew all he needed to know about the man.

"You can't ignore this," Grant spoke louder. "You can't bury it, or brush it under the rug."

John strode back to the table, set one hand on the surface, and leaned closer to the iPad. "You think I'm going to do that? The mayor needs to be dealt with."

"According to what he found on Mei, he's probably waiting for you to hire her to kill him. Or Ben will have her do it."

John shook his head. "I knew Ben had something to do with her being here. I asked him about it, but he gave me half a muffled answer and hung up. If he ever shows up here again I'm going to have to arrest him. I figured that's why he sent Mei in his place."

"I can't ignore this, John." Grant waved the paper. "I have to address each part, look into it, and probably conduct an investigation—"

The baby started to cry. John walked away, in the middle of Grant talking, and went to the crib. Andra sat up, so he waved her off. "Go back to sleep." She nodded, not even half awake. John gathered up the baby. "Good morning, Nicholas." He trailed back to the iPad, where Grant was still talking, and sat.

Grant's voice trailed off. "He's so tiny." Grant paused. "I don't think my girls were ever that small."

"That's because they're driving and going to college." John rubbed the baby's back. "Nicholas will be taller than them some day."

Grant smiled. "Good name."

"Give me some time on this. Let me talk to the mayor."

"I don't think—"

"Please," John said. "Something is going on, and I just need a couple more days to figure out what it is. Antonia is dead because of this. Xander saw someone try to kill Sam Tura. Things aren't normal in this town."

Normal was relative in Sanctuary, but still. Nothing was right.

"Two days. I can probably put the mayor off for that long. Then I'll have to tell him something."

John nodded. "Thanks, Grant."

"Don't thank me yet."

**

Gemma lay on her couch and tried to focus on the show. She'd been in the same spot all day, dawn to" —she looked at the window— "dusk now, doing nothing. She'd also been ignoring calls from Dan's extension. What was there to say? The two of them might have done a lot of life together, but they were in different places. Going different directions. *It's not You, God, it's me.* Her life was a cliché.

This was supposed to be a funny show, but mid-season four, it had taken a turn. Now it wasn't comedy, and there was way too much death. Gemma pulled up her TV guide and found a cartoon. It took a minute to load, but eventually that super annoying theme tune started, and she watched Pinkie Pie prance across the screen.

Much better.

Who wanted real life, when magical ones with guaranteed happy endings were so much better? If God could assure her that things on His team would be good, well she'd jump at the chance. Who wouldn't if they knew things were guaranteed to be golden? But alas, her dream was not to be. God wasn't going to promise her everything would be fine. People were way too unpredictable for that. And yeah, He knew the future and all, but why share the knowledge? They would only mess with what should have been just for kicks. Humans were mostly just about getting their kicks.

Except Dan.

As far as she could see, becoming a Christian hadn't made John Mason's life better. Or Nadia's. They'd still been through some crazy stuff. Sure, they each walked around with ridiculous grins that matched their other half's smiles, but what did that mean? Anyone could paste on a happy face.

Boy, Fluttershy was super annoying. She talked like Mei. Low, soft enough you had to strain to hear her. Fluttershy was probably a closet spy, too. Or at least some kind of off-books black ops agent on the side. That was totally plausible. Ish.

Gemma got up. She needed a change of scenery—or at least some popcorn—before she died of lonely, sad-and-single disease. It wasn't pretty, and there was an odor. She brought her notepad back to the couch with her because that wasn't a bad book idea. Melodramatic spinster. Cute doctor. He could diagnose himself with a broken heart, and hand her the prescription—with her name on it.

It wasn't Cherry Coke, but it would do for a short story at least.

The phone rang. Stopped. Rang again. Persistent, whoever they were.

It rang again.

Gemma blew out a breath and grabbed the handset without looking at the display. She lay all the way back on her couch to stretch the chord as far as it would go. "Yeah?"

She didn't really want to talk to Dan. But if she waited too long, then when they did, she would just give in. At least this way the good reasons why it wouldn't work were fresh in her mind.

"Gem."

"Mom?"

Janice made the *juh* sound of Gemma's name, as though she were trying to say it again. And then all Gemma heard was gurgling.

Gemma threw the phone aside and shot up. Halfway there she realized she had no shoes, but she didn't stop. Didn't go back. Main Street, then B Street. Why did her mom live so far away?

Gemma smelled the smoke before she turned onto her mom's street. Before she even saw the house. People emerged from neighboring homes. Gawkers. Gemma shoved them aside and ran toward the yellow glow in the night. The rising column that filled the air.

Her mom's house was on fire.

Chapter 20

Matthias exited the house, carrying Gemma's mom in his arms. He walked two houses down and deposited her on the lawn.

Gemma collapsed by her side. "Mom." She touched her face, surveyed her mom's prone form. Rumpled. Red marks on her wrists. "Mom, can you hear me?"

Her mom's eyes fluttered and opened. "Gem."

Relief flooded her. Gemma sat back on her heels. "Thank God."

Firefighters, residents who volunteered to serve the town that way, ran into the house. Matthias followed the line of her gaze and then said, "Doesn't look bad. I don't think it'll take long for them to put it out, but your mom's house is toast. These old buildings go up like a match."

A crowd had gathered in the street. People watching the drama because there was nothing on TV like the kind of drama that happened in real life—to someone else.

Someone dumped a red bag beside him. Matthias pulled out supplies, including an oxygen mask which he tucked on her mom's face. He checked her vitals with proficiency and no hesitation.

Gemma said, "You're good at that."

He ripped the Velcro of the blood pressure cuff and said, "Competent, maybe. Medical care in this town isn't guaranteed, and Frannie and I talked about it. We decided that since we were going to be parents I'd learn some basic stuff. Pediatric CPR, minor burns, wounds, that kind of thing. It was John's idea that I join up with the fire department."

"Good for you."

Matthias shrugged. "This town is what it is, but it's also our home. If we're not working to make it better then it won't ever be better."

"Makes sense." And yet she'd decided leaving was better. Or maybe easier. That wasn't the way to repair what was wrong with Sanctuary. "Have you thought about being the next mayor?"

He opened his mouth, but Janice let out a low moan. "Mayor."

Gemma leaned close to her mom's face. "Did he do this to you? Did the mayor set fire to your house?"

Janice frowned. "No. He… not do that."

"Okay."

"Friend."

Gemma said, "The mayor is your friend."

Janice shut her eyes and nodded her head slightly.

"He's not a good guy, Mom. He's done a lot of horrible things, or at least organized them and set them in motion." He had to be the one behind it, it didn't make sense that anyone else would be. Not when the mayor was so vocal, so dead-set against the direction the town was taking. "Did you see who set fire to your house, Mom?"

Janice opened her eyes. She seemed to rally for a second, then her chest fell.

"Be careful you don't make her strain herself. She needs to rest."

Gemma nodded, her gaze still on her mom's face. Janice opened her eyes. "I saw them."

"Who was it?" Gemma leaned closer.

"Two."

"There were two of them?" When Janice nodded, Gemma said, "Did you see who it was?"

"Masks. But man was tall. Like Dan."

"He didn't do it."

Janice said, "Or the sheriff."

"Because he's tall as well?"

Her mom nodded.

Gemma sat back. "Plenty of people in this town are tall."

Matthias nodded. "Just a couple more minutes here, Janice, and then we'll be ready to take you over to the medical center." He looked at Gemma. "I'm sure John will come and talk to her there, get a statement."

The first name off her mom's lips as to who had set fire to her house, and she said Dan? Her mom knew how she felt about him, and yet she still did that. Not that Gemma wanted her mom to be the kind of person who covered for a friend even when they were a criminal. But this wasn't a criminal, it was Dan.

"Matthias?" The voice was male, and crackly.

He grabbed his radio and clicked a button, held it to his mouth. "Yeah, John."

"Have you seen Dan?"

"He should be here, helping put out the fire. But I haven't seen him, just the others."

Gemma glanced around. Was the sheriff here? She scanned the crowd and saw John talking to the fire department's chief—not that you could really call him that when there was no fire house and no fire truck. Just the ranch truck, and some hoses half a step up from a garden hose. They didn't even have hydrants in Sanctuary. If a fire was bad enough, John could probably get a chopper from a neighboring county to drop water here. It had happened before with the old sheriff, years ago, and they'd covered the security breach so the person didn't blab there was a town over here.

Smoke would hang in the air for days before strong enough weather rolled through to empty the basin the town sat in. They needed a good storm, or the cloud cover would sit between the mountains like a blanket, and they'd be in an inversion until it was pushed out.

Fresh air. A breeze. Gemma glanced at the trees. *Thank You.* It was just like Him to clear the air like that.

The sheriff's voice came over the radio again. "Can you send Gemma over here?"

"I'll take care of your mom, Gem, don't worry. And I'll let you know when she gets to the medical center." Matthias motioned over his shoulder. "You go see what John wants, okay?"

Gemma stood. She wasn't fragile. A lot had happened over the past couple of weeks, but she hadn't broken down yet. Unless Dan had told his friends that she'd dissolved. Alone. With him.

John watched her make her way to him. The dark look on his face didn't bode well. "Gemma."

"Sheriff."

"Come with me."

Gemma followed him to her mom's front door, where he turned. "It's hot, but I want you to see this."

"The fire's out?"

He nodded and stepped inside. "It was all in one room—the dining room. Your mom was under the table. On top of the table, the fire had consumed a large quantity of papers that were used as kindling."

"Why was she under the table?"

"She was tied to one of the legs."

Gemma sucked in a breath laced with smoke. She coughed it out. "Tied?"

John walked straight to the dining room. The air was hot in there, and Gemma didn't want to stay. He motioned for her to step past the table and into the living room where papers had been laid on the carpet. "We pulled these out of the pile before the fire could get to them. I'd like to get your take."

Gemma crouched, already pretty sure what they were. But why would they be in her mom's dining room? She read one paper, moved it aside. The page was brittle, and even though she moved it as delicately as she could, it cracked under the pressure of her fingers. "These are papers from the radio station. I didn't read these specifically, but I did read one in this stack for sure."

John nodded. "Your mom is connected to this."

"She was a journalist in Vietnam and stumbled across a story. She was following Dan's dad, and he never saw her, but she knew who he was. It's how she met Hal." Gemma paused. "I can tell you the rest when we have more time."

"Let's go back outside."

Gemma led the way. Everything that happened just made it all even more confusing. What was she supposed to think now?

She stopped short, as she saw Dan walking toward her. Mei was right behind him. A curl of something nasty unfurled in her stomach. Had they been together?

"Hey."

Gemma couldn't smile, she just could not make her face do that right now. "Hi." She turned to the sheriff, but the huddle formed by itself, and Gemma found herself in between Dan and John, facing Mei.

The sheriff said, "Hal's papers were in the house. What I don't know is if they intended to kill Janice in the process of destroying the documents."

Dan set his hand on her shoulder and said, "She's okay, right?"

Gemma sucked in another breath. "She didn't have a good idea as to who did this." Matthias was gone from the spot where he'd set her mom. He must have taken her to the medical center already.

"I have two more names to add to the list."

Mei's words were clearly for the sheriff, but Gemma still asked, "Names for what?"

John said, "The list of people involved in this."

"With the mayor as the ringleader?" Gemma figured he would be, but had the mayor actually done anything bad yet?

"He's moving to have me removed as sheriff."

Mei snorted. "So he can be king of this tiny realm?"

"I guess." John stared at her. "I don't know what else he might have planned."

Gemma shook her head. "He can't just change the whole town because he feels like it."

Dan nodded. "Even if he does know about my father, and Hal, what does that give him?"

John folded his arms. "More information than the majority of the residents. Maybe he just thinks knowledge is power. Or, if he's not planning on blackmailing you with it" —Dan shook his head— "then he might use it to state his case with the committee."

"But why try to kill my mom? They got rid of Antonia and tried to kill Sam Tura. Terrence is wherever he disappeared to…" Mei shot her a weird look. Gemma didn't know what that was about. "Now Janice. People who are linked to them, or linked to Hal and Dan's father? Anyone who doesn't agree with them? I could totally see Sam Tura turning them down big-time."

Dan nodded. "The mayor tried to get me on board a couple of times, but I turned him down."

Gemma coughed out the lingering taste of smoke in her throat. "I should go check on my mom."

"Gem—"

"I'll see you later, Dan." Maybe while she was gone, he could spend some more time with his BFF, Mei.

**

Dan knew what John would say, so he didn't tell him where he was going. Mei had business. Gemma was at the medical center. He hadn't seen the mayor at all during the fire, while the rest of the town had been happy to come out to B Street and gawk at the event. Where was the mayor? Dan didn't really want to know what the man was up to, but there had to be a way to find out.

He lifted his fist and knocked on the mayor's front door.

It didn't take long, but it wasn't Collins who opened it. "Sal?"

The old Italian lifted his chin. "Pastor."

"The mayor in?" Dan needed to ask John if he had Sal Cordova on the list of the mayor's associates. People usually only called him "pastor" when they wanted to put distance between them. Which usually meant they felt guilty about something.

Sal stepped back and held the door open. Dan stepped inside. The mayor's house was considerably newer and twice as big as the rest of the town's residences. He'd heard the man paid for it himself. That was nice of him, to show everyone he had more money than them.

The inside was no different, though the cleaning lady hadn't been by in a while.

"Living room." Sal passed him in the hall and went to the back, where the kitchen was.

"Dan." The mayor sat on his couch, the lingering odor of a cigar in the air.

"Mind if I sit?"

"Suit yourself."

Dan was still covered in dirt from his farm, but he took a load off on the mayor's white suede couch. "Thank you. How are you, Collins?"

"Truth be told, Pastor, I'm taking Antonia's death hard."

"I'm sorry to hear that." That was what he was going with, grief? Dan didn't buy it one bit. The mayor had shown up right when Terrence had Gemma in that alley, and that had been only shortly after Antonia's death. He hadn't been grieving then, and Dan didn't buy it that the mayor hadn't known. The man probably ordered her death himself.

The mayor sighed. "The sheriff is too busy to find her killer. I find the man's work ethic questionable, and his ability to solve my wife's murder left me with no doubt he'd take his time solving Antonia's."

Dan listened to him rant longer. John had just had a baby, which meant he was completely at liberty to take a few days off. But he wasn't. Still, if Dan straight out said he agreed, Collins would never buy it. He had to go slow with this, introduce the idea of being sympathetic slowly so that Collins didn't get spooked.

The mayor nodded. "That's why I'm moving to have him removed from his position as sheriff."

"Really?" Dan couldn't over-sell his surprise even though John had told them about the mayor going to the committee. The mayor would be on his guard, watching Dan's reactions. "Who will replace him? Mei?"

The mayor snorted. "The Chinese girl is even less qualified than he is. I don't think she'll even be allowed to remain here as a resident after the sheriff is fired. Mei—whatever her last name is—will be another person on a list I've compiled whom I will be talking to the committee about. There are undesirable types in this town, and we cannot possibly have harmony if we allow them to remain."

Dan nodded slowly. "I understand wanting to clean up this town. It should be a place of harmony and cooperation."

"Oh, it will be."

"How can you be so sure? People are notoriously unpredictable. You can't expect them to simply fall in line with whatever you say." Dan paused. "And you are retiring as mayor, are you not?"

"The phase Sanctuary is moving into, we won't need a mayor. Maybe we won't even need a pastor." He sneered, which might have been meant to be a smile. It didn't work.

Dan had heard that before. People were fine, they didn't need religion. Dan didn't need religion, either—a set of rules to follow, and if they were completed righteousness could be obtained? He could never do it, and the reality was that no one on earth could because they were all flawed. Jesus was the only way any of them could have everything they needed to cope with this life, and the only way for hope of a life beyond it.

"The thing you need to be most concerned about is where you will fit in this new town. Will there be a place for you, or will you be one of those 'undesirables' who are removed."

"Was Antonia one of those?"

The mayor dredged up a sad look and shook his head. "Loss of life is never part of the plan. There has been too much death in this town already." His lips curled into a small smile. "As much as you can, live peaceably with all men. Isn't that right?"

Dan nodded. "It's from Romans. And I'm glad you feel that way, it's good to hear your intentions when there's so much conjecture flowing around town. People who dislike the way things are, pointing fingers at others, and blaming them for what is happening in town."

The mayor most of all. He'd hated John for a long time, probably since he showed up, but definitely since the mayor's wife was killed. The death had nothing to do with John, and he and Andra figured out who the killer was.

Then there was the other side, what he and his friends had been doing. They'd been quick to blame many things on the mayor, and mostly without cause. Before Dan came to this house he'd have wondered whether the mayor was going to do anything, but now it was clear. From what he'd said, it sounded like the man was planning a coup. Planning to take over the town—by force—and run out those he didn't think were worthy to live there.

"My father taught me many things," Dan said. It was going to be difficult to get the mayor to trust him without lying, but he had to find out details of what was going down. Antonia had died, and John would flip his lid if he found out Dan was putting himself in danger this way, but this was for Sanctuary.

His father's prison.

Their home.

"One of the things my father taught me, was that the town should be here to provide what we need. I don't think everyone feels that way. Some are simply… bottom-feeders who think Sanctuary, or witness protection, will provide them with the life they want." Dan chuckled. It sounded totally forced, but it was too late to back down now. "Sanctuary isn't here for them. It's here for those of us who want to see it succeed, who want to make it better."

"Exactly. And who will show them the error of their thinking?" The mayor motioned to Dan with his index finger. "I've long thought you should use that pulpit of yours for something more useful than talking about an old book. Stir people up! Help the town become better! There is so much you could do with the voice you have, Daniel. People trust you. They look to you for leadership."

"They do," Dan said. "And I think I need to consider ways I can utilize that to its maximum. Ways I can be on the ground, on the front lines, and really be effective." Dan was about to choke on his own baloney. He kept going anyway. "I've been thinking about your mayor position, but with what you said, I'm not sure that's the way to go now. You mentioned us not needing a mayor. Who will lead the town? I'd like to support whoever it is. To really come alongside them and encourage them as they take the reins." Dan lifted both fists in front of him for emphasis.

The mayor nodded slowly. "I think you might be a great resource, Daniel. Though in the past you've been misguided in terms of who you chose to impart your knowledge upon. Those you chose to help have been the less-fortunate, the ones struggling within the town. I can see how you would encourage them to make the most of their lives here, but we need a statement. I for one cannot live in a town where the sheriff allows people to be assaulted and lets the culprit go scot-free."

Dan nodded. "I'm so sorry that happened to you. Ben Mason is an unsavory character." That was enough of the truth he was able to sell it. "Anyone who commits a crime should pay the penalty and not go free because of any kind of nepotism. That's not right."

"It's good you think that. It will serve you well in the coming days."

"Days? So it won't be long, then?"

"Not long at all." The mayor's face lit up. "In fact, I got word just this morning that we will be moving to the next phase momentarily. It's going to be very exciting, and the new direction the town is taking will be undeniable."

"I see. Is there anything I can do to…prepare?"

"There is, actually." The mayor glanced once at the hallway, and then said, "You might want to think about keeping that deputy sheriff away from your house."

Chapter 21

Gemma sat beside her mom's bed. She still wore the oxygen mask, but she kept taking it off to talk. "It was for me."

Elliot hadn't given her anything but oxygen, but Janice sounded loopy anyway. "What was for you, Mom?"

"The music. Every song was mine. He played them all for me."

Shelby tapped lightly on the doorframe.

Gemma got up and went to her. "Is she okay? She's talking crazy."

Shelby glanced at the bed for a moment. "She had a traumatic experience. It could be she's still in shock, and she's processing what happened to her."

"By talking crazy?"

Shelby set her hand on Gemma's shoulder. "Allow her mind to work through this. To run its course so she can get to a place of peace and healing."

“Okay.” Gemma ran her fingers through her hair and tried to shake off the feeling, but it didn’t help. What was Dan doing now? He’d left the scene of the fire so fast she hadn’t been able to ask him where he was going. And why was it any of her business? They were broken up.

Her head was a mess. She wanted him with her, but she didn’t want to talk to him. She wanted to know where he was, mostly so she could make sure he felt as miserable as she did. He hadn’t looked like he was having a bad day. At least no more than usual. And what had he been doing with Mei anyway?

“Are you okay?”

Gemma shot her friend a look. “No. I’m really not.” She took a step back because she didn’t want to talk about it. “I’m going to sit with my mom some more.”

Shelby might have stood there for a minute, watching, but Gemma didn’t check. She sat where she couldn’t see the door and held her mom’s hand. “I’m sorry I moved out. I should have stayed.”

Since she’d been gone her mom had lost Hal, and now she’d been hurt in her home, tied under a table that was set on fire. Gemma should never have left, but she’d been so excited to get out on her own. It had taken years to decide she needed her own space. She’d never needed it before, and she’d been happy in her mom’s house. They’d both had their own lives, but Gemma felt like they should stick together. Then suddenly it was just time. Things were quiet, and Gemma had wanted her own home that she could put her personal stamp on.

Days later Hal was dead. Her mom was devastated, and Gemma still hadn’t unpacked all of her boxes.

She took her mom’s hand. “I think maybe I should move back in.”

Janice blinked. "That would be nice. I miss you."

"I miss you, too." Gemma studied her mom's face. The lines and creases. Had she always looked so old, or had the last few weeks of being so alone aged her? Janice had always been so active, working outside on Dan's farm. After retirement she'd helped out around town, and even helped Gemma landscape the library. Her mom had a healthy tan all the time and often smelled like dirt.

"I miss Hal."

"Tell me about him."

Janice smiled. "He loved me. But no one could know, no one could ever find out. Bill would know that Hal had a daughter. We were too much of a risk."

And yet he kept them both close. Her parents had spent years apart, never being a real family. She couldn't imagine what that would feel like now. All so a madman-murder never found out Hal had a weakness.

So instead of them, Bill Jones had simply tormented his own family. He'd tormented Dan.

Gemma sighed. "I know all this, Mom. Tell me what Hal was like. The good stuff."

"Every song he played on the radio was for me. Every flower I planted was for him. I wanted to write notes, but he didn't allow it. I wanted to go to the woods for the weekend, but he said it was too risky. He watched, he reported. He kept track of the CIA agents they brought down, and they were looking for us. A couple died. Cancer, a car accident. The rest never found us, though we'd get word every once in a while that they'd asked around. But none of them ever made a move on Sanctuary."

"Thank you for helping to keep us safe, Mom. I know what it feels like not having what you want. To have to watch other people have it while you stay on the sidelines in your own life. If he was here, I'd want to thank Hal, too."

Janice nodded. "You always were a good girl. Hal said that."

Gemma smiled. She squeezed her mom's hand.

"Bill said the same thing."

Gemma froze. She didn't want to talk about this.

But her mom continued, "I tried to look in his eyes, to figure out what he was talking about, but I couldn't read it. I thought he might have worked it out, that you were Hal's daughter. He never met me in Vietnam, and Hal and I were never together in town except in secret. But maybe he'd figured it out."

Gemma clenched her stomach. "He shoved me against a wall. Pushed me around, said horrible things. But that was it." It had taken her this long, and the perspective of an adult, to be able to say that. As a child she'd been traumatized. He'd seemed so much bigger than her.

"All because you stood up for Dan?"

Gemma nodded. She'd had good intentions, and God had saved her from something that could have been so much more horrific. But she'd never told Dan about it, and she wasn't going to. It wouldn't help.

"You aren't okay, are you?" Her mom started to cry.

Gemma didn't know how to answer the question. Dan had always been the one who wasn't okay. Was she allowed to not be okay as well? They couldn't both be messed up, and yet somehow they always had been. Not much in their lives had been right. It was why Gemma had asked him if he wanted to leave town. Wouldn't a clean slate, a new life, be better than what they had to live with here?

"I knew it," Janice said. "I went to talk to him, to find out what he'd done. When I saw his face, then I knew. Dan's mom made this squeaky noise, and I looked over at her. She knew as well, and a month later she was gone. I think you were the catalyst in her coming to Hal." Janice sniffed and a tear rolled down her face. "I'm sorry. I was with him that night, and I should never have left you."

"You couldn't be with me every second, Mom."

"But I wasn't there when you needed me." Janice squeezed her hand. "You've always been so strong. You never told anyone. I was so scared he'd done the worst thing, and I confronted him. He yelled at me until I spit it out, and then he punched and kicked me for interfering. Said you were a nosy little girl who got what she deserved." Her mom sucked in a choppy breath. "So I talked to Hal, and we decided that we'd take care of it."

"How?"

Gemma hadn't asked the question, though she'd been about to. She spun around.

Mei stood in the doorway. "How did you take care of it, Janice?"

Gemma didn't want her here. This was none of her business. And how long had she been listening, anyway?

Mei stood there until Janice spoke. "I told Hal. Maybe I shouldn't have, but I don't regret it."

"Did Hal poison Bill Jones?"

"He died of heart failure. Years later."

Mei shrugged. "Plenty of things can mimic heart failure, and an autopsy was never done. You yourself had access to herbs. Plants that can be used to heal, or kill."

Gemma stood. "Mei—"

Janice said, "He never told me if it was him or not, but I saw what it did to him knowing Bill had done something to Gemma. He waited years, but he couldn't stomach that man anymore. Arnold Walden. Bill Jones. Whoever he was, he had killed all the fight Hal had left. He wouldn't forgive himself. I think he wanted revenge."

Mei nodded. "Hal killed Dan's father. It's what I would have done." She glanced between them. "Some people are strong, but that strength has to be protected because it's a precious thing and its breakable. People like me, people like Hal, we don't need as much protecting. We're the line of defense for people like Gemma and Dan."

Right when Mei said her name, Gemma stood. She gritted her teeth together. "Outside. Now."

Mei shrugged and then followed her into the hall. Gemma spun. "You had no right to butt into that conversation. It was none of your business."

"You don't have to be embarrassed, and you don't have to hold onto that pain in silence."

"I'm not in pain, okay? But that doesn't mean I want to talk about it with you."

Mei shrugged. "Fine. We won't talk about Dan's dad, and we won't talk about Terrence."

"I cannot believe you asked her if she poisoned Dan's dad. My mom isn't a murderer." Mei was right, she didn't want to talk about Terrence. She just wanted Mei to find him already.

"Anyone is capable of killing if the right situation presents itself."

"I don't believe that." Gemma shook her head. "At least not without it destroying some part of themselves."

Mei's eyes flickered. "There isn't one person in this world who doesn't lose a bit of their soul when they kill another person. Taking a life is not free, and sometimes the price can be heavier than you want to pay."

"Am I supposed to know what you're talking about?" Gemma didn't even want to process Mei's words. She'd killed someone? That was the only way she'd know what she was talking about.

"Didn't you want Terrence to be dead after what he did to you?"

Gemma didn't answer.

"What if he'd done that to Shelby?"

Gemma rubbed her thumb on the inside of her left arm, where Terrence had marked her. Not in the same way Dan had done to the other arm, not the same at all. "I'd hate him if he did that to Shelby. Probably about as much as I do right now." She watched Mei's face as she spoke. "What did you do?"

"Terrence is alive. But you need someone to do what you're not capable of doing. And that's a good thing, Gemma. The world doesn't need more people like me, it needs more people like you."

Gemma didn't speak for a minute, then she said, "Don't speak to my mom again."

"Okay."

She thought there might have been a sad note in Mei's eyes, but it disappeared. "She's in a vulnerable place. I don't want you pushing her."

Mei said, "Where will you be?"

"I don't know." Why did Mei care where she was going now?

"Don't go to Dan. I don't think he needs to know that Hal killed his father. It probably won't help." Mei paused. "Besides, it isn't more than hearsay at best. None of it can be proved."

She didn't want Gemma to go to Dan? "You aren't the one who gets to decide what he knows and doesn't know."

"And you being forthright with him about everything but what his father did to you, isn't helping. He has enough on his plate without you adding stuff to it."

"What is that supposed to mean?"

"Just that you should give him some time, Gemma." Mei huffed. "I'm not good at this, so I don't really know how to explain it, but you should just be careful. Maybe wait until things in town are calmer."

"You're unbelievable." Gemma turned and started walking away.

"I told you I'm no good at this," Mei called after her. "I don't have many friends, Gemma. I don't know how it works."

Gemma glanced over her shoulder and delivered her parting blow. "We aren't friends."

She didn't wait around to see what Mei's reaction was. It wasn't like the woman would cry.

**

"Come on."

Dan walked faster to keep up with the two guys in ski masks. His itched, and he did not like walking around town dressed in black with his face covered, but the mayor had insisted.

Dan and the two men ran through the back streets of town keeping to the shadows. "So where are we headed?"

"The mayor said this was a test. Not supposed to tell you where we're going, but it's going to be good." He grinned. "The time has come to make a big splash and let the whole town know we mean business."

The man beside him laughed. Dan followed them to the library. Instead of skirting the building the first man stopped by the back door and pulled out a key.

"It's a shame we weren't allowed to smash a window. That might have been fun."

"This operation is at the library?"

The two men ignored Dan's question and went inside. "You find the door, I'm going to look around," the first man said to his buddy.

Dan followed them in and closed the door as quietly as he could behind him.

One of the men looked back and snickered. "No one's going to know we're here. Everyone in town is hiding at home so they don't get murdered like Antonia."

Dan said, "Don't forget Sam Tura. He was nearly killed as well." The gym and diner owner was recovering under armed guard—two of Frannie's old-man buddies apparently.

The second man put his arm around Dan's shoulder and pulled him deeper inside the Library. "Don't worry about Phil he's a conspiracy theory nut, and he wants to sensationalize every darn thing. He has all the classified documents from the moon landing. But you don't want to listen to his two hour speech about how it was all a hoax."

Dan just nodded, for want of something better to do.

Then he was shoved further toward the bookshelves. "You're the lookout, farmer-Dan. We have work to do."

Dan had been right. These two men weren't in this because they thought it would make Sanctuary better. They were on a power trip, and it was the ride of their lives.

They thought Dan would what, read a book, while they did whatever they had planned? Yeah right. This might be small in the grand plan the mayor had going on, given they weren't likely to test him on something big, but it was all information he could pass on to John and Mei.

Dan sat at a computer, tempted to fire it up and play a worship song from YouTube. They didn't buy his sudden allegiance to their side, but that didn't matter. It wasn't a fool proof plan because Dan was a farmer and not a professional whatever-they-were. Secret agent wannabes. Those skills weren't in his arsenal.

So Dan employed the weapons he did have and bowed his head

Snickers came from the other side of the large room, and then feet pounded downstairs. Minutes later there was a hum in the air and the computer turned off. Make that *all* of the computers turned off. Dan moved to the nearest light switch. Okay, that worked at least. All the power wasn't out.

"Turn the light off!"

"What did you guys do?"

They trotted up some stairs and through a door Dan was pretty sure hadn't been there before. Both men had grins on their faces. The first one into the room said, "Shut off the internet and the computers. It'll look like a brown-out."

Phil brought up the rear, still grinning. "No contact with the outside world."

His friend slapped him on the chest with the back of his hand.

Dan said, "Did you shut off internet to everything, or just the computers in here?"

Phil's friend frowned. "This is everything."

"The sheriff has an iPad. And he and Mei have satellite phones that call out of town."

Both men blinked. They hadn't known about the iPad at least. Phil rushed to say, "I bet the mayor knows. I bet he has a plan."

"Yeah, he has a plan."

Dan stared at them both.

"Now for the fun part." Phil raised his eyebrows. It was entirely disturbing.

"What?" Dan was just eager to go.

The other man strode to the bookshelves and swept the whole row onto the floor. "How about we make a pile and set fire to it?"

Phil strode to him. "Great idea."

There was no way he was going to let them do that, but how did he derail their plan without letting them know that was exactly what he was doing? "Uh, we might not have time—"

The front door handle rattled, and they all turned to look. Gemma was here and if she looked up, she'd see them all. It was dark, maybe they'd be obscured, but she would be able to see them.

A key turned in the lock. "Hide." But neither man moved, so Dan whispered as loud as he could, "Let's go!"

The lights flashed on.

Their boots pounded the carpet as they beat feet to the back door. Dan pumped his arms and legs, in danger of getting left behind by these two younger men.

"Who's there?" Gemma ran in their direction.

The two guys raced out into the night. Dan stopped to look back. He didn't want to. Would she know it was him under the mask? He wanted to pray she didn't recognize him, but he couldn't bring himself to think those words. God had asked for honesty as long as Dan had known Him—that was how their relationship worked. He wasn't about to start with deceit now.

She stopped short at the door. Her eyes widened. He saw the breath, the flash of recognition. "Dan."

He kept his voice low. "You got here right in time. I wasn't going to let them destroy any of the books, or your things, but they went in the basement and shut off the internet."

"I'll tell John."

Hopefully those two guys had run off and weren't listening to what Dan and Gemma were saying. Otherwise they'd probably tell the mayor, and Dan would end up at the lake with a bullet in his head. John would never forgive himself.

Gemma frowned. "Why are you here? Why break into my library?"

"To shut off the internet, apparently." Didn't he just say that? "I think it's another piece of this puzzle, like everything."

"That's not what I meant."

He didn't want to talk about the last conversation they'd had here. He wasn't ready to think about leaving Sanctuary. Not when so much was happening. "I'm not talking about us. I'm not even sure there is an 'us.'" It was a low blow, but if they were watching, then Dan had to make sure they saw what he needed them to see.

She stepped closer, but Dan shook his head. "I'm going to figure out this 'mayor' thing for John."

"Why you?"

"I live in this town, just like everyone else. I want to help, so I figured out a way to do that."

Gemma's gaze hardened. "Then why isn't everyone else helping? Why is it you that has to do it?" Her eyes were wet.

Dan could hardly look at them, or he'd want to hug her. She said, "Did Mei tell you to do this?"

"Don't worry about Mei." She flinched, but he continued, "You need to let me do this, Gemma. I already found out they're making a move soon."

"A move to what?"

"I don't know. Yet. But I'm going to find out." Dan needed her to understand. "I think it has to do with cutting off the town from the outside world, and I think they started with this."

"Disconnecting the internet?" When he nodded, she said, "That would be a good first move if they want everyone in town under their thumb."

"If that's the plan, it's a good one. A coup."

"But the mayor is quitting. Who will be in charge?"

Dan said, "That's a really good question I'm going to find out the answer to."

Gemma blew out a breath. "So what now?"

Someone shuffled behind the trees. They were probably watching, still testing him. Trying to find out if he was trustworthy. "I have to go. And I have to make it look good."

He closed in then, and backed her against the wall with one hand just below her throat. "Act like you're scared."

Gemma lifted her chin. "I could never be scared of you."

"Then act like I'm a bad guy."

"I don't think that would ever be convincing."

"Thanks for your faith in me." He pushed off her, turned and started walking away and called out, "Then quit stalking me, woman. It's getting old."

"Dan!" She called his name like she was distraught. Like he'd just told her he was leaving to be with another woman.

He strode to the trees. Before he reached it, a voice said, "She recognized you?"

"Yeah." He raised his own so they could hear. "Thinks she can claim me. Like I'd be seen with her."

Chapter 22

Gemma pulled her fist back, twisted her hips, and slammed her knuckles into the heavy bag. She pounded it again and again until her shirt clung to her back with sweat. If Dan wanted to put his life in danger for this stupid town who was she to stop him? Sure, he was probably going to pray through the whole thing and wind up fine, while Antonia had gotten killed for her trouble, but he would still be in danger every second.

Mentally she knew one person was not more valuable to God than another person. Intellectually, she got the point. And it wasn't like God had favored Dan's life all that much. It would never have gone the way it had with his father if God did that kind of thing. Dan told her about his "blessings," but it wasn't like God had saved either of them from his father.

Gemma stepped back and did her roundhouse kick over and over for thirty seconds. Then the other leg.

This was probably all because she'd pushed him. She did want to leave Sanctuary, and Gemma wasn't going to deny it. She was an artist. She wanted to travel, to find a place in the world that was *hers* and not just the home that had been given to her. Plenty of people left the town they'd grown up in to search for their own path. Why should she be denied that opportunity?

Dan wasn't punishing her, but he was trying to save a town Gemma was beginning to care less and less about. She had found some good things here, but most of those involved Dan so it was logical to ask him to come with her. If he wanted to get married that meant they needed to share each other's dreams. Why not travel together? Except that it would exclude them from being able to come back to Sanctuary.

Why did the government have to put them in this position in the first place? She'd have left years ago had the previous sheriff, Chandler, not denied her the chance. Now she was way too wrapped up in Dan to contemplate going anywhere that he wasn't there. Or to go on any journey when he wasn't with her.

Just the thought of leaving this place made her feel free, where Sanctuary had genuinely become her prison. Dan's father might have been the only convict in this town, but they were all inmates. Denied the ability to go where they wanted, to do what they wanted. Conditions. Rules. She was just completely stuck here, and she wanted nothing more than—for once in her life—to know she was free. To feel it the way she'd never been able to feel it before.

She might just have to take up skydiving while she was on the journey.

Gemma alternated sides until her left leg dropped, and she couldn't do any more.

"I'm tired just watching you."

She spun to find John in the middle of the gym. "Now you know how we all feel when you guys do those ridiculous strength competitions at the park, and try to one-up each other."

John grinned for a second, but then his "sheriff" face came back. "You know this is a crime scene."

"My house was a crime scene. The library is a crime scene. The lake. Is there anywhere I can go in this town and be by myself that isn't a crime scene?"

"Good point."

She motioned toward the office. "I'm pretty sure the crime scene is in there, anyway. And if I'd wanted to contaminate it, I'd have done that when I found Sam in the first place."

"I took a look at the library. You were right, they knew exactly what they were doing. Internet for the whole town is down."

"You're going to have a whole lot of crabby people on your hands."

"I'll deal with it. At least the satellite TV still works." He sighed. "I should get back to the sheriff's office soon. I don't know where Mei is, and people are going to show up since the town's internal phones are down, too."

Gemma sighed and unwrapped her hands, tossing the material on the edge of the ring. "Who is guarding Sam Tura?"

"Michael and Louis. I sent an update email to the committee, but I don't know if it went through at this point. I have to be real careful who I'm trusting. Dan saw Sal at the mayor's house, a man who went through the destruction of Bolton's house with Beth and Remy. I'd never have thought he would sell out to the mayor's grand plan."

Gemma liked fictional worlds and the interaction she had with the townspeople at the library. She wasn't trained for this cloak and dagger stuff, and she didn't have the first clue how to be some kind of covert agent. Neither did Dan. A farmer and a pastor and he was out there, playing undercover agent.

"This is all your fault."

John blanched.

"He only got the idea for this because of Antonia. You didn't see how he reacted when we found her. Dan can't handle this." She didn't like the fact her friend wasn't all the way mentally stable—who was?—but she was a realist. "You could have let anyone else do this, but you didn't. You swung him out there the same way you let Antonia swing."

"That isn't fair, Gemma. Dan did this of his own accord. Antonia knew what she was going into, and she thought it was worth the money and the chance to leave. I explained the risks to her so many times she could recite them back to me, and she trained with Sam Tura. She was as prepared as I could have made her. Now Aaron's taken my iPad for some reason. He knows he's not supposed to play with it, and usually he's good about that. I think he was coerced into it because he's vulnerable."

Aaron might be a young adult, but he was special needs. And though he'd thrived since he moved in with John, Andra, and Pat, he was still susceptible. There were people in town who would take advantage of that.

"Your list of the mayor's associates?" When John nodded, she said, "Does it include Phil and Matt?"

"Yes."

"You might want to add Dan's name to that list now."

He already knew, but she was mad enough at him that she needed to say it.

He'd made it sound like she was the last person he'd want to be seen with. Dan's parting words might have been a lie she hadn't known he was capable of speaking, but they still stung. Gemma shouldn't have been surprised it was an act. No one was good all the way through. Everyone had that seed of darkness inside them, some just chose to hide it less than others.

John ran his hand through his hair. "I didn't want him risking his life, but I also can't stop him. Believe it or not, he can handle himself. He's trained with me."

As if that was going to protect him against a gunshot like the one that had killed Antonia.

"Maybe you should figure out how to stop him," Gemma said. "He's not being smart. This is dangerous, and it's like he just doesn't care that people care about him." Her breath hadn't slowed from the workout, still coming too fast for her to try and calm down. If he got killed, what was she going to?

Gemma hung her head and tried to get enough air. She didn't want to leave if Dan wasn't going with her. How would she even do that when she needed his help to navigate the outside world? She needed him to be with her, to hold her hand. Ugh. Gemma didn't like being needy and helpless, but apparently she just was. Somehow she was going to have to find strength to do this.

"I'll talk to him," John said. "But I'm not going to tell you not to worry."

What good was that? She was freaking out here!

John stepped closer. "What would Dan do? What would he tell you to do?"

He'd tell her to pray. Of course he would. Gemma shot him a look. John grinned. "So let's pray." He set his hand on her shoulder. "Ready?"

Gemma nodded. As John prayed, she said her own in her head. She needed God's help to do what she wanted to do but didn't think she had the strength for. When John said, "Amen" she did the same aloud and then lifted her head. "I want to leave Sanctuary, and I want you to start the paperwork right away."

"Gemma—"

"I tried to leave years ago, but I wasn't given a chance that should have been mine."

"You'd have left forever?"

"I wanted out of here. Dan or not, I didn't want to be with these people. But Sheriff Chandler, either never filled out the paperwork and just lied to me, or he did and something happened. At first he told me to stop asking him about it, but then he just straight up told me my application had been denied."

It had hurt so much to even say that she wanted to go, but it had hurt more to stay and never get that opportunity to see the world. Dan would have understood. Eventually.

John frowned. "Can I look into that for you?"

Gemma shrugged. "As long as it doesn't delay my leaving. I want out, Sheriff. I want to leave Sanctuary."

**

Dan stared at the yellowing paper on the mayor's desk. It was the middle of a mess of papers, but this one was different. Instead of typed or hand-written words it was a pencil drawing. A map?

"Then he shoved her good, and we left." Phil had reiterated the story like they were the most important team in some elite army.

The mayor's gaze moved to Dan. "Trouble in paradise?" He sneered.

Dan said, "None of your business is what it is."

The sneer turned into a grin. "I'm starting to like you, Daniel."

Phil and Matt looked mad. Too bad they didn't have time to do something about it before two more guys walked in.

"You're back."

The first man nodded. Dan didn't know him well, but he worked construction around town. "It's all done."

"Good," the mayor said. "The internet is off. Phones are down, and it won't take long for people to realize they've been cut off from the world."

They'd hijacked the town. Dan fumed, but couldn't say anything else while the mayor stared at him like that. These men were taking this entirely too far, and he wasn't going to convince them that he was on board with it.

Dan gritted his teeth. "I can't be a part of this. I'm not going to stand around while you take people hostage."

He took two steps toward the door, but Phil moved in front of him. "Not so fast."

"You need to get out of my way."

"Don't think so." Phil folded his arms. "You aren't going anywhere."

"He's right, Daniel," the mayor said behind him. "You can't leave, not while the pieces are moving."

Phil's eyes narrowed. When they were done moving pieces this guy was probably going to take him out to the woods and bury him in a shallow grave. "You can't keep me here." Dan turned to face the mayor. "You were supposed to be about making the town better. That's what I signed up for, not this kamikaze, putting-people's-lives-in-danger business. I won't be a part of that."

The mayor sighed. "I guess it was too much to ask that there be even a little bit of your father in you."

"If there ever was he beat it out of me a long time ago."

No one moved. "Be that as it may," the mayor said. "You still aren't leaving." He motioned to an armchair. "Have a seat."

Phil moved to guard the door, and two more men strode in. "The charges are set."

Dan moved to get up, but Phil shifted toward him. Dan settled back down. "There haven't been enough explosions in this town already?"

The mayor shook his head. "That Navy SEAL was sloppy. Those boys are all about overkill, while I'm a man of finesse. Localized charges, just enough to get the job done."

"What job?"

Phil said, "You ask a lot of questions. Guess you like the sound of your own voice, but we all knew that. Running that church by yourself. Better than everyone else, holier than everyone else."

"I'm guessing you have some kind of problem with people who have faith."

"Faith in what? Ain't no one up there that's gonna save us," he said. "That's why we have to save ourselves. Make the world what we want it to be."

"That's an ideology which considers other people as inferior, nothing more than a stepping stone to a better life for yourself."

"And who's going to stop us? The sheriff?" Phil made a, "pfft" sound with his mouth. "Yeah, right. I don't see him here doing anything about it."

"Enough, boys." The mayor clapped his hands. "Besides, it's time for our next field trip." He opened the desk drawer and got out a phone that looked a lot like the sheriff's.

Dan filed that away in his head even, as he wondered how he could work it out so that he stayed behind. The mayor crossed the room. He nodded to Phil on the way, and the man opened the door for him. "Let's go, Daniel."

Phil strode over, grabbed his elbow and hauled Dan from the chair, halfway through the door. He wouldn't have thought the skinny guy had it in him. Two men in front, the other two—including Phil—walked behind him. Dan glanced back and then front, where the mayor strode ahead of them.

Dan couldn't get out of this huddle even if he tried, tripped or faked some kind of injury. They'd boxed him in, and he hadn't realized until too late. Dan reached back and found his pocket-size Bible in the backseat of his jeans. He needed that reminder. *You're in control, not them. As much as they think they've got this whole thing figured out. Bring the plans of man to nothing. Turn their hearts to You. Hosanna.* Save now. That seemed like an applicable prayer. God was their Savior, and sometimes that wasn't realized to its full potential until heaven, but it could be theirs now. Each of them, even these men.

Two golf carts took them to the farm. For the first time Dan was actually glad the mayor's house was on the same side of town as his farm. It meant no one saw him with this posse.

They drove past the caution tape, all the way up to the porch of his house. Phil smirked. "Time to go inside."

But he didn't know Dan wasn't afraid anymore. This house wasn't the source of his nightmares that it had been. *Thank You, Papa.* Dan had shed that fear once and for all, so it didn't matter what these men would throw at him, what they planned to do. Dan wasn't scared.

Not even when they led him to the basement.

Were they going to kill him and leave his body down here?

They waited by the tables, the men milling around clearly knowing what was about to happen. Dan watched the mayor, his attention on the tunnel. What was going to come through? That was when he heard it. Boots. Footsteps, getting closer and closer. Dan braced.

The man stepped into the basement room and looked around. "Good. You're all here." He was dressed in jeans and a blue shirt, not tired or sweating at all from that walk through the mine. Still, his hair was gray as it had been the day he left Sanctuary, diagnosed with terminal cancer.

Apparently, though, he wasn't dead.

"Sheriff Chandler."

He hardly moved, but the reaction was there. Then Chandler looked aside at the mayor, "And the girl?"

"Not hard to find."

"Good. Is everything else ready?"

The mayor nodded.

Chandler shifted a backpack off his shoulders and unzipped it. Out came two rifles, then four handguns.

"Grenades?" the mayor asked.

"I'll hang on to those." The former sheriff put the backpack on his shoulder. Everyone checked their weapons. No one gave one to Dan. "Now for the fun stuff." He lifted his chin to Dan, still playing nice despite the undercurrent. "You still have those horses?"

It had been more than two years since Chandler left town. "Yes."

Dan had figured the man would be dead by now. Not in a mean way, but it had been a pretty final diagnosis from what he knew. Why was Chandler here, alive? A person didn't just bounce back from terminal cancer. He'd gone out of town for some experimental treatment. Had it worked?

The group moved upstairs and outside. Dan stood on his lawn.

"Go saddle the horses, Daniel."

"Why? What do you need them—" A gun-butt connected with his temple. Dan's knees hit the grass, and he blinked away the pain that sparked through his skull.

"Saddle the horses, Daniel."

Hands hauled him to his feet. Not the first time, and he still didn't like the sensation of helplessness that came with being pushed around by someone bigger—or someone who thought they were bigger.

Dan saddled his horses and led them out one by one, saving Bay for last. Dan rode her out of the barn because he wasn't going to give these men any chance of being the one who did. She'd rear them off and then kick them. Bay didn't like anyone but him and—

Chase strode across the grass from the fields, pulling off his work gloves. Dan saw when he noticed the mayor and the group of men now on horseback. The hanger's-on waiting on the ground for orders because there weren't enough horses. The looks. The stances. The guns.

"Hey, Dan." Chase gave him a look like, *What is going on?* "You okay?"

"Yeah, Chase. I'm good."

"What are.... Sheriff Chandler? No way. It's um... good to see you, and so healthy."

Chase barely got the words out before Chandler lifted his gun and fired a shot.

Dan's friend fell to the ground.

Chapter 23

Gemma glanced through the peephole and sighed. "Great." She opened her front door and didn't bother to paste on a fake smile she wouldn't have meant anyway. "Mr. and Mrs. Evangeline." It wasn't good to see them. They hadn't had enough of slandering her for making that report about what their son had done? They'd raised the boy. What did that say about them?

Terrence's mom smiled, but there was something freaky about it. What on earth did this woman want? She'd used to be sweet, like a Sunday school teacher. Now she looked like the teacher you dreaded getting because she was going to make you write lines and rap your knuckles with a wooden ruler.

Mrs. Evangeline stepped forward. She couldn't think Gemma was going to actually let them in, did she? She smiled, but it was more like a grimace. Had she forgotten how to be nice? "Dear, we came to apologize. We treated you appallingly, and we're really very sorry for it. We should never have said that, just because you disparaged the good name of our only child."

"Apology accepted. Thanks for coming over." Gemma stepped back to shut the door, but Mrs. Evangeline put her foot between the door and the frame. The door bounced off her leather-upper shoe, and she pushed her way in.

"It's not necessary for you to come inside. Really."

Mr. Evangeline followed his wife in, determination on his face. "Okay, we're really doing this." He didn't sound so sure, and he'd lost that garden-gnome thing he'd had going on.

Mrs. Evangeline looked like something come to life in a horror movie. "We talked about this, dear. I thought you'd put your second-thoughts to rest."

Mr. Evangeline nodded. "You're the boss." He looked almost scared of her.

Gemma said, "I'd actually like you both to leave. I'm not feeling like company right now."

"I'm afraid that won't be possible, dear."

Gemma folded her arms. "Okay then, get out of my house." These people were dense, and devoid of common courtesy. "Is that clear enough for you? First your son assaults me, and then you slander me. Now what? Did you come here to make it worse some other way? Because I'm not in the mood. Now leave." She motioned wide with her arm just so they would get the message.

"It's there." Mrs. Evangeline glanced at her husband. "Just like he said."

"You know what that means," he replied.

"Guys—"

Mr. Evangeline stepped forward and grabbed her hand. "For whatever reason, the mayor wants you located. That means you're coming with us."

He held her hand so tightly in his it felt like all the little bones were breaking. Gemma cried out. He pulled her hand to him and turned it. He ripped off the bandage, the marks Terrence had burned into her skin in plain view.

"Let go of me."

Mrs. Evangeline grinned. "In the new Sanctuary, this means you've been claimed. If you want to make up with him later, that's your business. But since Terrence isn't here, and he was the one who claimed you, we figure that means now you belong to us."

"I don't belong to you. Get out of my house!" She screamed it as loud as she could, just like the last time someone unwanted had found her alone at home. Someone would hear. She had neighbors. One of them had to come and help her!

But they hadn't last time.

Mr. Evangeline didn't let go of her arm. He spun her, caught both hands behind her back and said, "Find something to tie her up with."

Mrs. Evangeline nodded and started to walk through her house.

Gemma fought as hard as she could, but his grip didn't loosen. She lifted her bare foot and kicked at his shins but found the legs of his boots under thick jeans. It was no use, but she didn't give up trying. There was no way she was going to freeze this time. Gemma had had enough of being the victim. "You're not going to tie me up!"

"Stop struggling and things will go a lot better for you." The warmth of his body came closer to her back. "It doesn't have to be all bad. Mama doesn't have to know what we get up to when she's not there."

Gemma screamed. *Please let someone hear.*

Mrs. Evangeline strode back into the room. "Loud, isn't she?" The gleam in her eyes was sickening. Like she was possessed. What had happened to these people?

"You were good. Nice. Church people! What happened to the two of you?" It was like they were drunk with excitement, adrenaline flowing through their veins like a high they'd never felt before.

"We saw it in Terrence. The rush and how it changed him. Then we got an offer we weren't about to refuse. All these years in this town, this prison. We're not about to end up on the wrong side of this fight. We're getting what belongs to us, and there's nothing anyone can do about it."

"Let me go!"

"No," Mrs. Evangeline said.

Where was Mei? For once she wished the little Chinese powerhouse was here. Why couldn't she bust in the door and start karate-kicking these two into next week? Gemma let out a cry of frustration. Nothing in her life ever went right.

"You belong to us now, and there's no use fighting it. That'll only mean we have to punish you." She giggled with a sick glee Gemma had only seen in horror movies. They tied her hands together, their disgusting paws roaming places they should not have touched.

Gemma kicked Mrs. Evangeline in the stomach. The older woman squealed out a puff of air as the wind escaped. She frowned, her face reddening, and grabbed a handful of Gemma's hair. Mrs. Evangeline slapped her, open-palmed, right across the face.

"Now for her mouth."

Gemma heard the words like she was under water, and then Mrs. Evangeline lifted a scarf Gemma had bought but never worn. "Right ahead of you."

Gemma struggled as hard as she could, whipped her head around so they couldn't cover her mouth. They held her face, crowding her so she couldn't move. Tears streamed down her face, and she cried behind the scarf so tight on her cheeks she could hardly breathe.

"The mayor was right. This is fun."

They took her out her front door, across the street, and down almost to the end. No one saw. Gemma struggled every step, until Mr. Evangeline stopped and put her over his shoulder in a fireman's hold.

Gemma craned her neck to see if anyone was watching. Someone had to have heard something? Where was everyone?

She thought she saw a curtain move, but maybe she was just imagining it.

Mr. Evangeline went inside. Their house smelled like something floral, so strong she got a headache immediately.

"Someone to cook and clean..." Mrs. Evangeline twittered.

Mr. Evangeline's response was to squeeze Gemma's rear. "I'm getting the hang of this. And I'll bet she'll turn out to be good for all kinds of things."

He walked to the back of the house, opened a door, and tossed her on the floor. Gemma hit the wood on her tailbone. Bare planks, no furniture. A boarded up window.

They slammed the door and locked her in.

**

John knocked on Mei's front door. When he was done being polite, and trying to get a polite answer in return, he pulled out his keys and used the master to get in. Sometimes it helped to have a key to every door in town. Too bad he couldn't just enter whenever he felt like it, search every house, and find the culprit to whatever crime had been committed. But the law didn't work like that, and people who felt their rights were trampled on tended to file lawsuits.

No one had seen Mei since she had taken Xander to Louis's the night before. John had a list of concerns about the woman, a lot of which settled around his brother, but he didn't want her to be hurt. Or missing. Or caught up in something that would get her killed. Or off doing something he would have to arrest her for.

With Mei, it could go one of several ways.

Fatigue weighed on him like a heavy coat. The morale in town was like Minnesota in January, and John was trying to figure out what to do about it, navigating being a new father again, working on keeping things good with his family, and trying to stay grounded in his faith, all while he figured out what the mayor was up to.

He rubbed a hand on the spot, high on his chest, where that rogue Navy SEAL had stabbed him. It still hurt sometimes, but he'd determined nothing like that was going to happen ever again. So he'd taken measures. He'd found that kid-size bullet proof vests had to be custom made. There would be as little vulnerability within his family as he could ensure. If they were going to live here then John would do everything within his power to protect them and pray for God to cover the rest that John couldn't.

He strode through the house. He knocked on the bedroom door before he entered. No answer. He walked through and checked the bathroom, half expecting to find a decomposing body in her bathtub. Mei was precisely the type of woman he'd imagine getting rid of her enemies that way. But the place was clean. So where was Terrence?

His phone rang. John looked at the display, *Private,* and didn't know whether to be glad, or annoyed that Ben would be calling right now. Because who else would it be?

He hit the button, praying he would get more than static this time, and said, "If you're calling to tell me why I'm standing in my deputy's bathroom I'm all ears."

"I've never understood that expression." Ben's voice was even, calm. "All ears. I mean, that's gross." In the background two gunshots went off.

"Where are you?"

"I can't—"

"Tell me. Yeah, I know." John sighed. He hadn't meant geographically "Where was his brother", or even "What was he doing." Just a general, "Why are you being shot at?" would have been nice to know. But whatever.

Moving on. "I need answers, Ben, and fast. The town is circling the drain, and maybe you sent Mei to do something and maybe you didn't, but whatever it is isn't stopping it. And she's now missing."

"She wasn't supposed to stop it. She was supposed to unravel the mystery in the first place. Find out why that town was there, who the original residents were. Why Hal left Gemma that room."

"And why would you need to know that?"

"It was designated part of what the committee needed to know, going forward. Just because we moved out from under the purview of the federal government doesn't mean we're just going to ignore unanswered questions. And you know I never take what they say at face value."

John sighed. "So Mei came here to unravel the mystery of Sanctuary."

"She's done pretty well, so far."

"Only because Dan talked to her, and Gemma told her what she found out from her mom. That was most of it."

"She found Dan's mom's body, didn't she?"

John wasn't going to get in this discussion with his brother. "Has she called in?"

"Why?"

"Because no one's seen her."

Ben was quick to say, "That doesn't mean anything's happened. Mei can handle herself, so if she hasn't shown up it's because she's busy."

John said, "Are you trying to convince me that's the case, or yourself?"

"Touché, little brother."

"If you don't have anything that can help me, why did you call?"

"How is Nicholas?"

"The baby is fine." John was ready to quit this gig and take his family to Hawaii to live on the beach instead, but he couldn't in good conscience do that. Ben was miles away living the secret agent life, and all he wanted to know about was his nephew?

"Mom sent me a picture. He's cute."

John was really trying not to get mad, but he was so tired. "Can you call me if Mei gets ahold of you, please?"

"Sure, br—"

John waited, but his brother never finished what he'd been saying. "Ben?"

A crackly voice came over the line, but John couldn't make out what his brother said. "Great."

John stowed his phone. The satellite must be having problems. Another thing to add to the list of problems he already had. His son didn't want to stay home. Townspeople wanted to know why everything was going haywire. Olympia wanted to know who had killed Antonia, and the search for Terrence was ongoing. All in the same week Andra had their baby.

Nothing in this town made sense at all. Least of all his deputy, who showed up out of nowhere, didn't fit the job, disappeared all the time, did no more than the minimum she was asked to do, and… it was the way she thumbed her chin when she was thinking. The way she worked her mouth back and forth.

He couldn't help it. She reminded him of Ben.

**

Dan knew they were moving. Intellectually he could feel the move of the horse underneath him. Bay held him centered when he would have split into dissonant fragments. The sight of Chase falling to the ground with blood covering his chest played over and over in his mind.

"Pick up the pace."

Dan focused at the other three horses in front of him. They were almost to town. He should tug Bay's reins and set her to sailing into the woods. She'd covered that ground so many times she could be blindfolded and she'd find her way.

Escape.

Then he saw the gun pointed at him. Dan didn't want to get shot in the back as he rode away, and he certainly didn't want Bay to get hurt. Miranda must be beside herself. She had to have found Chase by now. How was Dan going to explain to her what had happened? Nothing would ever satisfy her, no matter what answer he gave. Dan knew that, because he would never find peace after this, either. Except with Papa's help.

The squad of horses hit Main Street.

Businesses shut their doors. People on the street gasped, gathered up their children, and went inside. A group ran into the Meeting House. One by one the street descended into silence except for the rap of horse hooves on the concrete street as they slowed.

People watched from behind windows and doors.

Sheriff Chandler pulled to a stop in the middle of the street outside the sheriff's office, raised his gun barrel to the clouds, and fired off three shots. In the distance, Dan heard a baby start to cry.

He shut his eyes and prayed.

Sheriff Chandler yelled, "Time to come out, Sheriff Mason. Time to face me and explain to this town why you've let things get this far. Time to resign and let someone else take over. Someone who can do a better job than you."

No one moved. The sheriff never came out.

Dan couldn't see beyond the closed blinds of the sheriff's office. He looked up, but the curtains had been drawn upstairs. Was the sheriff even home? Dan didn't want to get in front of Chandler's gun, but if the man was going to go inside where John's family were no-doubt huddled together, Dan would do what he could to stop him.

The door handle turned. The door slowly opened, inch by inch and the sheriff strode out, wearing his uniform. Probably to make a point to Chandler as to which of them carried the authority. At least Dan hoped that was the case. John had to know what was at stake. He wasn't a stupid man, but Dan didn't know how far he would allow himself to be pushed. Or how he would react if Chandler leveraged John's family against the town of Sanctuary.

John's hands hung loose at his sides, his gun on his belt. Shouldn't he have brought a shotgun or something? Dan tried to communicate the seriousness of what was going on with his eyes, but John's gaze didn't settle on him long enough for him to read anything from Dan.

"Chandler. I thought you were dead."

The older sheriff grinned. "Guess I outlived my own mortality."

Dan figured he'd faked the whole thing, arranged exit out of Sanctuary and for John to replace him, and then spent the last two years orchestrating this whole thing. But Dan was just a farmer. What did he know?

"What brings you to Sanctuary?" John chatted like this was just another day, not a serious breach of security.

Dan tried to motion with his eyes and the jerk of his head that people had died and things were deteriorating fast, but John never looked his way after the first glance.

"I'm back for good," Chandler said. "I'm ready to lead again, to return Sanctuary to its former glory. No, to make it better even than before. Only a strong leader can possess the vision to usher these people and this place into the greatness that is possible." The old sheriff's eyes narrowed. "I admire the job you did for the marshals, but since you arrived your progress has been reported to me, and I'm sad to say things have not been impressive. You had a chance, John. A chance to really turn this town into something great! Instead you've let them erode it day-by-day."

"My job is to protect this town, not to govern their lives. They already have a mayor." He glanced at Collins. "Sad to say, he seems to have checked out in favor of his own agenda instead of doing what's best for the town."

Collins sputtered. "That's because you—"

The old sheriff lifted his hand. "Enough, Collins."

"That's not even my name," he yelled back. "I came here because they told me I'd be paving the way to a greater future. Instead I find a bunch of imbeciles, and not one of them has that vision of greatness you were talking about. I'm the only one who sees what could be."

"You are not the only one." The old sheriff shook his head. "And you will have a part to play in this, but patience is in order. People must be shown the right path in order for them to walk it."

John said, "You think this town is going to let you walk in illegally, set up shop and start changing their lives?"

"The manner by which I came to be here—"

John interrupted with, "You hiked through the mine."

"So you figured it out."

"Did you kill Mei?"

The old sheriff frowned. "Never mind the fate of that little chinky. She isn't important here."

John didn't look impressed. Dan tried to figure out what to do, and where this was headed. Chandler seemed so calm, but there was a nasty storm just below the surface. He'd seen it blow forth before, when Chandler was mad. He'd bet the man could be lethal if he wanted to.

"What matters is your fate," Chandler said. "This town is on the cusp of a new path, and it's time for you to decide. Are you with us, where you will share in what we're going to build beyond this town being a prison turned into a residence, or will you stand against us and face down the consequences? Can you resist what is happening, will you deny the greatness that we will surely mold this town into? Or do you choose your own fate?"

Dan held his breath. The whole of Main Street was silent, the horses' puffs and shifting seemed to cease as they waited for John's answer. Dan cleared his mind and let the Holy Spirit intercede on his behalf. There were no words. Surely John had to be praying, too. Yes. Dan saw his lips move. They needed God's help if they were going to emerge from this with the town and its residents out of harm.

What would Chandler do if John said no? How far was the old sheriff prepared to go in order to lead the town to a new era? Dan couldn't forget the man's reaction to his presence. He'd expected to be killed, and yet they'd kept him alive. They'd mentioned a woman. Gemma? He wanted her far from these men when he had no idea what was still to come.

John lifted his chin. "I won't let you railroad these people into a town of your design. They should be allowed to live the lives they want to in peace and safety."

"Very well." Chandler lifted his gun and pulled the trigger.

Chapter 24

Bolton's hand reached out and clasped Nadia's as she stood by him. He reached for his son with the other hand and the teen shot him a grim look, his eyes full of tears and ready to overflow. The town's fate had come to this, and they'd finally seen it play out.

Sanctuary had never been a safe place, but neither was the rest of the world. At least here he'd thought they had enough friends around them that they were strong to face whatever might come next.

Bolton glanced back at the Meeting House and all the people gathered inside. They'd been through so much already. Crazy murdering psycho's, crazier murdering psycho's, followed by a crazy murdering SEAL. Through it all several of them had found love. Made families. Forged some semblance of happiness out of everything that was right and wrong in Sanctuary.

He'd almost done it. Nadia Marie was here, his ring on her finger. Their wedding date would be set when she finally agreed they didn't need to wait any longer. Javier was here. Things were good between them, and while it would never be a perfect father/son relationship because of the years they'd spent apart, Bolton liked to think they were becoming good friends.

And now the town was overrun.

Sheriff Chandler had done little more than sit behind a desk when he had been here. He'd certainly never actually arrested anyone. Why did they think the crime stats had gone up since John arrived? Now the man was back? No cancer. No sickness at all that Bolton could see.

One shot, and now John lay on the street in the midday sun.

A tear rolled down Bolton's face, but he didn't have a free hand to catch it.

**

Matthias moaned, low in his throat. A gasp from Frannie set the baby to crying, but her gaze didn't move from across the street. Matthias went to her and took the child, then held them both close to his chest.

She'd had a hard time since Susan was born, but God had been so faithful to give them joy in spite of the bad days Frannie had. He'd seen her smile as many times as she laughed, and knew there was a measure of guilt there that she wasn't happier about their family. Matthias just reminded her that happiness was a human emotion, and those could change faster than the weather. What was true was that they had each other, and God had them. Their baby was healthy, they had another on the way, and they were together. Life was good.

The Meeting House was packed, most of the town already attuned to what was happening in Sanctuary, and while some crowded closer to the windows to attempt to see across the street, others backed up. Even before the posse rode down Main Street on horseback, armed. Before the former sheriff of Sanctuary had gunned down John Mason in the street. So many here had PTSD or other trauma symptoms. The sheriff's death was going to be a blow he wasn't sure this town could recover from.

Matthias's breath caught in his throat. Emotion. He squeezed his eyes shut.

God had them in His hands.

Over the murmur of dismay and disbelief of people in the room, Pat Mason screamed. Aaron sat crouched in a corner, rocking and talking to himself. Olympia crossed to the boy and pulled him into her arms. Matthias's sister was lost to them, but even with Antonia gone, his mom found a needy heart she could touch.

Andra sat on a plastic chair, holding baby Nicholas, her face completely pale. Who was going to help her?

The doors flung open.

People rushed back, and Phil and Matt entered. They dragged an older couple into the room, and then a young family.

Sheriff Chandler stepped up to the door. He surveyed the gathered crowd, all stood in stunned silence. Then he turned to his men and said, "Knock on every door. I want everyone brought here for a town meeting."

They slammed the doors shut.

Matthias glanced over at Bolton, and they shared a look. He squeezed Frannie and then moved so he could look down at her face. "I need to talk to Andra." She nodded her upturned face, and he kissed her quickly because he needed to, then touched his daughter's head before he walked to where Andra sat with her baby.

He crouched in front of her, not liking the look on her face. "Andra?" She was pale, too pale. Her eyes glassy. He touched her arm and found it cold and clammy under his fingers. She wasn't crying, she was in pure shock. "Tell me what you need."

He couldn't imagine what was going through her head. Brand new mom, nearly brand new wife. Seeing her husband shot down in the street right in front of her eyes. The whole room could hear Pat lose it, and Aaron wasn't any better though he was quiet and kept things to himself. Andra had some kind of mental strength Matthias had never seen before.

His sister hadn't been his best friend, but he hadn't held himself together when he heard Antonia had been killed.

Andra was going to lose it, too, and he'd bet money she wanted to do that alone.

He held out his hands. "Do you want me to hold Nicholas for you?"

She shook her head.

"How can I help you?"

Andra swallowed, then looked him square in the eyes. "Get my husband's body out of the street."

Matthias stood. "Okay."

He needed something to do, something practical that meant he was helping, even if it was only in a small way. He didn't want to see John like that, but if it was what she wanted then he would do it.

Matthias went to the door.

"Anyone out there?" Bolton had rolled over on his chair. Matthias saw Nadia with Frannie, and sent her a smile of thanks.

"Doesn't look like it." Matthias cracked the door and just listened. "Seems like they all dispersed on Chandler's orders." He stepped outside, and Bolton held the door open. "Yep, it looks clear."

"Be careful anyway."

Matthias stepped out from the cover of the Meeting House doorway, grimacing at the idea of what he was about to do. But Andra had asked. *Lord, help us all.* Whatever Chandler had planned wasn't likely going to be pretty.

But as he passed the flower bed in the center and approached the spot where John had fallen, he realized something.

The sheriff's body was gone.

Matthias's steps faltered, and he stopped.

"What is it?" Bolton yelled across the street.

Matthias was about to reply when movement at the end of the street caught his attention. Matthias saw Elliot and Shelby walking his direction, their steps frantic. Shelby glanced back over her shoulder, and Elliot urged her on.

Matthias met them outside the Meeting House.

"Men with guns dragged us out of the medical center. Never mind that we have patients, we're supposed to be over here for a town meeting." Shelby's words came fast, her skin flushed. She walked in and looked around. "Is she here?" She glanced around. "Has anyone seen Gemma?"

Janice got up from sitting with a group and walked over. "I haven't seen her." She held hands with Shelby. "I don't know where she is."

Matthias needed to talk to Andra. She was looking at him now, expectant. Did she think he'd bring John in here? Matthias held her gaze and shook his head.

Andra frowned.

Shelby glanced back at Matthias. "What about Dan?"

Matthias swallowed. He'd seen the pastor on the back of his horse. Janice answered for him, "Dan was with the mayor and Sheriff Chandler."

Shelby gasped. "What?"

Matthias nodded. "We all saw him."

"No, I don't believe it."

"He was," Janice said. "He betrayed all of us and joined them."

"He didn't look good." Matthias wanted her to know that. "Maybe he was even coerced into it. We don't know that he went willingly."

Shelby nodded. "He wouldn't have abandoned us. That isn't the kind of man Dan is."

"You don't know the kind of man he is," Janice said. "The son of Bill Jones could be capable of anything. And where's Gemma? He probably killed her and then joined Chandler!" Janice stumbled away, wailing.

Shelby turned into Elliot's arms. "He wouldn't have killed her."

Matthias said, "I don't believe it. Janice is distraught, but so is everyone." His voice cracked, and he walked to Andra. "He's gone."

"I know he's gone, Matthias." Her voice, thin and broken, made his chest ache. "I saw it just like you did."

"His body." Matthias's gut tightened. "It's gone."

Andra mouthed the word, *Gone,* but no sound came out.

"I'm sorry."

He heard Bolton behind him telling Shelby and Elliot what had happened. The noise in the room broke out into murmurs, disbelief that Dan had become one of the bad guys. People asking who had seen their friends, their neighbors. Janice yelled, "You never liked her anyway! What do you care what happened to my Gemma?"

Shelby and Elliot wandered to an open chair and sat.

Andra stood, the baby in a sling tucked close to her chest. She wandered to Aaron, crouched, and spoke quiet into his ear. Aaron glanced up, his face puffy and wet. She held out her hand, and he got up. Andra walked toward the door to the kitchen in the back, the bathrooms. The door to the bunker underneath the building. Aaron bent low in front of Olympia and took Pat from her arms. "Come on, little brother. Time to go."

"Go?" Bolton wheeled toward the family. "Where are you going?"

"To the bathroom." Andra's face was dead-pan. She never gave anything away. Ever.

"Time to go," Aaron said.

Andra said nothing, just turned and led her family through the swinging door to the kitchen.

"Chandler won't like it if they're gone when he comes back."

Matthias turned. He figured the look on Bolton's face was a lot like the one on his. "She knows what she's doing."

"Then we're agreed she's not just taking her family to the bathroom."

Matthias nodded. "John's body was gone."

"I don't want to know where Chandler took it."

Matthias didn't want to know what they were going to do with it. He'd seen enough blood and lived through enough death in his life to know that. So he bowed his head and did what Dan would tell him to do.

He prayed.

**

"Everyone reports to the Meeting House. No exceptions." The voice was muffled through the locked door that separated Gemma from the rest of the house, and freedom.

Gemma turned her head but stayed in plank position. Sweat beaded on her brow, but there weren't a lot of ways to burn pent-up energy that worked as well as doing a few push-ups. She sat back on her heels and blew out a breath. She'd worked her hands out of the bindings and taken off the scarf from her mouth, but she was still confined to this room.

"The mayor knows we're on his side. I'm sure he can explain to us what we need to know." It was Mrs. Evangeline.

Gemma was going to scratch that woman's eyes out if she got the chance.

"No exceptions. Now who else lives here? Anyone?"

"Just us," Mr. Evangeline told the man.

Boot steps pounded down the hall. Went different directions. Came closer to the room she was in. The handle twisted, caught, and was let go. "What's in there? I'm supposed to search everywhere."

"That's just a storage room," Mrs. Evangeline said. "All the sets from old theater productions. You know we run the Sanctuary art program. But it's so messy in there it would be like showing you my unmentionables drawer." She giggled, too fast and too fake.

"Yeah, I don't wanna see that."

The boots pounded away. "You two still come with me."

More footsteps, and then the front door shut.

Silence.

Gemma jumped up. They were gone? Really, seriously, gone? She pushed on the door. *Please let it be as well made as all the rest of the doors in town.* She'd been mad at her mom once, and punched her bedroom door. The thing had been hollow, and basically crumpled under her hand.

Gemma lifted her foot and kicked the door. Her foot went straight through until her leg up to her knee was on the other side of the door. She hopped and pulled her foot out, then kicked and kicked until there was a hole big enough to get through.

Thank You, Papa.

Gemma ran out the back door, jumped the fence. Through another yard. Between two houses. A dog barked, but she ignored it and sprinted as fast as she could into the woods.

You set captives free.

**

The baby stayed mercifully quiet. Andra took every back alley and short cut she knew and got her boys to the park. They couldn't go her normal route to the cabin. That would take them by the mayor's house. Chandler had probably set up shop there in order to oversee his hostile takeover of the town. Andra's hands clenched by her sides. She pushed aside the rage and took a cleansing breath. That was a feeling for later. When the kids were safe, and she had a gun in her hand.

"Mom." Pat's whisper brought her head around. She closed the gap between her and Aaron, who still held him.

She crouched so their faces were level. "Yeah, buddy?"

"Where's Dad?"

Andra put her arms around Aaron and Pat and pulled them both close to her. The baby stirred as she said, "Pray, okay?"

"Aaron pray."

Andra squeezed the older boy's neck. He was a man in age, but she prayed he'd never lose that youthful mentality even as she grieved the fact he'd always be childlike. She prayed both Pat and Aaron would be able to distance themselves from this. It was why they had her.

"Let's go," she said. "It's not far."

Her cabin in the woods had burned down, but when she and John had talked about weekend getaways and how they weren't really possible in Sanctuary, they'd decided to rebuild it. Between getting married, a rogue SEAL terrorizing the town, and then having a baby, they hadn't managed to start on the build yet, but they'd made some improvements.

And John had designated the cabin their rendezvous point. She'd scoffed at first, until she'd realized the wisdom of an "In case something happens" plan. Her eyes filled with tears. Something had happened.

His body. It's gone. Andra had never prayed as hard as she had for the last hour. God's action wasn't contingent on her prayers. That wasn't why she pleaded and begged for His help, for Him to have saved John somehow. She'd seen her husband get shot. Andra prayed because that dialogue with God was all she had to keep her going up the winding path that crept toward the mountains.

It was all she had to keep the hope alive.

**

"Thank you all for coming." Sheriff Chandler's voice boomed across the room and from the speakers. Someone had turned it up loud.

Beside Matthias the baby let out a mew. Frannie covered the baby's ear that wasn't pressed against her with the blanket, and then her hand. He shifted closer to her and held them both steady against his side.

Conversation broke out across the room.

"What's going on?"

"I thought you were dead."

"What's happened?"

"Where did you come from?"

Sheriff Chandler lifted his hand. "Today has been unpleasant for a lot of you, but it was necessary. I knew when I left that the situation in Sanctuary needed to change. For too long all of us lived under the thumb of the federal government. Now the committee wants us to bow to their whims instead?" He shook his head. "No. Not me, and I couldn't stand by and do nothing while all of you simply exchanged one dictator for another. You should be free."

Bolton shifted in his wheelchair and whispered to Matthias, "If he doesn't want to be lord and master of this town instead of the committee, then why did he ride in and shoot John?"

Matthias shook his head. He raised his hand and the old sheriff nodded. His men looked on, scattered around the room like sentries. Dan was outside. Matthias had seen him arrive, but he hadn't come inside. Did they keep the pastor out there on purpose, or was it his choice?

The sheriff glanced around, waiting for someone to oppose him.

Matthias wasn't going to stay silent. "If you're trying to convince us you're here to help, why drag people out of their homes? Why walk around carrying guns that are illegal in this town and kill the sheriff?"

Chandler didn't react, he stayed completely stoic and faced the crowd. "I'll prove my loyalty is to this town by proving to you all that the committee—particularly the Mason brothers—are not working for you. It's time for the truth to come out, and for Sanctuary to be revealed for what it was intended as."

Matthias said, "Everyone already knows it was a prison for Dan Walden's father." Frannie shifted in her chair and glanced at him for a second. She was upset? He rubbed her shoulder with his thumb. He had to stall long enough that Andra could do whatever she was doing, even if it was only so that she could hide her boys and be safe. All the sheriff's men were here which meant there was no one else stalking the town.

Matthias said, "What we don't know is how you got in here when no aircraft landed. Is there another way in and out of Sanctuary?"

"That is privileged information. Does 'everyone' also know that Mei Ling is an employee of Ben Mason, or that she was sent here to be the deputy sheriff, and none of the other applicants even had a chance?"

Matthias shrugged. He trusted John, and by extension his brother Ben. The man's methods were unconventional. If there was something Ben needed done in Sanctuary, then it needed done.

Sheriff Chandler waited for a second, and then said, "Didn't think so. There have been too many secrets in this town for too long. I'm going to bring the truth to light, and it's up to each of you to decide if you wish to remain here."

Matthias wanted to know what the plan was to allow those who didn't want to stay the chance to leave. The only problem was the reason why they were here in the first place—the fact that they weren't safe in the outside world. Would people choose mortal danger over living under this new regime, a regime that didn't seem to have their best interests at heart?

Sheriff Chandler continued, "Those who remain who truly threaten the safety of Sanctuary are not in this room, but they need to be found. Mei Ling must be brought to me. We will find out why she is here, and what she was sent to accomplish. This woman is armed and dangerous, and we believe she is responsible for the deaths of more than one person, including Terrence Evangeline and Antonia Hernandez."

"The other person we are currently looking for is Gemma. While unarmed, she is dangerous and believed to possibly be in league with Mei Ling. They could be plotting all kinds of things together, and so it is imperative they be found."

The room erupted into shouted questions and comments.

"Enough!" The mayor strode onto the stage and put his mouth right up to the mic. "Quit being so ungrateful when we saved you from them!"

"You seriously believe that?" someone yelled.

"Shut it, Hank!" The mayor's chest heaved. "Ben Mason is a thug, and Mei is as good as the same. Where is Terrence, huh? She probably killed him, too!"

The sheriff pushed him aside while everyone gasped. Even Matthias felt his eyebrows lift. He glanced at Frannie, whose eyes were wide as well.

"She needs to be found!" One of the men dragged the mayor from the stage.

Sheriff Chandler cleared his throat. "Until these people are brought to me, there will be a nine p.m. curfew in effect. After that time, no one is allowed outside of their homes."

Chapter 25

Belly to the dirt, Mei looked through the scope. Shadrach had talked her through the fundamentals of what it meant to be a sniper so many times she could hear his voice in her head as she lay there. *Wind speed. Distance. Angle.* The people of Sanctuary left the Meeting House looking like ants in a terrarium.

Mei pursed her lips, moved her finger to the trigger and blew out a breath. Low and slow. Her legs needed the break from walking. This was good. She'd been up the mountain and back down trying to get a signal to her phone. An ultra-marathon would have been easier than those sheer cliffs, in places dotted with ice and snow already, even though winter wasn't here yet.

She needed to be on a beach by Christmas. It was a vow, and she made it gladly. No matter what job she was sent on next, Christmas meant beach.

Mei sighed. There was no clear shot on Chandler. He hadn't come out of the Meeting House like everyone else. Two of his men had, and Dan watched on from the sidelines as they poked and prodded Bolton. The wheelchair bound man could stand, but evidently didn't feel the need to. Nadia and the boy were stiff, stood on either side of him. Seriously, Dan was just going to do nothing?

Mei adjusted her angle and looked back at the ringleader of this little tiff. It was a real shame that neither the sheriff nor the mayor had stepped outside the Meeting House. But she did not like this guy one bit, either, and hadn't since she'd seen him fixing the roof of a house in town, and he'd given her that look. The one he just sent in Nadia's direction. He would do for now.

Mei did the calculation in her head. She pulled half a breath of air into her lungs and held it. Three. Two. One. Squeeze.

His head exploded.

Mei hopped up, rifle in hand and sprinted, a grin on her face. This gun was messy. She liked it.

For ten minutes she ran as hard as she could. When they searched the woods for her they'd find prints, maybe an indent of her weight in the mud. But she would be long gone. Her orders were to protect the people of this town, and that was exactly what she was going to do. Finding out about Hal and Dan's father was secondary as far as she was concerned. At least she'd decided it was, and the boss man couldn't argue because Ben couldn't call her right now. When he asked, she'd show him the rock scrapes on her palms from climbing that mountain.

What bothered her most was why he thought they needed protection. Sure, this town had been through crazy stuff, but he couldn't have known that the old sheriff—who's file said he was *dead*—was, in fact, alive. That was a bone she intended to pick clean with Remy. Like the woman couldn't spot a faked death? Mei rolled her eyes as she ran. They should have known he was still around.

And if the boss man knew Chandler was alive, and that he'd been planning on returning to Sanctuary, he should have just told her that. Ben should have stopped it himself. She could tell in about thirty seconds of meeting someone whether they were going to harm another person. Why she could do this, or how, she didn't really know. But she could, and she'd spotted it with Terrence. Even Bolton, though it was muted. Then there was Ben. The fact her radar had pinged on *him* of all people wasn't lost on her.

Ben Mason was not a good man, but their lives were so closely intertwined she couldn't shake him off. She'd tried. Now she just avoided him instead. It was a good plan. Or she *had* been avoiding him until she'd seen his brother get killed. John's body was gone, and Mei couldn't even dispose of it respectfully for their family.

She was going to have to tell him what happened to his brother—what she'd allowed to happen. Because he would hold her responsible for it. They relied on each other like that, and it was good. Mostly, it was good.

It was all they had.

**

People scattered, but it was only a single shot. A sniper.

Dan waited for the horror of it to wash over him; the feel of hot metal in his hand. The ricochet. His mom as she fell to the ground. The gore. But the memory stayed tucked in his mind. Safe. *Thank You, Papa.* Dan shut his eyes for a second and then turned away from the sight of that man on the ground.

People ran away, Dan watched to make sure they got where they were going without being bothered by any more of Chandler's men. An older man fell. When Dan ran over to help him the man cowered, as though Dan was going to hit him. He crouched and forced himself to move slowly. "Timothy, let me help you."

The old man blinked and lowered his arms. "What are you doing?"

Dan took hold of his elbows and said, "Let me help you up."

Timothy allowed Dan to steady him as he gained his feet. "We're all in danger, aren't we?" The old man and his wife both looked on.

Dan nodded. "It would seem so. I'm trying to figure this out, to fight it from the inside."

Timothy said, "Well that's good. But who is going to help?"

"I'm sure there's a plan in place." John wouldn't have ignored the possibility this might happen. Even if the man was gone, there had to be a contingency. They'd had several for different eventualities when the federal government had been in charge. The committee must have put something in place, but Dan still prayed it hadn't slipped through the cracks as they transitioned to take over everything.

Timothy's wife said, "But the sheriff!"

Grief threatened to overwhelm him, but Dan locked his knees. It still made him sick that they'd shot John in broad daylight. He couldn't think about it, or he'd get lost in his own head. "Just keep praying."

"Oh, we are," Timothy said. The two both nodded, and Dan watched them go. He crossed back to the Meeting House and pushed his way through the heavy doors inside without looking at what was left of the man on the ground. Who had shot him?

The sheriff yelled, "Who shot him?"

Dan walked into the middle of the old Sheriff, the mayor and eight men all stood around. Most were armed.

The sheriff's eyes narrowed when he saw Dan. "Do you know?"

Dan shrugged. "Had to have been a hunting rifle of some kind. I think it came from the trees but that's a mile, easily. Maybe the ranch, or the lake?"

"One of you has to know who shot…whatever his name was!"

Someone said, "Cameron."

"Who cares? Mount a search. I want the woods scoured until you find that sniper!"

Dan stayed where he was while men filed out. He'd tied up the horses in front of the sheriff's office. When Dan wandered to the door to look out, he saw them race for his animals. Three men climbed on horseback and rode off.

Dan blinked. Where was Bay?

Peace flooded Dan like he'd jumped into a swimming pool full of it. He held his breath as it resonated through him. Okay, so… Bay was fine? *Papa, is Bay fine?* Dan heard nothing, but the sense of peace didn't leave him. Bay was gone, but it wasn't reason to panic. Did it have to do with the fact John's body was now gone?

Dan didn't want to entertain the false hope that the sheriff had somehow climbed on Bay and left. Someone would have seen him, wouldn't they?

Peace.

Okay, so it was possible John was okay. Somehow. Dan shook his head. It was so hard to believe, but if there was anything he'd learned since he first heard about God it was to trust Him. So that was what Dan was going to do.

He turned to look at the sheriff, facing him, the mayor's profile. The mayor only had eyes for Chandler. The peace retreated somewhat. *Not fine.* Dan reached back to touch the edges of the pages of the Bible tucked back there. He prayed.

The mayor had abdicated all authority to Chandler. The older sheriff was definitely in charge of this operation.

Collins said, "It was that deputy. Mei. It had to be her. Ben Mason probably trained her to kill and then sent her here to take care of all of us."

The sheriff didn't move his attention from Dan. "That infers he knew about the plan all along. Which he could not have, as the only ones who did were you and I and a select few others."

"And they sent me here to take care of things. To give you the freedom to leave and formulate a plan since Bill Jones was dead. I should be rewarded for my part."

The sheriff turned his head and faced the mayor. "I always knew you'd be a liability."

"I've done my share. You would never have known what was happening in town if I hadn't been here while you were gone. For *two years* I took care of business, I kept things running. I got you your own army!" The mayor huffed. "You need me."

"Maybe."

"I want to kill the Chinese girl myself."

Dan took a step back. He didn't want to be a part of this. He knew how to use a rifle, and if he could get his hands on one then he would end Chandler and Collins. He could do it.

The ricochet. *His mom's eyes flashed, and she fell. Hit the floor with a sickening thud.*

"Not so fast." Chandler lifted a hand, palm out.

Dan's feet halted. He didn't want to be here. He wanted to leave. *Papa.* The plan to stick around, to be in the inner sanctum and try to help from the epicenter of trouble was unravelling. They were looking for Gemma and Mei, and Dan wouldn't be able to stop them from doing whatever they wanted to the two women when they were found. He had to kill these men, but he wouldn't know if he could until it was too late. What if he froze? What if he couldn't pull the trigger?

A million thoughts raced through his head. Would God help him kill these men? Would he be able to do it if it saved Gemma's life?

Dan cleared his throat. He had to stall them until he figured out a plan. "This is about my father?"

The sheriff said, "Is there anything in this town that isn't about your father?"

"Yes, plenty. But you wouldn't know that, because you haven't been here." Dan motioned behind himself. "These people have lives, and so do I. But you don't care about that, do you? I don't think you ever did, or you wouldn't have ignored child abuse. You wouldn't have let a million other things pass by un-investigated. You'd have done something good for this town. Now you want whatever it is you want, and nothing is going to hinder you getting it."

Chandler said, "You're beginning to figure it out."

"Figure what out?"

The side of Sheriff Chandler's mouth curled up. "Your father made me a promise, and he reneged on that deal. So I sold him out to the very people he was hiding from. Bingo. Dead in the lettuce."

"And the town?" Him, Gemma—what about them?

"Sanctuary took forty years of my life. Now I'm going to get what *I* deserve." He glanced once at the mayor. "Retirement in a place of my own making. And I choose here."

"So you'll torture and torment these people until they do whatever you say, and then you'll kick back and live your golden years stuck here, just to spite us?"

"Life is what I make it. This town took a pound of my flesh, and now I intend to take back that pound from this town."

Dan took another step toward the door.

"But the son of Bill Jones isn't going anywhere. You see, I found something out while I was gone from this town. The CIA agents who were hunting your father? They are very much alive. And they might be old, but they still hate your old man for ruining their lives. They want the papers Hal kept to be destroyed—"

The mayor butted in with, "I took care of that."

Sheriff Chandler shot him a disapproving look. "Any living family members, or any other persons with any knowledge of what happened, are to be taken care of. And the photo of the CIA agents that was in Bill Jones's possession—a photo that was not in the radio station room—is to be found and turned over. They paid handsomely for the promise that I would take care of their problem once and for all. And I'm sure I'll find time for their task while I set up my regime here in Sanctuary."

He stepped closer. "Now tell me—"

The door behind Dan slammed back against the wall. "Sheriff Chandler!" Terrence Evangeline's parents raced in, flushed and sweating.

"We didn't know." Mrs. Evangeline rushed to the mayor, completely ignoring Sheriff Chandler. "After you told us about Terrence and Gemma we decided that meant she—"

Chandler cut her off. "Get to the point."

"We had Gemma."

Everyone waited for more.

"And now she's gone." Mr. Evangeline pressed his lips together, more in tune with what was happening in the room than his wife, and knowing he should tread cautiously.

Dan stepped forward. "What do you mean you had Gemma?"

The mayor said, "She's gone?"

Mrs. Evangeline nodded. "We went home to get her for you, so we could bring her back here, but when we got there she was gone. She broke free and escaped."

Mr. Evangeline was a deacon in Dan's church. "You were holding her captive?"

The sheriff said, "If you don't know where she is then maybe you should go and look for her. That would be more useful than you standing around here trying to convince me I shouldn't kill you for being imbeciles."

"But the mayor said—"

Chandler didn't let her finish. "Seems like Collins made a whole lot of promises. But I'm in charge here, and I want the two of you out of my sight. Bring Gemma to me, and I won't kill you."

"Yes, sir."

"Yes, sir." Mrs. Evangeline echoed her husband. They bowed and scraped their way back out of the door. The sight of two people he'd respected in a posture of obeisance to the man who was destroying their town made Dan sick. Where was Gemma? If she'd escaped there were only a few places she might go to hide.

"You know her." Sheriff Chandler stalked toward Dan. "Where would Gemma be hiding? Where did she go?"

Dan wanted to shrug.

"I know you're friends. Probably lovers, too, with a special place you go to be together."

The tent.

For whatever reason it sprang to mind. He hadn't been in that part of the woods for so many years. Not since he discovered how he felt about Gemma, realized it wasn't okay for them to be alone for hours with no one knowing where they were—or what they were doing.

Chandler palmed his gun and waved it toward Dan in a loose grip. "Tell me."

Dan wasn't going to lie and say he didn't know where she could be. He was pretty sure that even if he wanted to, he couldn't lie that well. "The library. Her house. The radio station. My farm. She could have gone anywhere."

"We'll find her."

"I'm sure you will." He hoped that wasn't true, because when Chandler did they would both be dead.

**

Gemma collapsed between two trees. Twigs dug into her knees as she crawled, her breath heaving, into the spot where the tent had been tucked. This was the right place. She looked around, but there was no material left. Even more bizarrely, branches covered with leaves had been woven together to obscure the inside.

She collapsed onto the ground. Soft grass, cleared of rocks and sticks. Gemma rolled over, uncaring that grass and mud were going to cling to her hair. She wasn't going to get caught, and she'd had to dodge two sets of men out searching. For her? For someone else?

Now she just wanted to rest.

She hadn't been out to the site of her tent for years. What had happened to this place? Someone had cleaned it up, for sure. Did they use it? Probably she couldn't lay claim to it anymore, given how long it had been. Still, part of her would always think of this place as "hers." Gemma lifted up on her elbows and looked around. Four-by-six, the light was dim but still peeked through the tightly woven branches. Whoever they were, they'd spent a phenomenal amount of time here perfecting the design to keep the person inside hidden.

When she found out who, she needed to give them a gift basket. This was a wonderful place to hide.

In the corner sat a lantern, one she remembered immediately. Dan had given her that smiley face sticker. Now it was worn on the edges and the yellow had dulled. Gemma sat up and looked around. Nothing else remained, though at the edge behind her head there was a spot which had been cleared and then layered over with pine needles. The difference was purposeful, and she moved toward it.

Leaves rustled.

Gemma's hand halted four inches from the pine needles so purposefully arranged. She waited, hardly daring to breathe for fear of being heard. And what was she going to do, stay here forever? It would get dark in a couple of hours, and really cold tonight. She had no food. No water. And meanwhile the town was under siege with no one to save them.

Gemma wasn't a hero, or a fighter, or even that good at making plans. When she wrote, she could brainstorm for an hour the best way to get the hero out safely. There was no such luxury to save Dan. She needed help. She just didn't know how she was going to get it, or where to get it from. So Gemma prayed and asked God to help her and the town of Sanctuary because as far as she could see there might not be a way out of this. Sheriff Chandler wanted the town he wanted, and there was nothing anyone could do to stop him.

Leaves. A branch shifted, and foliage to her left was disturbed. She'd been in here with small animals before, but the movement lengthened. Stretched from her left all the way to in front of her.

She reared back. Was there someone in here? It looked like they were emerging from beneath the ground.

There was a low moan, and the movement dropped back down to the ground.

"There you are."

Gemma squealed and fell aside onto her hip. Mei crouched in the entrance, one knee to the dirt and the biggest gun Gemma ever saw in her hand. She set it down in the far corner. "Man, that thing is heavy. There's one thing they don't tell you, that you'll end up tromping around with tons of gear that makes you feel like you weigh another hundred pounds."

Gemma whispered, "What are you doing here?"

"Duh, helping." The Chinese woman frowned. "Obviously."

Gemma touched pine needles on the ground. She swept them back with her hand to reveal the dirt underneath.

"Hey, there's something I should tell you."

Her fingers sank into the soft earth, and whisked around the frame of something cold. Metal.

"Gemma? You listening to me?"

She dug the box from the ground with their bare hands. Little bigger than the cash box she kept at the library to collect late fees, it was heavy. She set it down and clicked the latch. It popped up. Gemma stared at the lid but didn't move to open it.

Mei reached past her and grabbed it. She flipped the lid. "Letter. Some papers. Whoa." Mei lifted a gun. "It's a Barak." She caught Gemma's gaze and said, "Not an American weapon. Whoever got this wants something with power and zero flash." She held it out. "Guess it's for you."

Gemma stared at it so long Mei set it on the dirt in front of her.

"This has your name on it." Mei handed her a folded piece of paper. "There's also a passport in here. American. Has your picture, but with the name Elaine Leonard."

"Hal."

"Your father left this for you?"

Gemma nodded. She fingered the paper, but didn't move to unfold it. "He buried it here." The words washed over her as she said them. Her father had found her secret place, he'd preserved it as a haven of safety. And he'd written her a note.

The leaves shifted once again. Gemma dropped the box and scooted as far back as she could in the small space. "What is…"

"That's what I was trying to tell you."

Gemma stared. The figure sat up. Leaves and branches fell to the ground and she saw his face, blood covered. Eyes nearly swollen shut, red had pooled under his nose and dripped down his chin. He looked like he'd been in the ring for two rounds already.

"Terrence." She breathed his name as fear raced through her. His hands and feet and knees were all tied up and his elbows had been taped to his body in a binding that wrapped around his stomach. There was little shirt still visible with the amount of blood on him.

Mei lifted that giant gun and pointed it at his face. Even with his eyes like that, he had to be able to see it.

"Don't move."

Chapter 26

Every foot John placed on the ground was agony. Every breath shot fire through his lungs. That thin body armor might be almost invisible, and it had stopped the bullet, but it had left a bruise the size of Montana on his chest. Sweat poured from his temples but he kept walking. It was the only way to get help for his town. One step at a time, all the way through this mountain that would never end.

He'd followed the tracks for what felt like ever before he saw sunlight on the other side. John hadn't been out of Sanctuary in more than two years. He didn't miss it, even with what was happening now.

His knees buckled, and he planted his hands on the grass as he sucked in clean, fresh air. Ground angled down, away from him. This side of the mountain didn't look too dissimilar to his side. Ponderosa trees. Rocks. Probably a deer, or mountain lion. If he never saw another tunnel in his life, it would be too soon. He didn't know how he was going to walk all the way back through the mountain to town after he made his call, but God would figure it out.

John rolled to his back and slipped his phone from his belt. "Please work." The words were barely audible. He coughed, pulled the water from his backpack and drank the last couple of drops. He held the bottle above his mouth and waited for that last drip. He'd gathered enough intelligence over the last couple of weeks to figure out where the way out of town was.

Thank You, Lord. Now God needed to bring another miracle, because John was all out of steam and strength and ideas.

He lifted the phone again and tried to make out what was on the screen. Signal, but barely. He dialed, praying as it rang that he'd get through.

"Grant Mason." His brother's voice was like a fresh bottle of water.

"It's John."

"Are you okay? What's happening?" The words came out like a rush, and then Grant went silent.

"I'm probably the only one that is okay."

"We've been trying to reach you all day. Ben is freaking out. Mom has been calling me every half an hour, and even Nate was on the phone, saying he can't get through to Pat."

John ran down what had happened.

"Okay, I know 'siege' was on the list, but I never thought it was actually a possibility."

"It happened. Chandler shot me, and now he's claiming the town as his." John took a breath so he could continue. "Please tell me we can deal with this."

The fear was like a voice, screaming into his ear. *You aren't strong enough to save them. They'll die, and you'll be alone forever.* Andra. Pat. The baby. Aaron. His family was back there, and John was out here. "Please tell me I did the right thing." Tears spilled onto his cheeks. John squeezed the bridge of his nose and tried to get ahold of himself.

Grant spoke in his ear. "Brother, you did the only thing you could. Staying there, you could save one. Maybe you could save your family. Now you're going to save the whole town."

"And if Andra dies? Or any of the boys?" None of them would forgive him, and that was fine. John wouldn't forgive himself. "How do I go on after that, Grant?" He choked on his words. "You need to get a helicopter here. I can't even get up. I'm useless. I walked all this way, and for what?"

"To get word out," Grant said. "We're calling everyone in now. We'll come and get you, and then we're going to retake that town. We're going to work together, not alone. This team will get Chandler and get the town back. Okay? Us. Not you, alone. Not Ben. Us, together."

John squeezed his eyes shut and fought back the emotion. "I have to get back there. Now."

What was Andra thinking? Did she believe he was alive? No one had seen him, no one saw Bay. It was almost like God had shielded him from their eyes just so that he could get out. Could it be possible? He didn't know, he'd never experienced anything like it. But now that he was out, it burned in him to get back there. Sanctuary had fallen, and they had to save the people.

"I'll have you picked up. Don't move. We need a static position."

"We can't just fly into town. Chandler will start shooting them like hostages."

Grant said, "When we go back in we do it with a plan. Fast as we can, but not without making sure everyone knows what we're doing."

"Get Ben on it."

"Soon as he calls me back, I will."

John nodded even though his brother couldn't see him. He clenched his free hand into a fist. "I have to get up. I have to move." If he couldn't function, how could he help? The bullet had slammed into him with a force that felled him. Stunned, he'd lain there with his eyes closed, waiting for the bullet to the head which would finish him off. But it never came. Sheriff Chandler had gone onto his next task and left John in the street.

He collapsed back onto the grass and a breeze drifted over his face like a kiss. John held the phone to his ear. "I have to be able to do this, Grant."

"You will. Just rest."

Rest? Nothing to do but wait. John hung up the phone and dropped it on the ground before he threw it at the nearest tree. He looked up at the sky and let out a frustrated cry. Everything he wanted to be, everything he wanted to do. All those people to save, and he might only be able to save some while he lost the ones who meant the most to him.

**

Gemma sat frozen. "Terrence is in my tent."

Mei flipped the gun backwards and slammed the handle part into his temple. Terrence fell back on to the grass. "Are you going to read that letter?"

She looked up, ready to snap at Mei for being so uncaring about what Gemma was feeling. Then she saw the look on the

Chinese woman's face. Her eyes shone, almost childlike under the emotion that swam there.

Mei said, "I'd want to read a letter my father sent me. Even if it was bad, I'd still read it. I'd probably carry it with me, forever."

"Then you know how I feel. But you need to give me a minute." She scooted back as far as she could go to get away from Terrence. He'd still be able to reach her when he woke up. "I don't like him being here."

Mei nodded. "I'll get rid of him for you. But you should know, there could be something in that letter which might help the people in this town live to see tomorrow. So read it now, before we do anything else."

Gemma looked through the other papers that were with the gun and the passport. A photo of five men; on the back their names were listed along with *Saigon Base, March 1976.* These had to be the CIA agents Bill Jones had testified against—the ones Hal kept him safe from. It grated on her that a murderer could be protected, but it wasn't for her to decide. No one person was more or less valuable than anyone else, but people seemed to assign more value to the victim. Or an innocent. People who couldn't protect themselves.

"Why are people in power always so much worse than the bad who have no authority? Instead of just being mean, they make people's lives a living nightmare and we can't avoid them."

Mei took the photo. "That's why there are people like me in the world. We do what we can, dispensing justice where it would otherwise never have come in this life and trying to save just one more person who can't—or won't—save themselves. It's what I was born to do."

"Don't you ever want to just walk away? Disappear and go live another life."

"Sure, but then I'd have to live with the fact that there would come a time when I didn't do anything, and I could have saved someone."

Gemma stared at the woman who just might turn out to be a friend. "So you're basically a superhero."

"You forget. Superheroes are all good all the way to the center of who they are. That's why there aren't any in the world. And I'm not one of them."

Gemma didn't know that she agreed with her friend. Plenty of people were many shades of good and bad. She looked at Terrence, still unconscious. Some were a lot worse than others, but the rest were all a work-in-progress moving toward who they wanted to be. She'd always figured those who accepted they were evil, like Bill Jones, were the ones she was sad for. They couldn't get better, because they'd given up and surrendered to it.

"Now read the letter."

Gemma unfolded the paper and read aloud,

"My dearest Gemma,

For years I have prayed for one chance to tell you who I really am. Your father. For years I have watched you grow, not just in height and age but in character. In strength. You have stood up for the ones who couldn't protect themselves and been hurt because of it. I tried to shield you the only way I knew how, with secrets. But it didn't work.

There is nothing worse in this life than realizing the worst you could have imagined has come true. If you're reading this, things are bad enough in Sanctuary—or for you personally—that you have sought solace in your tent. I tried to build a place of protection, a Sanctuary, for you but I could not. It was beyond my power, but you carved one for yourself in the middle of my nightmare."

Gemma swiped a tear from her cheek and kept reading.

"Even now that Bill Jones is dead, I'm afraid for us. For your mother. For you. The world is full of evil, a dark stench that creeps into our lives and corrupts even the best of us. I have allowed an evil man to hurt everyone I love because it was my duty to ensure he remained in Sanctuary. I thought the town would heal something in him, and it was too late before I realized it had not. Things were the same as ever, maybe worse.

Bill Jones has, for years, spread his evil to others and to you. Dan suffered because of it. His mother was a casualty of my war, and I allowed it. For that I will always be truly sorry. Because of it, I can never have the happiness I desired for myself and for our family. If Dan Walden cannot have peace and love in his life then neither will I.

My prayer is that you will leave. I know you have lived in town your whole life, but I wish for you to see the world. There is beauty in it, and I believe that you will find peace, because I fear that you won't find it here. That is why I have left you this gift, a way out. Protection.

The photo enclosed in this box will save your life when those who hunt me for my part in the betrayal against them come for you. Maybe they are all dead. Maybe my era is over now. But if it is not, use this photo to bargain for your life. There is nothing more important to me than that you live. Leave. Be free when I could not. Love when I could not. Find a Sanctuary of your own.

Your father always and forever,

Hal Leonard."

Gemma snatched up the photo and scrambled to the lantern. She found the matchbook she'd always used to light the wick. Mercifully, it was dry.

She struck a match and held it to the photo.

Mei didn't move. "Are you sure about this?"

Gemma was glad the woman didn't try to stop her. "I don't want this. It isn't going to be a bargaining chip, as much as Hal might've wanted that." The corner curled up toward where she held it. When the heat hit her fingers she dropped the photo on the ground. "They want it, they can't have it. I won't give up something Hal spent his life keeping out of their hands."

Mei's face shone with something that looked a lot like respect. Gemma couldn't decide whether she cared or not what the woman thought.

"I'm not giving it to Chandler. I'm doing what I should have done with all those papers in the radio station in the first place."

"Good."

She didn't need the woman's approval, either. "But now—"

Mei slapped her hand over Gemma's mouth. Before Gemma could react she touched the index finger of her free hand to her closed lips.

"I swear I saw someone go this way." A man, outside their hiding spot, crunched through the pine needles. A branch cracked. More than one set of footsteps.

His cohort said, "I smell burning. Is something on fire?"

"You mean like Janice's house?" They both snickered. Gemma wanted to launch from their spot and punch the guy in the face.

Mei shook her head.

She wanted to do it, but that didn't mean she was going to.

Mei dropped her hand. She patted the photo and the ground around it to extinguish the fire. Her sleeve pulled back with the movement, enough that Gemma saw a stripe of skin around her wrist. It matched the circle of red on her own wrist from being bound by Terrence's parents.

Mei looked up and Gemma realized the woman knew she'd seen it. Mei pulled her hand back and adjusted her sleeve.

Terrence's leg moved.

The footsteps outside got closer. Gemma's stomach knotted as Mei moved again. What was she doing now?

Mei took items from her pockets and set them gently on the ground, no sound emanating from her movements. A granola bar. Another one—birthday cake flavor. A metal pen. A knife in its own sheath. Mei tucked that in her boot and motioned to the gun still lying in the box. Gemma lifted it out, but Mei mouthed the word, *Yours.* Did Mei think she was actually going to use it? Dan had taught her how, but that didn't mean she liked guns.

Terrence shifted and moaned.

The footsteps were right outside now. One of the men said, "I think there's something in here."

Gemma reached over and put her hand on his mouth. She could hold his nose as well, but he'd thrash as his body searched for air.

Mei pulled her pant leg down over her boot to hide the knife and then blew Gemma a silent kiss. She crawled to the entrance, rocked back on her heels like a sprinter and then burst out of the hiding spot.

"Hey!"

Over the man's yell, the sound of a gunshot made Gemma's whole body jerk. *Please don't let Mei get killed.*

"Stop!"

Feet pounded the dirt away from her. Mei wasn't dead.

More shots rang out.

"Okay, I'll stop!" Mei's voice drifted back, her yell quiet over the distance she'd run. "Don't shoot me, I'll go with you."

"The sheriff wants to talk to you."

"Okay. Just don't hurt me."

"Sure," the man's voice wavered on a laugh even as he said it. Gemma heard an "oof" and someone thumped onto the ground.

She lifted her hand from Terrence's mouth and moved away as quietly as she could. She sat again and bit her knuckle to keep from crying out and giving away her position. *Please don't let Mei get hurt.* The woman had given herself up to save Gemma. Probably there was an ulterior motive of taking that knife and being brought to the sheriff. Mei wasn't going to go down without a fight. But what was Gemma supposed to do? Hal had told her to leave. To live.

She wasn't going to leave without at least telling Dan where she was, but how could she do that when all she had was one gun?

Gemma glanced at Terrence.

His eyes were open.

**

A soft knock on the door. Matthias was leaning against the counter by the coffee pot. The Hispanic man shrugged, so Bolton wheeled across his kitchen to the back door. "Who is it?"

The voice beyond the door said, "Sergeant Pepper's lonely hearts club band."

Matthias shook his head. "What?"

Bolton just smiled and opened the door. The general—or at least he used to be—strode in, followed by a former air force officer who was now his assistant. Behind him was Michael, Louis, and Maria's husband, Tim.

Michael and Louis made a bee-line for Matthias. They were godfather's to his daughter, only they took that in the full Italian meaning of the word Godfather. And everyone in town knew it.

Major General Halt pulled up a chair and his assistant, in her forties and never outside without her uniform of a pant suit or skirt suit, found his stash of coffee and set the carafe under the sink to fill. *Guess we're having more coffee.*

Bolton turned his chair to face the table. "Is there a reason why you're invading my kitchen this evening?" Though he figured he knew why, considering they'd broken curfew and snuck in the back instead of ringing the doorbell in front.

Halt cleared his throat. "To make a plan, of course."

"A plan for what?" Matthias folded his arms. Beside him, both Italian men did the same, even though Michael only had one arm. Matthias rolled his eyes. "Bolton and I have been friends for years, you know that. Why would we be planning anything?"

"You're going to let Chandler run this town?"

Matthias didn't answer. Bolton pulled forward to the spot at the table where there was no chair and set his hands on the table. A mug of coffee was placed in front of him. He told the general's assistant, "Thank you" and then said, "This is an extremely delicate situation, Halt. Matthias isn't going to put his daughter in jeopardy."

"She's already in jeopardy," the assistant said as she took her place at the table. "We all are. The young, the old, the infirm, and those entirely capable of taking care of themselves. Now, the sheriff isn't here, so it's up to us."

"If he was, we'd be right beside him." Bolton glanced at the general, and then back at his assistant. "You know that. It's exactly what we did when that rogue SEAL had the town under his thumb."

The general said, "Well then why stop now? We can do this if we team up, just like last time and every time. Chandler is only one man. His army? Maybe ten at a push, and I can count on three fingers how many of them have military training."

"They have guns." Matthias's Italian buddies nodded at his words.

"So do we."

Bolton stared at him. "Where did you get weapons? The mayor and Chandler's men took all mine, all Matthias's. Probably all of Dan's. I saw one take the gun from John's hand after they killed him." He prayed something had happened and John was okay. It was a long-shot, but the man's body hadn't disappeared all by itself, and Andra's leaving the town with the kids was way too planned.

There had to be something going on. It was what he and Matthias had been talking about before they were invaded—John bringing the cavalry.

Major General Halt grinned. "Battle night."

"Those are paintball guns."

"That we've now converted into AR-15's." The general's expression stayed neutral, like he was discussing what kind of sugar to buy. "Expensive, but possible."

Bolton felt his eyebrows rise. "When?"

"Since the SEAL went rampage. People are dying, Bolton."

"You want to start a war? What, roll into town and start shooting up Chandler's men? You're going to start a blood bath."

"Do you want to take the town back, or not? It's really that simple, Bolton. Some of us are willing to risk our lives to win this town back." The general paused, way too accustomed to the dramatic effect of his voice. "We'll split up, A team and B team, just like every time we practiced. The underlings can be overpowered easily. We just need a place to contain them. Then we go after the top dogs."

Bolton didn't even know where to start. This was the craziest idea of all the crazy ideas he'd ever heard in his life. Sure, they needed something dramatic to happen, but Nadia had just encouraged him to pray, saying that was all they needed to do. "Major General—"

"Son, what do you think Battle Night was for? Years we've been training for this."

"We have no advantage."

"We have surprise."

Matthias interjected with, "It won't be enough. People will get hurt. Maybe even killed."

"War is never free of casualties."

Bolton watched the fight range across Matthias's face and knew exactly what the man was feeling. Was Matthias going to go out and fight when it could cost Frannie and the baby their lives? They'd all seen John fall. The likelihood that he'd walked away from a chest shot and that he'd managed to get to help. That the help was then actually coming. It was a long-shot.

And the best chance they had.

Matthias said, "I'm in."

"Me too." "Yeah." The Italians would die side-by-side with him if it took that.

The general's assistant said, "Me."

"Me." The general turned to Bolton and gave him a pointed look.

Movement at the doorway brought his attention around. "Me."

Bolton stared down his teenage son, the boy he hadn't even met until a few months ago. "No."

"This is my home, too, Dad."

He'd never even called Bolton that. Not until tonight.

Chapter 27

Dan pushed through the door to the Meeting House kitchen. Olympia's face glistened with sweat, as she closed the cupboard below the sink and turned to see him. Her eyes flashed with something he couldn't pinpoint, then he lifted a dish towel tucked in her skirt and wiped her forehead. "Dan." She half-whispered his name.

The big soup pot on the stove was full of a broth in which she'd put sausage and potato. The liquid bubbled, giving off a cloud of steam that filled the room. It smelled good but since it was for the sheriff and his men who cared what it tasted like? Dan wanted to grab the handles and throw it on the floor. They could starve for what they were doing to the people in this town.

Olympia lifted a wooden spoon and stirred the pot. He glanced around the room. There was no time to make a trip to the farm and pick some herbs. Not for flavor, no. He'd pick the ones that shouldn't be consumed. Dan didn't grow everything for food. Some plants had other jobs—and some were toxic in varying quantities. But they would notice his absence.

He wondered if there was anything in here that would have the same effect. Cleaning supplies. Rat poison. A wave of guilt rushed over him at even thinking it. *I'm sorry, Papa. I shouldn't even be thinking this, even if I could find the courage to do it. Even if killing might save the lives of more innocents.*

Olympia didn't look over. "I told them you hadn't joined the sheriff. I knew you'd never do that. There had to be some other reason you were with them."

"They killed Chase." That wasn't the reason, but he needed to ask his next question. "Has anyone been to the farm to check on Miranda?"

Olympia nodded. "Louis went out there earlier. When he came back he reported to Matthias, who told me, that Miranda was dead. Her body was on top of Chase's. He said a gun was next to her hand."

"She killed herself?" Dan's thoughts spooked like a horse and bolted.

Olympia's eyes filled with tears. "I won't let them take anymore from me. I won't let them destroy this town when I can do something to stop it."

Dan saw the darkness in her eyes. He'd never known her to be anything other than warm and caring, though he'd seen her get frustrated with her kids and the fact they were adults who sometimes had to be left alone to make dumb adult decisions on their own. Olympia only wanted good things for everyone she knew, and often went out of her way to give that to them.

What could have put that darkness in her eyes now?

"Olympia—"

"It's done. Too late now. There's nothing to do but let things take their course. If God doesn't like what I've done then he shouldn't have put me in the situation where this was my only option." She moved close to whisper in his face, her voice vehement. "Damned now, or not. I will have no regrets. These men murdered my child, and I'm past the point of caring about my future. I'll plead my case with Almighty God."

"Olympia." Her name broke from his lips like a warning. Had she done what he'd thought of doing himself? And how could he blame her for it? "What did you—"

The door swung open. "What's taking so long? We're hungry." His face was set, uncaring that his friend had been shot in the street by a sniper. This man only cared to fill his belly.

Olympia said, "It's almost ready."

"Good. We gotta eat before they bring the China girl in. Then it's fun time."

Dan's stomach churned. He fought to tense it enough he didn't hurl up nothing. A growl erupted from his middle. Olympia went to the counter and tore off a roll from a bag. She handed it over. "Eat this. Not the soup."

Dan held the roll in his hand. "What did you do?"

"Maybe nothing. Maybe something bad. However it turns out is up to the Lord. I don't know what affect it will have on them, but I put plenty in."

His stomach flipped. What had she done? "Plenty of—"

Olympia cut him off. "Don't ask questions you don't want to know the answer to, Pastor. Just carry out the soup so the men out there can eat."

Dan glanced at the circular window, the men beyond restless to eat when the rest of the town suffered at home. Cut off. Shut out. Oppressed. Overtaken.

Dan grabbed the pot and pushed through the swinging doors. *Papa, forgive us.* "Soup's on."

He set it on the table beside where Olympia had laid out bowls and spoons. She set the rolls beside it and handed him a ladle. It shook. Was she having second thoughts about what she'd done? Dan prayed no one would die. If she'd poisoned the soup, this could be bad. As he served the soup, he asked for God's intervention. Olympia had surrendered her life to Him, and Dan wanted only what God desired for this situation. He would continue to pray, for however long Chandler insisted on lording it over the people who lived here, and Dan would never let them walk all over anyone. He should have stopped them from shooting John, and that would forever now be his biggest regret—he hadn't stood up to them.

Could he do it now?

Men filed past them. Dan handed each a small bowl of soup. If there was too much poison, they could die. He didn't want to be a murderer, but this was war and they'd declared it as such with their invasion. Wasn't killing justified in wartime? People's lives were at stake, and these didn't care who was hurt. Men, women, children. Young and old were in danger.

Dan could attempt to justify it in his head as much as he wanted, and he could come up with a solid argument. But that didn't remove the lump in his throat at the idea that he could be complicit in anyone's death. It never would. Some were meant to be soldiers, caretakers of the weak, and those unable to defend themselves. Dan wasn't. He shepherded, he had to. He safeguarded, because that choice had been taken away from him, and he hadn't been able to protect his mother.

The rest of the town needed his help now. Olympia had made a decision, but Dan intended to follow through. How it would turn out was up to the Lord, and Dan trusted Him that it would honor Him. That was Dan's chief desire.

He turned his back to the now eating men, and leaned close to Olympia's ear. "I need a minute to slip out the back. If they have Mei, then I need to find Gemma."

It had been driving him crazy wondering if she was okay after she'd escaped from the Evangeline's house. What was she thinking? Was she hurt? It was like she'd disappeared, and unless someone was hiding her in their home, there was only one place he could think of that Gemma would have gone to.

Olympia leaned back, a blank look on her face he didn't know how to read. "I don't feed traitors like you. Go clean up the kitchen."

Someone snickered.

Dan nodded. "Yes, ma'am."

He strode to the kitchen and pushed at the door. A scuffle brought his attention back around. Two men hauled Mei in by her arms, her legs dangling on the floor behind her. Limp. Both men had blood on their faces—one a nasty gash, the other a broken nose from the look of it. They looked like they'd been in an MMA fight.

Chandler lowered his spoon. "What happened to you?"

"She put up a fight, but we knocked her out." One man let go. Mei's body swung toward the man holding her other arm, and he let go so that she hit the floor on her shoulder. She didn't move.

Chandler said, "Tie her to a chair, and then get something to eat. We all need our strength. This isn't going to be over for a while."

Dan wanted to know what more he thought was going to happen. Or did he just mean dealing with the town? Perhaps he was just prepared for the resistance people would show them all as they weren't prepared to simply submit to a new authority. He didn't like the way Mei's shoulder was angled. Had they dislocated it? The two men looked like they'd been put through the ringer, which meant she'd put up a good fight. How badly had they hurt her just to get her knocked out?

He should be out the door, looking for Gemma. Something held him there while everything in him cried out for him to go. To find her. Dan's gaze didn't move from Mei's prone body. He had no idea what they had planned, but he wasn't going to let them hurt her. Gemma—wherever she was—likely was a whole lot safer than Mei was right now. *Papa, is she safe?* Dan felt the war in him battle between going to Gemma and staying to make sure Mei was guarded.

The men lifted Mei into a chair and taped her to it. The way her shoulder looked, there was something seriously wrong. Her head hung down, her hair obscuring her face. Dan walked over. He touched her cheeks and lifted her chin. Mei's face was a mess of bruises, swollen cuts, and abrasions.

He lowered her head gently and glanced back at the sheriff. "This woman needs a doctor."

Chandler sneered. "She can handle it. You just worry about that bleeding heart of yours."

So now caring about people was a weakness? Dan didn't worry about his "bleeding heart" one bit. The compassion he had for others was God-given in a world where he'd been classified a victim.

Dan strode to the door. "I need some air."

Whether he took off to see Gemma or not, Dan needed to get out of this room. The air felt like it was choking him, like he was right back with his father. The recipient of that man's harsh words and violent temper.

"Not so fast."

Dan turned, one hand on the front door. The cool, dark night air only inches beyond the wood under his palm. Air. Freedom. He looked back across the room. Chandler had stood, Mei halfway between them. Two of the men now pointed their guns at him.

Chandler said, "No one gave you permission to leave."

"I need some air, that's all."

"Sit down, Daniel. It isn't time for you to go just yet."

**

"Everyone has their list of names?" No one indicated they didn't. Bolton bit his lip. Were they really going to do this?

The general leaned against the counter. "We're all set. Everyone has their quadrant to take care of."

But this wasn't Battle Night, it was real. "We should pray before we go out."

Javier walked over, so Bolton held out his hand. When the boy took it, Bolton bowed his head and prayed. There was a limited amount of things he could do from his wheelchair, but that might work to his advantage. Helplessness gave him the element of surprise. He was counting on these guys seeing only the chair—and not remembering the fact he could walk a few steps.

When he said, "Amen" and lifted his head, Nadia stood in the doorway, a gun held loose in her hand. She lifted her chin. "If you're doing this, so am I."

**

Andra kissed Nicholas on his perfect cheek. His skin was warm and soft, there was really nothing in the world like the feel of a baby. She re-adjusted the blanket that didn't need fixing and left him to sleep on her coat that she'd bundled up on the floor. Wide awake, Andra surveyed the room. Pat, asleep on the floor in the corner. Aaron, two feet away from his brother, the comic book they'd been reading between them.

She walked through the shell of the building John had begun constructing. He'd made more progress than she'd imagined, and the bag had been under the new floorboard right where she'd had it stashed in the cabin that had burned down.

He'd put it there. For her. He'd been here—but when?

The gratitude sat in her stomach along with all the questions. The mix was like a tart dessert. Not all the way sweet and satisfying when the first taste was too sharp to enjoy. *John.* She wanted him there with her, not who knew where. Dead or alive. There could only be one reason his pack was gone while hers had been under the floorboards. He'd been here before he went… wherever he went.

Lord, where did he go? Andra wandered to the door and picked up the shotgun that leaned against the wall inside. There were no windows, just openings that let the air in. The wind. The rain. Exposed with little protection from the elements.

That was how she felt. Exposed. Alone, protecting her boys. Wondering if her husband would ever come.

She stepped outside onto the grass and over the exposed frame of the porch. She'd be able to hear if the boys were hurt, or disturbed somehow. That was one good thing to come from the cabin being far from finished.

She was, what…seventy-eight percent sure he was alive? Factoring in any injuries he might have sustained. The new vest he'd ordered and been wearing since he was stabbed in the chest. Well, that wasn't totally true. He'd been wearing it since she told him she was pregnant. Not that their child made more of a difference than Pat, or even Aaron, but there was something in John that had changed with everything that had happened in Sanctuary and culminated in Nicholas's life. John was no longer prepared to take chances

Which meant that if he was alive, he was doing everything possible to return and save them.

Andra looked up at the sky and watched the stars for a moment. The flashing lights of an aircraft interrupted her musings. The outline got bigger, the lights brighter. It circled, as though surveying the area. In the dark. From that high?

Andra kept watch. The plane kept its steady course, and then she saw the first one. Another. Then another. Five total that she could see, descending into town under cover of darkness and making the stars wink out for a second as they flew through the sky.

Parachutes.

**

"I won't let you hurt any of these people."

The sheriff sneered at Dan's words. "As if you can stop me?" He snorted. "That's funny coming from the son of Bill Jones. Do you know how many people your father murdered? Massacres. People slit open from nose to navel just for the fun of it. He told me about it once, he did. The way blood runs out, warm. Seeping from a person the same way life bleeds from their eyes. I didn't believe it until the first time I saw it for myself." He paused. "And you'd know all about that, wouldn't you Daniel? He told me what you did to your mother."

Dan didn't let his words penetrate. Instead, he glanced around the room. The sheriff's men listened, waiting for instructions. Olympia watched the scene play out with her dish rag over her mouth. Mei was in the center of the room, still tied to that chair.

The mayor strode through the kitchen, a satellite phone in his hand. "They aren't happy." He went directly to the sheriff's side. "They want proof it's been taken care of, and they want it by dawn."

Sheriff Chandler didn't take his attention from Dan. "Then that's what they'll have. Afterward we get on with our lives. With rebuilding this town to its former glory."

"What former glory?" Dan genuinely wanted to know what Chandler thought was so great about the way town used to be run. "We don't get supplies from the military, or funding from the government. It's all private now. What if the committee decides they aren't going to give you any money?"

Chandler said, "Where do you think your father hid all his money?"

"How would I know?"

"I do, and I persuaded him to give me access to it. So you see, we don't need anyone's help."

"Because you're going to spend your own money buying toilet paper for the people who live in this town?" Dan didn't think he was that benevolent.

Mei let out a low moan. She shifted in her chair, and then her head came up. Her gaze swept the room and then zeroed in on Chandler. "We meet at last."

The mayor palmed a gun, walked across the room and pressed the gun against Mei's thigh. He pulled the trigger.

"Collins! What are you—" Dan made it two steps before the mayor lifted the gun and pointed it at him. He fired a shot at the floor in front of Dan that made his steps falter. He stopped.

Mei gritted her teeth and cried out, her body taut like a wire. She pushed out a breath, turned her head to the side, and was sick on the floor.

"She works for Ben Mason," the mayor said. Then he turned to her. "Where is he?"

Mei's gaze lifted. "Who?"

The mayor didn't move. "Like you don't know."

"Well he isn't here." Sweat rolled down Mei's cheeks. "Because if he was, you'd be dead."

The sheriff smirked. Dan had to do something, the two of them and their rampage was out of control. But what? He had no weapon. No skills. All he could do was pray, but that didn't stop the blood pooling from Mei's leg onto the floor. How could she talk? How could she sit there?

The mayor said, "I'm waiting for him. He'll come."

Chapter 28

John's brushed off his brother's hand and continued along the path toward town. "I'm fine."

Grant shot him a look that said he wasn't convinced at all. John didn't much care. They were back in Sanctuary, by parachute of all things. The landing hadn't done his injuries any favors. John had blacked out for a minute and woke up to Grant shaking him and yelling. Now he just wanted to get this done and get to Andra. He had to take care of the town before he could find his family and make sure they were safe. For right now he was trusting God, and trusting in Andra's ability and all the will she possessed to safeguard their kids and Aaron, to keep them safe, and out of harm's way.

He'd never prayed so much as he had since the second he realized the situation in Sanctuary was beyond his ability to take care of and that he needed help. *God is my help.* John had arrived here as a nonbeliever, and over the last two years had journeyed with every step toward the solid relationship he now had with the Lord. His Lord. Not just other people's God. Jesus was now personal to him, and part of his life. And John didn't understand everything about God and the Bible, but he believed.

And that was a good thing, because they needed Him now more than ever. The future of Sanctuary was on the line, not just the people who lived here.

His boot hit a rock, and he stumbled. Grant reached out and grabbed him, one arm around his waist. The motion shot pain through John's torso, and he cried out.

Grant jumped back. "Sorry. Sorry."

John put everything he felt into the look he sent his brother's way. "We're supposed to be keeping our voices down."

"I'm just trying to help."

"Well stop trying. Don't worry about me, worry about all the people who've been stuck here with Chandler and the mayor the whole time I've been gone."

John started walking again, his flashlight bobbing on the gassy dirt beneath his feet. The temptation to go to Andra and forget the rest of the town was strong—which was why Ben put him on this side of town. He'd even thought about angling his parachute toward the cabin, even while he prayed she'd made it over there. The rest of them could take care of—

John lifted his fist. Grant halted at the same time—he'd heard it, too. John studied the area around them, listening as intently as he could for what it was that he'd heard.

A whistle, one long and two short. It wouldn't mean much to anyone, but it was the signal he and Bolton had used during the last Battle Night. Bolton had gotten all-terrain wheels for his chair just so he could participate. Much to Nadia's dismay. Though likely only because they were on different teams.

He called out, "It's John." Grant reacted to his shout, but John slammed his arm across his brother's chest to stall him. "It's fine." Always the big brother, finding fault with everything John did without asking questions so that he could understand.

Bolton pushed out from behind the cover of the trees. His smile stretched wide. "It's really good to see you, friend."

John strode over, and they shook hands.

"You got shot. We all saw it."

John rubbed the spot on his chest where the bruise was a ripe blue color. "Broke a rib. Hurts like the dickens."

Bolton shook with laughter, though no sound emerged. "So you're back?" He glanced at Grant and lifted his chin. "Ben here, too?"

"The whole team." Grant said. "Shadrach, Daire. And Malachi." His disapproval of that was plain on his face.

"Malachi?"

John said, "You met him in Hawaii. He just called himself Colt."

"The biker dude?"

John nodded. "There's a story for you."

"You're gonna want to tell me that story later."

"Deal." Malachi—Colt—hadn't been allowed to live in Sanctuary, but Ben had recruited the man for his team. "I'm ready to get to work." John had to ask, though. "Have you seen Andra?"

"She disappeared out of the Meeting House with the boys."

"Good."

"It was foolish. She should have stayed here. Safe."

"You think they'd have left her alone?" Especially with him gone. There was no way the sheriff and his army would have steered clear of her. They'd likely have harassed her. Which was why they'd formulated a plan for Andra to get the boys to safety. They'd agreed that while helping the town was a priority, it was better for her to make sure their family was safe than put them all on the line.

Kind of like the plan he'd formulated with Bolton for precisely such an eventuality as the hostile takeover of the town. "Did you set everything up?"

"You were dead. You know that, right?"

"Does that mean you didn't?"

Bolton stared him down. "It means Major General Halt took it upon himself to put together a vigilante army to take back the town."

"Good," John said. "That means we're here just in time to help."

"The major general's plan is in place, but there's no way to communicate a change to any of them. None of us have radios." Bolton glanced at his watch. "And I have one minute to get to Main Street since I already put my man down."

He wheeled the chair down the path a ways where they found a resident on his face, the back of his head bloody from what John figured was blunt force trauma. The man's hands had been tied behind his back—his feet, too—and he was tethered to a tree. "How'd you reach up that high?"

"I had the element of surprise on my side."

At Bolton's words, Javier stepped out from between the trees. "Dad distracted him, and I hit him over the head." He glanced at his father. "Coast is clear."

Bolton nodded, and John shook the boy's hand. He knew it had been a long road for Javier to trust Bolton. Calling him "Dad" was a huge milestone.

Grant leaned down and checked the man's pulse with two fingers. "You didn't kill him?"

Javier blanched. Bolton shook his head. "We want the town back, but we don't want anyone dead."

"I'll let Ben know to expect additional clean-up and the transportation of detainees." Grant clicked his radio and talked to their brother as he walked away from the group. John heard the conversation at low volume in his earphones.

He turned back to Bolton. "Tell me what you know."

Bolton ran down the situation for him—though John had seen Dan with the old sheriff with his own eyes—and then said, "Now they're holed up at the Meeting House. We think they're waiting for something."

John nodded. "The sheriff wants a photo that was kept here, one the mayor didn't find in Hal's radio room. He's supposed to deliver it to the people Dan's father testified against." John took a second to compose himself before he said, "He's also supposed to kill anyone remaining alive who knows about Bill Jones and Hal Leonard and the CIA agents they brought down."

Bolton's jaw muscle twitched. "We can't let them kill Dan and Gemma."

"I know."

"But Dan's with him, and I don't even know where Gemma is. No one's seen her."

"We have two priorities. Then we take back the town." As soon as it was done he would find Andra and the boys.

Whether Dan's defecting to the sheriff's side would be a problem or not, they still had a job to do. Lives to save.

A town to take back.

**

Gun in hand, Gemma turned the corner behind the mayor's place. What she should be doing was going to Terrence's parents' house. But putting a bullet in each of them wasn't on her bucket list. Neither had it been on Gemma's, which was why she'd held the gun on him but not fired that shot.

She might have been discovered because of it, so she'd simply left him there. Discarded like the nothing he was.

Gemma wasn't entirely sure what she was going to do now, but she could wave this thing around. She could confront the mayor, and get Mei back. Gemma wasn't going to let the deputy sheriff get hurt on her account. She had a feeling there was a lot of good Mei could do in the world—even if that good was simply disposing of some bad.

She'd never been flippant about killing before, but Gemma had lived in this town before. She didn't figure it was much like the real world, and their lives were in danger now. If ever there were extenuating circumstances these were those.

Mostly though, she figured that when it came down to it, she'd freeze up the way she always did. That was why she wasn't going to sit around and do nothing. Gemma was going to put up what fight she could, and let God take care of the rest. Dan probably wouldn't agree with that theology, but it was all she had right then. Hal had loved her, he'd given up nearly all that he had in order to make sure she was safe. To still be able to be close to her.

What had she ever done for someone she cared about?

She heard two people go in, and the screen door slammed behind them. This had to be a spot they were holed up, maybe even where they were keeping Mei. If she could slip in a window, she could get Mei out of here. Then the deputy could help her figure out a plan. All her brain seemed to want to do was go back over the words of her father's letter. She ached to stop, pull it from her pocket and read his words over and over again. But she couldn't. Not now when the town was in so much trouble.

Inside, she could hear muffled voices. Gemma crept along the siding to the rear of the house. Maybe she could sneak in through the patio door and look around. If she was found she could play dumb, but it would be hard to come up with a plausible story when she had no idea what had been happening in town since she escaped from the Evangeline's house.

She still shuddered just thinking about what they'd been planning on doing with her. If she ran into them, it wasn't going to be pretty—and it depended a whole lot on whether she was capable of killing them. She might want to. Her dad might have armed her. But pulling the trigger was another story altogether.

"Come on. We're going to miss dinner because you're taking so long in there."

A toilet flushed, and a door lock clicked. "All right, all right. Keep your panties on."

Gemma figured she didn't need to look in the frosted window. She wouldn't see anything good, if she could make it out through the distortion. The front door opened and boots tromped down the front steps. Gemma held the gun in front of her, just in case they came around the back way, and then sprinted to the front of the house.

Two younger men she'd never seen in the library strode toward town. Gemma waited until they were a good distance away, and then set out after them. If they turned she'd be seen, but she had to figure the dark and the distraction of impending dinner on her side.

Main Street was quiet except for the lights and noise inside the Meeting House. Gemma ducked in the alcove of Sam's gym and watched them go inside.

"Guess I lucked out."

She spun, but he was too fast. A flat palm hit her forearm, and the gun skidded across the floor. She dashed away, got two steps, and he tackled her. Gemma hit the concrete with the man's body on top of hers. He laid there, his breath hot on her ear while Gemma struggled. "Shame. No time to play."

The man hauled her to her feet. Gemma twisted and tried as hard as she could to get free of his grip. He marched her to the Meeting House and strode inside. "Lookie what I found creeping around outside."

The room was full, most of the men were sweating, and a couple looked very pale. Olympia stood by the kitchen door, hands twisted in her apron. Mei was tied to a chair, blood in a pool on the floor beneath her wet leg. Gemma broke out of the man's grip and ran over. She touched Mei's shoulder and her knee. The Chinese woman didn't stir. Gemma twisted to the sheriff and yelled, "What did you do?"

But it was Dan her gaze snagged on. Sitting in the corner where she hadn't seen him.

A gun to his head.

He mouthed her name. The man with the gun grabbed Dan's shirt over his shoulder and fisted it in his hand.

Gemma stood, taking one step back on reflex. "What's going on?"

Okay, that was a dumb question. They were taking over the town. But why target Dan and Mei? There were much more important people in this town. People capable of fighting back. Why was Dan being held at gunpoint? Why did Mei look like she'd been tortured?

Sheriff Chandler stood. He wobbled a little before he found his footing, but wiped his moist brow with his sleeve and walked over to her. "I was sent here with a task. One I think you might be able to help me with."

"Me?"

Chandler nodded. "Your father had a photo Bill Jones *retrieved* from Saigon CIA base. The photo is a group of men. Agents. The remaining ones would like their identities to remain a secret."

"A bunch of old guys don't want it to get out that they hired Bill Jones to kill people in Vietnam, or that they were in bed with Vietnamese drug dealers?"

"Let's put it this way," Chandler said. "There are some constituents in two different states who would frown upon such things being revealed about their representative's days as young men in Vietnam. Not to mention the ramifications if the Pentagon found out, and what would happen within the Justice Department."

"So they want a photo? That's it?"

"I get the town. They get the peace of mind their problem has been…resolved."

Yeah, they were going to kill her. And Dan. Probably Mei, too. If she wasn't already dead. Gemma sniffed. "Fine. Let's make a deal."

The mayor snorted. "You want to make a deal?"

Gemma ignored him the way the sheriff was, and said, "That's how these things work isn't it? You get hired to do something. Well, I want to bargain as well."

The sheriff opened his mouth. He didn't speak for a moment, but lifted his hand and pressed it against his stomach. "I'm listening."

**

What was she doing? More than one man had a gun pointed at Gemma. *Papa, what are we going to do?* Dan stood waiting for Gemma's bargain. While thoughts rushed back and forth across her face, Dan prayed. The man beside the door leaned over and retched. Phil's grip on Dan's shirt loosened. He turned to the side and did the same. The gun lowered.

Dan wasn't going to waste an opportunity that Olympia's actions had given him, but that he wasn't going to discount God's hand in. He twisted, grabbed the gun from the man's hand, and punched Phil in the head. He dropped to the floor like a pile of hay.

Dan spun to the room. Four guns pointed at him. Someone was sick, and at least two men moaned.

"Enough!" The sheriff's yell wasn't directed at anyone, just the room in general. Then he turned to Dan. "Drop the gun."

"No way."

Gemma stood in the center. All the weapons in the room were either aimed at her, or would be in a matter of half a second.

"Gemma, walk to me."

She ran over, grabbed his free hand, and moved around to stand behind him. Neither of them let go. From behind him, she said, "The town for the photo. I give it to you, and you leave them alone. Let them live in peace." She paused a second.

"And you get medical attention for Mei. Actually that's my first condition."

Except that they had little leverage. If the sheriff decided he could protect himself from the former CIA agents who had sent him back here, he wouldn't need to return the photo. Betrayal would mean they had nothing left he needed. The sheriff could simply order them all killed and set up the "new" Sanctuary he wanted without anyone willing to oppose him.

Dan wasn't willing for that to happen to the people who remained. A life of oppression wasn't something he would wish on anyone. Not when he had intimate knowledge of what it was like to live under the rule of someone who wanted their way and would do anything to get it.

The sheriff walked to Olympia. She let out a squeak right before he grabbed her upper arm in his grip. He held his gun to her head and strode back to the middle of the room. His steps faltered, and he swayed. Olympia tumbled to the floor while the sheriff moaned.

He couldn't start shooting. They would get shot. Mei would get shot. Olympia. It would be a blood bath. And while Dan felt better about having it in his hand, it was likely not going to do him any good.

"This is not an impasse!" The mayor waved his gun violently around the room and walked over. "You two die right now. Olympia dies. Mei dies. When Ben Mason gets here, I'll kill him, too."

He thought Dan was just going to let them kill him and Gemma without doing anything back?

"No." The sheriff stood. "We need the video."

"What do you care about making a video of it? Keep the money. Kill them and we don't need that photo. Job done."

"And days from now when a drone on a 'training mission' jumps its programming and drops a bomb on this town, what then? Will you care when we all go up in a ball of flames? You have no idea who these people are."

Another man collapsed. The mayor shook his head. "I knew not to trust you." He hauled Olympia to her feet. "Guess who dies first."

"Wait." The sheriff strode over. "I have an idea. A way to draw out whoever opposes us, using their beloved matron to send a signal. We cannot be stopped." He pointed at Dan. "They're right to be afraid. And we're going to make sure everyone else knows it."

Of course they were afraid. Dan could feel Gemma trembling behind him, and he was sure he was doing the same. And why not? Fear was good, especially when the situation warranted it. And it didn't change the fact he knew where his security lay. Dan would be safeguarded by God, and Gemma would be as well.

Whether they lived or died, they were in His hands.

The mayor stopped the sheriff with a hand. "You're in no condition. I'll do it."

Dan tried to remember if he'd seen the mayor take a bite of Olympia's contaminated food but couldn't remember.

The sheriff nodded. "I'll call in the doctor. You take her outside."

"I know how to make a statement, Chandler. Don't worry about that."

**

John looked through his binoculars. "I see movement. The Meeting House door is opening." He was crammed in the corner of Sam's gym by the window. The rest of them were scattered around Main Street, Ben's men filling in the holes where Bolton and the general hadn't been able to cover every spot.

"I see them." Shadrach's voice came through the radio clearly.

Grant said, "Let us know when you have a shot."

"Copy that."

"I vote we move in. Take them out hard and fast." Daire's reputation wasn't one John knew well, but what he did know fit what he had seen of the man so far. He had no tolerance for anyone who put a woman or child in jeopardy.

John didn't want that unless he absolutely had to give the order. "There are innocent people in there. I don't want a blood bath."

Olympia exited the Meeting House. Her hands were clenched in front, her face pale and eyes wide. Dread. She knew what was about to happen, and she was convinced. She was going to die.

John shifted before he even registered the intent to move toward the door. He didn't want to start a war, but these people had trusted him and the committee—and beyond them the US Marshals—with their safety. He didn't want to let them down. Besides, Olympia was a wonderful woman who blessed others without expecting anything in return. She was rare in a world of selfish people out for only themselves.

John heard a mic being cued, and then Matthias's voice came on. "No one shoot. That's my mom." His voice was laced with dread. "No one shoot."

The mayor was with her, one hand on Olympia's shoulder. A gun in his other hand. Collins shifted and pointed it underneath her chin. John's first thought was, if he fired at that angle the bullet would go through Olympia's head and probably hit the mayor, too. The man might wield his power like a pro, but he wasn't a gunman. More like a politician with an evil bent. Okay, so basically just a politician then.

"I know you're out here," the mayor yelled. "I know you can hear me!"

He shuffled forward, moving Olympia to the center of Main Street. The woman was going to be collateral damage in this war, if John didn't give the order to move forward.

"Back off!" The mayor spun, keeping Olympia in front of him.

John leaned out of the gym's front door. Matthias stood at the other end of Main, gun raised at the mayor.

"Let her go!" Matthias's voice rang out down the street.

John stepped out. "All units converge, but give them space."

He moved first, as far in as he wanted them to move. The rest of the men would get the idea. Matthias kept his attention on the mayor, but the man spun as he took in the multiple men all congregating around him now.

"If you all want to die, feel free to get closer."

John cued his radio. "Shad?"

A second later, the former Marine replied, "Still no shot."

The mayor started to back up toward the Meeting House. "In a second, men will pour from this building and kill all of you!"

The situation had turned, and Collins knew it. Faced with the force of who John had brought back with him, he was making a retreat.

"Let her go!" Matthias moved as well.

Collins fired a shot. It hit the ground in front of Matthias. The young man jumped back, gun still aimed at the mayor.

"I don't have a clean shot." Daire was to John's left.

"Don't hit her."

Matthias's order was obeyed. Grant was between John and Matthias, and said, "I don't have a shot, either."

John could fire, but he'd hit Olympia's shoulder. Any one of them could minimize the damage to her, but Matthias's order counted. No one fired.

Bolton was at the medical center, rallying help. They were spread thin, but they'd made it this far. One last stand off outside the Meeting House and they would be in. These men would be caught. The mayor neutralized. The old sheriff arrested.

John wanted them all taken down.

"Enough, Collins." John didn't want anyone getting hit. "Drop the gun and let Olympia go. This has gone far enough. It's time to surrender."

Collins's eyes narrowed on him. "This town is ours now."

"It will never be yours."

The mayor shifted. His back hit the door. He moved his gun, fired off a group of shots across the ground that made them all back up. No one wanted to get their toes shot off.

Collins grinned. "Wanna bet?"

He squeezed the trigger of his gun, buried in Olympia's side. The woman went stiff as the life bled from her face.

The mayor slipped back inside the Meeting House before Olympia dropped to the floor.

Gunshots erupted as Matthias fired on the door. Grant tackled him to the ground. "There are people in there!"

John held down the button on his radio and ran to her. "Everyone take up positions around the Meeting House. And get me the megaphone. We're going inside."

He reached down and touched her cheek. Felt for a pulse.

Olympia was dead.

Chapter 29

Dan gripped the gun so hard his hand was beginning to cramp. Mayor Collins raced through the room. He slammed into the swinging doors to the kitchen and kept running.

"Collins!"

He ignored the sheriff's yell. Chandler hadn't called for Elliot to come and take care of Mei. Instead, he'd watched the mayor go outside, and they'd all heard him make his "statement." Hot tears spilled down Dan's cheeks. Collins had shot Olympia.

Dan whispered, "Glory to the Father and to the Son and to the Holy Spirit, both now and ever, and unto the ages of ages. Amen." He took a breath and continued through the prayer to, "…for Thy Name's sake. Lord, have mercy."

Behind him, Gemma whispered, "Lord, have mercy."

The sheriff's eyes narrowed at the aim Dan had on him. All he had to do was pull the trigger.

Across the room one of his men groaned and then fell to the floor. Then another. The sheriff pressed his lips together, and his torso jerked like he was going to throw up.

"Sheriff Chandler, we have you surrounded!" John's voice boomed from outside. "Surrender now. Your army has been incapacitated, and there is no one left to fight for you."

Inside the Meeting House another man fell to the floor. John didn't know how right he was. The sheriff took one step and collapsed to his knees, moaning. His gun wavered, but he didn't lower it. Gemma gasped as it centered back on the two of them again.

Dan should simply shoot the man. Plant a bullet in the sheriff for everything he'd done, and finish this. Finish the man. A person. Dan saw his mother's face in his mind, even while he stared at the sheriff's nasty sneer. *Her body jerked from the impact of the shock, her eyes widened, and surprise washed over her face.* Gemma shifted closer to him. Her arms came around his waist from behind, an embrace, and she surrounded him with her caring and support.

John's voice infiltrated the room once again. "This is your last warning!"

Dan shifted his finger on the trigger. The sheriff was going to kill them first, and Dan couldn't let that happen. He needed to do this even though his heart pounded. Dan heard every beat in his head. Every intake of breath rushed through his ears. Gemma's arm tightened on his diaphragm, and her other arm moved, covered his arm that held the gun. Her hand slid down his forearm to cover his.

Dan's breath hitched.

The sheriff's eyes narrowed. "Where is the photo?"

Gemma spoke to the man, over Dan's shoulder. "I burned it, Sheriff. Your campaign of terror is over."

Chandler zeroed his gun's aim on them. Dan tried to pull the trigger of his weapon, but his finger wouldn't move. Gemma's hand moved over his, just as his father had done. But this was nothing like that day, this was for them. Together. For Sanctuary.

A door slammed behind them, and Dan fired the shot. Another gunshot immediately followed at almost exactly the same time. Chandler flew backward and hit the floor as men poured in the room.

"Guns down!"

"On the floor."

Dan dropped his weapon and heard it clatter on the floor. People ran around them, but Gemma didn't let go. They stood still in the midst of the chaos, still in their embrace. He shut his eyes, and Gemma put her head on his shoulder. He heard her whisper quietly, "Thank You, Lord."

Dan echoed her words. God had given him Gemma when he needed her most, to give him the strength to do what he'd needed to do.

"We need to talk."

Dan opened his eyes to find John stood in front of him. Dan nodded, and then said, "Are you okay, Sheriff?"

"I'm having a real bad day, Dan. I'm not gonna lie." John blew out a breath. "I'll be glad when I can get to Andra and be done with this."

Men, some of whom Dan knew and some he didn't, ran around them, scooping up the sheriff and his men. Securing their hands behind their backs.

"Maybe we can talk tomorrow."

John studied his face, then he nodded. "Okay, that sounds good." He strode away and crouched beside Mei as one of the men cut her bonds. John pulled her arm around his shoulder.

"Come on, partner. Let's get you some help." He stood, then slipped his other arm under her knees.

Mei glanced up and looked around. "Is he here?"

**

Ben watched the mayor round the corner from his position, tucked behind a door. The mayor's face was flushed. His eyes flicked around frantically as he raced down the alley. Ben stepped out from the cover of the door, gun raised, and waited for the second the mayor spotted him in his way.

Collins cried out and pulled up short. He brought his gun up, and they faced-off against each other. "I've been waiting for this moment for two years." His lips curled up, but not with humor.

"Put the gun down."

The mayor shook his head. "Why would I do that when I have two years of pent-up revenge to satisfy?"

"Been up to a few things in the meantime. Bored, so you jumped on Chandler's bandwagon. But not because you had the brains to figure out a coup all by yourself. No, you're only a follower. Why anyone ever elected you leader over this town is a mystery to me. Probably always will be." Ben sighed, feeling every one of his forty-six years at that moment. "I know who hired you and sent you here to Sanctuary. I know you owe a debt you can't pay, and Chandler was part of appeasing them. I know you were sent to infiltrate this town, to make sure Chandler was doing his job—and to watch over things while he was gone. And I know you made a deal with them. One, sorry to say, you won't be making good on."

Ben should kill him right now. "I told you two years ago not to mess with my family, and I meant it. You've gone too far, haven't you, Thomas Fingerling?"

The mayor gasped.

That was the last card Ben had left to play with the man. The game was over now. All he had to do was pull the trigger, and the mayor would hit the ground, dead.

And yet, he couldn't. Had he lost his mojo?

Thump.

The mayor's mouth dropped open, and he slumped to the floor. Daire stood behind him, jeans and T-shirt. That ugly, scuffed leather jacket. Ben's associate shook his head. "What is wrong with you?" He shrugged, gun in hand. "A lifetime of being verbose and suddenly you're giving him a long-winded speech. Bang. He's dead. Conversation over." Daire shrugged again.

"It isn't like you killed him."

Daire cocked his head to one side. "Why bother when he'll be dead the minute his name hits the prison system database?"

"Then why are we arguing about killing him?"

"Because you've been in a funk since Nadia Marie's thing, when you saw *her* in Denver."

Ben turned to walk away but Daire's phone rang. He didn't want to talk about that, but nothing had been right since then. Daire was right, Ben was in a funk and it was starting to affect his work.

Ben waited through the short conversation, then Daire hung up. "Remy said Bogota checks out."

"Then let's roll."

Daire said, "You don't want to check on Mei?"

Daire's feelings about his family weren't a secret, but that didn't mean Ben ran his the same way. He didn't need Daire to tell him how to do this when it would only remind him how much he sucked at it. Ben could infiltrate anywhere, get information out of anyone, and complete every mission ever assigned to him. This, he couldn't figure out.

"I'll check in on her when I have more time."

**

John stood out front of his office and watched Grant gesture wildly to the Air Force colonel who'd come with military police. He'd directed the entire town, organizing removal of every man that worked with the mayor. John was beyond grateful for his help, even if Grant had retired from the Marshal's Service and gone to work for Ben. At least one of his brothers had stuck around. Ben had left for Bogota, of all places.

The Meeting House doors opened and two men walked out, escorting the mayor between them. Matthias broke from his conversation with Bolton and ran over. "You killed her!"

John sprinted over faster than his bruises wanted him to and intercepted his friend. He hugged Matthias around the middle. "Easy."

"Easy? He shot my mother in front of all of us."

John didn't let go of his friend. "I'm sorry."

"You're not the one who should be sorry."

At Matthias's words the mayor lifted his head and smirked. A baby started to cry. That was what broke through the rage which coursed through Matthias. John felt the shift in him, and Matthias glanced back over his shoulder. Frannie stood watching, a worried look on her face. The baby in her arms squirmed and let out another cry.

"Go to your family."

Matthias nodded and then heeded John's words.

The mayor let out a snicker.

Matthias halted and turned back, halfway to his family. John didn't wait for him to come back over, he strode to the mayor, balled his fist, and punched Collins's cheekbone. The impact reverberated up his arm, and the men holding the mayor both took a step back.

John walked away.

Grant waited for him. "Feel better now?"

"You don't know these people." He got in Grant's face. "You've never lived here, so don't ask me if I'm going to *feel better* when people are hurt, and others are *dead*."

Grant backed up and raised his hands.

John snapped, "Don't you have some secret mission to go on with Ben?"

"He feels my skillset would be better used here." Grant looked around. "Even though I never lived here, these people know me. I was there for each of them in some of the scariest times of their life." He paused. "I sent them here, I put them in danger."

"You didn't know this was going to happen. How could you have?" If they had, then John would have protected them. Olympia wouldn't be dead.

A muscle in Grant's jaw flexed. "Bill Jones compromised this town. That's the problem with putting criminals in witness protection. They don't want to follow the rules."

"A man like Bill Jones was never going to tow the line. It was a disaster waiting to happen. Just like the idea of a secret town."

"And I put all these people at risk because of it." Grant glanced over to where Dan stood, Gemma under the circle of his arm. "I didn't even think much about the ones that were born here. How could they be in danger when this was a place of safety? I might as well have held a gun to their heads myself."

"You aren't to blame."

"Well it feels like it." Grant squared off with him. "And maybe it should. Maybe someone should feel responsible."

John understood that need, the one which held him accountable for the authority he had within this town. The people who lived here hadn't elected him sheriff, but they had trusted him to keep them safe. He grabbed his brother by the back of the neck, squeezed the tension he found there, and then pulled Grant in for a hug.

"Dad!" Pat's voice brought John's head around. Behind his son, Andra carried Nicholas in a sling. Aaron was with them, a wariness in his eyes John wasn't sure would ever go away. John walked toward them. Pat started to run. John did the same. He caught up his son in his arms and hugged him. When Aaron got close, he pulled him and Andra and Nicholas into his arms.

"You're back."

John shifted his head so he could see in his wife's eyes. He gave her a quick kiss. "I'm back."

The question was, what would happen to Sanctuary now?

"I know that look." Grant grinned, said, "Hi, Andra." He turned back to John. Pat launched himself from John's arms to his uncle Grant, who chuckled. "Hey, kid." To John, he said, "The town is a mess, and this is going to take time to repair. But the advantage we have now is that exit plans are in place. If people want to stay here because it's their home, we can do that. If they want to leave then they can opt out. There are also some other… *options*."

"Which are?"

Grant said, "I'll have to discuss those with you at a later date."

Which meant, when they were alone. Which meant, after Grant told him, John would go home and tell Andra.

She smiled at him.

John would never, not ever in his life, get tired of seeing his wife's smile.

**

Dan waited for a break in conversation and then pulled Gemma aside so he could talk to her without anyone listening. Yes, they were only curious because of the suddenness of their relationship, but there was plenty of time to explain that, in a way, Gemma and Dan had been together for years.

"Are you okay?"

Dan kissed the frown above her eyes because he could. "No, but I will be."

He tugged her all the way to the sheriff's office and into the alley so they could have some peace and quiet. Gemma touched his cheeks, lifted up, and planted a kiss on his lips. "So will I."

"A while ago…"

"Yes?"

"You said you were planning to leave Sanctuary."

She pressed her lips together.

"Gemma…"

"Looks like I'll have to save you all over again."

Dan froze and turned. He shoved Gemma behind him before he even processed the fact that Terrence stood there. Blood dripped down his face and sliced strips of tape clung to his clothes. He'd freed himself from his bonds.

"No." Gemma's voice was breathy and full of terror.

Dan saw it then, the gun in Terrence's hand. He was really sick of having a gun pointed at him.

Terrence clicked his fingers. "Next to me, Gemma. Or he's dead."

She didn't hesitate, just scrambled over there.

"Gemma!" Why did she do that?

Terrence grabbed her arm and pulled her to him. "You belong to me." His free arm across her, he pulled up her arm and showed it to Dan. "This mark means she's mine."

"I'm not yours." Gemma struggled.

"Fight and I'll shoot him. I will. Do not test me." Terrence narrowed his gaze on Dan again. "You don't win. I got her first, and you can't have what's mine."

"Because you stuck me with a cigarette, you coward?"

Dan stared, unable to process what he should do. If he called out to anyone for help Terrence would shoot him and then take Gemma. He was not going to take Gemma anywhere. Dan wasn't letting her out of his sight this time.

"Well guess what, moron?"

"Gemma," he cautioned her. She shouldn't push the man. Gemma had gone over there to save Dan's life, he knew that. Now her plan was to antagonize him?

She didn't listen. Go figure.

Gemma lifted her other arm, shoved Terrence's arm enough she could show him the tattoo on the outside of her right arm. "Guess what?"

"WHAT?" Terrence was losing patience.

Please let that have been loud enough that someone heard.

Gemma's smile was hard to see, it was so full of love for him. "You aren't the first one that 'marked' me. Dan is. This tattoo covers a scar far older than the ones you gave me."

Dan's stomach dropped. He'd seen the scar, and asked her about the tattoo. She'd told him it was an ugly cut she got hiking that she wanted to cover up. "Gem…" He did that? Not recently, it had to have been years ago. He didn't even remember. How could he not remember?

She shifted to face Terrence. "So I guess you lose and Dan wins. Boo hoo."

His face morphed into rage, and he lifted the gun. Gemma kicked him in the stomach.

Terrence grunted but brought the gun up. Dan raced over, pulled her out of the way. The gun went off. Dan shoved her out of the line of fire and jumped on Terrence. He wasn't going to hurt her, not if Dan had anything to say about it.

He punched and kicked. The gun was dropped and a crowd raced around the corner. Boots. Dan saw them out the corner of his eye, but he didn't let up.

"Enough."

Dan stilled at the sheriff's voice.

"That's enough."

He dropped Terrence on the floor, each breath like shards in his throat.

"Dan."

Her voice was soft. When he turned to her, Gemma ran into his arms. How could she even touch him after everything he'd done to her?

She burrowed into him. "Do you want to stay?"

He wanted to be where she was, wherever that might be.

"I hurt you."

"I don't care. You didn't know, and you didn't mean it. It was an accident, and I forgave you a long time ago."

Over the years, Sanctuary had torn him open and wounded him down to his soul.

"I…"

Dan wanted peace. He wanted to marry Gemma. He wanted to find a quiet mountain where he could farm the land and she could write books from the kitchen table. Or the porch, where he'd be able to see her when he rode Bay back to the house.

She moved back and then pulled him from the alley back onto the safety of Main Street. "What?"

Dan glanced toward the farm, where Chase and Miranda lay dead on the dirt. "There's too much death here." He didn't even know if he could stay here and face it every day.

Gemma hugged his middle. "Do you want to see the world with me? Get married. Settle down somewhere quiet; you can farm and I can write."

"On the porch."

Her smile was blinding. "From the porch."

Dan leaned in and kissed her. When he was done telling her everything he had to say, he leaned back.

Gemma chuckled. "I'm going to take that as a yes."

Dan lifted her in his arms, spun around, and kissed her again.

Epilogue

Eighteen months later
Red Butte, Wyoming

Dan rode Bay across the flat of their land between the creek and the house. His horse was hot beneath him, sweat covered. He wasn't much cooler. It was a scorcher today, and he was seriously ready for fall. Hot apple cider, blankets. Gemma.

She was on the porch in a rocker, her laptop on her knees because her belly was so big she had to hold it away from her stomach. She'd told him yesterday the baby had been kicking the corner of it while she wrote her first cutesy rom-com. Apparently the love-interest guy wore a flannel shirt.

He put Bay away and strode over there without running, even though he wanted to do it. Still, he hopped up the stairs and planted a kiss on her lips. Gemma shifted the laptop onto the coffee table and lifted her feet so he could sit and she could rest her swollen feet on his lap.

Buford looked up from his sentry in the corner, the big hound eyeing him and then settling back down. "Some guard dog." He chuckled, then turned to her. "Good afternoon, Mrs. Smithfield."

She grinned. "Good afternoon, Mr. Smithfield."

Dan shook his head. "That's still super weird." But he didn't have his father's name anymore, even if it was only because of witness protection rules.

She grabbed his hand and thumbed his ring. Hers glinted in the sunlight, which made Dan lean over and kiss her. He couldn't resist.

They ate dinner, and then sat on the porch again to watch the sun go down over their tiny plot of land. He wasn't running a business anymore. They owned the land free and clear, courtesy of the US government, and grew enough food to sell at a local farmers market to make a little cash to put gas in the truck. Money from Gemma's book sales went to renovating the back room into a nursery.

Life couldn't be better.

As the sky turned from orange to gray, Gemma leaned over. "It's time for bed, Mr. Smithfield."

Dan grinned, got up, and lifted her into his arms. Once in a while the past reared its head, but weekly Bible studies online with all their old friends meant people like John and Bolton, who knew him inside and out, could offer counsel. He needed it sometimes, and he knew Gemma got the same from Shelby. They were making it work.

One day at a time.

Dan kissed her before she went inside. "Time for bed."

**

Lanikai Beach, Oahu

Nadia ran to the porch. The wind ruffled her hair, and she grinned, her face aglow from the sunset. "They're on!"

Bolton set his fishing line down and wheeled his chair across the porch back inside the house to find Javier already at the desk. His son smiled. His skin was dark from all the surfing he did, and Bolton thought he might have a girlfriend. The kid spent practically all his time texting someone. Javier said, "It's working now."

"Great." Bolton put the brake on beside his son and smiled at Matthias and Frannie on the screen. "Hi, guys!"

"Hi!" Frannie waved, a tiny baby bundled up and held close to her chest.

Nadia set her hand on his shoulder and leaned down to see her friend. "How is she?"

"Good."

Two girls climbed on Matthias. "Dadda!" One snuggled his face, and the other shoved her smaller sister aside. "Where Javier!"

Everyone chuckled. The girls grinned with Frannie's smile, and they settled in to catch up. Nadia shifted beside him, and Bolton pulled her onto his lap. She was just starting to show, but only he could tell. Soon enough they would tell everyone, but he liked it being a secret just between them.

He kissed her shoulder at the edge of her tank top and then set his chin there, holding her against him as they caught up with family.

As Frannie told Nadia Marie all about the newest baby, and the birth, Matthias sat still. A smile stretched his face wide, two little girls in his arms.

Bolton said, "Dude."

Matthias chuckled. "I know."

They both smiled. All those years working the ranch alongside each other, who'd have thought they would be family men now?

Frannie turned to her husband. "What? What did I miss?"

Nadia shifted on his lap. "Yeah, what did we miss?"

"It was man stuff," Javier said with a grin. "You wouldn't understand."

**

Unnamed town, Montana

John sat at the head of the table. His boys on one side, Nicholas in his high-chair. Nate sat on the other side, Cyan beside him smiling. Dinner was over, plates cleared. Andra lifted Nicholas from her chair. "Finish your peas, Pat."

His son groaned, making Nate laugh. John's brother's peas were still on his plate.

Grant got up as well. "Can I talk to you for a minute?"

John nodded. They got up and walked through the house. He wasn't unhappy that Grant had visited, but he didn't think his brother had flown across the country just for dinner.

A group of Sanctuary residents had wanted to remain together, and so they lived in a small community in Montana. You could find it, if you left the highway in the right spot and drove off a couple of beaten paths. John wasn't their sheriff, but they still looked to him nonetheless. He supposed they always would.

Grant closed the door to the study behind him. He'd brought his briefcase from the hall where he dropped it when everyone converged on him to say hello. John didn't know how things were with his brother's kids and his ex-wife but the man had soaked up the affection like a starving man at a buffet.

John settled on the edge of the desk. "Everything okay?"

"Sure, why not. Just wanted to check in and let you know things are good with the former residents. Everyone is settling in nicely."

"So why the secret meeting?"

"Ben asked me to go on an assignment for a while. No contact."

John nodded. He knew what those were like. "Be careful, okay?"

"I'll try." Grant blew out a breath. "While I'm gone, you'll be the one people call if they need outside assistance." He pulled a satellite phone from his briefcase and held it out. "If any of the residents have a problem, this will ring."

"A problem like, my cat got lost, or a problem like they're being hunted down?"

"Code red problems."

"Okay." John didn't like going back to those days—not when he was living his peaceful life, but duty called and he would answer. It was their way.

Grant got out a paper file and handed that over as well. "They're spread out, but this is a list of everyone and where they're at, so you know where you're headed if you need to leave. Put it in your safe."

John nodded and opened the file. He glanced down the sheet and gaped.

He looked up from the paper. "I thought these people were being relocated into witness protection like the others."

"They have targets on their backs. It's our job to keep them safe."

"I know, but—" John blew out a breath. "Exactly how many Sanctuaries are there?"

"You don't have the security clearance to know the answer to that."

Thank you for giving of your time and money to read Sanctuary Forever

I hope you enjoyed it.

Reviews tell other readers what you thought of a book. I know they help me decide what to read next. If you would be so kind as to visit Amazon or Goodreads, or even share your thoughts on Facebook, I would very much appreciate it—both as the author, and as a fellow reader of good Christian fiction.

Made in the USA
Middletown, DE
12 August 2021